RESCUED BY THE GUARDED TYCOON

ROSANNA BATTIGELLI

MAKING ROOM FOR THE RANCHER

CHRISTY JEFFRIES

MILLS & BOON

First Published in Great Britain 2021
by Mills & Boon, an imprint of HarperCollins*Publishers* Ltd,
1 London Bridge Street, London, SE1 9GF

www.harpercollins.co.uk

HarperCollins*Publishers*
1st Floor, Watermarque Building,
Ringsend Road, Dublin 4, Ireland

Rescued by the Guarded Tycoon © 2021 Rosanna Battigelli
Making Room for the Rancher © 2021 Christy Jeffries

ISBN: 978-0-263-29924-3

0221

MIX
Paper from
responsible sources
FSC™ C007454

This book is produced from independently certified FSC™
paper to ensure responsible forest management.

For more information visit: www.harpercollins.co.uk/green

Printed and bound in Spain
by CPI, Barcelona

RESCUED BY THE GUARDED TYCOON

ROSANNA BATTIGELLI

For my beloved granddaughter Rosalie,
who fills my life with joy and laughter. xoxo

CHAPTER ONE

RONNIE'S EYES WERE blinking as fast as the wipers on her car. The fast-falling snow, mingled with the freezing rain pinging against the windshield, was making it hard to focus on the road. Her stomach muscles tightened as she gripped the steering wheel.

She should have checked the weather before heading into town, she berated herself, biting her lip. She had been unpacking boxes from her move to Parry Sound, and oblivious to anything but her task at hand, she had decided to give herself a break and venture out. Her intention had been to treat herself to some books downtown, pick up a pizza and to go back to the cottage at Winter's Haven, where she would spend the rest of the evening relaxing.

It had been snowing when she had started out, but nothing that had caused her to worry. Snow was a given in these parts, sometimes even starting in October. After purchasing the latest Giller Prize–winning novel at Parry Sound Books, Ronnie had continued down the street into Bearly Used Books, a sprawling store with a bear as its mascot. She had floated contentedly in and out of the themed rooms, taking her sweet time searching for a new treasure.

After happily selecting three books—two for herself

and one for her son, Andy—Ronnie had proceeded to the front counter. She had vaguely noticed that the number of customers had dwindled, and as she had paid for the books, Melissa, the store owner, had announced that she would be closing shortly because of the freezing rain.

Ronnie had hurried out to her car, her vision blurred by the sleet and gusts of wind. The noticeable drop in temperature would make the ride back to Winter's Haven downright dangerous if the wheels hit black ice on the winding road. She would have to slow right down and pray that other drivers would do the same.

Inside her car, Ronnie wiped her face with some tissues and turned on the ignition. As the car warmed up, she dashed outside to brush the snow off the windshield and windows. She realized how futile it was, though; she would just have to start driving and keep her wipers going, and hope she could make it back before dark, when the roads would be even more treacherous.

Ronnie breathed a pent-up sigh as she left the downtown, a blur of traffic lights, slick streets and glistening vehicles reflecting the illuminated storefronts. There was no way she'd be able to stop at Maurizio's Pizzeria, she thought, wistfully conjuring up the authentic Sicilian pizzas that her cousin Casson had ordered when she had first arrived a week ago. Her mouth watered at the memory of the spinach and ricotta pizza that she had anticipated enjoying this evening, and then she started as her car swerved as it caught on a patch of ice.

Righting the vehicle, her heart in her mouth, Ronnie slowed down even further.

Concentrate, just concentrate, she kept telling herself, her mouth dry. Her eyes felt itchy from the strain of trying to focus on the road, but she didn't want to lift her hand from the steering wheel to rub them.

Thank goodness her son wasn't with her right now. She would have been twice as terrified if Andy had been in the car with her. Squinting, Ronnie could understand how a person could become totally mesmerized by the hypnotic swish of the wipers as the snow and ice pellets lashed at the windshield.

A sudden beam from a vehicle's headlights jolted her and she shot a glance in her rearview mirror. An enormous black truck with a massive chrome grille seemed to be approaching fairly quickly. Ronnie frowned. Perhaps the driver wasn't particularly concerned with the road conditions because he or she had studded tires. But even so, he—she was willing to bet the driver was male—should have some consideration for people driving a much smaller vehicle. Especially in this brutal weather...

Ronnie considered putting on her hazard lights and slowly driving off to the shoulder to let the truck go by. She didn't want or need the pressure of driving with an impatient driver behind her. It would be unnerving, to say the least, especially if he decided to pass her. And from the looks of it, he was aiming to do just that.

She would be proactive, she decided. She pressed the hazard lights on, and then veered toward the shoulder. And then it felt like the steering wheel jerked from her grasp and the car was moving of its own volition. It was spinning, she realized numbly. Black ice! Losing all sense of balance and control with the kaleidoscope that was flashing in her eyes, Ronnie closed her eyes and braced herself for the inevitable impact.

She opened her eyes timeless moments later, realizing there hadn't been a life-threatening impact. In fact, there hadn't been a crash at all. Her car had simply skidded onto the shoulder of the road and then come to a stop in the snow-covered field, several yards from the stand of pine trees parallel to the road. Thank God, she thought, her jaw muscles unclenching. She was unhurt but her stomach was coiled in a tight knot, and her heart, which she suspected might have frozen for a few seconds, was now clanging in post-shock alarm.

Blinking, she peered out the window and saw the black truck that had been behind her was slowing down and coming to a stop on the shoulder. Her jaw dropped. "Jerk," she muttered. He could have been going slower, in which case she wouldn't have felt the compulsion to let him drive by.

And she wouldn't be stuck in this mess right now.

She felt her cheeks burn at the thought of what might have happened, how she could have been killed if her car had slammed against a tree trunk. Or an oncoming vehicle. Some angel had been watching out for her.

And Andy...

Ronnie took several deep breaths, trying to calm herself. The worst hadn't happened, thank heavens. She had to concentrate on what she needed to do *now* to get herself and her car back on the road.

She watched as the door of the truck swung open and the driver emerged. Her view was diminished by the icy drizzle accumulating on her windshield, but when she tried to start the car to get the wipers going, the noise her car emitted made her turn off the ignition right away. Muttering an expletive, she waited for the driver to approach. She squinted, catching a glimpse of russet hair before the man whipped the fur-trimmed hood of his parka over his head and started walking toward her vehicle.

He was a giant, well over six feet, and the size of his green parka and jeans-clad legs hinted at broad shoulders and an athletic physique. He took huge strides, but sank with each step into the knee-high snow. Which meant that *she* would be sinking up to her thighs if she ventured out.

Ronnie shivered. Her fingers were starting to feel numb, even with mitts on. The freezing rain pelting down on the hood of the car seemed to have intensified, and she felt her stomach muscles tighten.

She had to call Casson. She hadn't told him or his wife, Justine, that she was heading into town...

She fumbled to get her cell phone from her handbag, and groaned when she saw that the compartment where she usually kept it was empty. It must still be on the kitchen table, where she had absentmindedly placed it before searching for her boots. She was stranded in a town she had just moved to, and the truck driver was getting closer, now just a few giant steps away. She would have to rely on him to help her. The first thing she needed to do was to call her cousin. Then she'd need a tow.

Ronnie took a deep breath, trying to steady her jangled nerves. She was irritated with herself on several counts. First for being oblivious about the weather conditions, and second for skidding off the road, and third for forgetting her phone and being in a position where she had no choice but to depend on a stranger for help. Trust that he meant well...

She had always prided herself on being self-sufficient, but even more so when her husband had decided that he couldn't handle dealing with their son's life-threatening illness and abandoned her and Andy when he was midway through his series of chemo treatments.

The fact that he had found solace with another woman before he left her had been just as hard a blow, and Ronnie had had to wrestle through alternating feelings of shock, sadness, anger, disbelief, resentment and self-pity.

She had struggled, but she had been fiercely determined to carry on, for the sake of their son. Ronnie had vowed to herself that she would never depend on a man again. *For anything.* And now here she was, vulnerable and helpless, with no choice but to depend on this mountain of a man. It was a situation that could have been prevented, she berated herself for the umpteenth time.

Ronnie tapped her fingers against the edge of the steering wheel. They slowed as the man came into view. She could make out his furrowed eyebrows, caught glimpses of startling bluish green in his narrowed gaze, a straight nose and ruddy upper cheeks, and glistening, golden-red scruff that covered his upper lip, well-defined jaw and chin. It matched what she could see of the guy's hair under the hood of his parka. Reluctant to let in the freezing rain, Ronnie waited until the man was a couple of feet away before rolling her window down a few inches. She felt a flutter shimmy down the length of her. He looked like a Viking. A Viking in a Canadian parka.

"Hey there, are you okay?"

His voice was baritone deep, the kind of voice that matched the height and breadth of him, and for a few seconds her words caught in her throat. She was tempted to ream him out for being the cause of her decision to get off the road, which led to her spinout, but conversely, she was grateful he had stopped and had been concerned enough to come to see if she was all right.

Maybe he wasn't a complete jerk…

She stared at him, mesmerized by the crystal clarity of his eyes and the genuine concern in them. "I—I…"

"Did you hit your head?" he asked, leaning toward her. "I don't see any blood from here, but you might have suffered a concussion."

"I—I— No." She blinked up at him.

ROSANNA BATTIGELLI   13

His frown deepened. "You might be in shock and can't remember. I think it's best if I take you to the hospital immediately. Your car will have to stay here until you can get a tow tomorrow. I doubt anyone would come out now in this weather." He stepped closer to peer in through the opening, surveying her as if he were looking for signs of broken limbs. "Does it hurt anywhere? Your neck? Chest? Legs?"

The warmth of his breath fanned her face. For a moment all she could process was the emerald brilliance of his eyes. And then she heard him asking her again if she was hurt.

"No, no, no." Ronnie shook her head and then winced. "But I have a headache."

"Which is why you need to get checked. You might have hit your head when you spun out, and can't remember, which is common with head trauma... Thank goodness your car didn't flip over," he added huskily. "What did you say your name was?"

"I didn't." Ronnie hesitated. Why would he want to know that? And then it hit her. Of course; he was wondering if she was suffering from a concussion. "Veronica," she said. "Or Ronnie."

"Okay, Veronica or Ronnie. It's not nice to meet you under such circumstances, but it's still nice to meet you. My name is Redmond. Or Red," he said with a smile.

She blinked, and the sudden image of him in a Viking warrior tunic and chain mail ignited a swirl in her stomach. Maybe Erik the Red was one of his ancestors... Ronnie shook her head and met his gaze, her cheeks flaming with the realization that he had noticed her lingering gaze.

"Your eyes look a little glassy," he murmured. "We'd better get you to a hospital and make sure you're okay."

"I—I don't need to go to the hospital. I need to call my—my—"

"Husband," he finished for her. "Of course. But let me get you in my truck and you can call from there. And warm up. I'll have to clear the snow around your tires first, though. And from the looks of it, I may have to carry you over…that is, if you allow me to…"

Ronnie felt her cheeks tingle. Surely she could manage to trudge through the snow on her own.

As soon as Ronnie rolled up the window, he used his gloves to brush off enough snow to allow him to open the door. It made a crunching sound from the built-up ice along its edge. She shifted in her seat to ascertain if she could walk to the truck herself, but realized that the depth of the snow and the quickly darkening sky would make it very difficult. At least there was already a path made by her apparent rescuer.

She had no choice but to trust this stranger. And let him carry her to his truck.

She swiveled in her seat, grabbed her handbag and one of the book bags and hooked them over her right shoulder.

"That'll be an extra freight charge," he said, his tone serious.

Ronnie's jaw dropped. "You've got to be kidding." Her brow furrowed at the teasing look in his eyes. *She* was not in a joking mood.

"Did you actually believe me?" he chuckled.

"Well, I don't know you, so I wouldn't know if you were joking," she returned coolly. "And I'm not in the habit of jumping into a stranger's arms, either." She gestured toward the snow. "But I can see I'd be swimming in the stuff if I don't take you up on your offer, which is really the least you can do."

He looked at her quizzically. "I'm not sure I follow

you on the last bit, but you can clarify it in my truck. In case you haven't noticed, I've been getting pelted. I feel like I'm about to become an ice sculpture."

Ronnie's mouth twisted, and she bit back the reply on the tip of her tongue.

"Okay, you can shift your body into my arms and put your arms around my neck. Let me know if anything hurts, all right?"

Ronnie shifted slightly and felt his arms immediately slide under her legs to support her weight. She managed to click the door lock on the key before she felt him straighten. Her arms instinctively flew out and up to entwine themselves around his neck. As he began taking big strides back toward his truck, she automatically pressed her head against his chest to shield her face from the elements. She closed her eyes and a shiver of relief ran through her. His broad chest was like a protective wall shielding her from the forces of nature. A wall softened by a big warm comforter.

It was an odd feeling, that of being protected. Taken care of…and by a complete stranger. From the crunch of his every step, Ronnie realized that the drop in temperature had caused the top layer of snow to become hardened with the freezing rain. The roads would be like a skating rink. And the country roads would surely be worse.

How would he be able to get her back to Winter's Haven?

Her eyes flew open when he stopped. She felt an unexpected sense of disappointment when he set her down on the shoulder of the road, a couple of feet away from the passenger door of his truck. She shot a glance at the road. Very little traffic, and the cars that were there had all reduced their speed. She eyed his truck. He had left it turned on, so the windows would stay defrosted, and it thrummed like a sleeping monster. Its wheels came up to her waist, but Ronnie still had doubts that it could maneuver its way safely on the winding road toward her cottage.

"I'd ask you to jump in, but after spinning out, you'd better not," he said, his husky voice pulling her back to reality. He opened the door and held his hand out as she stepped up into the truck.

The warmth of the interior blanketed her immediately, and releasing a pent-up sigh, she sank into the passenger seat. Her nose immediately reacted to a familiar scent. *Pizza?* She turned and saw the large box on the back seat with the words *Maurizio's Pizzeria* on it.

The door on the driver side opened and Red quickly settled in behind the wheel. His face broke into a grin. "Hungry?"

Red almost laughed out loud at her expression. It was one of mingled disbelief and something else—like maybe envy...

"I was going to pick up a pizza there," she murmured wistfully. "But I changed my mind when I heard about the freezing rain."

"Well, I don't mind sharing," he said, feigning solemnity. "But first things first. Don't you have to call your husband? And then you can let me know your address. I can either use my GPS or you can tell me where to go." He smiled, turning on the windshield wipers.

"If I wasn't at your mercy right now, I'd probably tell you where to go," she blurted. "Pardon my bluntness, but your monster truck was getting too close for comfort. It made me nervous and I wanted to move onto the shoulder before you zoomed by me and caused an accident." She crossed her arms and tilted her chin defiantly at him.

"Ouch. I left myself wide open for that, didn't I?" He

rubbed his jaw. "But let me set the record straight, Veronica or Ronnie. I was approaching because I wanted to let you know that one of your taillights wasn't working." He leaned toward her. "And believe it or not, I was going under the speed limit." He surveyed her flushed cheeks, and eyes which reminded him of chestnuts glistening in the sun. They matched her hair, or what he could see of it under that toque. It looked like she had it up in a ponytail. And her mouth…right now her lips were pursed, but rosebud pink and lovely…

"I forgot my phone. May I use yours, please?"

"Of course," he said, stifling his desire to chuckle. He found her honesty refreshing. He stretched out to reach into his pocket. "Your hubby must be worried about you."

A frown immediately creased her forehead. She took off her gloves and reached for his cell phone, giving him a clear view of her left hand. *No ring.*

The sound of a male voice was loud and clear. "Hey, buddy, what's up?"

Ronnie looked at the phone as if it were something from outer space and then put it back to her ear. "Hey, when did I become a 'buddy'?"

"Ronnie, is that *you*? And why are you using my friend's phone? Where are you? I didn't know you were out in this weather!"

Red exchanged a confused look with Ronnie. They had a mutual friend?

"Friend?" Ronnie's jaw dropped. "My car spun out and got stuck in a stretch of deep snow off the shoulder. He was behind me on the road and he stopped to help me. I forgot my phone at the cottage."

"Are you all right? Are you hurt?"

"I—I'm okay."

"Are you sure? Let me talk to Red."

Red took the phone. He was curious to find out which one of his friends Ronnie had contacted. And why they had never mentioned this lovely lady sitting next to him now, her chestnut eyes fixed on him with just as much curiosity in their glistening depths.

"Hello? Hold on a sec, I'll put you on speaker. Okay, which one of my 'buddies' are you?"

"Red, it's me, Casson."

"What the—" Red frowned.

"And you've rescued my cousin. Thank God she's safe."

"Cousin?" His gaze flew to Ronnie. Casson *had* mentioned a cousin by the name of Ronnie.

"Are you sure she's okay? She didn't hit her head?"

Red's gaze flew to Ronnie, who was rolling her eyes. "She insists she's fine. There's no sign of bruising. And no bruises on her car, either. Just wheel-deep in snow."

"I'll arrange for a tow tomorrow," Casson said. "As for driving her back to Winter's Haven, I wouldn't advise it. The country roads are iced over. How are they in town?"

"Getting bad. I'll be taking my time getting home."

"Can you put Ronnie up for the night? I'm sure you can find a corner for her in that shack of yours, Red." Casson laughed.

Red chuckled, aware of Ronnie's sudden scowl. "I suppose I can put up with Ronnie for the night," he said, deliberately switching the words.

"Excuse me, *gentlemen*," Ronnie cut in sharply. "Red can just drop me off at the nearest hotel, if you don't mind."

"Okay, call me when you get there, Ronnie," Casson said. "Thanks, Red. Drive safe."

"Will do. Catch you later."

Red put his cell phone down and turned on the radio,

catching the last segment of the sports news. "Weather's next," he said, buckling up. Moments later, they heard the warning to stay off the roads, as the quickly dropping temperature was causing flash freezing and dangerous driving conditions.

Red turned off the radio. "Well, that clinches it," he said, shrugging. "I have no choice but to drive you to my place. The nearest hotel is much farther away." He saw her look of dismay. "Don't worry. It's not that run-down of a shack. Sure, it needs a little TLC, but I'm sure there are worse places to be stuck in…"

"I can't believe this," Ronnie muttered, shaking her head. "What rotten luck."

"It's not *that* bad," Red said consolingly, flashing her a grin. "You get to have some of that awesome pizza. Man, it smells so good. Let's get outta here…" He rolled down his window to make sure the way was clear. The air was remarkably colder, and the freezing rain lashed at his face. He quickly shut the window. "You buckled up?" Nodding his approval, he slowly veered back onto the road and concentrated fully on driving. Recalling everything Casson might have told him about Ronnie would have to wait until much later…

CHAPTER TWO

RONNIE STARED NUMBLY AHEAD, the wipers swooshing hypnotically left and right. So much for a relaxing evening at the cottage… She was heading to the "shack" of a virtual stranger. The fact that he and Casson were friends was somewhat reassuring, but she didn't relish the thought of spending the night in what sounded like a ramshackle bachelor pad.

At least, she figured, he must be a bachelor. There had been no mention of a wife or girlfriend…

Ronnie stole a glance at Red. He had flipped back the hood of his parka, revealing a shock of hair the color of burnished copper, with curling ends. His jaw and chin had scruff that hadn't seen a trimmer in at least a week. Yet she couldn't deny that he was…kind of cute. Okay, maybe *cute* wasn't the right word for this…this *Viking*.

He turned and caught her staring. She felt heat swooshing up into her cheeks and she blinked, trying to come up with something to say. He smiled, and the heat spiraled back down her body to her limbs. She resisted the temptation to roll the window down to cool her flaming face. "Um, how far is it to your place?" she blurted.

"Can't wait to dig in to the pizza, eh?" he teased, his smile widening into a grin that showed his perfect teeth.

He turned his gaze back to the road. "Just a few more minutes before we get to my humble abode—"

The truck suddenly veered to the left and Ronnie cried out, her head swerving against Red as he maneuvered the truck out of the skid. For a few seconds her cheek was pressed tightly against his upper arm, and she closed her eyes, afraid to look. When she felt Red's arm ease up again, she ventured a peek. He was turning off onto a road with no houses in sight, just streetlamps. She righted herself and squinted through the constant swiping of the windshield wipers. Where on earth was he taking her?

Ronnie's heartbeat matched the staccato rhythm of the ice pellets pinging against the truck. And then she caught sight of an ornate Victorian-style gate directly in their path, flanked by sturdy lampposts. Her gaze flew to Red, who had slowed down and was aiming a device toward the gate.

"Open sesame," he ordered dramatically, and Ronnie's eyes widened as the double gate swung open and then closed once they were inside. Moments later an immense three-story Victorian mansion with gables and arches came into view, its bay windows lit up like bright eyes in the dark. A string of lights hanging above a wraparound porch twinkled as they moved with the wind and freezing rain. Red came to a stop in the circular driveway adjacent to the front steps. "Welcome to my 'shack,'" he said, grinning. "I'll get your door."

He put his hood back on and leaped out. He opened the door and put out his hand to help Ronnie down the step, which was already glazed over with ice. "Let's get you in the house, Miss Veronica or Ronnie, and I'll come back for the pizza." He held out his left arm protectively as they went up the half-dozen stairs to the doorway. "I don't want you to slip and get hurt. Your cousin would have my head!" He opened the stained-glass door and motioned for Ronnie to enter.

The foyer was breathtaking, with its carnelian-and-black-tiled floor, creamy white leather high-back chairs and gleaming antique armoires opposite each other that reminded Ronnie of one of her favorite books: *The Lion, the Witch and the Wardrobe* by C. S. Lewis…

"I'll take your coat, Ronnie," Red drawled.

She snapped out of her thoughts and took off her parka, and realized that while she was in Narnia, Red had already hung up his parka in the armoire behind her. She couldn't help noticing the perfect fit of his cable-knit sweater and straight jeans. The forest-green of the former suited him and enhanced the color of his eyes. Now that her boots were off, he was even taller, with a broad chest and defined shoulders that made her wonder if he was a football player… And his hair, ruffled and the color of burnished oak leaves in the fall, had her guessing that his heritage was Irish.

"I'll go and grab the pizza and you can make yourself comfortable in the salon in the meantime." He chuckled. "I guess I shouldn't have hung up my parka…"

She followed Red into a spacious salon with an ornate fireplace flanked by built-in bookshelves that were stocked with some classics as well as some recent titles. Two dark brown leather recliners were positioned side by side opposite the fireplace. An elegant mahogany desk and padded leather chair sat in an illuminated alcove with a large sash window. The curved wall boasted more bookshelves and hundreds of gilded volumes. A couch with a William Morris design and mahogany accents lounged nearby. Ronnie blinked, feeling as if she had entered another century.

Her gaze shifted to the sweeping staircase and upward

to the immense vaulted ceiling embossed with roses. She could only imagine what the second floor was like... *And that's where you're probably going to be sleeping tonight*, her inner voice whispered.

"How do you like my new digs?"

Ronnie started. She hadn't even heard him come back in. "Um... It looks like a 'shack' out of a fairy tale," she said dryly. "I was almost expecting Beauty to float down the staircase in her lovely gown, with the Beast right behind her."

Red chuckled. "Well, I can assure you there are no beasts in this place. Unless it's a full moon, and then—" he rubbed his chin and looked at her with narrowed eyes "—my fur grows exponentially."

Ronnie's brows arched and she cleared her throat. How was she supposed to respond to that?

"And I might turn into a beast if I don't satisfy my craving for pizza soon," he said, feigning a growl. "Come on, let's have a bite, then I'll show you to Beauty's quarters." She followed him into a spacious kitchen with a charming hearth and live-edge harvest table, and what looked like brand-new appliances. Red followed her gaze. "I know. You're probably wondering why I ordered pizza when I have a setup like this... Well, I need a break once in a while. I can't cook gourmet meals *every* day of the week."

Ronnie smiled cynically. This Viking friend of Casson's had a joking way about him that she suspected he used to charm the ladies and maybe even distract them from his defects of character. *Which are...?* Her inner voice pressed her for an answer, but she brushed it away.

Ronnie watched as Red pulled off his sweater, revealing a plaid shirt that was now partially untucked. He casually pulled out the rest of the shirt and then went to the sink to wash his hands before getting out some plates and cutlery. He had already set down a bottle of wine and two glasses next to the pizza. "May I?" he said, lifting her glass.

She shook her head. "Just water, please." She sat down at the table.

He complied and then poured himself a glass of wine. "Cheers. We made it home safe and sound."

"To *your* home," Ronnie said. "I'll celebrate when I get to *my* place."

"Speaking of which—" he stroked his chin thoughtfully "—you're staying at Winter's Haven?"

Ronnie had a drink of her water. "For a while," she said casually. She averted her gaze and helped herself to a slice of pizza. She hoped he'd get the hint that she didn't want to talk about her personal life. Instead, she wished she could just blurt out the questions that were piquing her curiosity about *him*. Like what did this guy do for a living? How did he know Casson? Was he from the area? Was he in a relationship? What was he doing in this Victorian mansion?

"I called Casson," he told her before biting into his slice. "He was happy to know that you're safe."

Ronnie nodded and glanced at the leaded casement windows. They could hear the wind driving the freezing rain against the panes. It *was* a relief to be off the roads.

"And *I'll* be happy when you forgive me." He cocked his head at her.

Ronnie stopped midbite and shot him a bewildered look. "Forgive you?" She finished chewing. "Oh, for your part in my spinout? I suppose I have. More or less."

"Aha! I knew it! Some lingering resentment." His green eyes narrowed. "Have you no mercy, woman? I *did* rescue you from the snowy depths of despair and bring you to a safe haven."

Ronnie shook her head in disbelief. Was this guy for real? Perhaps he was an actor for the local theater. He certainly had a flair for the dramatic… She blinked at him, not sure how to respond, and saw his lips twitching.

"Uh…well, I guess I *could* find it in my heart to forgive and move on," she murmured, shifting her gaze to her plate.

"Great—I'll be able to sleep now," he said dryly, reaching for another slice of pizza. "Come on, eat up, Veronica or Ronnie."

She pursed her lips. "Okay, you can choose one or the other. My name, that is," she said pointedly. "Although I generally prefer Ronnie."

"Ronnie it is, then." He nodded, suppressing a smile. She seemed a little tense, but he couldn't blame her, having been spun around in that little car. Thank goodness there hadn't been any oncoming vehicles or sharp rock cuts, like on the highway. Maybe she needed something to relax her. "Since you're not having wine, how about a cup of herbal tea?"

"Thanks, but I think I'll just finish my water, and then, if you would be so kind as to show me to a room…" She pulled back her chair. "And hopefully not a haunted one…"

He chuckled. "The only spirits in this house are in my cabinet over there." He watched her cradle her arms apprehensively. He couldn't help thinking how young she looked, with her hair in a ponytail and wearing a plaid flannel shirt and jeans. He guessed her to be no more than twenty-seven or twenty-eight.

She looked at him intently. "Are you sure? A *mansion* like this must have quite a history. It must be close to a hundred years old." She glanced upward to the decorative tin tile ceiling.

"A hundred and five to be exact. And very well maintained over the years. It's an art designated home."

Red sensed that Ronnie wanted to know more about the place, and maybe even about *him*. "I'll take you for a tour tomorrow, if you'd like," he told her. "I think I'd better get you to bed now."

Her eyebrows lifted and he berated himself silently for his choice of words. The last thing he wanted was to make Ronnie uncomfortable. Or more uncomfortable than she already was. "Okay, Ronnie, let me just pull my big foot out of my mouth, and then I'll take you up to Beauty's suite. Unless—" he cocked his head "—you'd rather stick around and we can twiddle our thumbs by the fireplace."

Her lips twitched. "Sorry. I've got some books I'd like to delve into." She took a couple of steps toward the doorway and then stopped to look back at him. "You'll have to twiddle all by yourself."

Red laughed. "That's no fun. But I will graciously accept your decision, Ronnie. Now let me lead you to a guest room."

A couple of minutes later they were in the hall on the second level, with its original narrow-slat oak flooring and elegant gold-embossed wallpaper. They passed several open doors, revealing fully furnished rooms. He had been lucky to purchase the house with all the antiques and furniture. The elderly previous owner, whose great-grandparents had built the house, had decided to sell when he was told that his condition was terminal. It would make him happy, he had explained to the Realtor, to find someone who would genuinely love and preserve the Victorian home that had been passed down to relatives over the years, since there were no longer any heirs.

Red had been in the right place at the right time. His old university friend, Casson Forrester, had gotten in touch and had hired Red's architectural firm to design Franklin's Resort, a getaway for children who had finished their chemotherapy treatment. They and their parent or parents would be treated to a week at the luxury resort. Red had visited Parry Sound himself, fallen in love with the area, and had decided to invest in a property in the little town known as the "jewel of Georgian Bay's Thirty Thousand Islands" and located inside the UNESCO-designated Georgian Bay Biosphere Reserve.

When he discovered that a Victorian mansion had been listed, Red had immediately made plans to check it out. He would be interested in renovating it, and perhaps designing some unique architectural features for the property. Although his flagship firm was located in Toronto's Harbourfront, with offices in major cities around the world, Red had been charmed by the idea of spending time in picturesque Parry Sound when he needed a break from big-city living. And when he had gone through the house and surveyed the property, complete with a picturesque pond and a stunning view of the channel that fed into Georgian Bay, Red had been hooked.

He had taken possession of it a month earlier, but had only moved in two weeks ago, in plenty of time to settle in and attend the grand opening of Franklin's Resort. He had hired a company to give the interior a fresh cleaning, and the only rooms he had made any changes to were his bedroom and the two guest rooms, with the purchase of new beds and linens, and the washrooms on both levels. He had plenty of time to consider any other modifications. For the next couple of weeks, all he wanted to do was enjoy his new estate and let some design ideas germinate…

"We're almost there," he said, slowing suddenly and turning. Ronnie, whose gaze had been drawn to the open door—and *his* room—across the hall, collided squarely with him. She stumbled backward, dropping her bag of books, and his arms instinctively flew out to grasp her firmly. As her head skimmed his chest, he felt a spike in his pulse. And then she pulled away and his arms dropped to his sides.

"Sorry about that," she said with an embarrassed laugh. She picked up her bag.

"No worries," he said lightly. "But I think we need to practice a little more if we want to perfect our tango for that dancing show on TV…"

Red saw Ronnie begin to frown and then her brow relaxed and she laughed. He was glad she was taking his comment as a joke, and as nothing more suggestive. He stopped farther on in front of a closed door. "This is one of the guest rooms," he said.

He turned on the light switch just inside the door, and gestured for her to enter the room. He felt a tug of satisfaction at the look of wonder and surprise on her face. "I wanted to maintain the Victorian features in most of the place," he said. "This room has just been refreshed— new wallpaper, draperies, linens. In fact, you're the first guest to sleep in the new bed…"

"Wow, I guess I'll know what Queen Victoria felt like," she murmured.

"Enjoy the experience," he said with a half smile. "And make sure to turn on the gas fireplace if you find it cool during the night."

"I'll be fine. I'm always hot at night." She averted her gaze immediately, and Red suspected she was regretting the phrase.

"Okay, then, good night."

She glanced back at him. "Good night," she said, before shutting the door firmly.

Red stood for a few moments, staring at the door, and then went downstairs to the grand salon. He ambled to the window seat that looked out of the huge bay window onto the channel. The freezing rain hadn't abated; in fact, it had intensified, and Red's view was obscured by the accumulation of ice on the pane.

Even with the limited view, Red felt himself relaxing. He would enjoy visiting this place regularly and experiencing a taste of all the seasons, he thought, inhaling and exhaling deeply. Mr. Cameron Doyle—the previous owner—had wanted to personally meet whomever was interested in buying his mansion, and after chatting an hour with Red over afternoon tea, he had accepted Red's offer, expressing his delight that "a young man of the same Irish heritage" would be purchasing it, with the intention of maintaining it as his family had done for a hundred years.

"And maybe you can find yourself a bonnie lass to marry and have a half-dozen children to liven up the place again." He had slapped Red heartily on the back, and Red and the Realtor had laughed before taking their leave.

Red's smile faded as another memory popped up. The image of his ex-girlfriend, Sofia, whom he had dated for over a year. Red had met her when her family had contacted his firm to redesign an estate and winery they had recently purchased in Italy's Tuscany region. Sofia helped run her Italian Canadian parents' wine business, which encompassed vineyards in Niagara-on-the-Lake, Ontario, and in the Okanagan Valley of British Columbia.

After focusing exclusively on his graduate studies and then his family business, Red had allowed himself to reconsider dating…

It hadn't taken him long to be captivated by Sofia and her little boy, Marco. Red had spent many hours with Marco while Sofia dealt with business calls and regular trips to the family's various wineries. They had agreed to maintain their separate condos, especially since Sofia had a five-year-old son. After she had returned from the ribbon-cutting ceremony at the official reopening of the Tuscany winery, she had dropped a bombshell: she had been seeing the Italian lawyer handling the sale, and she was sorry, but she and Red had been drifting apart in the last little while, and the best thing was to accept it and get on with their lives.

Red remembered blinking at her and thinking: Drifting apart? Yes, she had been spending more time at work, but he had continued to spend time with Marco…

As the weeks went by, Red's initial shock and surprise—even sadness and occasional anger at Sofia's betrayal—had eventually begun to subside. The hardest part was missing Marco. He soon realized that the only genuine love that had existed in the relationship had been that between him and the boy. His sadness over Marco had lingered, but he had realized that he had no choice but to accept the situation and get on with his life.

And he had vowed he would never again get involved with a woman with a child or children.

Not that he didn't want kids one day. And he wanted to experience a close bond with them, something he hadn't had with his own parents.

They had been affectionate and loving when they were home, but as a couple whose award-winning architectural firm had been commissioned to do projects around the world, they had enjoyed extensive traveling and had often left Red in the care of his full-time nanny. They had missed special occasions and milestones in his life, and although his nanny had to be credited with trying to make the events memorable for him, Red had felt the absence of his parents. As he grew older, he became better at masking his hurt and disappointment by pretending to be cheerful and happy-go-lucky.

Red had been popular with the girls in high school— they had liked his easygoing personality and humor— but that facade had threatened to crumble when a date eventually invited him over for dinner. Meeting her parents and witnessing the interactions of a "normal" family would make him a little edgy and he would shift uncomfortably at their probing questions about his family. Despite the impressive meal and their congenial banter, Red would leave with an unsettled feeling in his stomach…and not long afterward, he'd break up with the girl.

Red hadn't realized the true source of his discontent at first. As he continued to date, he'd experience similar feelings of discomfort, followed by a lingering malaise, followed a short time later by him breaking up with the girl. He had always been the one to initiate the breakup. By the end of his final year of high school, the girl who had been his prom date hadn't accepted his excuse for breaking up—the fact that he was studying architecture out of town and it would be too hard for him to keep up with a relationship. "You just want to keep stringing girls along." Sherry had hurled the accusation at him. "You're obviously not the kind to want a serious relationship with anyone, from the look of your track record. Well, go, then!" She had leaped out of his Mustang convertible and slammed the door. "Have a happy life. *Alone!*"

Red had watched her for a moment, a burning feeling of frustration and anger rising into his throat. He stepped hard on the gas and screeched away.

As he drove back to his parents' house—he couldn't call it a home—he had forced himself to take deep breaths in and out. He had parked, strode through the empty house—his parents were in the South of France—and stretched out on his bed to think about what Sherry had said about his track record. There *had been* a pattern. A string of dates…that hadn't lasted.

And it had finally hit him. He had broken off with every date before he could become entrenched in her domestic life. Red had wanted to be a part of his own family, not anyone else's.

Spending time with *them* had emphasized the emptiness in his own familial situation even more.

And he hadn't liked the feeling in his gut…

Red had immersed himself in his studies at the University of Toronto. Despite the invitations and hints from female classmates, he had stayed clear of relationships. Other than group get-togethers on a Friday night, he had focused on his academic goals.

When he had graduated summa cum laude, his parents had been on the opposite side of the world. Red had paused on the stage during the convocation ceremony, putting on a smile for the commissioned photographer, but his happiness at his achievement had been diminished by their absence. As families had rejoined afterward to take photos and enjoy the reception after the ceremony, Red had instead made his way past his friends and colleagues who were hugging their relatives and quickly returned his robe before driving in his midnight-blue Porsche back to his penthouse condo, both graduation gifts from his parents.

Red had placed his diploma in his desk drawer, opened the sliding doors to his spacious patio and stared at the city lights. Despite all the material comforts he had enjoyed in his youth and the luxury grad gifts, he had felt there was something missing in his life emotionally. He had gone to bed shortly after, telling himself that the position he would be assuming in a couple of weeks' time in his parents' firm would keep him busy, with little time to think about anything else.

Red had focused entirely on the business these past eight years, and his parents had bestowed upon him the role of president when they retired. He had proven his competency, they had told him, and they had every confidence in his ability to continue the Brannigan legacy.

And he had. He was on top of all his firm's ventures. It was just so ironic that when he had finally thought he could seriously commit to a relationship, Sofia had been the one to break it off.

Now, a year since the breakup, Red was excited about his new investment in Parry Sound and the possibilities for the future. He was intent on focusing on his job and leisure time. Alone.

Red left the window seat and headed to his bedroom. He was pleased with the changes he had made to it. A sturdy king-size bed with a slate headboard, extra long, with more of a cottage vibe than a Victorian one. A huge horizontal dresser had been custom-made by a local craftsman, and Red admired its rich grain and live-edge feature every time he entered the room. A sitting area by the bay window featured a pomegranate recliner with a pine-green throw and a coffee table that matched the dresser. The original wood floor gleamed under a Muskoka-themed area rug displaying loons on a lake edged with pine trees.

Under his warm duvet, Red thought about his unexpected guest. The last thing he had expected today was to spend the evening with a lady…and one related to a friend of his. Gazing at his ice-encrusted window, he thought back to what Casson might have told him about Ronnie. He had met with Casson a couple of times during the contractual stages of the project. Red's Toronto team was handling the venture, but Red had taken a few days off to drive to Parry Sound to catch up with his friend from university.

He stretched out his arms and linked his hands behind his neck. He thought back to when he had met up with Casson and his wife and their new baby at Winter's Haven after taking possession of his new house. His brow furrowed as he remembered another person who was there, a little boy Casson had introduced as his nephew... Adam? No, *Andy.*

After Andy had left the room, Casson had told Red about Andy finishing his treatment, and that he'd be one of the first kids to stay at Franklin's Resort when it opened in the New Year. With his mom, Casson's cousin Veronica.

Ronnie.

Red's heart began to pound. And he didn't exactly know why...

CHAPTER THREE

RONNIE LISTENED TO the freezing rain striking her window as she changed into the guest robe she had found hanging in the luxurious en suite bathroom. As soon as she had stepped into the room earlier, she had felt that she was stepping into another century. Her gaze had immediately flown to the elaborate four-poster with its ivory lace-edged canopy panels and plush bedspread with gathered ruffle. A rich Aubusson carpet with floral accents and cream, coral, and light green hues covered much of the polished wood floor. An elegant coral wingback chair and matching ottoman were positioned in one corner by an ornate porcelain fireplace, along with a gleaming coffee table and vintage lamp. On the ceiling, an intricate rose-gold chandelier shimmered with dozens of lights.

After Red had left, Ronnie had checked out the spacious en suite bathroom, a mix of modern and vintage, with its elegant marble and glass features, claw-foot tub and mosaic-tiled shower.

Tightening the belt of the robe around her waist, she padded to the window, shivered at the sight of the freezing rain, and was glad they hadn't ventured any farther. Hopefully, the temperature would rise in the morning, melt the accumulated ice on the roads and Red could drive her back to Winter's Haven…

Red. The name suited him. He was tall and strong. And damn good-looking. An image of the way his broad chest and shoulders had filled out his plaid shirt, and his long legs in jeans, popped into her mind… It reminded Ronnie of a drawing of Paul Bunyan in one of her childhood books. She wondered if anybody called him *Big Red…*

What silly musings, she thought, shaking her head. Why was she even conjuring up such images? She turned off the chandelier and switched on the bedside lamp before shifting the pillows and slipping under the covers. She sighed. The bed was heavenly, and she *did* feel like a queen. She'd have to recount her adventure to Andy when he returned from visiting his father in a few days.

Ronnie's smile faded as she recalled the shock of Andy's diagnosis, their lives instantly changing, the harrowing trips back and forth to the Hospital for Sick Children, Toronto's SickKids, from their home in Gravenhurst, the building tension between her and her husband and the final blow: her husband, Peter, "needing a break" and moving out, leaving Ronnie with the bulk of the responsibility.

He announced months later that he had been seeing a nurse called Meredith, and that she had accepted his proposal to become Mrs. Walsh after his divorce. What had surprised Ronnie the most during this time was that Meredith, to her credit, had encouraged Peter to devote more time to his paternal responsibilities. As a result, Andy was now spending alternating weeks and every second weekend with his dad. And new stepmother.

Ronnie turned off the lamp and listened to the tinkle of ice pellets against the bay window. She felt safe and cocooned under the bedspread. Protected, just like she'd been when Red had carried her to his truck…

Her pulse quickened at the memory of her head pressing against his chest as she tried to shield herself from the slanting freezing rain. A coil of heat spiraled through her, and she brought her palms up to her cheeks. What on earth was happening to her? Surely she wasn't allowing herself to be physically affected by a virtual stranger who had swept her up in his arms for no other reason than to bring her to safety?

Her body was betraying her. Responding to a man's touch—no, to the *memory* of his touch, as if she were starved for a man's caress...

Stop! The last thing she wanted—or needed—was a man's touch. She had come out of a broken marriage. She had continued handling her parental responsibilities independently. Why would she get herself entangled again? And what if—and she prayed it would never happen— Andy got sick again? She couldn't take the chance that whoever she was with would not be capable of sticking it out through the tough—and scary—process of treatment. She wouldn't do that to Andy. Or herself. They had been abandoned once. She would not allow it to happen again.

Ronnie inhaled and exhaled slowly a few times. Her mind knew what it wanted. And didn't want. It was her body that was waffling. Reacting to a tall, strong, dashingly handsome Viking type with Irish eyes and red-gold hair that curled this way and that, and scruff the same color.

So you noticed a hunky guy, her inner voice whispered nonchalantly in her ear. *It means you're normal. Nothing to get worked up about; it's not like the Viking is out to conquer you...*

Ronnie shivered. She pulled up the covers around her face but couldn't get warm. She considered getting out of bed to look for a blanket but another series of shivers kept her huddled under the sheets.

And then she started at the sudden knock on her door.

"Excuse me for bothering you," came Red's husky voice. "I just wanted to let you know that some power lines have collapsed from the weight of the ice. Electricity's out. And you're on the north side of the house."

Ronnie blinked.

"Ronnie, did you hear me? Are you awake?"

"Yes, I heard you," she called out, sitting up. "Now what do we do?"

"Well," he drawled, "I can see only two options at this point—huddle together under some blankets, or make a roaring fire in the salon…"

Ronnie knew he was joking, but the image of the two of them under a blanket made her pulse jump. She cleared her throat. "I… I'll opt for the fire."

"Right. Okay, then. I'll wait here until you're ready to come down. My cell phone is charged. I can hand it to you now if you need a light…"

"Sure, thanks." Ronnie managed to find her way to the door without tripping or bumping into anything. She opened the door a few inches and in the bright light of his phone, Ronnie's gaze flew over Red's tousled hair and quirky smile. He had changed into a plaid shirt and a blue-gray cardigan, and in his other hand he held a green cardigan.

"I thought you might appreciate this also," he said. He held out both hands, and Ronnie realized that she'd have to open the door wider. She pulled back to ensure her robe was wrapped snugly around her before doing so. Somewhat subconsciously, she reached for both items. "Thanks," she murmured again and closed the door. "I'll just be a minute."

It was going to be a long night. No power, no heat, and instead of a good night's sleep—which she had just been about to embark on—she would be sitting by the fireplace, trying to keep warm next to a guy she knew next to nothing about, other than the fact that he was a friend of her cousin's and that he obviously made a good living, being able to afford a place like this.

She quickly changed back into her clothes and then glanced at the cardigan. Why not? The chill had already settled into the room, and she imagined the roomy salon downstairs would be even colder until Red got the fire going.

A few moments later, she headed toward the door; then, as an afterthought, she grabbed her bag of books. If the fire was bright enough, she might be able to read a bit, instead of being forced to make awkward conversation with Red.

Ronnie handed the cell phone to him and he nodded, his gaze sweeping over her. She followed him down the winding staircase and into the spacious living area. She was relieved to see a healthy supply of wood stacked in an alcove next to the fireplace. "Oh, good, I won't freeze to death tonight," she said, hugging her arms.

Red paused as he was arranging the logs in the grate to cock his head at her. "I wouldn't let that happen, Miss Ver— *Ronnie*. Casson would have my head." He gazed at her and looked like he was going to add something, but then he gave a rueful smile and concentrated on adding bits of kindling and newspaper to the pile. "Good thing I made sure it was in working order when I bought the place," he said, lighting a long fireplace match.

In minutes the fire was crackling and roaring. Red had turned off his cell phone light, and the illumination was bright enough to read by, but Ronnie sat in one of the high-back recliners flanking the fireplace and just stared at the flames, mesmerized. Her heart twinged at the thought of Andy, and like other times when he was away, she felt like a part of her was missing. A loud crack diverted her attention and she rose in alarm.

Red strode to a nearby window to peer through the ice pellets hitting the pane. "Looks like some branches have snapped off the big oak. The weather's gotten worse. And it's windy as hell. It'll be a nightmare tomorrow…" He returned to sit by the fire. "Well, I don't know about you, Ronnie, but I'm not sleepy at all. How about a glass of wine and we can chat a bit?"

Red had to stifle a smile at the way Ronnie's eyes had expanded at his suggestion. She blinked for a few seconds and then she shrugged. "Sure—why not?"

"Red or white?"

"I prefer white, thanks."

"I won't take it personally." He laughed, and after a couple of seconds, her frown disappeared and she smirked.

"Okay, Ronnie, I'm leaving you to keep the home fire burning while I take care of your order."

"Um…okay." She looked back at the crackling fire, and for a moment Red sensed a wistfulness in her profile, or maybe even sadness. Was she missing her son? She looked so petite, leaning forward to warm her hands. She had let her ponytail down, and her dark hair now fell to her shoulders. The glow of the flames danced across her features, and Red found himself holding his breath for a moment. Reluctant to let her turn and catch him staring, he turned on his cell phone light and strode to the wine cabinet in the kitchen.

As he gathered a tray, glasses and wine, he thought

about the details that had come back to him after Ronnie had gone to the guest room. He had taken a quick shower, changed into a robe and stretched out on his bed, not bothering to pull back the covers. He had returned to the conversation he had had briefly with Casson after Andy had left the room. Casson had expressed his displeasure with Ronnie's husband, who had been unable to cope with the situation, and had gotten his own apartment.

"The poor guy wasn't getting enough attention," Casson had muttered sarcastically. "Well, Ronnie doesn't need a guy like that. She has enough on her plate, dealing with a very sick little boy." He had gone on to say that he loved his cousin and godson and that when Andy had finished his treatment, he was going to suggest to Ronnie that she move to Parry Sound to be closer to him and Justine and the baby they were expecting.

Ronnie had been manager of Casson's hardware store in Gravenhurst, and he would offer her a position as Provincial Marketing Manager, which she could do from any location. She was more than qualified, having graduated with a master's in Business Administration and Marketing, and the bonus was that their kids could grow up together. She needed family to be around her and Andy, Casson had said, emotion catching in his throat. And when Franklin's Resort was built, they would be among the first to stay there for a week's rest and relaxation.

Red had been seeing Sofia at that time, and the news about Andy's illness had made him sad, thinking about how devastated he would feel if Marco were undergoing treatment for a life-threatening illness. Red and Casson had moved on to other points of conversation, but after he had left to drive back to Toronto, Red hadn't been able to stop thinking about Andy. And his mother. Casson had pointed to a picture of both of them from when Andy had turned two. The boy was standing up on a chair at the kitchen table. His little cheeks were puffed up, about to blow out the cake candles, and Ronnie was standing behind his chair, her hands around his waist to ensure he didn't fall. She was beaming at Andy, and Red remembered thinking what a lovely woman she was.

His memory sharpening, he recalled that in the photo her hair was styled in a pixie cut, which suited her heart-shaped face. Now she had let it grow out. Either way, she was a beauty. A wholesome, natural beauty…

Red started as another branch clattered onto the roof. He forced himself to suspend his daydreaming and fixed a plate with a variety of cheeses and crackers. When he returned to the living room, he set down the tray on a small table between the recliners.

He poured the wine and handed Ronnie a glass. "Cheers," he said, grinning. "Might as well make the best of this adventure."

"Cheers," Ronnie said, giving him a curious look as they clinked glasses. "Is your disposition always this cheerful in the midst of environmental adversity?"

He burst out laughing. "Nobody's ever asked me such a question. Hmm." He stroked his jaw. "I generally like to stay positive in adverse environmental conditions and other trying situations," he said. He twirled his glass and met her gaze, amused that she was still looking at him as if he were some incomprehensible species from another planet.

"Are you following some kind of Eastern philosophy or something like that?" she said, genuine curiosity in her voice. "Surely you can't stay positive *all* the time…"

"Well, now, to answer your first question, I do occasionally meditate," he said. "And as for the second, I *have* been known to slip into the dark world of negativity when my hockey team is losing zero to three."

"So you're a hockey fanatic," she said, raising her eyebrows.

"You mean hockey *fan*," he corrected. "Go, Leafs, go!"

"A Toronto fan…" She smiled. "Just like my son."

"Since I was a kid. Forever a faithful fan of the Toronto Maple Leafs." He lifted his glass in a mock toast.

Her lips quirked. "A fan with astounding alliteration ability."

He chuckled. "And you're a lady with a lovely literary lexicon."

She laughed. "Okay, enough. I don't think I can top that." She took a sip of her wine and then set it down as the pelting against the windows intensified. "If this freezing rain keeps up, you'll have your own skating rink in your driveway."

Red saw her brows knit together. "Are you worried about your son?" he said gently.

Her gaze flew to his. "How do you…? Of course. Casson told you about Andy…"

She looked at him with narrowed eyes, almost as if she were speculating how much he knew about her personal life.

"No, I'm not worried about *him*. At the moment, that is." She glanced at her watch. "By now, he's been fed, bathed, read to and tucked into bed." She shifted her gaze to the fire for a few moments and then suddenly turned toward Red again. "Do *you* have any kids?"

Red's eyebrows went up. Ronnie was treading in sensitive waters. The relationship that he and Marco had shared had felt close to a father-son relationship. In fact, they had done what most dads seemed to do with their kids: play sports and games, go to the park, read, help with homework, go fishing… The thought that he wasn't doing any of those activities anymore struck him hard. *Again.*

A year may have passed since the breakup with Sofia, but his feelings about Marco hadn't dulled or changed. He missed the lad. *A lot.* And he vowed to himself every night that he would never cause himself this kind of grief again… Realizing that Ronnie was waiting for him to respond, he shook his head. "No, I don't have any children," he said with feigned lightness. "Or a wife."

Something flickered in Ronnie's eyes… Was she curious whether or not he was seeing anybody? "Or significant other," he added with a twist of his lips. "You know the saying—once burned, twice shy. To be more accurate, I've been scorched…"

Ronnie's eyebrows tilted slightly. "Sorry to hear that," she murmured, and turned to gaze into the fire.

"And yourself?" He might as well ask, since she had delved into *his* personal life.

She turned swiftly to face him again. "I went through a few flames myself," she said, lifting her chin. "Things have cooled down though, and I intend to keep it that way…"

"So does that mean you're with somebody but are giving him the cold shoulder?" he said wryly. "Or are you freezing out any and all would-be suitors?"

She frowned, then laughed curtly. "They're not exactly knocking at my door."

"Their loss," he heard himself say, and watched as a coral flush bloomed on Ronnie's cheeks.

"My gain." She shrugged nonchalantly. "Andy is my main focus, and his welfare and happiness are all that matter to me. I don't want—or need—any distractions from people who look like men but who are really needy little boys that can't cope when your attention strays from them…" She shifted and looked as if the cardigan she was wearing was making her itch. *Ouch.* He could almost envision the protective enclosure around Ronnie. With barbed wire on top…

"Casson had mentioned something about you moving to Parry Sound…" he said casually while placing another log in the fire. "So you're staying at Winter's Haven?"

"For now." Ronnie nodded. "I want to take my time looking around before I buy a house. I'll probably wait until spring. After all the snow is gone." She fixed him with a curious stare. "So what made you buy *this* place? It's rather large for just one person…"

"It is, isn't it? I'm looking forward to designing some new features and redesigning other areas. This is an art designated home, or 'heritage home,' so there are laws as to what can or can't be done. I just moved in two weeks ago. And I plan to entertain eventually—that is, if I can manage to make any friends," he said, chuckling. "I'd like to hold old-fashioned garden parties in the summer, skating parties on the pond in the winter—"

"There's a pond?" There was a note of awe in her voice.

He nodded. "Like something out of Currier & Ives."

"So you bought this place because…?" She gestured around her.

"First, because I have this thing about Victorian homes. When I was a kid, I always thought they looked enchanting, with their turrets and gables. I imagined all sorts of secret rooms and underground tunnels that led to caves in the hillside. I wanted to build a house like that when I grew up. And second, because I fell in love with the area when I first came to visit Casson after he got in touch with my firm in Toronto."

"Your firm?" Ronnie's brow furrowed momentarily before her eyes widened. "Do—do you mean the firm that designed—" She broke off, emotion catching in her throat.

"Franklin's Resort," he finished. "And I'm looking forward to the grand opening…"

CHAPTER FOUR

RONNIE REALIZED HER mouth was gaping. She closed it promptly and tried to process what Red just told her. Discovering that her rescuer's architectural firm had been the one chosen to fulfill Casson's dream—and that he would be at the grand opening... It was all too much. "So you're Red Brannigan...of Brannigan Architects International..." she said wonderingly.

"The one and only," he chuckled. "Actually, that's not true. I'm named after my father, so I'm officially Redmond Brannigan II. But since everyone called him Redmond, I became Red. And to tell you the truth, I much prefer it. Redmond sounds kind of stuffy, don't you think?"

Ronnie just shrugged, at a loss for words.

"Although 'Red' and my glorious mop of hair did leave me open to some childhood teasing," he said, his mouth twitching. "I remember that during an art lesson in grade three, a new kid in my class called Ivan started teasing me about my hair when the teacher was distracted. He called me 'Carrottop Four-Eyes'—not the most original of insults—and then crossed the line when he added, 'Your mom and dad must be ugly carrottops too.'" Red's eyes glinted with amusement. "He hurt my feelings, of course, and I did what my inner warrior instinctively told me to do: I dipped my paintbrush in my jar of orange paint and managed to give his blond hair some nice highlights." He laughed, shaking his head.

Ronnie couldn't help but burst out laughing. "That must have landed you in hot water."

"Indeed." He grinned, showing perfect teeth. "We were both sent to the principal's office immediately. But seeing the look on everyone's faces in the class—some of them had been insulted by Ivan the bully, as well—made it all worth it. In fact, I think I remember our teacher trying to hide a smile. I have a feeling that she and others might have been glad that he had gotten his just deserts."

"Did he plan his revenge?"

"Actually, he left me alone after that. Which is what bullies often do when you stand up to them. Not that I condone what I did," he added wryly.

Ronnie pictured Red as an eight-year-old with his russet hair and glasses, and couldn't help smiling. He must have been a cute kid...and an adorable baby, with a head of soft, reddish brown curls...

"What are you smiling about?" He fixed her with a piercing gaze.

Ronnie hesitated for a moment. "I was imagining you as an eight-year-old. And as a baby." She let out a chuckle. "I'm sure you were cute back then."

His eyebrows lifted. "Are you implying I'm no longer cute?"

Ronnie felt her cheeks begin to ignite. "I—I didn't mean... I mean, I wasn't... I—"

"Okay, sorry, Ronnie." He leaned toward her, grinning. "I didn't mean to put you on the spot. I don't expect you to comment on my current state of cuteness or lack thereof."

The heat in Ronnie's cheeks intensified. The crackling

of the fire seemed to synchronize with the sparks dancing along her nerve endings. With the darkness around them, with only the light of the flames illuminating them both, it felt as if she and Red were in the spotlight like two actors in a play, his body so close that his energy was palpable. He was looking at her squarely, his leprechaun eyes glinting mischievously from only about a foot away, the firelight flickering over the strong lines of his face. He was close enough for her to reach out and run her fingers through his—

She blinked and cleared her throat. "Well, I wouldn't exactly call you Ugly Carrottop Four-Eyes," she replied lightly. "I only see two eyes…"

"I'll take that as a compliment." He smiled. "How about you? I mean, were *you* teased as a child? I can't imagine that you had anything to be teased about…"

His eyes swept over her so quickly that Ronnie wondered if she had imagined it…

"Well, actually I was," she said, drawing herself up in the recliner. "Some kids tried to torment me with a couple of names: 'Shortie' or 'Rabbit.'" She tilted her chin defensively. "But I didn't care. I liked rabbits." She took another sip of her wine.

"So we have something in common," he said softly. "You were the rabbit and I was the carrottop." He continued to gaze at her intently, and then gave his head a slight shake as if to redirect his thoughts. "I've never met a rabbit that *wasn't* cute…"

Ronnie felt her pulse quicken. Was this his enigmatic way of saying that he found her cute? Did she want him to find her cute? "Um, well, I'm sure Beatrix Potter would agree with you," she stated matter-of-factly. "I just wish I could hop home…"

"What? I may not be as cute as a bunny, but I didn't

think my company or conversation were *that* bad…" His lips drooped into a pout and he blinked dramatically.

She couldn't help but laugh. "Now you look more like a sad puppy dog." *Still cute, though. More than just cute…*

Red burst out laughing. He held up his wineglass. "Let's toast to bunnies and puppies, the cutest little creatures in the world."

She held up her glass and realized in embarrassment that there was barely a mouthful left.

"May I?" Red reached for the bottle.

"Ah, no, thanks, I'd better not." She leaned toward the fire to glance at her watch. "I think it's going to be a long night…" She shifted in her recliner. "I feel like I'm on a night flight on an airplane. I doubt I'll be getting much sleep tonight…"

"The recliner does recline," he said. "Here, just press on this." He stood up and leaned over to indicate the hidden button. "And keep your finger on it until it's as far back as you want it to go."

Ronnie's pulse quickened as his arm brushed hers and she caught a whiff of his cologne, an exotic spicy scent. When she pressed on the spot, the recliner glided back. She felt self-conscious with Red towering over her while her body moved back with the chair.

"Try to catch some sleep," he said huskily before throwing another log onto the grate. "I intend to do the same." He strode over to a couch on the other side of the room and came back with a thick scarlet throw. "This should keep you warm, especially if I fall asleep and the fire burns out." He smiled, unfolding the throw and placing it over the length of her body. "Good night, Ronnie."

Something fluttered in her chest as Red looked down at her, his face reflecting the shifting light of the fire.

"Good night." She closed her eyes until she heard his recliner slide back. She stole a sideways glance at him and saw that he had stretched out without a throw, and his arms were crossed over his chest.

And he was looking right at her.

Red smiled and turned his head away from her. He certainly didn't want to make Ronnie feel uncomfortable. He imagined it was already awkward enough for her, being stranded in a stranger's house in the middle of an ice storm. Well, at least knowing that he and Casson were friends would have eased her mind somewhat.

He listened to the crackle of the fire. The room had warmed up, especially around their recliners. Outside, the freezing rain was still pelting the windows, intermittent gusts of wind making it sound intense.

He had absolutely no inclination toward sleeping. How could he, with a woman he didn't want to be attracted to lying not three feet away from him? She was easy to look at, with her dark hair and dark almond-shaped eyes. He had never seen lashes that long, and he was pretty sure they weren't fake. She was petite, but Red had sensed her inner strength even before he discovered she was Casson's cousin. The cousin with the little boy who had undergone treatment for leukemia. He felt a surge of empathy for what they must have both gone through. It had been hard enough for Casson…especially after having lived through the experience with his younger brother. And losing him.

Red was glad Casson had thought of him and his firm when contemplating his dream of building a resort in Franklin's memory. It had led him to reconnect with his university friend in the picturesque town of Parry Sound and eventually invest in the Victorian home he had always dreamed of but never got around to building himself. He traveled extensively around the world, keeping abreast of the many projects being developed by his firm's international branches, and when he had visited Casson, he had realized that he needed a place where he could truly take a break from business and just enjoy a more relaxed lifestyle.

Scenic Georgian Bay and the Muskokas had hooked Red immediately. As his pilot had flown Red's private plane to Parry Sound in the middle of autumn, Red had been mesmerized by the forests ablaze with brilliant hues of red, orange and yellow. And now that he had moved in, he was taking a month off for the simple pleasure of making this house a home.

And now, he couldn't deny that he was attracted to Ronnie.

And he was fighting it.

She wasn't free. Whatever fates had decided to slide her into that field and send him trudging through knee-deep snow to rescue her, had just complicated his life. He had thought that after getting over Sofia, and reconciling himself to the sad fact that his relationship with Marco was over, as well, he would be immune to another relationship if it involved a child. He had been adamant that it would never happen again. He couldn't take the thought of building a relationship with a girlfriend's child, only to have to deal with the acute grief of having it come to an end. He had vowed over and over again that any future relationship would happen only if the woman were free. *Childless.*

So even if his body *was* physically attracted to Ronnie, his mind would not allow him to encourage any emotional attraction. He had had to ignore the spike of his pulse when he had lifted her and carried her to his truck, the thud of his heart when she had huddled against him, the empathy that had stirred in his chest at the thought of what she had had to endure, and the pleasure of laughing with her…

Red shifted in his recliner. It *was* going to be a long night. He closed his eyes. His thoughts flitted back to the moment he had seen the vehicle in front of him begin to skid. His heart had jolted, and he had immediately slowed down, hoping the driver wouldn't careen into him. He had been more worried about the impact on the smaller vehicle than on his considerably larger truck. And not for the vehicle itself, but for the passenger or passengers inside. Were there children in the car? Elderly folk?

He had watched it spin out and stop, still upright, off the shoulder and in a field, its tires buried in deep snow. It had all happened in mere seconds. And in a matter of seconds he had maneuvered his truck safely onto the shoulder, leaped out, and trudged through the snow to make sure the driver and any passengers were okay. He'd call 911 if he had to, although with the icy conditions it would certainly take longer for an emergency vehicle to get there safely.

He had proceeded to the car with his head down to avoid the sleet, his heart thumping erratically. Through the partially glazed windshield, the female driver sitting with her hands on the wheel had looked dazed but unhurt. But he had needed to make sure…

Discovering Ronnie's connection with Casson had surprised him, but the memory of some of the details about her and her son had jolted him. It was one thing to have had Casson tell him about his remarkable cousin who was tiny but tough, a real "mama bear," dealing with her son's illness and treatment, but to be with her in person was even more revelatory. He could sense her determination and desire to be independent.

Despite the fact that she had allowed him to carry her back to his truck, he had no doubt that she would have trudged through thigh-deep snow herself had he not stopped to check on her.

Red closed his eyes. He wondered if Ronnie was asleep or awake and thinking like him. And if she was doing the latter, who was she thinking about? Her son? Probably. Him? Probably not.

He couldn't hear the sound of her breathing with the crackling of the fire. After what he felt was a reasonable amount of time, Red turned in his recliner to glance over at Ronnie. Good. Fast asleep. "Sweet dreams," he whispered.

She had pulled the blanket up to her chin, and gazing at her small outline and the way her long lashes rested on her heart-shaped face, Red felt a surge of protectiveness.

And contentment, knowing she was safe.

He inhaled and exhaled deeply, and allowed himself to drift off, hoping his dreams would be just as sweet…

CHAPTER FIVE

THE TANTALIZING SMELL of food cooking woke Ronnie up. Disoriented, her eyes opened to take in an unfamiliar ceiling, an unfamiliar room and a crackling fire. A turn of her head revealed an empty recliner. And then awareness returned.

She was in the home of Red Brannigan, her Viking rescuer...

From the amount of light in the room, she figured it must be midmorning. She couldn't believe she had managed to sleep that long. Or even that she had fallen asleep so quickly. After turning to find Red's gaze fixed on her, she had felt a shiver running through her. He had given her a casual smile before turning the opposite way, no doubt having sensed how awkward she had felt. She had turned the other way herself, and closing her eyes, had wondered how she could possibly fall asleep with the vision of those intense blue-green eyes imprinted in her memory.

She had pulled up the blanket, feeling somewhat vulnerable. Not because she felt frightened in any way; knowing that Red was a friend of Casson's was enough to reassure her of Red's character. Rather, it was more of a feeling of suddenly being aware of a few uncontrollable physical reactions she was experiencing in Red's proximity. And not wanting him to know it. It was silly, really. How could he possibly know how his presence—his height, his strength, the way his russet hair looked after he ran his fingers through it, his crystal-clear Viking eyes—was affecting her?

Her body was a traitor. She didn't *want* to be attracted to Red. She didn't *need* that kind of distraction in her life. Her life was full. More than full. Her responsibilities as a mother were her top priority. She had no business investing any of her thoughts in any man right now.

You have nothing to worry about, she told herself. Red would be driving her back to Winter's Haven, and there wouldn't be any reason for their paths to cross again, other than at the grand opening of Franklin's Resort.

His husky laugh nearby startled her. "Hey, do I have to cook *and* bring you breakfast in bed?" Red was standing in the doorway, a whisk in one hand. His hair was damp, and he had changed into a pair of black jeans and a teal pullover.

Eye candy.

She felt a rush of heat at the unbidden thought and hastily brought the recliner up, realizing she must have undone her ponytail during the night. She smoothed her hair down self-consciously and shot back, "I didn't expect or ask you to cook. I expected only a ride back to Winter's Haven. But since the power has been restored and you have gone to the trouble, I will help consume your culinary creation."

He burst out laughing. "Oh, no. We're not starting the day with literary linguistics, are we?"

"Actually, I prefer to start my day with a strong cup of coffee. And then another. Hopefully coffee's on?" she said, tilting her chin imperiously.

His mouth quirked. "It's waiting for me to pour it in a

cup for you, *Miss Veronica*. And I'll be waiting to serve you in the kitchen." Flashing her a grin, he gave a bow, turned and disappeared into the next room.

Ronnie smirked. He seemed to enjoy flinging teasing remarks at her. Well, she would fling them right back at him, at least up until the time he drove her back to her cottage. She folded the blanket and placed it back on the recliner along with the cardigan Red had given her, before striding to the nearest window, anxious to see the aftermath of yesterday's freezing rain and snow. Her hope that she'd be able to get back to Winter's Haven sometime that morning plummeted. At some point during the night, the freezing rain had solidified with the considerable drop in temperature. The limbs and branches of the oaks and maples flanking the driveway were encased in ice. The sky was clear, and the bright sun made the trees glisten as if bejeweled. The snow that had remained on the ground was coated with an icy sheen, as was Red's truck.

Ronnie didn't need to hear the weather report to know that she wouldn't be leaving anytime soon. It might be different in town and on the main roads, where the sand trucks had probably already passed over, but this place was obviously not in a high-priority area, being situated on the outskirts…

She took a deep breath and let it out in an exasperated puff. Along with being a little stiff from sleeping on a recliner all night, she felt out of her comfort zone. And she didn't like it.

Although she hadn't been that long at her Winter's Haven cottage, she had felt at home right away. Casson and Justine had had it refreshed with new furniture and linens, and some homey touches. They could stay in the cottage as long as they wanted, Casson and Justine had reassured her. And, her cousin had added with a wink, she and Andy could babysit A.J. when he and Justine needed a date night... Ronnie couldn't help smiling at the thought of Amy Jay. She was an absolute doll, with Casson's dark brown hair and Justine's blue-gray eyes.

Ronnie turned away from the window. Like it or not, she had no choice but to spend the next few hours in a stranger's home. The last thing she had envisioned when she had left the cottage yesterday was being stranded in a Victorian house with a Viking type who seemed to take everything in his stride. What on earth would they do while waiting for Mother Nature and the town crews to make driving possible?

She would have breakfast and then find herself a spot where she could bury her nose in one of her newly purchased books. And, like it or not, she'd have to be patient. With any luck, she'd be back at Winter's Haven sometime in the afternoon...

A wave of longing washed over Ronnie. She wished Andy was with her, at the cottage, sipping hot chocolate and doing a jigsaw puzzle together, or making peanut butter cookies, his favorite. She gave her head a shake. She should be glad—and she *was*—that Andy's father was taking responsibility and regularly spending time with him. But even so, there were moments where she missed Andy's presence. Many moments...

Casson had given her a reassuring hug when she had voiced these feelings to him one day over coffee. "You may be small," he had chuckled, "but you're still the protective mama bear. You've always put Andy first. He's been the center of your world. Of course it feels strange now to be on your own for blocks of time without him..."

Ronnie sighed and made her way to the kitchen. To her embarrassment, her stomach gave a loud grumble as she entered the room.

Red's eyebrows lifted. "I guess I'd better feed you before there's an aftershock," he chuckled. He gestured for her to sit down at the sturdy oak table, where he had arranged two place settings, two mugs and a carafe. He filled Ronnie's mug. "Enjoy," he said. "I'll be back with the breakfast special." He winked conspiratorially. "And then, since the roads are still a skating rink, we can talk about what we want to do…"

Red watched as Ronnie took her first bites of the mushroom and cheese omelet and nodded when she gave him a thumbs-up.

"Whew! Thank goodness I passed *one* test, anyway…"

Ronnie's brows furrowed. "And what is the other test for? Doing a good deed of the day?" She took a sip of her steaming coffee. "I believe rescuing a stranded driver *does* fall in that category."

He grinned and gestured at his head. "My halo should be lighting up any minute. So—" he gazed at her "—since we are housebound for the moment, we might as well have some fun…"

Ronnie's fork paused in midair. She stared at him as if he had suggested something wild and inappropriate.

"I don't need to be entertained," she said stiffly, her expression wary. "I'll be quite content reading one of my books." She lowered her gaze, concentrating on cutting her omelet into small, precise pieces.

Red gazed at her thoughtfully. She wasn't going to allow herself to relax. She had just given him the not so subtle hint that she didn't need his company while stuck in his house. A sudden thought occurred to him. She hadn't had a lot of time for "fun" while dealing with her son's illness and treatment these last couple of years. She had probably forgotten what having fun was…

"Hey, I could bury myself in one of my books, too," he said lightly. He had stocked the built-in bookshelves on either side of the fireplace with several boxes of his own books as well as a dozen from his recent trip to the local bookstores. "But why not live a little?"

He watched her as she dabbed at her lips with her napkin, avoiding his gaze.

"You can tell me to mind my own business if you want, Ronnie, but I think maybe you've had to put life on hold while caring for your son—"

"Andy is my life," she blurted defensively. "He's my priority and always will be."

Red felt a twinge in his stomach at her words. "You're obviously a good mother. A very good mother," he said softly. "Andy's lucky to have such a devoted—and strong—parent."

Ronnie's eyes flickered. "I *had* to be strong. I had no other choice."

"Everyone has a choice," he said, unable to keep a hint of bitterness out of his voice. "My parents chose to prance around the world on business and pleasure. That was *their* priority. I guess they figured their only son would have no problem growing up mostly with a nanny…"

She frowned. "I'm sorry…"

"Don't be," he said bluntly. "Thank goodness I was healthy and they didn't have to spoil their plans to come back and take care of me. Besides, I had a great nanny."

"I… I…that's too bad." She shrugged and shook her head. "The first part, I mean."

"It could have been worse," he said, making his voice sound cheerier. "I never lacked for food, clothes, or money. In fact, I shouldn't really complain. It's not everyone who ends up with a Porsche and a fancy condo as grad gifts."

Her brows lifted and she blinked at him. "Yes, but—"

"Let's not talk about me," he said firmly, reaching for his cell phone. He texted something, waited, then looked back at Ronnie. "Just what I suspected," he said, rubbing his chin.

"What do you mean?"

"You said you had no other choice. Well, you didn't, not with a name like Veronica."

"I don't get it."

"I just looked up the meaning of your name. It says here 'Veronica—she who brings victory…and true image.'" He turned off his phone. "Well, it obviously takes a strong person to bring victory…and everything you've done to support your son has helped to bring that about." He felt his gaze soften as her eyes misted. "Andy's in remission. Don't underestimate *your* part in his recovery, Ronnie."

"I did what I had to do," she said, her voice wavering slightly. "My hus—*ex*-husband couldn't handle it. He left, and found comfort crying on the shoulder of another woman. And eventually moved in with her." She inhaled deeply and exhaled slowly. "I took a leave from work. I had to travel back and forth to Toronto's SickKids, watch my little boy subjected to treatment that left him weak and vulnerable. It was—" she bit her lip "—heartbreaking. And then for months, Andy couldn't leave the hospital, and so I ended up staying at Ronald McDonald House. It was…tough."

Red felt a surge of anger inflaming his gut. He could only imagine the emotional ordeal she had experienced, having her husband take off, unable to cope. Coping had fallen completely on *her* shoulders. His gaze took in the decisive tilt of Ronnie's chin as she speared a piece of her omelet. His anger gave way to admiration. Despite her petite size, she exuded an air of inner strength and determination. She had carried on without her deadbeat of a husband.

Well, at least the guy had smartened up and had resumed his parental responsibilities. And if Ronnie had chosen to forgive him and move on, Casson had told Red, then *he* would have to, as well. At least now, Ronnie could have some time of her own. Time to enjoy life—especially since Andy was in remission—and have some fun.

Red dug into his omelet. The weather report earlier had indicated that the temperature was warming up. The crews were still out sanding the side roads. By sometime in the afternoon, driving should be able to resume all over town.

So they had about three and a half hours left in each other's company. And as much as he loved to read, he had other plans. The challenge was getting the determined woman sitting across from him to consider what he had in mind.

Ronnie looked up suddenly and met his gaze. She swallowed and set down her fork. "Thanks, it was good," she said. "A treat not to have to make my own breakfast," she added with a soft laugh.

Red felt a warmth radiate in his chest. She deserved to be treated. "Glad you enjoyed it," he said casually. "I'll treat you to lunch if the roads aren't cleared by then."

She smiled, but Red could tell she was uncomfortable at the prospect. She stood and tucked her chair back in. "Since you cooked, I'll be glad to do my part and wash the dishes."

"Not a chance," he laughed. "The dishwasher will take care of that. But—" he stood up and crossed his arms "—I'm hoping you will accept my challenge to change your plan to read since that can be done any time and come outside with me instead…"

"Outside?" Her gaze flew to the window. "For… what?"

"Let's just say, I'd like you to experience the magic of this place. The conditions are perfect, with last night's freezing rain…" He gave her a warm smile. "Trust me, it'll be a lot of fun…" At her look of suspicion, he chuckled. "If you don't enjoy yourself, I'll give you your money back."

Ronnie gave him a measured glance. "I don't know what I'm getting myself into, but I hope you have good insurance."

He burst out laughing. "Come on, Ronnie," he cajoled, "grab your coat and mitts. You won't regret this."

Moments later, carrying her boots in one hand, Ronnie followed Red past a series of rooms to a hallway that led to the back porch. The sun was streaming through the decorative leaded windows, dotting the wall with prisms of light. Ronnie sat on the long upholstered bench and, still mystified, began to put on a boot.

"You won't actually need those," Red said. "Because—" he opened the doors to an antique armoire and gestured to the contents "—we're going skating!" He grinned. "I invited Justine and Casson over last week. I suggested they leave their skates here for the next time."

Ronnie's jaw dropped. She told Red that *she* had babysat A.J. with Andy last week. Casson had told her they would be out skating, but A.J. had started to fuss and he and Justine had been too busy trying to settle the baby down to give any further details. As soon as she had settled, they had hurried out the door, reassuring Ronnie that they'd be home in a couple of hours. And when they did return, Ronnie didn't linger, as Andy had complained of a headache, and she wanted to get back to the cottage so he could rest in his own bed.

She looked at Red and at the skates and then back at Red. "But I… I haven't skated in years. Besides, I doubt Justine's skates will fit…"

"Justine has small feet. Try them out." He handed her the pair of white skates that were comfortably broken in. His pulse skipped a beat as her hand brushed his. The fact that Ronnie had agreed to go outside instead of reading, as she had originally intended, pleased him. A lot.

He took out his own pair and sat down next to Ronnie to put them on. As he was lacing up his right skate, he glanced up at her. "Well, Cinderella? Does the shoe—I mean skate—fit?"

"Wow; I can't believe it," she said. "We actually take the same size."

"Fabulous. Lace 'em up, and in the meantime, I'll go check the surface of the ice." He finished lacing up his left skate and then gave her an appraising glance. "When you're ready, just come on out." His lips twitched. "You can't miss the quasi-Olympic-size pond."

"That's what I'm afraid of," she retorted, "when I face-plant."

"I'll be on standby," he assured her. "I'll scoop you up before you do…" And with a wide smile, he went out.

CHAPTER SIX

She watched him through the windows. He was impossibly tall, and he strode toward the pond. Her gaze went from the blue-and-white Toronto Maple Leafs toque on his head to his wool-lined denim jacket and jeans, and finally to his black skates. When he had sat next to her, leaning over to tie them up, she had almost laughed at the sight of her diminutive pair next to his. But when his thigh had momentarily pressed against hers, the amusement she had felt changed to a pulse-quickening sensation that left her immobile. And then he had made the Cinderella comment, and she had responded casually, although inside she had felt a tingle go through her…

Satisfied that her laces were tied snugly, Ronnie stood up, testing her balance on the plank flooring. She proceeded cautiously to the door. She had been a decent skater in her youth and teenage years, and even in the early years of her marriage to Peter, but after Andy was born, skating had not been a priority. And when she had contemplated introducing Andy to the national sport, he had been diagnosed with leukemia.

She sighed. It had been heartbreaking, seeing how restricted Andy's life had been for the last couple of years. While other children were enjoying all the traditional activities of childhood, Andy was undergoing his chemotherapy. She had spent countless hours at his bedside at SickKids, reading to him, singing, and dreaming of the day when he would be able to go home and be a kid again.

Those dreams had come true. She was filled with gratitude every day for the success of his treatment, and she prayed that he would continue to get stronger. And eventually catch up with his friends.

And now that they were settling into Winter's Haven for the next few months, she could even contemplate getting Andy a pair of skates and taking him to the arena…

She smiled, mentally conceding that it was a good thing that Red had gently pressured her to do this. If she was going to take Andy out on a skating rink, then she'd better brush up on her skating skills.

Knowing that the property included a pond and actually seeing it were two different things. Ronnie paused in the doorway, momentarily stunned. Who had a pond this size in their backyard? The previous night's freezing rain had turned it into a giant, polished mirror. Squinting from the glare of the sun's reflection on the ice, she diverted her gaze to the current owner of the place. *Redmond Brannigan II.*

He was skating around the perimeter of the pond, and when he caught sight of her, he sped toward her in long, confident strides, coming to a dramatic sideways stop, the edge of his skates skimming off the top layer of ice.

"Don't expect any Ice Capades maneuvers from *me*," she declared, stepping gingerly onto the ice. "I don't do any of that fancy stuff."

"I'm not expecting anything other than you having fun," he said. "Just enjoy." He flashed her a smile. "I forgot to do something," he said enigmatically. "I'll just be a moment."

He went back inside, and for a few seconds Ronnie

stared at the huge expanse of ice before her. A swirl of
anticipation ran through her. Who wouldn't want to have
this entire pond to themselves? She started off slowly, re-
acquainting herself with the feel of the ice and the rush
of cool air on her cheeks as she picked up some momen-
tum. She felt like she was in another world, the sun dazzling her and turning the ice surface into a sparkly glass
lake. She breathed in the crystal cool air as she began her
second lap, her strides more confident. For a moment she
tilted her face to the sun, daring to close her eyes. She
felt bold, free and an exhilaration she hadn't felt in years.
Her heart racing, she opened her eyes, and, with a jolt,
realized that Red was at the porch door, watching her.

As he stepped out and approached the pond, a popular
rock song came on out of nowhere. When he was near
enough to Ronnie, Red pointed to the speakers on posts
around the pond. "They obviously enjoyed their skating
parties here," he said. "I thought you might enjoy a little
musical interlude while we skate."

Ronnie had slowed down, but the beat of the song
was catchy and made her want to keep skating. She nodded and zipped past Red as he flashed her a Cheshire
cat grin. Her heart flipped. Was she dreaming, or had
he just said, "That's my girl?" She shook her head, her
heart pounding in synch with the bass, and berated herself for even thinking such a thing. The movement compromised her balance and she felt the edge of her right
skate wobbling and lifting off the ice. And then she was
falling. Backward…

She closed her eyes, bracing for the fall. But instead
of landing hard on the ice, she felt herself being swooped
upward. Her eyes flew open and all they could register at
first was the sight of the boards whizzing by.

And then it hit her. She was in Red's arms as he skated around the pond.

"I told you I'd scoop you up if you fell…" he murmured in her ear without stopping.

Ronnie was speechless. The sensation of being carried—no, *swept away*—in Red Brannigan's arms was heady. He held her in strong arms, his long strides never faltering as he skated around the pond. Like the day before when he had carried her effortlessly to his truck, she found herself leaning against his broad chest.

Was he going faster? He was. Her arms flew up and involuntarily encircled his neck, her hands clasped together. He suddenly veered toward the center of the pond and as he circled in a figure eight, Ronnie couldn't help letting out a high-pitched yelp. She closed her eyes, convinced he would take a misstep that would send them both tumbling down. Her heart was drumming so hard, she could barely hear the music. She felt terrified and excited at the same time. At the next swirl, she felt her cheek pressed against Red's neck and she couldn't pull away from the centrifugal force.

His neck was warm, and the sensation took her breath away. Her lips were close enough to—

She gasped as he spun her around in a dizzying on-the-spot rotation, forcing her to shut her eyes again, and when he finally stopped, a few seconds passed before she tentatively opened them. He was looking down at her, his sun-flecked eyes glittering above a crooked smile that she could only describe as impish. No, *devilish*. And then he set her down slowly, her hands unclasping and falling limply at her sides. He kept a steadying hand under her left elbow, and she couldn't help but feel relieved, not knowing if her feet would hold her up after that…

"I can't believe you did that," she said breathlessly.

"I should be mad at you for scaring me half to death…"
She paused at the unapologetic twinkle in his eyes. How
could she be mad, though, when the last few minutes had
been nothing short of exciting? Unbelievably exciting,
activating sensations throughout her that she had never
felt before… "I suppose I should just be grateful," she
said, feigning a scowl, "that you didn't toss me up in the
air and then attempt to catch me…"

He threw back his head and laughed. "Maybe next
time," he said huskily. "But seriously, Ronnie, I hope
you can forgive me for my impetuous skating maneuvers." He gazed down at her, his hand still under her
elbow, despite the fact that she felt steady on her feet. "I
just wanted you to have a little fun…especially after the
stress of yesterday…"

There was a warmth in the depth of his eyes that Ronnie knew she wasn't imagining. They were the color of a
tropical lagoon…inviting and startlingly beautiful.

And sexy, an inner voice whispered.

His eyebrows lifted, and with a jolt she realized that
he was waiting for her reply, not reading her thoughts.

"I do," she blurted. "Forgive you."

His mouth curved into a smile. "Great, now let's seal
it with a…"

Her heart stopped.

"…hot chocolate. *And*, since you've been such a good
sport," he added, a twinkle in his eyes, "I'll add some
marshmallows on top."

Red placed the steaming mugs of hot chocolate on a tray
and brought it to the living room. Ronnie had replied to
Casson's text on Red's phone, and was standing by the
window, a wistful look on her face.

She walked over to the recliner she had slept on the

day before. He set the tray on the side table between the recliners and sat down. "I checked the weather report, Ronnie. The roads are much better in most places. I'll be able to drive you back to Winter's Haven whenever you're ready."

She nodded and took a sip of her hot chocolate. "Nice," she murmured. "I can taste the cinnamon and something different in here. Nutmeg or cloves, maybe?"

He gazed at her pensively. Her tone was pleasant, but he sensed that something was off. She seemed more subdued…maybe even a little sad…

She took another sip, and when she looked across at him, her brows tilted as she waited for his reply; he couldn't help smiling at the puff of melting marshmallow on the tip of her nose.

She cocked her head at him, and he felt something undeniably sweet tingling through him.

Something dangerous…

Yet some other force made him lean toward her, his hand ready to—

And then she became aware of the white puff and wiped it off herself with a nearby tissue.

He leaned back again, not sure if he felt relief or regret. He took a sip of his hot chocolate and wondered what she was going to do once she got back to Winter's Haven.

"What are your plans today?" he said casually. "Will your son be back?"

Her head shot up, and the look she gave him made him realize that he had ventured into private territory, territory that she was very protective of…

Of course. She was the mama bear, and naturally, she would be vigilant over her little one. And of their privacy, as well. "Sorry, I didn't mean to be nosy," he said gently.

Her features relaxed. "It's all right. For a moment I

forgot about your connection to Casson and that he had told you about Andy…"

And about his remarkable mother. "Yes, and what a brave little boy he is…"

Ronnie's eyes misted. Damn, he didn't mean to make her emotional. He opened his mouth to apologize, but she put up a hand.

"I'll be okay." She sighed. "There are days when I can think or talk about what he's been through and not fall apart." She pressed her fingertips against her closed eyelids for a moment. "And then the slightest words or memory will—" Her words caught in her throat, and she looked at him and shook her head. "It's been hard. Really hard." She swallowed. "On both of us. And scary, worrying every day about the future…" She shook her head. "No, it hasn't just been hard. It's been hell…" A few tears slid down her cheeks.

"Falling apart is okay, Ronnie," he said gently. He wanted to reach out, wipe her tears, put a comforting arm around her, but something held him back. "It's good to get your feelings out. That's part of the healing process." He gave a slight grimace. "I'm sorry. You've probably heard this all before."

"I have," she said, nodding. "But it doesn't hurt to hear it again." She inhaled and exhaled deeply. "It's amazing what some people say to you, though, like 'You have to be strong.' If I had a dollar for every time that was said to me…" She bit her lip. "I know people were just trying to help. It's just that sometimes hearing those words really got to me. I *knew* I had to be strong. Nobody had to tell me." She traced a finger over the rim of her mug several times while her forehead creased. Red wondered what memories she was revisiting.

Suddenly she set down the mug, her gaze riveting

back to Red. "But to answer your question, Andy won't be back from his dad's until the end of the week. So my plans are to keep unpacking—not everything, though, since I'll be looking for my own place in the spring. How about you?"

"Me? I'll probably continue working on some of my renovation ideas. This place is in great shape, but I'd like to make a few changes, if I can. Maybe replace some of the wallpaper. Since it's a heritage home, there are laws as to what can or can't be done."

Ronnie nodded. "There must be a lot of fascinating nooks and crannies in a place like this." She looked around appreciatively.

"I'd be happy to show you around," Red offered.

"Thanks, but I think we should head out," she said. "I really have a lot to do still."

"No problem," he said, rising. "Maybe another time," he added impulsively. "And—" He stopped himself. What was he doing? He had almost said "And bring Andy too."

He shouldn't have even suggested that there might be "another time" to Ronnie. Much as he had enjoyed her company—maybe too much, especially when she was in his arms—he had to remember that she had a child. A sweet little boy. And that's why he had to stay away. Or make sure *they* stayed away. He couldn't risk getting to know another boy who wasn't his. And although he probably couldn't avoid them at the opening of Franklin's Resort, there was no reason why he would be seeking Ronnie's company otherwise…

She was looking at him, waiting for him to finish his sentence. "And…good luck with your unpacking," he said brusquely.

Moments later, as he drove out of his neighborhood, Red sensed a different dynamic between them. He and

Ronnie had been in each other's company for less than twenty-four hours, and yet he found himself experiencing the anticipatory awkwardness of saying goodbye.

Was she feeling something similar? She had been subdued since getting into his truck. But then again, she was probably missing her son.

He turned on the radio. Might as well liven up the atmosphere… He switched a few channels, and settled on the classic rock channel. He couldn't help singing along to some of the catchy tunes, and several times, he caught Ronnie's amused glances in his direction. When one of his favorite songs came on, "Small Town" by John Cougar Mellencamp, he got through the entire song, and at the final harmonica segment, he whistled along.

As Red turned into the winding road on the final stretch to Winter's Haven, Ronnie gave him directions to her cottage. He slowed down even more, conscious of the intermittent patches of ice on the path flanked by trees. A final turn brought him to cottage number three. Ronnie's car was sitting in the driveway and she clapped when she saw it.

"Casson deserves a batch of cookies for this," she said, grinning.

"He's quite a guy." Red smiled back. He parked behind it and turned off the ignition. "So if *he* gets cookies for arranging a tow, what do *I* get for my heroic rescue? Not to mention my culinary effort and the outdoor entertainment I provided?" He batted his eyelashes as he looked at her pointedly. "I think I deserve at least a cookie or two. Or maybe twenty…"

Ronnie burst out laughing. "If I had my phone, I would have taken a video of you. I'm sure it would have gone viral."

"Really? Well, here's my phone. Let's give them something to talk about…" He sang the last phrase. He pulled off his toque and ran his fingers through his hair, making it stick out, before batting his lashes at her again.

"I'm going to pass," she said, holding up a hand. "Besides, I don't think that performance would do anything for your image as the owner of Brannigan Architects International."

"Fine!" He patted down his hair. "But don't get distracted from the fact that you offered to make me a couple of dozen cookies."

"What?" She looked at him with an exaggerated frown. "Casson should have warned me about you…" She opened the side door and glanced back at him. "But I do offer you my thanks and appreciation for your aforementioned heroism and associated efforts."

She walked gingerly up the steps to her door, then turned and waved, a slight smirk on her face.

He rolled down his window and waved back. "Peanut butter cookies are my favorite," he shouted. Grinning, he backed up before driving off slowly, conscious of Ronnie watching him until he turned and disappeared from view.

CHAPTER SEVEN

RONNIE SHOOK HER HEAD and unlocked her door. She took off her coat and boots and put on her fleece-lined slippers. Feeling a little cold, she turned up the heat and then sat down on the couch, covering her legs with the checkered throw. She gazed at the dozens of boxes that still needed to be unpacked and sighed. It was a task that needed to get done, but somehow, she had no desire to get to it right now. Or anything else. Except maybe baking a batch of cookies for Casson later in the afternoon.

There was no way Red had been serious about baking him cookies, as well…

Peanut butter cookies, his favorite. Just like Andy.

He had been in a joking mood; he was just teasing her…

Or maybe not, her inner voice suggested.

Ronnie frowned. She wouldn't think about it for now. She'd rather read. She glanced at the doorway for her bag of books. Confused, she wondered in dismay if she had left it in Red's truck. And then she realized she hadn't remembered to take the bag with her. It was on the floor next to the recliner she had slept on.

Damn. Now she'd have to make arrangements to get it from Red. A thought occurred to her. Maybe Casson was planning to meet him before the grand opening, and if so, Red could give it to him.

Her cell phone suddenly rang, and she jumped up to get it on the kitchen counter where she had forgotten it. It was Casson. He had seen Red's truck go by. He asked if she was okay, and if she wanted to drop over for lunch.

"Thanks, Cass. Yes, I'm fine, and thanks too, for getting the car towed. Um, I'll pass on lunch... I had a big breakfast, so I'll just munch on something a little later, but I will drop by this afternoon, okay?"

After hanging up, Ronnie stretched out on the couch and gazed out the huge living room window that looked out onto the water. It had started to snow again, and as she watched the flakes tumbling gently down, she was glad she had some time to herself. She felt bad about declining Casson's invitation, but she needed to process everything that had happened since her car had spun out of control. It was true what she had said about breakfast, but she couldn't exactly tell Casson that this architect buddy of his had spun *her* around. Literally and figuratively.

And much as she loved Casson, Justine and the baby, Ronnie knew that she'd have little A.J. in her arms immediately if she went over. She would delay that pleasure until the afternoon, once she had baked the cookies.

Okay, start processing, her inner voice urged. *Start with his looks.*

Ronnie closed her eyes. She could see him approaching in long, purposeful strides, assaulted by the freezing rain. His dampened russet hair and piercing blue-green eyes. The strength in his arms as he carried her to his truck. His broad chest in that teal pullover and perfectly fitting black jeans today. She had had no problem with the way he looked...

What about his personality?

He was positive, creative, attentive, daring, funny, a good listener, empathetic, silly, charming…

What are his negative qualities?

Ronnie frowned. She tried to think of something Red had said or done that had irked her.

His teasing? Mmm…no, she hadn't minded it; in fact, it had made her feel a swirl of different emotions, but none of them were bad.

What he *had* done was make her feel something that had been missing in her life since Andy had become seriously ill. The feeling of being lighthearted. *Alive*. When Red had swooped her up, preventing her from falling on the ice, and then skated around the pond with her in his arms, she had felt like a switch had been turned on inside her.

She could keep the truth from Red, but she couldn't keep it from herself. Red had turned her on. Made her remember that she was a woman. And that life was fun.

She had lost her sense of play, of adventure, of joy. Of course she had felt joy at the success of Andy's treatments, but all the other emotions before that—worry, fear, despair, loneliness, sadness—had weighed her down. Peter taking off had made her cynical. Cynical about men, about ever putting her trust in any of them.

And she had been determined *never* to allow herself to get involved in another relationship. She wouldn't risk it. She had Andy to think about. She couldn't put him through that. His little heart had had enough to deal with…

And *her* heart had been bruised enough.

Ronnie took a deep breath and strode into the kitchen. She and Andy would have a good life in Parry Sound, and enjoy being close to Casson and his family. They would share seasonal traditions and celebrate their children's milestones together. She was so looking forward to this new chapter in their lives…

Ronnie began gathering the ingredients for the peanut butter cookies. For the past year, she had been adamant that she didn't need or want a man in her life. So why, then, did she now feel her resolve suddenly wavering?

Ronnie glanced out the window, her gaze dropping to Red's tire tracks on the snow-packed driveway.

You have Red Brannigan II to blame for that, an inner voice replied.

Red's grin lasted for about a minute after leaving Ronnie's cottage until he realized he had done what he had vowed not to do. Suggested a way for him to see Ronnie again. Over cookies, for heaven's sake. Although Ronnie hadn't really taken him seriously. How could she, after he had made it a point to act like a clown?

He liked to joke around, that was part of his personality, and his business associates and employees appreciated his easygoing attitude, but what exactly had he been trying to accomplish with Ronnie? Yes, she had been amused, and just seeing her lose her preoccupied expression and laugh outright had sent a tingling pleasure through him.

Nevertheless, his words and actions were going against his vow not to become interested in a woman with a child. And getting involved with Ronnie and Andy could be even more problematic than any relationship he had had with Sofia and Marco.

Marco had been healthy. Under no restrictions or limitations. Time spent with him had been carefree, with no worries about the child's immune system being compromised. And Marco's mom had been even more carefree, having no problem leaving him under Red's care while she conducted business out of town or even out of the country. Getting closer to Ronnie and her little boy would not be a carefree situation. They had both suffered a huge ordeal in their lives. Emotionally and physically. Andy was in remission, but that didn't mean there were no conditions that they still had to be mindful of.

So what was pulling him toward Ronnie's sphere? What had he been thinking about, offering to give her— and almost inviting her son— a tour around his mansion? Had he taken leave of his senses?

When exactly had his plan backfired?

He *was* interested.

His brain was swirling with so many emotions. Desire. Desire to stay away. The instinct to protect and the instinct to withdraw. Didn't he have enough on his plate, being the president and owner of one of the most prestigious architectural firms in Canada and around the world?

He had to go back to the house and think about this. Deep down, it worried him. Worried him because being with Ronnie had felt good. *Really good.* He had enjoyed being with her, listening to her share her story, her feelings. He had felt a surge of excitement sweeping her up and skating around with her in his arms. It had been a heart-racing, exhilarating experience, and he was almost sure that she had felt the same way. He had liked the way she had clasped her hands around his neck, with her body pressed against his.

His imagination began to wander…

He gave his head a shake. He needed to concentrate on the road, not fantasize about how it would feel for him and Ronnie to be pressed against each other in different circumstances…

A few minutes later he pulled into his driveway. Inside, he strode into the grand salon, got the fire going and then decided to make himself a strong, dark coffee to clear his mind.

He sat on the recliner that Ronnie had used and, sipping his coffee, spotted a bag on the floor nearby.

Ronnie's book bag.

His pulse spiked. Now he would *have* to see her again. He doubted that she would drive all the way to his place to get them back. He set down his mug and picked up the bag. He withdrew the books and smiled at the first one, *Decorating Your Country Cottage with Nature's Gifts*. He lifted it to see what her second selection had been. *Adventures with Hercules the Hamster*. He flipped through the pages, chuckling at some of the illustrations. Andy would have fun with this one.

Red stared at the title of another book: *Moving On: Embracing a New Chapter of Your Life*. He flipped the book over to read the blurb on the back cover.

> You've chosen this book because of circumstances in your life that have either forced or compelled you to move on. A separation or divorce, perhaps, or the loss of a loved one. The end of a job or a friendship.
>
> Whatever life challenges or ordeal you have faced, this book will help you to move forward physically, mentally and emotionally, and to embrace this new chapter in your life.

He opened the book and scanned the table of contents.

Chapter One: Accepting the Past.
Chapter Two: Looking at Your Options.

Chapter Three: Packing Up and Moving Out.
Chapter Four: Becoming the Author of your New Life.

And so on…

Red pictured Ronnie flipping through its pages in the bookstore, her gaze resting on the chapter titles. Had she accepted the past? Was she looking at her options? She had packed up and moved out of her previous town, so maybe she'd skip that chapter.

Red turned to chapter one. Had *he* totally accepted his past? With a cynical twist of his lips, he started reading…

Disoriented, Red realized he had fallen asleep. The book was resting on his chest, pages down. He closed the book. The intermittent sleep he had had the night before—ensuring the fire didn't die out, and due to his inability to stop thinking about the dark-haired beauty an arm's length away—had caught up to him, and he had nodded off on the third page.

He checked the time on his cell phone. Really? He couldn't believe it was midafternoon. In a few hours it would be dark. He should really head out to Winter's Haven now. He didn't have Ronnie's cell number, so he couldn't text her to let her know he'd be dropping off her bag of books. By now she would have realized she had forgotten them. She didn't have his number either, but Casson did. Yet she had not thought to get it from her cousin. Or maybe she just didn't want to…

Red strode to the washroom and splashed some cool water over his face. He examined his reflection in the mirror. His scruff could do with a trim. He could do that himself now. And maybe he'd go for a haircut tomorrow, before driving back to Toronto midweek for an important meeting with his team and a prospective client. He put on his parka and boots, pressed a code into his phone to activate a set of intermittent lights inside and left, bracing himself against the cold wind.

Hopefully Ronnie would give him a warmer reception…

CHAPTER EIGHT

RONNIE GAVE AMY JAY a gentle kiss on the forehead and handed her back to Justine. She had been quite content sitting in her high chair and playing with her while the adults had their cup of coffee and some of the peanut butter cookies Ronnie had brought over.

She had put some in a tin for Casson and Justine, and some in another tin for when Andy returned. Somehow, there was still a dozen left over.

Red's request had popped into her mind. Or maybe it had always been there.

With a flutter in her chest, Ronnie had left the extra cookies on the tray and had walked over to Casson and Justine's to fill them in on her rescue by Red.

There were some details she had chosen to keep to herself… Feelings that had sprung up from out of nowhere, that were too new, too private to share. How could she possibly tell Casson and Justine that something crazy and magical had happened out on the pond with Red? Something she still needed to make sense of…

It had started with the feeling of freedom as she skated around the pond, a feeling that somehow had been buried under all the responsibilities she had had to manage over the last few years. And then that feeling had catapulted to a whole new level when Red had literally swept her off her feet.

Casson's questioning look drew her back to the present.

"So what did you think of Redmond Brannigan II?" Casson said after Justine had left the room with the baby.

The sudden question made her start. "Um…well," she said, shrugging, "he… I thought he was decent enough to stop and see if I needed help…especially since…"

Casson's cell phone buzzed. His eyebrows lifted and his gaze flitted back to Ronnie before he texted back and then put his phone away.

"By the way, Cass, I forgot a bag with some books at Red's place." She paused, thinking how "at Red's place" sounded so…*familiar*. "If you're in the area, could you maybe stop and pick it up?"

Casson finished his cookie. "No, I can't, sorry."

She stared at him blankly.

His eyes crinkled in amusement. "I can't because Red just texted me. He said he was around the corner and was going to go to your place to drop off something you had forgotten, and then stop by here to discuss some business, if I was free. I texted him that you were at my place. He'll be here any minute."

Red pulled into the driveway. His headlights shone into the kitchen, and he could see Casson and Ronnie looking out toward his truck. There was a look of surprise—or was it shock?—on Ronnie's face.

He shut off his lights and ignition, grabbed the bag and made his way to the door. "Long time no see," he said, a corner of his mouth tilting upward as the door opened. "Hi, Ronnie."

"Hi." She looked down at the bag he was holding.

"Sorry you had to come out all this way to bring these back…"

"I'm not sorry," he said, handing her the bag. "Casson texted that you had come over with some cookies. I couldn't get here fast enough," he laughed.

"Hey, what's so funny out there?" Casson's voice boomed from the kitchen. "Come on in; coffee's on."

Ronnie stepped back to let Red in. She set the bag down by the door. He hung up his parka and followed her to the kitchen, where Casson was filling a mug. He set it on the island and then walked over to shake Red's hand.

"Have a seat there, Mr. Brannigan," he said, grinning, "and grab a cookie."

"Only one?" Red complained. He tilted his head toward Ronnie on the stool next to his. "Perhaps I can find a way to convince your cousin here to perform an act of charity and make me a batch of my own…"

"Good luck with that," Casson laughed. At Amy Jay's sudden wail, he excused himself to assume his parental responsibilities.

"I should head back to the cottage, Cass," Ronnie said. "I still have boxes all over the place."

"What? You're leaving, too? Is it something I said?" Red held his half-eaten cookie in midair. "If you both desert me, I'll have to drown my sorrows by eating the rest of these cookies."

"I'll let *you* handle this drama," Casson laughed, giving Ronnie a hug. "See you later."

Red's gaze swept over Ronnie. She had changed into a pair of maroon jeans and a black long-sleeved shirt that accentuated her feminine curves. An inner voice prompted him to offer to help her with the unpacking. He started to open his mouth, and then he snapped it shut.

Stay away, Brannigan, his common sense warned.

You'd be entering a danger zone. Remember your vow? She has a child. You can't take this kind of a risk. Don't. Get. Involved.

Ronnie was looking at him quizzically. "I *did* end up with some extra cookies," she said nonchalantly. "You can have them, if you'd like."

Something leaped in his chest. He blinked wordlessly for a moment, then nodded. "I'll just take care of some business with Casson, and then I'll come by."

Common sense be damned, he thought, watching her leave. What fool would pass up a batch of her cookies?

CHAPTER NINE

RONNIE'S HEART WAS pounding all the way back to her cottage, and it wasn't due to exertion from speed-walking or running. She had barely acknowledged the fact that it had started to snow, and when she arrived, she was surprised at the snowflakes that had accumulated on her coat and hood. She quickly removed her coat and boots, and after setting her bag of books down on the kitchen table, she hurried to put the cooled cookies in a small tin. She would hand them to Red as soon as he arrived, then he would be on his way, she would close the door, and she would have the rest of the evening to herself.

She peered out the window of the front door. No sign of him yet. She caught a glimpse of herself in the small oval mirror on the wall adjacent to the door. Her hair was wind-tossed, her cheeks were rosy and her eyes looked darker than usual. She patted down her hair and walked over to turn on the gas fireplace. She sat down on the edge of the couch and picked up the *Parry Sound Life* magazine on the coffee table, flipping through the pages but not really processing what she was seeing.

The sound of wheels crunching along her driveway startled Ronnie. She stood up and then promptly sat down. She picked up the magazine again, and a few moments later she heard the knock. Taking a deep breath, she walked to the door and saw Red's profile through the transparent curtain. She opened the door. Red had his hood off and the plump snowflakes were drifting onto his head and face.

"Hi again, Ronnie," he said, smiling.

"Hi." She noticed that he hadn't left his truck running…

"May I come in?" He shook the snow off his hair and shoulders.

"Um, sure," she said, stepping back awkwardly. She hadn't intended for him to come in, but how could she say no?

Red closed the door behind him and stood on the mat. Ronnie saw him scanning the boxes piled along the living room wall, and then his gaze shifted to the kitchen counter where she had placed the tin.

"I'll grab the cookies," she said. As she began to move toward the kitchen area, he put a hand on her arm.

"Hold on, Ronnie. I *did* come here for your cookies, but I also wanted to ask you something."

"Oh?" Ronnie frowned.

"Would you like some help?"

"Help? With what?"

He pointed to the boxes. "With *those*. Unpacking can be a drag when you have to do it by yourself. Besides," he added with a glint in his eye, "I need to perform my one good deed of the day."

"Says who?" She looked at him skeptically.

"It's a universal law," he said. "Has to be done—" he checked his watch "—by 5:00 p.m. Which means I still have time."

"I'm sure you have more important things to do with your time, Mr. Brannigan. But if you're willing to help, I'd be silly to say no. So…yes, I'll accept your offer. You can hang your coat up on that hook."

While Red took off his parka and boots, Ronnie went over and transferred a few boxes from the stack near the wall to the living room carpet. She opened the first box, labeled BOOKS. "Those can go on the mantel for now," she told him. There was actually a bookshelf in her bedroom, but she felt awkward sending him there.

She grabbed the second box labeled in red crayon with Andy's name and smiled. He had wanted to help pack his things, and she had indulged him. He hadn't quite followed any particular folding technique, but that hadn't bothered her. She had watched him out of the corner of her eye, proud of her little guy as he rolled up pants and shirts, socks and underwear. And she had been both amused and touched when he had raced to get one of his plush animals to pack into each box, hugging them before closing the box.

Red had finished unpacking the books and had knelt on one knee across from her. She handed him Andy's box.

"You can unpack this directly into the chest of drawers in Andy's room," she said. "Down the hall, first door on your right."

Ronnie saw something flicker in Red's eyes. Was that a look of dismay? His smile faded for a mere second before he smiled brightly, making her dismiss her initial notion. It must have been the play of light on his face…

Red took the box and strode down the hall, his jaw muscles tensing. He had gotten himself into this, and now he had no choice but to carry it through.

He stole a sideways look at Ronnie before entering Andy's room. She had opened another book box and was looking through the pile she had lifted out, her lips curved into a smile. Red stepped into the boy's room. The comforter on the twin bed had a space theme, showing planets and galaxies and shooting stars. A plush bear was plopped against the bed pillow, and instead of the usual pads on its paws, four red hearts had been sewn on. Another heart filled the center of the bear's chest. Red felt a twinge in his chest. Had Ronnie bought Andy the bear while he was at SickKids? He set down the box and he picked up the bear. It was soft, and Red found himself pressing it against his cheek.

That was when he felt his own heart crack. He had given Marco a bear for his fourth birthday, only it was much bigger, like an actual bear cub, and Marco had wanted it placed in a corner of his room, near his bookshelf. When Red had asked him to think of a name, Marco had scrunched up his face and tapped his chin, and suddenly, he had grinned from ear to ear. "Red!"

"Yes?" Red had replied and Marco had laughed. "No, I'm calling my bear 'Red'! That way, you'll always be with me, even when you're not!" And then he had plopped himself down into the bear's lap and asked Red to read him a story before bedtime.

Red had laughed at the time, but now the memory sent sharp spears into his chest.

How could he not foresee that Andy's toys would trigger such memories?

He had to get himself out of there…

When Red had impulsively jumped at Ronnie's offer, he had been thinking primarily about himself. And not just because he'd be ending up with a batch of her cookies. If he had to be completely honest with himself, the main reason was that he'd get to see Ronnie alone again. In *her* space.

Something was drawing him to her, and he was having a hard time resisting the magnetic pull. Now, immersed in memories activated by entering Andy's room, Red felt regret washing over him. He looked down at the box that he had set down.

Just do it, his inner voice prompted.

He strode to the dresser and pulled open the top drawer. He tried to swallow the lump in his throat from handling each rolled-up little item. This was exactly why he should have heeded his common sense and stayed away.

He couldn't handle this. At least not now.

Too many emotions were surfacing, feelings that he had convinced himself were resolved when it came to Marco...

He had to leave.

He would tell Ronnie that he had a very important meeting in Toronto with a client from Melbourne the day after tomorrow, and he needed to go over the files.

It *was* true. There was no way he could tell her the real reason...

Red returned to the living room with the empty box. He saw Ronnie perched on a chair by the fireplace, arranging some books on the mantel. His gaze fell on one chair leg, positioned unevenly on the raised edge around the porcelain tiles at the base of the fireplace. When he saw it start to wobble a moment later, he let the box drop and leaped to prevent Ronnie from falling. The chair tipped and fell over, but Ronnie was already in his arms.

She had let out a cry at his sudden intervention, and her arms had instinctively entwined themselves around his neck. For a timeless moment, their gazes locked and their bodies pressed against each other. He couldn't tell if the wildly beating heart was his or hers. Her eyes were dark pools, their pupils expanded. He wished he could read their impenetrable depths...

And then he had no choice but to release his hold

around her waist, letting her slide down his body until her feet touched the floor.

"Sorry," he said gruffly, righting the chair. "You could have fallen and hit your head on those tiles." He pointed to the raised border around the tiles. "The chair leg wasn't positioned on the flat part."

"Thanks," she said breathlessly. "I feel like such a klutz. I seem to lose my balance every time I'm around you," she added accusingly.

"And fortunately for you, I've been successful in preventing you from falling," he replied smoothly. "You might want to consider protecting yourself with bubble wrap as a preventative measure," he said with a crooked smile, gesturing toward a pile of it in a box Ronnie had unpacked previously. "Especially since I can't stick around to save you again."

Her brow furrowed momentarily, and she took a step back. "No problem. I wouldn't want to keep inconveniencing you," she replied tersely. "I'm sure I can manage to save myself."

"No inconven—"

"I'll get your cookies." She turned away sharply and returned with the tin, avoiding his gaze.

She had taken offence at his words. But what had he said that could have bothered her?

"Thanks, Ronnie. I have a very important meeting coming up in Toronto and—"

"You don't need to explain. It's none of my business." She crossed in front of him to open the door, letting in a snowy gust of wind.

She was figuratively and literally giving him the cold shoulder. He brushed the snow off him and bent to put on his boots before reaching for his parka on the wall hook.

She obviously didn't want him around…

"Thanks for your help," she said stiffly, holding out the cookies.

"No problem," he said, attempting to sound casual. "Good night, and thank *you*." As he stepped up into his truck, he glanced back at the cottage. He waited a few moments, then turned on the ignition and drove away. What had he expected? That Ronnie would rush to the window and wave him off?

Don't be a fool, he scoffed inwardly. And why would he expect or want Ronnie to do such a thing?

On the way home, his thoughts vaulted between his reaction in Andy's room to what it felt like holding Ronnie in his arms. He tried to divert his thoughts to what he hoped would be accomplished at his upcoming meeting in Toronto with the Australian tycoon. If all went as planned, he'd be approving a billion-dollar account, toasting the success of the project, and then driving back to Parry Sound for the rest of his holiday.

With one important event on the agenda at the end of the month: the grand opening of Franklin's Resort.

The thought of the resort made his thoughts return to Andy, and how being in his room had triggered emotions he thought he had resolved. Red wondered what Marco was doing now. Had his mother flown to Italy with him over the summer? Had she decided which school to enroll him in? Was Marco happy? Did the boy ever ask about him? Did he think about Red whenever he looked at his bear?

Red clenched his jaw. He had to stop. Stop wondering. Stop tormenting himself. Marco was young. He wouldn't have suffered from the loss in the same way Red had suffered... Or had he?

Maybe he needed to talk to somebody about this. He

had believed that he had worked through his grief, but putting himself right into another child's space and doing the seemingly innocuous task of putting away some of Andy's clothes and picking up his plush toy had rocketed some feelings that he had obviously buried right back to the surface…

What he *didn't* need to do was get himself tied up in a relationship when a child was in the picture. And although there was no relationship between him and Ronnie, why tempt fate and let himself get drawn into her life? She had moved to Parry Sound permanently, and *his* permanent home base was Toronto. He'd be back more often now that he had bought the Victorian mansion and was making plans to renovate it, but with his business dealings and travel around the world, he couldn't see himself even considering a long-distance relationship with anyone.

But even more than these kinds of logistics, Red had to seriously consider whether he could risk encouraging a relationship with Ronnie and consequently getting close to her little boy…a boy who could end up with a relapse. Could he face that kind of responsibility? The uncertainty? Could he allow himself to open his heart to the kid—as he had done with Marco—and then risk having it broken again if Andy—

No! He wasn't even going to go there…

At home, Red got a fire going, poured himself a brandy and sat by the fire and stared into the flames. He could repress some of his fears, but he honestly had to search his soul to see if he could cope with such a dire situation… Or would he end up quitting on her, like her ex-husband had done?

No again! He was not that kind of a guy…

But one part of him was pulling him one way, and

the other was pulling him in the other direction. Red swallowed the last of his brandy. He was in a tug of war. With himself.

He'd eventually have to let go…

Letting out a soft growl, he strode to his desk and opened his laptop. He needed the distraction of work to blot out the duel playing out in his brain.

CHAPTER TEN

RONNIE CONTROLLED THE impulse to go to the window. She heard Red's truck starting up and driving off, and when she was sure he was out of sight, she went and looked out. It was still snowing and the image of Red at her door earlier, shaking the snowflakes off his head and shoulders, made her heart skip a beat. Again. His physical presence moments later in the cottage had made the space suddenly seem smaller.

She had been very conscious of his proximity as she opened up the boxes and handed him the books. A couple of times, her fingers had brushed against his, and she had deliberately avoided glancing at him. But she hadn't been able to avoid meeting his gaze when her chair had caught the edge around the tiled fireplace base and he had leaped to prevent her from falling.

It had happened so quickly. Her brain had hardly registered that the chair was tilting when his arms reached out and braced themselves around her waist. The few seconds that it had taken for him to do that and then set her down had, at the time, seemed to play out in slow motion…

Her initial gasp as his strong arms closed around her had given way to a heavy heart thumping at the impact of her body being pressed against his. Her eyes had melted into the mesmerizing landscape of his eyes. And the slow, *very slow*, descent of her body sliding down his had sent a surge pulsating throughout all her nerve endings.

And was sending a shiver through her now…

Her reaction to his proximity was one-sided, no doubt.

Ronnie searched her memory to find out if Casson had mentioned Red having a current girlfriend or having been married. Of course he hadn't. Casson hadn't shared much about Red, other than the fact that he was a friend from university, and that it was *his* firm that would be designing Franklin's Resort.

She pictured the woman who would most likely be Red's type: tall like him, probably, wearing exclusive fashions and mingling in upscale social circles. She could see the woman linking her arm with his as they strode into an invitation-only event at Roy Thomson Hall or some private party after a movie premiere at the Toronto International Film Festival, rocking her European designer gown and killer heels.

Would. You. Stop!

Why on earth was she even spending any energy on such thoughts? What difference did it make to her whom he was seeing?

Ronnie sauntered to the kitchen and scanned the contents of the fridge. She wasn't really in the mood to cook anything. She fixed herself a peanut butter and jam sandwich and ate it at the kitchen table while looking through some files on her laptop related to her new position as Provincial Marketing Manager for the Forrest Hardware chain. She was looking forward to working from home, with occasional trips to the stores across the province. Some of her out-of-town meetings could be accomplished in a day trip while others might take a couple of days or more. She was happy that with both scenarios, she could leave Andy in Casson's and Justine's capable hands.

Ronnie looked forward to using her university training and skills in this new position.

She smiled. She was excited about starting her new job and implementing some of the innovative marketing strategies she had been working on.

Ronnie finished the last bite of her sandwich and her glass of milk. She shut down her laptop and reached for the bag of books, and immediately the image of Red popped into her mind.

Well, she didn't want Red in her mind. He had already taken up too much of her headspace…

Ronnie sauntered over to the living room and set the books on the coffee table before going to her bedroom to change into her pajamas. She would relax with one of her new books for a bit until she felt ready to go to bed.

Moments later she curled up on one corner of the couch. Pulling the books out of the bag, she smiled at the cover of the one she had picked up for Andy. She would enjoy reading it together with him soon. Ronnie set aside the Giller Prize–winning book, wanting to savor it when she had a bigger block of time. She stared at the title of the next book. *Moving On: Embracing a New Chapter of Your Life.* Hmm. Did she really want to get into that now? She reread the blurb on the back cover and skimmed over the table of contents.

Serious stuff.

She could actually skip over the first three chapters. She had accepted the past and looked at her options, which had led to the packing up and moving out theme of chapter three. Now she considered herself happily at the unpacking stage.

Ronnie yawned. She'd pick one chapter to read and then call it a night. But which one? Her gaze flew over the next few chapter headings and stopped at chapter seven, *Learning to Trust Again*. Was she ready to do that? Did she want to?

Trusting again… That implied a desire or readiness to invest in a new relationship. Which meant that reading this chapter would just bring Red back into her headspace…whether she liked it or not.

Red had said he didn't have a "significant other" and had referred to himself as "once burned, twice shy." And then he had gone on to say that he had been "scorched." She couldn't see him being ready to trust again. Why would he want to get involved with someone else after such a terrible experience?

Why would she? After all, like Ronnie had said to Red, they weren't exactly knocking at her door.

Well, not "they," actually. Just Red.

And all he had wanted was her peanut butter cookies. Not her.

With a wistful sigh, she started to read the chapter anyway…

Red shut down his laptop and got ready for bed. Minutes later he was staring at the ceiling, his brain a jumble of conflicting thoughts. Maybe he should have had a cup of herbal tea instead of the brandy…

Impatiently, he threw back the covers. Running his fingers through his hair, he strode to the large casement window that overlooked the expanse of pond. Snowflakes were drifting gently down, occasionally sticking to the window. They were tiny and intricate. Beautiful.

Like Ronnie…

But out of reach.

The metaphorical glass between them was a little boy. No—two little boys. Andy and Marco.

Andy was Ronnie's shield against the intrusion of another man in her life—or so he had inferred from her comments about Andy being her priority. And even though Marco was no longer in his life physically, he was still in Red's mind…and heart…

A knot nudged its way into his throat, helped along by twinges of guilt.

Perhaps he should have never encouraged Marco to get so close to him. Maybe he should have kept his distance more, until he and Sofia had been on the same page when it came to their feelings for each other.

He had assumed too much. He had thought that once she had taken care of business in Italy, they would move forward in their relationship.

Red felt a surge of anger shoot through him. He had been so naive when it came to Sofia. He had trusted her, believed her when she had told him that all those trips back to Italy were absolutely necessary. Four trips in two months…

He gave a cynical laugh. What a fool he had been!

And he had innocently encouraged the bond between himself and Marco to grow…

How could he not feel guilt now over the fact that it must have exacerbated the loss and confusion Marco would have felt at Red's sudden disappearance from his life?

Red turned away from the window. Sofia hadn't been the only one to blame in all this. He had to accept his share of it, even though he had only ever had the best of intentions when it had come to Marco…

Taking a deep breath, he walked to his dresser and picked up the photo of him and Marco. He stared at it for a long time, forcing himself to accept his conflicting feelings. He really had no choice but to move forward with his life…

The photo became blurry. "I'm so sorry, Marco," he rasped. "I never wanted to hurt you." He set it back down, wiped his eyes and went to bed.

CHAPTER ELEVEN

FROM THE BRIGHTNESS in her room, Ronnie realized that she had slept in. She had obviously needed it. She stretched languorously before reaching for her cell phone on her night table to check the time. Nine twenty…

She padded to the living room and looked out the bay window. Last night's snow and wind had come to a stop. The surface of the bay and the dense woodlands beyond the blanketed shoreline were glistening with pinpoints of sunlight. It would be a perfect day to go for a walk in the woods—do some "forest bathing," as she had heard it called. Refresh her mind and spirit out in nature. Maybe she'd even spot a snowshoe hare or a fox…

You have work to do, her inner slave driver reminded her. *Boxes to unpack, shelves to line, clothes to hang, laundry to do...*

She would put on some coffee, have some toast and head out. The work wasn't going anywhere, but she was! Passing by the coffee table on her way to the kitchen, Ronnie's gaze dropped to the book she had been reading last night and the chapter about learning to trust again.

She stooped to pick up the book, then changed her mind and continued on to the kitchen. She didn't want to think about trusting, or taking chances, or anything that had to do with contemplating a new relationship. There was no contender presently in her life, nor was there the possibility of anything changing soon. After the week-long stay at Franklin's Resort, she would be starting a job that would require some traveling back and forth to Toronto, and when she wasn't doing that, she'd be at home in Parry Sound. Hopefully, once she was in a routine, and after the snow melted, she could start looking for a place of her own.

Casson and Justine had actually offered to sell her the cottage she was staying in…and she *was* seriously considering it. It would be great to be close to family. By spring, Justine's mom and dad would be back from their three-month vacation in Arizona, and Justine had already told Ronnie that her parents would also be happy to babysit Andy when Ronnie was out of town.

And Winter's Haven was a fabulous property. Cottages were in high demand in Parry Sound and Georgian Bay. Cottagers who lived in Toronto and tourists caused the town's population to soar in the summer. Casson had mentioned that the few property owners who *were* willing to sell their cottages, were getting their asking price or even higher. Buyers were willing to pay the big bucks for cottages on the pristine waters of either Georgian Bay or the many inland lakes. They could enjoy the natural beauty of mixed woodlands, smooth or granite shorelines and breathtaking sunsets under a canopy of stars on a sultry summer night.

She had it made, she thought, putting on the coffee. Her little boy was in good health, her family was close by and so supportive, and she was about to start a big new job. What more could she want?

A man, maybe? A little voice edged its way into her thoughts. *Companionship? Love?*

The two slices of bread she had plunked in the toaster

popped up, startling her. She brushed away her thoughts and focused on buttering her toast and filling her mug with coffee.

As she ate her breakfast, Ronnie's gaze took in the cozy ambiance of the cottage. Maybe she *would* stay put here for a while. Enjoy the seasons as they changed. Go cross-country skiing, ice fishing, swimming, blueberry picking, hiking… And in a few minutes, a glorious walk through the forested property.

Ronnie put her dish and mug in the sink and went to change out of her pajamas. She *was* moving forward, like the blurb said on the back cover of her book, and embracing the new chapter in her life.

The only thing she didn't have in her life was *someone* to embrace…

Red thanked Casson and Justine and put on the snowmobile helmet. Casson had said he could try his snowmobile out, and he had, several times since he had arrived in Parry Sound. Red had enjoyed riding along the Seguin Trail, which, Casson had told him, linked sledders all across Ontario. Red was happy to have been introduced to a new adventure into a winter wonderland of snow-frosted forests and ice-etched lakes and rivers, a magical place when the sun glinted through the evergreen canopies onto the smooth trail route. Red planned to purchase a sled of his own to enjoy on winter weekends in Parry Sound in the future.

He had woken up this morning with the intention of getting some fresh air on the trail. Once he had arrived at Winter's Haven, he had had a coffee with Casson and Justine, and as he was getting ready to head out on the sled, Justine had innocently suggested that he ask Ronnie to go sledding with him.

He had looked blankly at Justine for a moment and then at Casson, who had shrugged and given him a silent *I don't know what that's all about* look.

"Um… I don't know if she'd even be interested in—"

"She needs a little fun in her life," Justine urged. "It's a double seater, and she can borrow my helmet." And she had swiftly pulled it out of the hall closet before handing it to Red.

After thanking them, he climbed aboard the red-and-black snowmobile and headed to Ronnie's cottage. How had he allowed himself to be roped into this situation? Could he not have just said "No"?

He stopped the machine and in a few strides he was at her door. He gave a couple of knocks, and then another couple of knocks, and when she didn't answer, he figured she was either sleeping or pretending she didn't hear the door. And then he noticed her boot prints on the steps leading in the opposite direction from the way he had come.

Red considered his options. Return the helmet to Justine or head out in the direction of the tracks Ronnie had left.

Another mental tug of war…

He sighed, put his helmet back on and moments later was following Ronnie's trail.

A mile down the road, he spotted her. She was staring up at something in a tree, and as he approached, she turned to watch him. Red brought the machine to a stop and pulled off his helmet.

"Oh! I thought you were Casson!" She frowned.

"Understandable mistake," he drawled. "Are you enjoying your walk?"

"I am," she said. "Actually, I was enjoying the solitude and quiet of the forest…"

"Forgive me for the raucous intrusion."

At that moment a blue jay let out a squawk. "Hey, it's getting really noisy out here. Want to go for a ride?" Red gave her a tentative grin.

Ronnie looked at him as if he had suggested something improper. "Have you had enough practice on that beast?" she said doubtfully.

"Well, if you don't trust me, why don't you take the reins?"

Her brows furrowed. "Um…don't be offended, but… okay, I will!" She took the helmet and Red caught the sudden gleam in her eyes.

"Should I be afraid?" he laughed, handing her Justine's helmet.

Her brows arched but she didn't respond. "Give it up, Brannigan," she told him, with a curl of her lip.

Red scooted back in his seat.

Ronnie checked the throttle and turned the key to start the engine. When it was idling smoothly, Red had just enough time to straighten in his seat before she zoomed off, sending a spray of snow over him from both sides.

CHAPTER TWELVE

RONNIE HAD NO IDEA what had come over her…deciding
to take Red up on his offer of a ride, and then impulsively taking the driver's seat. Something had risen up
inside her, made her want to show Red that she was in
control of her life, that she was perfectly capable of taking charge…

She had had plenty of practice riding on and driving
a snowmobile in the past throughout the Muskoka trails,
especially before Andy was born, and the temptation to
show Red her ability—given that he was a relative newbie at sledding—had been too hard to resist.

What she hadn't initially thought through was the fact
that the Viking would be pressed against her, his hands
alternating from the side hand rests to her waist…

She had tried to ignore the sensation of having Red so
close, and focus instead on the exhilaration of the ride
with the sun streaming over them and the dazzling views
of the woodlands on either side of them as they sped by.
Ronnie had done the loop through Winter's Haven and
then proceeded to the route that led to the Seguin Trail.
After about a forty-five-minute run, they were back in
front of Ronnie's cottage.

Red climbed off the sled, pulled off his helmet and
waited for Ronnie to do the same. He nodded slowly with

an enigmatic smile, and she smiled back, the adrenaline still pumping through her.

"Thanks for the thrills and chills," he said dryly. "I'd invite myself over for some hot chocolate, but I have some business files to look through. So I'd better take the sled back and head home…" His eyes narrowed. "But you'll have to show me a little trust the next time, Ronnie, and let *me* drive…"

Her pulse skipping a beat at his words, Ronnie watched him drive away. Once inside, she immersed herself under a hot shower and unsuccessfully tried to put Red out of her mind. But how could she when she had felt his Viking presence both physically and emotionally on the snowmobile…

Ronnie's cell phone rang, startling her. She saw that it was Casson and reached over to put the phone on speaker mode. "Hey, Cass, what's up?"

"Hi, Ronnie. I need you to do me a favor…"

"Sure; do you need me to babysit A.J.?"

"No, it's not that. The baby's running a fever, and Justine thinks *she's* coming down with something, too."

"Oh, my goodness, what can I do to help?"

"How do you feel about starting your new position sooner? Like tomorrow. I have a meeting with the Toronto store manager to discuss some of those new marketing plans outlined in the file I sent you two days ago. But I don't want to leave Justine and the baby. It's just for tomorrow, Ronnie. You can take over completely when you actually start in a month's time."

Ronnie thought fast. She'd have to get up at the crack of dawn to either beat or join the early-morning commuters going to Toronto. She had really hoped to sleep in and have a leisurely day unpacking the remaining boxes and then going for a long country walk. But she'd have to delay those plans now. There was no way she could turn Cass down. She didn't blame him for wanting to stay close to his wife and baby in their time of need. That's what a devoted husband and father did...

"Of course I'll go, dear cousin. You just worry about taking care of your beautiful girls. I've got this."

"I know you do, Ronnie. By the way, when I was talking with Red earlier he mentioned that he was heading to Toronto tomorrow morning for a meeting himself. I hope you don't mind, Ronnie, but I just gave him a quick call a minute ago—hopeful that you would say yes—and asked if he wouldn't mind driving you also, since you're both heading downtown. It'll be safer traveling in his truck."

Ronnie's brain swirled with this sudden rush of information. "What did he say?" she said, keeping her voice casual.

"He said it would be his pleasure...and that *he* would drive," Casson chuckled.

"Um...*okay* then." Her cheeks burned at the knowledge that Red had told Casson about their ride...

"Thanks, Ronnie. I'll keep you posted about the girls."

"Give them hugs for me, okay?"

"Will do, and, oh, Red said to be ready by 6:00 a.m. sharp. He'll be waiting outside 'with bells on.'"

Ronnie set her cell phone down. The thought of traveling with Red for a couple of hours to Toronto and back in such proximity sent a series of bells clanging in her chest...

Red's personal black limo pulled up to the estate at the exact time he had specified to the driver the night before after deciding against taking his own truck. "Good morning, Liam," Red said, as the driver stepped out of the limo.

"Top of the morning to you, sir!"

As Liam briskly opened the door for him, Red placed his garment bag and black leather briefcase in the back seat. He would change before his meeting in his Toronto office. Pulling up the collar of his jacket, Red got in and put on his seat belt before giving Liam directions to Ronnie's cottage. It was dark, as dark as it had been at midnight when he had still been up, thinking about Casson's request the evening before.

Since returning home yesterday, all Red could think about was the rush he had felt riding on the sled with Ronnie, and how his intentions to keep his distance from her always seemed to go awry. He had just finished choosing his suit and tie for the next day when his phone had buzzed.

Casson had explained what he needed and Red had groaned inwardly. It seemed that every time he had convinced himself to stay away from Ronnie, the universe contrived to throw them together.

Red hadn't been able to come up with a reason why he couldn't take Ronnie with him. "No problem," he had told Casson, making an effort to keep his voice light.

Of course it was a problem.

But he couldn't turn Casson down, even if it meant being thrown together with Ronnie for a good part of a day. Casson had thanked him and promised to have him over for his homemade chili one night soon.

Red had hung up the garment bag with his suit in the foyer armoire, leaving the door open so he wouldn't forget it in the morning. Shortly after, he had tried to push away thoughts about Ronnie while he was going over his files, but their constant intrusion had forced him to shut down his laptop.

He had poured himself a brandy and had tried to process the impact of Ronnie Forrester in his life since he had stopped to rescue her. He had only known her for a little over forty-eight hours, but Ronnie had landed in Parry Sound like a meteorite, making a sizable dent on the surface and sending chunks flying in every direction.

And one of those chunks had hit *him*. *Hard.*

Red had swallowed the rest of his brandy and headed to his en suite bathroom for a quick shower, the quickest he could manage, so he wouldn't be tormented by the memory of his body pressed against hers...

He hadn't been successful. The torment had been sweet, and the possibility of his imaginings becoming a reality had steamed up his consciousness more than the way the hot water had steamed up the shower.

Afterward, he had put on a robe and decided against driving to Toronto himself. He would employ the services of his private limo driver...

Liam now turned into the winding road that led to Ronnie's cottage. His pulse spiked when Liam made the last turn. Ronnie was waiting at her doorstep, wearing a short red coat over a dark gray dress or skirt, and short black dress boots. She had a red-and-black scarf tied around her neck, and her black winter cap matched her black gloves. She had a briefcase that she had set down, and was peering down the driveway, her eyes widening as the limo glided toward her.

Well, at least she was on time. "I'll get her door," he told Liam.

"Good morning, Ronnie." He opened the door on the passenger side for her and held out his hand to take her briefcase, which he set down on the seat opposite his. Red tried not to let his gaze linger over the way her dress or skirt tapered to just inches above her knees, and at the generous glimpse of her legs below... He held out his hand, instinctively guessing that she might need it to prevent slipping, especially with those heels…

"Good morning." Ronnie took his gloved hand and gave him an awkward smile as she stepped into the limo, her cheeks flushed.

CHAPTER THIRTEEN

"I HOPE CASSON warned you about my strict rules for passengers who travel with me," Red said wryly, while he buckled up across from her.

Ronnie's eyebrows shot up. "Actually, just one. And I *did* comply, being outside at the precise time you had specified. Although I had expected you to drive up in your truck, not in *this*."

"I appreciated that," he said, nodding to Liam through the glass partition to proceed. "Although, if I was driving by myself, I would have probably left at least an hour earlier."

Ronnie stared at his profile, wondering if he was annoyed with having had to alter his plans to include her. She caught the slight tensing of his jaw muscles. He *was* annoyed.

"Well, Casson didn't have to go and ask you to include me in your travel plans," she blurted defensively. "I would have been okay to travel on my own… You'd think he was my parent at times, instead of my cousin, worrying so much about me."

Red glanced at her, his brow furrowing. "Well, you *did* have a recent incident with your vehicle," he reminded her pointedly. "But no need to bring up the past. You might as well sit back and enjoy the ride."

Ronnie stifled the response she wanted to articulate and settled back against the plush leather upholstery, wishing she had thought to sit next to Red, instead of having to face him the whole trip. It was disconcerting. His face scruff had undergone some trimming. If he had been good-looking before, now he could join the ranks of hunks in magazines, or in commercials for high-end cologne… And whatever cologne he was wearing at the moment, the refreshing scent of pine trees, seemed to be encapsulated in the limo with them.

"Can I get the driver to stop at a coffee shop before we hit the highway?" He slid open a temperature-controlled compartment in the limo that held bottles of champagne, wine and assorted liquors. An adjacent section held a variety of fluted and other glasses. "I don't imagine you'd be up for one of these." A corner of his mouth curved upward.

"You imagine correctly," she said curtly. "That's not my style."

Red switched on the intercom and instructed Liam to stop at the coffee shop coming up on their right.

"Large coffee your style?" He glanced at Ronnie.

"Yes, thanks. Double milk, no sugar," she said, zipping open her handbag to grab her change purse.

"I think I can handle paying for an extra cup of coffee," he said, grinning.

"I didn't want to be presumptuous," she said, lifting her chin. "But I *will* split the limo bill with you."

"No worries," he laughed, "I've saved for that, as well. Are you hungry? Can I get you anything else?"

Ronnie shook her head. "No, thanks. I'll wait until we get to Toronto."

As the driving resumed out of town and onto the highway heading south, Ronnie sipped her coffee and kept her gaze outside the window. The traffic wasn't bad; they would feel it in about an hour, though, once they approached Barrie. From there on, it would be pretty congested alongside the regular commuters.

Ronnie stole a glance at Red. He seemed immersed in thought, and she wondered if it had something to do with his business in Toronto. Her gaze dropped to his wool jacket, blue checkered shirt and jeans. She had noticed the garment bag hanging up next to him and imagined what he'd look like in a suit and tie. Something dark would be perfect for him, she thought. Pine or teal green. Or classic black. With that hair of his, he'd look—

"Are you all set for your meeting?"

Her head snapped up to meet his. A transport truck drove by them, illuminating them both for a few moments. Ronnie was mortified, having been caught staring. She could feel a spiral of heat rising to her neck and cheeks.

"I'm as ready as I can be," she said lightly. "My job as Provincial Marketing Manager will officially start in about a month. I'll go at it full tilt then."

"I'm sure you will. Congratulations. Casson had told me about your new position."

"Thanks. Um…what time is *your* meeting? Maybe I'll have time to do a little shopping. My son's birthday is coming up." She bit her lip, a wave of emotion engulfing her. This birthday would be different. Finally. Gratitude for the end of Andy's maintenance treatment. And joy in the miracle of his remission. Ronnie turned to look out her window, her eyes misting. The sudden raucous honking of horns jarred her back to the moment, and she turned in alarm.

"Just a couple of idiots trying to pass a transport truck," Red said, shaking his head. He gave her a look of reassurance. "Don't worry; you're in good hands." He looked away before she could.

She was glad, because her cheeks were flaming as an image of herself in *his* hands, or rather, in his arms, as she had been two—no, *three*—times now, popped into her mind. Despite the coffee, she felt fatigue from too little sleep last night weighing down her eyelids. She had woken up twice during the night, and when the alarm had finally gone off, she had bolted out of bed, afraid to press on the snooze button in case she slept through the next alarm. She had had a quick shower, dried and brushed her hair, and gotten dressed in less than half an hour. And she had been out the door with her briefcase in hand two minutes before Red had appeared.

She had stood in the frosty stillness, looking up at the black sky and breathing in the crisp pine-scented air. Inhaling and exhaling deeply, she had felt a sense of peace come over her. And a tingle of anticipation at the same time. She looked forward to the upcoming meeting, and afterward, exploring some of the shops in the area to find something special for Andy's birthday.

While she was picturing Andy's little face shining with pleasure as he was about to blow out his birthday candles, the sleek limousine had appeared in the driveway. For a few moments, his headlights had blinded her and she had stood there stunned, having expected Red to drive up in his truck. She still hadn't moved when Red had jumped out to open the door on her side of the vehicle.

As she had handed Red her briefcase, Ronnie hadn't missed his gaze casually sweeping over her.

And approval in the dark, enigmatic depths of his eyes…

* * *

Red gazed at the woman across from him. She had removed her coat and had fallen asleep just before Barrie, an hour from Toronto. Her arms were crisscrossed against her chest. She looked so vulnerable, her long lashes resting on her face like a…like a sleeping angel.

His gaze dropped to the locket around her neck. He hadn't noticed it earlier. The latch wasn't completely closed and the locket had opened to reveal a tiny photo. Her son. On the other side, nothing.

Had it previously held the photo of her husband?

He felt his jaw muscles tightening. Why did he feel so conflicted?

You know why, his inner voice murmured. *You're attracted to Ronnie, but you don't want to be. Because of her little boy…*

Red glanced again at the photo. A feeling of guilt washed over him. The kid didn't deserve this kind of rejection. Neither did Ronnie. They both deserved to have someone who could accept them both. *Together.*

It was just too bad that *he* had had such a heartbreaking experience in the past. An experience that was affecting his choices now. The choice to risk again.

There was only one thing stopping him. *Fear.*

The realization stunned him.

Fear had essentially kept him from even considering another relationship since his breakup with Sofia. He had purposefully buried himself in work so as not to even be tempted to get involved with another woman. Why would he? He had been burned. *Scorched.* And he hadn't been ready to trust again.

Fear had succeeded in freezing his emotions. But something was changing. Something was chipping away at the hard layer of ice that had formed around his heart. Or rather, someone.

Ronnie Forrester. Even though she wasn't aware that she was holding a hammer and chisel…

He saw Ronnie shifting in her seat and the movement roused her. She glanced out the window. The sky had lightened and she blinked before checking her watch. "Wow. I—I guess I needed that snooze."

"No worries. That's part of the passenger perks," he said, flashing her a teasing grin.

She responded with a crooked smile and noticing her open locket, she clasped it and snapped it shut.

Red saw her briefly hold up the locket to her cheek. She was such a devoted mother. That little boy was everything to her. And Red knew she was the kind of mother who would put Andy's needs and welfare before her own.

He felt an overwhelming desire to gather her up in his arms and just hold her. Cradle her against his chest and show her how much he respected her for everything she had done for her son. For her selfless, loving presence and care. She was the kind of mother every child should have. The kind of mother he wished he had had when he was young.

The kind of mother he'd want for his children…

CHAPTER FOURTEEN

THE LIMO STOPPED and dropped Ronnie off right at the Yonge Street store. Since Red's meeting was scheduled at the same time, he had suggested they join up afterward for lunch. When he had found out she had never been to 360, the CN Tower revolving restaurant, he called and made reservations. "Might as well do something new while you're in town," he said. "Good luck with your meeting."

An hour later, Ronnie walked out of the hardware store with a light heart. Mr. Kennedy had been very open and receptive to what she had to show him. He thanked her for being Casson's emissary and told her that he would arrange a final conference with Casson.

Ronnie headed toward the downtown area. She had time to peruse a few shops before heading to the CN Tower. She ambled along Yonge Street near Bay. Ronnie wasn't sure what she was looking for, but she was determined to go back to the cottage with something unique that Andy could cherish forever.

Ronnie arrived at the Eaton Centre. She would surely find something here, she thought, striding toward the navigation screen that listed the stores and boutiques on each level. She searched for children's novelty shops, made a note of where they were located and set off.

Ronnie entered a children's store that, at first glance, seemed to offer a wide variety of gifts. She walked up and down the aisles slowly, hoping something extraordinary would catch her eye.

And it did, near the back of the store. Her eyes widened. It was the last thing she had expected to see. An enclosure with a kitten in it. No, several kittens. They came out from behind an elaborate scratching post, tumbling into each other and scampering off, only to dash back moments later, ready for another tumble.

One particular ginger kitten caught Ronnie's attention. It was the most playful of the bunch, and most vocal, mewing as it leaped from one spot to another, and doing the most comical acrobatics.

Ronnie laughed. Its fur was just about the same color as Red's hair. And as it came closer, she noticed its eyes were blue-green, also like his. Maybe *he* should buy this kitten. They would be a perfect match.

No. *She* should buy it. Andy had asked her for a pet while he was at SickKids, but there was no way she could have dealt with such a responsibility at that time. But now things were different. Andy was back home, and taking care of a kitten would be manageable. He would love it. It would be the best surprise she could think of for his birthday…

But how could she keep it a secret till then? A sudden idea popped in her head. She could ask Red if he could take care of it until Andy's birthday. It was a long shot, but she could try…

With excitement swirling in her veins, she strode over to a staff member. She was going to do this! "Ginger" was coming home with her. After lunch.

* * *

Red's meeting with the Australian magnate had gone longer than expected, but with superlative results. All of his projected outcomes of the meeting had been achieved. And more. His legal team had been present to see to the technical details of the contract, and after heartily shaking the magnate's hand and wishing him a good flight back to Australia, Red had left the meeting, elated at having secured this new project for his Melbourne office, a world-class art gallery with specialty restaurants, gift shops and teaching studios.

Red placed the garment bag with his jeans and shirt in the back seat of the limo. Not wanting to keep Ronnie waiting, he had decided not to change. He instructed Liam to head to the CN Tower as the gold stylized letters of Brannigan Architects International receded in the rearview mirror.

He was ready to celebrate, and he was looking forward to celebrating with Ronnie.

She was waiting just outside the main entrance. After exchanging greetings and the news that their respective meetings had gone well, they proceeded into the building and reached the glass-fronted elevator that would take them up the iconic tower to 360, the restaurant 1150 feet above ground that revolved every seventy-two minutes. But first, Red wanted Ronnie to experience the first view of the city at the LookOut. As they rocketed upward amid gasps and a few excited shrieks, Ronnie did what many did the first time in the tower: instinctively move away from the glass panel as the elevator shot up. It was packed, and as she stepped back, one foot landed on Red's shoe and she faltered, her body pressing against him. Red's arms instinctively encircled her waist, and the rest of the visitors in the elevator disappeared as his mind and body registered only the sensory impact of Ronnie in the tight circle of his arms.

And then he promptly dropped them as Ronnie gained her balance. The door opened and the visitors surged toward the floor-to-ceiling window walls, while others ventured to the glass floor, showing the dizzying vertical view.

Red was glad it was sunny, so Ronnie could have the experience of enjoying a magnificent view of the cityscape. She was leaning toward one window with an expression of childlike awe, and the thought suddenly occurred to him that her son should have this experience also. He saw her reaching up to clasp her locket wistfully before turning to face Red. "I will definitely have to return with Andy," she declared. "He'd love it!"

"He's not afraid of heights?"

Ronnie laughed. "My little guy isn't afraid of much. He's tougher than he looks." Suddenly she unclasped her locket and opened it before handing it to Red. "The origin of Andrew is Greek, *Andreas*, and it means strong, courageous, brave. That's him," she said, her voice softening.

Red gazed at the photo. It was tiny, but he could see the resemblance to Ronnie. "He obviously takes after you," he murmured, handing it back to her.

She snapped it shut and put it back on. "I don't always feel strong and courageous."

"I don't think you give yourself enough credit," he shot back. "But I was actually referring to his looks. He's a cute kid."

Seeing the emotions play on her face, Red suddenly regretted his comments. He was venturing into sensitive territory for both Ronnie and himself, and should not have given Ronnie the opening to talk about her son, let alone offer an opinion about her. And letting his tongue slip about Andy resembling her was even worse.

He turned sharply away from her as she opened her mouth to respond. He felt like a heel, but he wanted to keep things between them as neutral as possible, and discussing her son, or making inferences about how he felt about her appearance, was only going to complicate things.

As Ronnie moved stiffly past him to navigate her way around the LookOut, Red suspected she had felt rebuffed. He saw her proceed to the glass floor and ten-tatively step onto it, and then his memory flooded with the image of Marco doing the same thing a year and a half earlier. A pang ripped through him, and as Ronnie turned to rejoin him, he forced himself to repress the memory and paste a smile on his face. There was no reason why he couldn't be civil during their time here. And even friendly without crossing personal lines. "Are you ready for the Sky Terrace next?" It was outdoors, one level below, still a refreshing one thousand plus feet above the ground.

"Uh…*no*! I'm quite fine inside, thank you," Ronnie replied. "I think I'd like to just sit for a while."

"So I guess the Edge Walk is out of the question also?"

Her wide-eyed response indicated she knew of the CN Tower's most extreme attraction: the world's high-est hands-free external walk around the tower on a ledge five feet wide, situated even higher than the restaurant, 116 stories above the ground. The most daring visitors would be attached to an overhead safety rail by means of a trolley and harness system and walk around the tower in groups of six.

"Okay, lunch it is," he said, nodding. "I don't think I'm quite up to circumnavigating the tower in the middle of winter either."

Minutes later they were seated at a table in 360 The Restaurant. Ronnie had preferred it over a booth, so she could enjoy the view even more.

"Do you know that the CN Tower has the distinction of holding the Guinness World Record as the World's Highest Wine Cellar? So how about a glass?" Red suggested a white from the Niagara Peninsula and waited for Ronnie to approve before he nodded to the waitress.

His gaze couldn't help taking in the gray woollen dress Ronnie was wearing. It fit her body perfectly, and her ruby red lipstick matched the short coat she had just removed and placed over her chair.

After ordering, Red lifted his wineglass. "Cheers for us both having had a successful meeting."

She hesitated, eyeing him warily for a brief moment before nodding and clinking glasses. She took a sip. "Yes, I have good news for Casson."

"And we are going to have a fabulous lunch to celebrate getting what we wanted today…"

Ronnie's eyebrows arched. "This *is* a treat," she said, with a wave of her hand. "And I did manage to find something special for my son." She had another sip of her wine. I *was* going to get around to telling you about it," she murmured, her cheeks flushing, "especially since we'll be traveling back with you…"

"We?" Red frowned.

Ronnie bit her lip. "I couldn't help it. She was so sweet. And I know Andy will absolutely love her…" She gave Red a tentative smile. "I have to go pick her up after lunch…"

"Pick up who?"

"Ginger."

"Ginger?"

Ronnie nodded. "Our new…kitten," she said, breaking into a grin.

CHAPTER FIFTEEN

RED'S BLUE-GREEN EYES seemed to match the slate gray of his suit. He leaned forward, his brows furrowing, and Ronnie couldn't help thinking how distractingly handsome he was, with that black shirt and burgundy silk tie—

His frown dissolved. "Okay, I've heard of impulsive shopping, but this is…" He laughed.

"I hope you don't mind me bringing it back with us in the limo… You're not allergic to cats, are you?"

He waited until the waitress set down their plates, thanked her and gave Ronnie a bemused look. "No on both counts," he said. "I had a cat when I was a kid. He was round and orange, so I named him Pumpkin."

"Cute. Same as Ginger. She's got the most adorable coloring…" Ronnie smiled, her gaze shifting to Red's hair, and when she looked across at him, she realized he had noticed.

"Are you thinking Ginger and I might be related?" he said, eyes narrowing. "I don't have any kids, feline or otherwise, and I intend to keep it that way."

Ronnie's smile froze momentarily before fading. So Red Brannigan II didn't want kids. Was it because the responsibility would interfere with his jet-setting lifestyle, or was it simply because he was too self-centered and en-

joyed freedom and relationships with no ties? Her gaze
flitted over him. He was smart, handsome—no, damn
handsome—and wealthy, but whoever ended up with him
would have to be happy to have him alone, with no little
Reds to carry on the Brannigan lineage…

Not everybody had a paternal or maternal instinct…

"So you're okay with this?" she said brusquely. "Me
bringing Ginger back in the limo?"

"I'm not an unreasonable guy," he said, smirking.
"I'm sure the three of us can get along in the close confines of the limo for a couple of hours…" His mouth
curved into a smile, and Ronnie caught a flash of a
dimple in one cheek. She reached for her glass of water,
suddenly feeling too warm, and decided to delay her proposal to have him keep Ginger temporarily until they
were back on the road. She surveyed the sweeping view
again. "I can only imagine how stunning the view must
be at night, with the city all lit up…" she said, changing the subject.

"Would you live here?" Red said, eyeing her intently.

"I… I'm more of a small-town girl. Living in Parry
Sound works perfectly for me and Andy, especially since
I have family there. But I do like Toronto… I'll be traveling here more often once my new position officially
begins."

"Well then, you'll be able to return to 360 for a night
view…" He lifted and swirled his wineglass, the movement of the wine almost as hypnotizing as the laser gleam
in the ocean-like depths of his eyes…

Would she return by herself? It would be bittersweet,
enjoying the dazzling lights of the city while dining
alone. Like watching a midnight indigo sky studded with
stars, and having nobody to share the magic of it.

But you didn't want another man in your life… Her

inner voice was right. Until a few days ago, she hadn't had time to think about sharing her life with anybody other than Andy.

And then a spinout in bad weather had forced her to share space and time with Red. She blinked with the sudden awareness that there was a puzzle piece missing in her life, an empty space that had gone unnoticed during Andy's health crisis.

Ronnie had put her entire focus on Andy's treatment and recovery. She had had little time to think about or worry about anything or anybody else, including herself.

You have time now...

"Do we have time for a coffee? Dessert?"

Ronnie was jolted out of her thoughts. Those eyes fixed intently on her sent her emotions into a spin. "I'm fine," she said. "The desserts look amazing, but I couldn't eat one more thing."

"Next time, then." He nodded, a glitter in his eyes. "You're probably anxious for us to pick up the new addition..."

"Oh, are you new parents?" The waitress arrived at their table. "I couldn't help overhearing. How wonderful!" she gushed. "Is it a he or a she?"

"A she," Red answered before Ronnie could correct the waitress.

"How lovely. Girls are special."

"Very." Red smiled as he looked straight at Ronnie.

"What's her name?"

"Ginger." Red was grinning now, his gaze flicking from the waitress to Ronnie.

"Aww. Does she have hair like her daddy?"

"She does, indeed," Red chuckled.

"She must be a pretty little thing, if she takes after both of you! Congratulations!"

"Thank you," he said, taking the credit machine from her. "And lunch was excellent."

Ronnie was speechless, embarrassed and self-conscious that Red would let the waitress think that they were married and new parents.

"I can't believe you just did that," she said when the waitress was out of earshot.

Red just laughed and stood up. He walked around and leaned forward to pull out Ronnie's chair as she got up. "Shall we go? But before we fetch our little darling, would you mind if we make one stop?"

Red hadn't intended to check out Brannigan Architects International's latest accomplishment during this visit, but something made him want to show Ronnie the luxury condo residence he had designed and would be moving into at the end of the month. He had decided that it was time to move out of the condo his parents had gifted him, and into one of the penthouse suites of the residence. They didn't mind; they told him they'd be happy to keep it for out-of-town friends and guests who came to visit them.

Red suppressed a cynical laugh. His parents were hardly ever back in Toronto; they were too busy traipsing all over the world. He had accepted their perennial absence for the most part; when it did irk him, he repeated his vow to himself that unlike them, he would be very present in his future child or children's lives…

The residence, which he had named the Four-Leaf Clover to honor his Irish heritage, was a decadent Harbourfront development that was actually shaped like a clover, with each of the four circular leaf sections boasting floor-to-ceiling windows, and rooftops surfaced with green solar lights that illuminated at night. The opulent entrance, designed to represent the stem of the plant, had a massive Canadian maple-leaf-shaped double door of Waterford crystal that opened to a luxurious marble foyer with Waterford chandeliers. The residence, scheduled to officially open at month's end, included two gourmet restaurants that would feature Canadian and international cuisine, and an authentic Irish pub.

Red had designed the sprawling suites with high-end features: hardwood floors, vaulted ceilings and private terraces with spectacular views of the city and harbor. The amenities that residents could enjoy were those that Red appreciated himself: infinity pools, a state-of-the-art gym, a conference suite and library, and a meditation room.

The official opening would take place a week after the grand opening of Franklin's Resort, and Red felt a surge of excitement at the thought of starting a new chapter in his life with the move.

Red had told Ronnie about the residence, and that he wanted to have a quick glance before returning for the grand opening, but he hadn't revealed that he was the principal designer, and that he would be moving into one of the penthouse suites. As he pressed a special code to enter the building and walked through the grand foyer, Ronnie's wide-eyed expression gave him a tingling pleasure that superseded his previous sense of satisfaction with his accomplishment.

"Wow," she said, her gaze flying between the chandeliers and the opulent decor. "I've never been in a place like this…"

Something in her tone caused a strange twinge in his chest as she preceded him into the gleaming brass and marble elevator. As Red took her on a tour of the pool room, gym, conference and meditation rooms, she sporadically commented on the choice of colors, styles, floor coverings and features of each room, nodding her approval. It was the library that rendered her speechless for a few moments. She pivoted to take in the floor-to-ceiling bookshelves already stacked with new books, the luxurious high-back armchairs and recliners, and shot Red an appreciative grin.

"Whoever designed this is my kind of designer," she murmured, swirling around again to take it all in.

"And mine," he said, chuckling. "Are you ready to continue skyward? You've been in the CN Tower. I'd like to show you another spectacular view."

Ronnie's eyebrows lifted. "Why not? I doubt I'll get this chance again."

As they returned to the elevator, Red thought about Ronnie's words. They had been uttered without bitterness or longing. She had simply stated a fact that she believed to be true, a fact she accepted with calm practicality.

This was a side of a woman he was unfamiliar with. Sofia had grown up having and expecting luxury and extravagance in her life. It had become obvious to Red that she was never satisfied. The more she had, the more she wanted.

That was not the kind of woman *he* wanted in his life... and sooner or later, he would have realized that, if she had not broken up with him first.

As the doors opened to the penthouse level, Red ushered Ronnie toward his suite. While he had been settling into the estate in Parry Sound, his personal administrative assistant had arranged for the new furnishings to be delivered here and arranged where Red had specified. She had also arranged for his personal belongings to be transferred from his previous condo to this one, unpacked and put in their assigned places. He had only to walk in and enjoy life in his new penthouse.

Red was looking forward to checking it out…

He was not disappointed. As he scanned the sprawling open-concept space, Red nodded in satisfaction at the gleaming European kitchen, the sleek, Northern Italian furnishings in the living area, the heated hardwood floors, exotic area rugs and the eclectic decor. Perfect. Minimalistic but not stark. Comfortable. He turned to Ronnie. "Comments?"

"Stunning. Sleek and elegant, but not stuffy." She walked to the nearest floor-to-ceiling window. "Breathtaking view…" She stared out at the cityscape and the impressive view of the CN Tower. "Awesome."

Red joined her, and for a few moments they looked out together. He had chosen this suite for its spectacular positioning and iconic views.

"Come out on the terrace," he murmured.

Ronnie followed him past a spacious bedroom and as she took a few steps forward onto the terrace and looked down at the dizzying view, she suddenly swayed. Red reached out to help her steady herself.

"It's a different sensation, being out here, as opposed to looking out the window," she said apologetically, inhaling deeply. "I'm feeling a little light-headed."

Red steered her inside. He led her into the nearest room and had her sit down on an upholstered bench at the end of the king-size bed. He sat next to her and looked at her closely. "Are you feeling dizzy now? Light-headed still? Close your eyes and tilt your head forward."

She closed her eyes and when she swayed away from him, Red's arm shot out to stop her. He moved her gently back against him and kept his hand clasped around his arm. "Okay, take a deep breath," he murmured close to her ear. "Nice and slow. And let it out…"

As she inhaled, her head came up and his lips brushed

against her temple, igniting a thudding in his chest. Her skin was so soft and rose-scented, and Red instinctively felt the urge to kiss her.

Don't...

Ronnie turned her head and opened her eyes at that moment. Those bright chestnut eyes with the soft fluttering of her eyelashes were his undoing...

CHAPTER SIXTEEN

RONNIE BLINKED, DISORIENTED. Red's arm was around her, holding her as if he were afraid she would fall off the seat, and he was looking at her in a way she had not seen before. Was it concern? The intensity of the fathomless depths of his eyes sent a shiver through her. If she didn't know any better, she'd think it was more than just concern. Tenderness, maybe…

She could still feel his breath fanning her cheek, and the sudden swell of his chest as he inhaled deeply himself. Her heart did a pirouette, followed by a tap dance across her chest. She couldn't deny that she liked the feel of Red against her, the protective clasp of his hand on her arm, the red-gold hair and scruff she'd be tempted to reach up and touch…if they were more than just acquaintances.

"Are you okay, Ronnie?"

His voice was husky, and the way her name tumbled out of his mouth so easily made her pulse leap. "Um… I'm fine now. I'm okay with heights…but it's a whole different feeling when you're actually *outside*."

Ronnie saw Red's mouth quirk at her choice of words. And couldn't stop staring at his lips. She felt her stomach muscles contracting. A sensation of desire swept through her, and as she gazed upward at him, her cheeks burning, she could tell that Red was all too aware of her state of being. His hand slipped from her arm to cup her head gently as he leaned down to grant her unspoken request.

The gentle pressure of Red's lips on hers galvanized her. Ronnie's arms moved of their own accord around his neck. She felt herself sinking into a wonderland, her body drifting into the depths of pleasure…a pleasure she had believed herself to be immune to.

If she had been light-headed moments earlier, now her whole being felt as if it were in a no-gravity universe, with nothing but the pull of desire between her and Red…

She was floating on clouds…

And then the clouds darkened. She wasn't dealing with reality.

She pulled away from Red and she met his questioning gaze, trying to unravel her jumbled thoughts.

What was she doing? She was totally out of her element. Red was single, free and had said he didn't want kids, or something to that effect. So he was obviously just attracted to her physically.

But it wouldn't be right to encourage that attraction, or succumb to it. There was too much at stake. She had a kid, and playing around with a multimillionaire bachelor whose lifestyle was totally different from hers was not something she could allow herself to do. Her first priority had always been Andy…and she had no intention of doing anything that would change that. Even a little.

She stood up and raised her chin, shooting him a frosty look. "Let's forget what just happened." As she strode to the glass doors, she glanced back, adding, "Being this high up must have depleted the oxygen to my brain."

Making me lose my common sense and respond to your kiss, she added silently.

* * *

The limo stopped at the Eaton Centre. "I'd better come with you," Red said, and leaped out before Ronnie could reply.

"I'm pretty sure I can handle this by myself," she said, once he had come around to where she stood.

"I'll be there to make sure that you don't get all soft when you see those little fur balls, and decide to adopt more than one. I wouldn't want to have too many feline claws ready to strike in the limo," he added with a smirk.

Ronnie raised an eyebrow but chose not to reply. He followed her quickened pace with a leisurely stride, occasionally sweeping an appreciative gaze over her. She seemed not to notice the heads that turned to glance at her…

Minutes later they were watching the antics of half a dozen kittens in the enclosure. "That's her!" Ronnie said excitedly, pointing to a kitten that had pounced on a sibling and then scampered away with a triumphant meow.

"How can you tell?" Red frowned. "They all look the same to me. But maybe you should pick out a kitten with a more subdued character." He pointed. "Look, she's tormenting her other sister. Or brother. Maybe you should consider changing her name from Ginger to Tiger."

"A mother can always pick out her own," she retorted. "And I want a kitten with a little spunk. She'll be great with Andy."

"Ah, I see there has already been some bonding," he chuckled. "Okay, Mama, is there anything else you need to pick up before we head back? A carrier, food, litter box, protective gloves, face guard?"

Her jaw dropped. "Really?" She rolled her eyes. "It's all taken care of and put aside for me. I paid earlier. I just need to get Ginger." She waved over an employee, who reached for a carrier and a leash behind the counter and headed their way.

"Aw, are you Ginger's daddy?" The employee grinned as he approached. His gaze shifted to Red's hair. "Looks like you're the perfect match!"

"Indeed," Red replied dryly. "I just hope she takes to me as well as she took to her mama here…"

Red was relieved that they had left the midafternoon city congestion and were now just past Barrie on the 400 North, heading back to Parry Sound. A little over an hour to go. Ginger had initially expressed her displeasure at her new confinement, mewing incessantly for the first half hour, but was now napping.

Since they had left the penthouse, and for the last hour, Ronnie had been quiet—actually, more like aloof—and had directed most of her communications to the kitten, which she had finally released from her carrier and snuggled in her arms, murmuring to her as she stroked Ginger's fur. And after Ginger had fallen asleep, Ronnie had avoided his gaze, preferring to look out the window, when not glancing down at the puff of orange in her arms.

Ronnie was obviously not happy that he had kissed her. And maybe she was upset at herself for having responded.

He should be upset, too. Kissing Ronnie had been an impulsive and dumb thing to do.

Exciting, yes; it had ignited a flame that had begun to sizzle through his nerve endings in the most provocative way…but still dumb.

Although the silence was awkward, he decided it was best to try to focus on something else. He snapped open his briefcase, and at that moment Ginger woke up with a plaintive meow. And wouldn't stop.

"Okay, Mama, can you do something to pacify your little one? I'm sure she'll sense your motherly empathy and experience and settle down." His brows furrowed. "I don't know if I can take this the whole way back home."

"I suppose I could try to give her some milk from the carton I bought," Ronnie said coolly.

"Well, do whatever you think will work," he drawled. "Or I'll be needing a drink from the minibar. Or two."

"I can understand why you wouldn't want kids," she said, not bothering to conceal her disapproval. "It takes a lot of patience to be a parent."

His frown deepened. He had no intention of getting into a conversation about kids. Or parenting. "That's why you're adopting the kitten and I'm not," he said lightly. "And hopefully she'll get used to your place quickly and not keep you up during the night…"

Ronnie blinked at him but didn't reply. She put Ginger back in the pet carrier and reached for the carton and bowl from one of the bags on the floor beside her. She poured a small amount of milk in the bowl and carefully unlatched the carrier. "Well, hello again, little darling," she crooned, stroking the kitten's head and back. "No need to fuss. Drink your milk and we'll be home soon…"

Red felt something flicker in his chest at the tender scene. Despite the current friction in the air between them, he couldn't help thinking again that Andy was a lucky little boy to have her as a mother. Getting him this kitten for his birthday was sure to add to Ronnie's responsibilities, especially with the new job she would be starting soon, yet she had seized the opportunity to get him this special gift, knowing it would bring her son happiness.

What puzzled him, though, was her assumption that he didn't want kids…and then, while he watched Ginger slurping up the milk, he recalled the comment he had made in the restaurant, about not having kids or cats and intending to keep it that way…

He hadn't added "for now" at the end of his statement…

That explained her judgmental and disapproving opinion of him, but Red couldn't attempt to change what she thought of him without going into explanations about his past, and that wasn't going to happen.

"Speaking of home…"

Red started and turned to see Ronnie's dark eyes fixed intently on him. She was biting her lip and her brow was creased, as if pondering whether she should go on.

"My home or yours?"

"That is the question," she said, stroking Ginger, who was now back in her arms and purring. "I have something I need to ask of you, and I know it might seem a little presumptuous, but I really want everything to be perfect for my son's birthday, um…and so, I need to ask you for a favor, just for a few days. Two, or maybe two and a half at the most. I'd be eternally grateful and it would just make the surprise even better—"

"What can I do for you, Ronnie?" he said dryly. Her previously cool tone was now sounding more civil. And maybe even a little humble.

"Would…would you be willing to keep Ginger at your place until Andy's birthday? He's back tomorrow and his birthday is the day after. I want to keep it an absolute surprise. I'd really appreciate it. And I'd pop by a few times to take care of the litter box…"

Red stared at her, stunned. This was the last thing he had expected to hear from her. "I'm not used to having a pet in the house," he said slowly. "I haven't taken care of a kitten since I was ten. I might forget to feed it or something."

"You can just leave the food out for her."

"Um..." He glanced away.

Liam turned on the windshield wipers as big snowflakes started coming down. Red turned back to Ronnie. "Have you considered offering this...exciting prospect... to your cousin?" He couldn't keep a slight note of sarcasm out of his voice.

"I actually had, but Andy would want to go see his little cousin right away when he gets home. And I don't want him to see Ginger until his actual birthday." Her dark eyes held an anticipatory gleam.

"Right." He pursed his lips. "Way to pull on my heartstrings, Forrester, although it sounded like you didn't think I had a heart when it came to kids and kittens..."

"You're putting words in my mouth," she murmured defensively. She shifted in her seat, and the movement caused Ginger to slip out of Ronnie's grasp. The kitten jumped across onto Red's lap and crawled upward, rubbing her face against his. Ronnie pulled her away and cringed when Ginger's claws dug into the fabric of his suit jacket. She extricated the kitten and looked ruefully at Red. "Sorry. She's just doing what kittens do..."

"Right." He indicated the decreased visibility ahead. "It's a good thing we're almost home. I don't think the snow is going to let up."

"And speaking of home..." Ronnie's brows lifted hopefully.

Red let out a big, dramatic sigh. "Fine, I'll take her home."

"Aw, thank you! I'll think of some way to repay you…"

"Just be on standby in case I need you," he warned. "Especially if she starts crying in the night. I need my beauty sleep…"

CHAPTER SEVENTEEN

RONNIE FELT A surge of happiness at Red's words. And an acceleration of her heartbeat. She couldn't remember when she had last felt so happy or excited, other than when she had heard the wonderful news about Andy's remission.

She gazed at Red's profile as he looked away to focus on the road as Liam drove through a particularly snowy stretch.

He had a strong, firm jaw and features that she was sure had caused a spike in more than one woman's pulse… And he did have a kind heart, she admitted grudgingly to herself. Who else would have agreed to keep a kitten for someone they had just met a couple of days earlier?

Ronnie placed Ginger back into the carrier when they approached the exit that would take them into Parry Sound. Snow was falling at a much gentler rate than the almost whiteout conditions around Barrie. She shivered and hoped that Red would start the fire while they set up Ginger's corner…

The thought gave her a jolt. It had sounded like a statement someone might have made if they had been married or living together. And the image it suddenly triggered in Ronnie's mind made her blush. How ridiculous to picture herself cradling Ginger, snuggled under a cozy throw that Red had placed over her shoulders.

Okay, this has to stop. Just because Red agreed to keep Ginger for a couple of days didn't mean he had any domestic inclinations where *she* was concerned…

But would you like there to be? a rogue inner voice pressed her.

Ronnie stole another glance at Red. He had looked mighty fine in a cardigan and jeans, but in that tailored suit… Her gaze slipped from his broad chest to the way his long legs filled out his trousers and an undeniable shiver went through her.

Maybe there *was* something going on. In *her*, anyway.

The snowflakes were coming down soft and wet when they arrived at Red's place. Red thanked Liam and wished him a good night before jumping out to get Ronnie's door. She handed him the carrier and stepped out carefully. Red motioned for her to precede him and once inside the house, he invited her to join him in the salon. "The first order of business when I get in is to get the fire going," he said brusquely. "And then I need to insist on a transition period for Ginger before I let you go home…"

"What…do you mean?" Ronnie said, her brow wrinkling.

Ginger began to meow in her carrier, which he had set down on one of the recliners. He gestured toward it. "I have to make sure Ginger is happy here. So after I start up the fire, you can get her litter box set up and let her out of her carrier while I boil some water for tea. See how she takes to her temporary digs. And if she shows me a reasonable amount of love—and doesn't tear my place apart—I'll be happy to keep her."

"You didn't tell me there would be conditions," she protested, shooting him an accusing look. "I thought her staying with you for a couple of days was a done deal."

Red gazed at her for a long, worrisome moment. She couldn't believe that he had first said yes, only to now reveal that things might not work out after all…

"It is," he said, grinning. "I just couldn't resist teasing you."

Red was acutely aware of Ronnie shuffling about, setting up Ginger's food and water dishes. He felt warm and rolled up his sleeves, but he suspected that it had little to do with the fire. The warmth was inside him. Despite the warning voice telling him he should remain detached, he knew deep down that he liked having Ronnie around. In his house, in his truck, on his pond. In a restaurant. Sleeping by the fire…

Maybe "liked" wasn't the right word…

A couple of glances over his shoulder as he arranged the kindling on top of the logs in the grate revealed Ronnie preparing the litter box and placing it in a corner behind a large potted plant. He heard Ginger's contented purring as she lifted her out of the carrier and set her down in the litter box. When the fire was robust, Red drew the panels of the safety screen together and stood up. He walked over to where Ronnie was and they both watched as the kitten leaped over to the area rug, surveying her new surroundings and emitting a few plaintive mews.

He and Ronnie exchanged bemused glances, and he couldn't help thinking how natural it felt to be doing this with her. Watching their new kitten together.

Whoa. *Her* new kitten.

"Oh, look, Red!" Ronnie clasped his forearm. "She's

rolling like a little ball. Oh, my gosh, she's so cute!" And then she let go to kneel down on the rug beside Ginger.

Red watched her playing with the kitten, his pulse elevated from the brief touch of her fingers on his arm. He smiled at Ginger's antics and at Ronnie speaking to the kitten as if she were a child, and stroking her after each roll or tumble. In the background, he could hear the intermittent crackling of the fire.

Anybody looking in on them would think they were a happy family…

That's all he had ever wanted growing up…to do normal things with his parents, like the other kids in his class and in his neighborhood. Simple things.

Things that Ronnie probably did with Andy…

And things that he could imagine himself doing one day. With his own kid…

CHAPTER EIGHTEEN

CLASPING RED'S FOREARM had been involuntary. It had happened before she could even think about stopping herself. The feel of his bare arm under her hand had instantly restored her awareness, though, and she had casually let go and knelt on the carpet with Ginger, making sure that her flaming cheeks were not in Red's line of vision.

Ronnie watched Ginger as she then ambled toward the pet bed that Ronnie had placed a comfortable distance from the fireplace. The kitten sniffed curiously around it and explored other nooks and crannies around the room before returning to curl up in it. Ronnie cheered inwardly and as Red excused himself to go to the kitchen, she sat down on one of the recliners. She would leave after a quick text to Casson.

She was happy to hear that the baby's fever had gone down, and Justine was feeling better. Relieved, Ronnie texted that she'd be over in the morning to share the details of the business meeting with him. A glance toward the cat bed made Ronnie set down her cell phone quickly. Ginger was gone. A quick scan of the room showed no sign of her.

She had to find her. Ginger could get into anything in such a huge place and ingest something that could be harmful… Her heart drumming, Ronnie dashed into the kitchen, breathlessly told Red that she was looking for Ginger, and dashed out again. The doors down the foyer were all closed so she headed to the carpeted stairway. Ginger was small, but she could have managed the trek upstairs.

Ronnie's dismay grew as she inspected the first two rooms and found no sign of Ginger. And no luck in the room she had occupied her first night in the mansion. She entered the open double doors of the room opposite that one, and with a jolt realized she was in the master bedroom. *Red's room.*

She had never seen such a huge room. It incorporated a living space with an amber leather couch and chair. The king-size bed with what she realized, as she stepped closer, was a live-edge slate headboard. The floor was a gleaming expanse of dark hardwood. The entire wall behind the bed consisted of floor-to-ceiling window panels, providing a view of the pond and a majestic stretch of snow-dusted pines. Two of the side panels were actually doors leading to a balcony jutting out in a spacious half-circle.

As she turned away from the view, her gaze fell on a photo frame on the night table near her. Someone had taken a photo of Red and a little boy, probably four or five years old. They were both wearing Toronto Maple Leafs caps and were sitting in a stadium. They had smiles on their faces and were making a thumbs-up sign. Ronnie's heart skipped a beat. Was this cute little boy with the ruddy cheeks and dark brown eyes related to Red? A nephew, perhaps?

She knew next to nothing about Red.

Perhaps he was separated or divorced… The thought created a funny swirl in her stomach, but she would have to process her feelings later. She needed to find Ginger.

A ripple of the bed skirt caught her eye. And then the unmistakable flash of a ginger-colored tail. Ronnie quickly turned around to close the double doors before crouching by the edge of the bed, calling Ginger's name softly. A responding meow followed, along with the appearance of Ginger's little face. Ronnie lunged forward to scoop her up, but lost her balance in the process, and she found herself sprawled on the bedside floor mat, kitten in both hands.

And then her gaze flew to the doors as they clicked open, Red framed in the center, a crooked smile on his face.

The last thing Red had expected to find was Ronnie lying flat on the floor next to his bed, holding Ginger.

After she had run in and out of the kitchen, he had turned off the boiling kettle and then gone upstairs to join in the search. The closed double doors had puzzled him and he had reopened them, doubting his memory. And there they both were, on the floor.

He strode over to Ronnie and offered her a hand to assist her in getting up, but instead, she handed him the kitten. She shifted awkwardly to right herself, her cheeks flushed. "I'm sorry. This little rascal was under your bed."

"Don't be sorry," he said with a chuckle. He lifted Ginger in front of his face. "It's this little rascal who should apologize." The kitten meowed and licked his chin. "Now don't try to sweet talk me, Miss Ginger." Red caught Ronnie's eye. "I think she's trying to tell me she'd rather sleep with me in my nice big bed instead of her teensy one. Not a chance."

Ronnie's eyebrows lifted. "Well, you might want to put her bed in a corner of your room. You could keep a better eye on her."

"What?" He feigned a frown. "This was not in the original contract."

"She'll be lonely downstairs. And she'd wander," Ronnie said authoritatively, walking toward the door.

"I see." Red followed. "Why don't you just stay the night?" he said impulsively. "You can have your room back and she can sleep with *you*?"

Ronnie stared at him, blinking. "You're kidding, right?"

"I'm not. This way, we both get to sleep."

"Why do you think I wouldn't be able to sleep at my place?" Ronnie frowned.

"You'd be too worried about Ginger."

Ronnie shook her head and continued out the door and down the stairway. "I'm not at all worried," she said, turning on the last step to smile brightly at him. "I can see that Ginger is in very good hands."

He was losing all control, Red thought repeatedly as he followed Ronnie back downstairs. What inner sorcerer had made him ask Ronnie to stay? His invitation had slipped out of his mouth before his common sense could intervene…

He set Ginger down in her carrier as Ronnie watched. He straightened and looked at her curiously. "What time do you expect your son to be back tomorrow?"

Ronnie's face brightened as she clasped her locket. "Around noon. I can't wait." At the entrance, Ronnie slipped on her coat before Red could help her. She put on her boots and then turned to him. "Thanks again for doing this," she said, offering him a tentative smile. "Um, I… I hope you don't mind me asking…but I couldn't help noticing the photo of you and a little boy upstairs. Is he a relative?"

Red could feel the smile that had started to form freeze on his face. "He could have been," he replied brusquely.

"Oh." She shook her head, her forehead creasing. "I'm sorry; I shouldn't have asked—"

"His name is Marco. He's my ex-girlfriend's son." Red looked away. Just saying the words had precipitated an unexpected wave of emotion that hit him like a punch in the stomach. Only, instead of a fist, it was a jagged hunk of meteor, piercing him with all the feelings that he had experienced in the past year: sadness, bitterness, loss, helplessness. He glanced back at Ronnie, and another wave hit him when he saw the empathy in her eyes.

CHAPTER NINETEEN

RONNIE WISHED SHE hadn't brought up the photo. It had evoked painful memories for Red and she felt terrible, but she couldn't take the words back. She looked at him helplessly. It was strange to suddenly see a different side to him. And to catch the flicker of hurt in the depths of his eyes, as if invisible arrows had struck their exact target.

She pulled the collar of her coat. "Sorry it didn't work out for you."

He gave her a piercing stare, as if he were trying to decide whether he should say more.

"I'm not," he said finally.

Her eyebrows arched uncontrollably.

"I don't regret that it didn't work out with *her*. The hard part was that it meant I wouldn't be able to see her son anymore."

And Marco had meant the world to Red. It was in his eyes…

He turned to the fire. Kneeling on one knee, he placed another log on the grate.

Her heart suddenly swelled as she gazed at his broad back and stooped head. He was a guy with a sense of humor, but now she knew that there was also another part of him that he probably hid from most people. A part that hurt like hell.

She understood what hurting felt like. Especially these past two years. The cause of her pain was different to his, but pain was pain.

Right or wrong, she went over and reached for Red's hand and gently squeezed it. His body swiveled toward her, and in the firelight she could see his eyes had a misty sheen. Suddenly he had both her hands in his and he was pulling her to him. And she had no desire to pull away. In seconds she was kneeling on the mat with her head pressed against his chest and her arms around his waist, with his clasped around her back. His body was solid, warm, and felt…nice. *Very nice.*

Was that his heart drumming against her ear, or was it her pulse? She breathed in the scent of his cologne. Intoxicating. A warning light flickered in her brain, but she ignored it, wanting this rush that she was feeling to continue…

She lifted her face and at the brush of her jaw on his chin, he leaned down and a second later, his lips were on hers. They both froze at the initial impact, and then Ronnie felt the gentle pressure of Red's mouth inviting her to respond.

She wanted to. *Needed to.*

Ronnie closed her eyes, immersed in such waves of pleasure that she thought she was spinning, airborne. She thought she heard her phone buzzing, but she ignored it. Inside, a hunger was gnawing at her, a hunger that she never thought she'd feel…

Her heart was thumping so loudly that she had to take a breath. Red's lips trailed down her neck, each kiss activating a sizzle that radiated throughout her body.

His cheek descended farther, brushing against her locket.

And that was when common sense flooded her.

She stiffened and pulled back, forcing herself to ignore the flash of hurt in his eyes. She should have never allowed herself to get to this point. She rose and turned away from Red, trying to get her breathing back to normal.

But how could life ever be normal after tonight?

"I think—" she paused shakily "—that it's best if you stay away from women like me until you figure out a way of getting over your past relationship."

"I am over it," he rasped, also rising.

"Over *her*, maybe. But not over her son…" She bit her lip. "You need to let go… Because otherwise, I don't think you can move on." She stopped as his eyes narrowed, his expression fierce. A sudden thought came to her. Red was attracted to her but inevitably pulled away, and Ronnie could see now that Andy was probably the reason. How could Red even contemplate the idea of another child in a relationship, when he hadn't let go of Marco?

And perhaps there was even more to it than that…

She saw the muscles in his jaw flicking. He might not want or be ready to hear anything else, but she felt compelled to try.

"Red, can I just say something else? You mentioned that you were an only child, and that your parents had often been absent when you were young, traveling around the world." Ronnie paused as his gaze turned sharply to her. She bit a corner of her lip. "Have you ever thought that…that maybe you're not only still trying to heal from the loss of Marco, but also from the physical and emotional loss of your parents during much of your formative years?"

Something flickered in Red's eyes, and Ronnie knew her words had touched a nerve. He was still hurting…

Ronnie felt his ache in her own heart. Imagined what he must have felt as a child. He turned away.

"I think," she said softly behind him, "that accepting your loss doesn't mean you have to forget Marco. Or feel guilty that you might have caused him to feel hurt over the breakup…"

She saw his shoulders stiffen. "There are people… professionals who can help with any lingering feelings you might be experiencing…and losses that go farther back…"

Moments passed and Ronnie wondered if maybe she had said too much. "I'm sorry," she murmured.

Red slowly turned around to face her. "I never thought about it—all of it—in that way before…" He nodded slowly. "I might just see who I can talk to when I get back to Toronto. But what you said makes a lot of sense." He held her gaze for a few moments. "Thank you, Ronnie."

She nodded, and bit her lip. "It's a lot to deal with. Look, Ginger is sleeping. So if you don't mind, Red, I'd like to head back home. I'll just take a cab."

Red felt a lurch in his stomach muscles as he stared back at her. He didn't want her to leave. Moments ago, Ronnie had offered her perspective on a condition that had previously seemed hopeless to him. He had been struggling with the challenge of letting go of his recent past. He had accepted the end of his relationship with Sofia, and maybe even with Marco, but Red hadn't been able to stop thinking about him.

Accepting your loss doesn't mean you have to forget Marco.

No, he didn't have to try to forget Marco, he now realized with wonder. He could cherish the memories they had shared. His loss might still make him sad at times, but perhaps he could let go of his lingering feelings of guilt, and now move forward and allow a new relationship to develop…including one with a child.

And maybe Ronnie was right about his unresolved issues with his parents, and their connection to his loss of Marco…but he would deal with that later…

"No. *I'll* take you home."

But first he had to deal with what had happened between him and Ronnie earlier…

How had he ended up doing what he had vowed never to do? Kissing her like he had been stranded in a desert for weeks and she had just brought him water. He had to try to apologize. Red inhaled and exhaled deeply. "Look, Ronnie, I'm sorry if I made you uncomfortable earlier. It wasn't my intention."

She didn't respond.

"I'm sorry," he repeated. "I—I just got caught up in the moment… Can we just forget it happened?" What a stupid thing to say. How could he forget any of it? And it was the same request Ronnie had made after their kiss on his terrace…

She nodded slowly "I'm sorry, too." Minutes later, as he held the door of his truck open for Ronnie, Red caught a whiff of her perfume, a delicate rose fragrance that he had trailed along her neck and—

It was just beginning. The torture of remembering…

He turned on the radio to an easy listening channel. It would relieve them both of the effort to make small talk on the way to Winter's Haven…

Ronnie's phone buzzed, and he turned off the radio. He was able to hear the muffled voice of a man, but not the message.

"Oh, my God, Peter," Ronnie gasped. "Oh, my God. Will he be okay? Are they doing tests? Does he have a concussion?"

Red felt his heart begin to thud. Something had happened to Andy…

He glanced at Ronnie. She was staring straight ahead, her face creased with worry. She listened intently to her ex-husband while blinking rapidly.

"I'm going home to get my car and I'm heading to Gravenhurst right away," she blurted while he was still talking. "My poor baby. Tell him I love him. I'll be there as soon as I can!"

A few seconds later she hung up and turned to Red. "Andy fell and hit his nose on the edge of the coffee table. It started to bleed and he also had a gash that needed stitches. They're doing more tests, given his health history." Alarm flickered in her dark eyes.

"Did Andy's father feel it was serious?"

"He said it was under control, but still, I should be there… What if there are complications?"

"It's late, and by the time you get there—it'll take you more than an hour in this weather—they might already have discharged him," he said gently. "Perhaps you should let Peter handle this. I'm sure he would let you know if there's a more serious issue." He activated the windshield wipers as the snow started up and then glanced over at Ronnie. "It's not the best weather to be traveling at night on the highway…"

"I could have been on my way already if I had answered my phone earlier." Her jaw clenched.

He frowned. When had her phone rung? Oh, yes… when they were—

"And he wouldn't have had to go through this ordeal by himself."

"He's not by himself, Ronnie; his dad is with him."

She waved a hand dismissively. "I shouldn't have been

distracted. What if something worse had happened? I'd never forgive myself."

"It sounds like things are under control, and something like this could happen with or without you being there, Ronnie, so you don't have to beat yourself up over this," Red said in a nonjudgmental tone. "Kids fall, get stitches and need to go to the hospital."

"I think I have a little more experience with kids than you," she blurted. And then she shook her head. "I'm sorry. That was insensitive. I shouldn't have said that."

"Apology accepted. You're under stress."

Ronnie nodded. "Can you go a little faster?" She leaned forward, tapping nervously on the glove compartment.

"Ronnie, if you're that intent on driving to the hospital, I'm not letting you go alone." His tone was firm and her gaze shifted to him, her brows furrowed. "But the wisest thing to do—in *my* opinion—is to go home, wait for updates from Peter, and once he reassures you that Andy is fine—which I'm sure is the case—then you can go to sleep with peace of mind, and tomorrow Andy will be back in time for lunch and your hugs."

Red turned into Ronnie's driveway, and brought the truck to a stop near the doorstep. He switched off the wipers and in seconds the windshield was covered with a layer of snow. He swiveled in his seat to look Ronnie in the eye. "Why jeopardize your life by driving at night in these conditions? Andy needs you to stay safe…"

From the outdoor light that illuminated the interior of the truck, Red saw that Ronnie's initial glare had changed to a look of thoughtfulness as she weighed his words.

"Let Peter handle it," he murmured. "Let him be a dad…"

Ronnie stared out the window. She let out a long sigh.

"Okay," she said, nodding slowly. "I'll call Peter. But if he calls back later and tells me I should go, I'll go…"

"Of course. And that's when you'll call *me*, and I'll pick you up and drive you there."

The drive back home was long, dark and lonely. When Red opened the front door, Ginger's mewing actually cheered him up. He opened up the carrier and lifted her out. She nuzzled his face and he stroked her head and back, marveling at how relaxing it felt.

He needed to relax. Think things through. Figure out how Ronnie Forrester had, in the three days since she had spun into his life, taken up residence in his mind.

Along with her son.

He hadn't wanted to complicate his life again by pursuing a relationship that involved a child.

But now…he was ready to open the door—if only a crack—to that possibility.

Ronnie had been very perceptive about the dynamics of his relationship with Marco. And something inside him had let go at her advice.

Lying in bed a little later, Red recalled the feel of Ronnie pressed against him and her response to his kiss that had sent ripples of desire through him. He could only imagine what might have transpired had she not pulled away…

CHAPTER TWENTY

RONNIE WAS ABOUT to put her finger on the snooze button and then remembered that Andy was coming home today. Peter had called shortly after Red had left last night, and said that Andy was fine and they would be heading home. Ronnie had changed into her pajamas and made herself a cup of chamomile tea, hoping it would settle the agitation in her stomach and chest caused not only by the initial worry over Andy but also by the ambivalent feelings churning up inside her over Red's embrace. And kiss.

But she couldn't just blame *him*.

She had started it, letting her empathy for his pain over Marco compel her to reach out and squeeze his hand. And then he had literally taken her breath away.

Unfortunately, the tea hadn't produced the results she had hoped for, and she had spent a good portion of the night shifting from side to side, while her thoughts kept turning to Red…

As she got out of bed, Ronnie reminded herself that she had Andy to think about. And she could not—*would not*—get involved with Red. No matter how much she was attracted to him.

She had no intention of trusting her deepest emotions to any man and then getting hurt if it didn't work out. More importantly, she didn't want Andy to get hurt.

Ronnie removed her locket before stepping into the shower. She really didn't have to worry that Red would be pursuing her. He had made it clear that he wanted them both to forget what had happened. And he obviously had trust issues, as well. His previous relationship hadn't worked out, and Ronnie didn't blame him for not wanting to repeat that kind of scenario with someone else.

So why, then, knowing all this, did she feel a twinge of hurt over his readiness to forget?

Red shut off his laptop and gazed at the ball of fur resting in her pet bed. Ginger had been surprisingly quiet during the night, so he couldn't blame the kitten for his lack of sleep. What had kept him awake were the images that kept popping up in his mind. Dozens of images of Ronnie that circulated in his memory incessantly: her dazed look after spinning out; her peaceful expression while sleeping on the recliner; the breathtaking skate on the pond; the wonder on her face at the CN Tower; her pleasure as she watched Ginger's antics; and her luminous brown eyes that had seemed to melt into his when he had leaned forward to kiss her…

Declaring that he and Ronnie should just forget what had happened between them had been unrealistic. At least for *him*. She had seemed to have no problem agreeing that it would be best to forget.

He sighed. Why did thinking about Ronnie hurt?

Because you want her…

He blinked. He *did* want her. In his house and in his life.

Child and all.

It was time to stop living in the past. He had to accept that Marco had been a temporary gift in his life. Someone who had shown him that he had the capacity to love a child who wasn't biologically his and that he would be loved back. After considering what Ronnie had told him, Red knew it was time to accept the past and let go. He would never forget Marco, but he could move on and not feel guilty about it.

And now Red had the opportunity to accept and love another child simply because he was in love with the child's mother.

The realization shook him to the core. He didn't just *want* Ronnie; he was in love with her. He just had to come up with a way to make her feel the same way…

But would Ronnie trust him to stick around, even if times got tough? The stakes were high for her too, but he had to find a way to show her that he'd be there for the long run, through sunshine and storms. In sickness and in health. For both her and Andy.

There must be some way he could make her believe…

CHAPTER TWENTY-ONE

ANDY WAS FAST ASLEEP before Ronnie had finished the first song. Her heart swelled at the sight of his long, feathery lashes on his flushed cheeks. She was so glad to have him home. Earlier, when Andy had pulled open the dresser drawers to get a fresh set of pajamas, Ronnie's heartbeat had accelerated at the sight of his clothes arranged in neat piles. By Red. Knowing now that his past relationship had included the woman's child, for whom he had cared a great deal, Ronnie realized that going into Andy's room must have brought back some bittersweet memories...

And perhaps the reason Red had been ready to leave after that...

Ronnie's thoughts went back to the afternoon she and Andy had spent with Casson and Justine. They were perfect for each other, and they were so in love with their adorable baby. They deserved every happiness.

And so do you, her inner voice murmured.

Yes, she did. And she *was* happy. But she couldn't deny that there was a hollow in a corner of her heart, and wondered if it would ever be filled by love of a different kind...the love of a partner. A man whose love could encompass her son, as well. Without it, there would be no relationship.

But you didn't want a relationship...

Her inner voice was right. She hadn't wanted one after her marriage had ended, hadn't had time to even consider fitting another person in her life.

And now?

Now, nothing. Red Brannigan II had entered her life and there had been a mutual physical attraction between them, but he had clearly stated that they should forget what had happened. Ronnie put away her mug and got ready for bed, deliberately shifting her thoughts to Andy. She couldn't wait for his birthday tomorrow. He would be turning seven and celebrating with his family at home, unlike last year.

This birthday would be his best so far. He deserved it. Ronnie vowed that every birthday after that would be better than the last. This year, a kitten… What she needed to think about was whether she would go and pick up Ginger, or if she should just call Red to see if he could drop the kitten off at Casson's. If she went with the latter, she could avoid seeing him.

Why did she feel so conflicted? She sighed. Tomorrow was a big day and she hoped that, unlike the night before, she'd be able to have a decent sleep.

Without the memory of those blue-green eyes and that red-hot kiss breaking into her dreams.

Red had spent half the night at his laptop, playing around with ideas for renovating the mansion and developing some of the acreage. And then some wild ideas had taken hold of his imagination…

In the early hours of the morning, Red had nodded off at the keyboard, and when he had awoken, he had surveyed the design templates he had created. Plans for all the things a little boy would get excited about: a water slide and pool; a basketball court; a treehouse; and a mini movie theater. It was crazy, and his plans might never be realized, but he was going to wait for the right time to show them to Ronnie…

Red knew very well that kids today liked their electronics, but if they were like Marco, they would enjoy all these activities, too. The thought had galvanized Red. It was the first time he had remembered something about Marco and felt happiness instead of grief. Happiness knowing he had played a positive part in the boy's life, at least for a while. He had shut down his laptop and gone to bed, knowing in his heart that he had come to a turning point. He had finally let go…

And maybe now a new chapter in his life could begin.

With a contentment he hadn't felt in a long time, Red felt himself drifting peacefully toward sleep.

CHAPTER TWENTY-TWO

RONNIE WOKE UP EARLY to a pink and baby blue sky. It promised to be a beautiful clear day. No snow, no freezing rain, just a whole lot of sunshine. Her little guy was seven today. And this was a birthday she hoped he would always remember.

Ronnie put her hair up in a ponytail and dressed quickly in jeans and a red T-shirt. After she made breakfast for Andy, she drove over to Casson and Justine's. Andy went off with Casson for a walk in the woods. Ronnie strode to the big living room window with its gorgeous view of the frozen bay and the section Casson had cleared off for skating. It immediately evoked the memory of Red sweeping her up and skating effortlessly around his pond, with her clasped tightly in his arms…

She was flooded with a longing that she never thought she'd feel again. But this longing was much stronger, perhaps because she knew it would not be fulfilled by the man who had caused it…

A man who had helped her make a giant step yesterday… to let go and not feel she had to be with Andy every waking moment, guarding him, protecting him from getting hurt, or being there when he was hurt. Red had made her realize that she had to relax and let Peter be a responsible parent too, without her hovering over them.

Red had taught her a lesson about trust.

She had to try to give up the reins of control and trust that Peter could do the job of looking after Andy as well as she had done. And even if he couldn't, she'd have to let go and hope that he would do the best he could.

Ronnie sighed. Red had given her a new perspective. Letting go was hard, though. But like it or not, she had to try. Perhaps now she could continue to let her guard down more, have more fun in her life, do things for herself.

And maybe the time would come when she'd be able to trust another man in her life…

The doorbell sounded. She strode to the door and when she opened it, her heart clanged at the sight of Red holding Ginger in her carrier.

She swallowed. "I—I thought… Casson told me *he'd* be driving over to pick her up…"

"I called him to say I could drop her off. He said he'd text you…"

Ronnie glanced across the room at her cell phone lying on the kitchen table where she had placed it upon arriving. Red stood on the doorstep, his eyebrows arching. "I'll get Ginger's bed in a minute… It's in the truck."

"Okay, thanks," Ronnie said, snapping out of her stupor. She set the carrier down in the foyer and watched as Red returned with the pet bed and a bag with the rest of the items for Ginger. Ronnie reached for the bed, but Red wasn't letting go. His brow was furrowed and he stood there blinking at her, with a steely intensity in his eyes. Eyes that seemed darker, the color of the stormy waters in some of the paintings of Georgian Bay by the Group of Seven.

"Ronnie, is there a chance we can talk before Andy's birthday?"

"Talk? Here?" Justine would be coming down with the baby at any moment…

"How about in my truck? We could go for a short ride, if you have time."

Ronnie's heart began drumming. "I—I'm going to bring Ginger upstairs and I—I have to let Justine know." She lifted the carrier and Red released his hold on the bed.

"Okay; I'll wait in the truck."

When Red saw her leaving the house a few minutes later, he jumped out to open the passenger-side door. "Okay if we just drive around the corner?" he said.

"Um, sure."

He drove out of Winter's Haven and down the highway. After a couple of minutes, he turned into a road through a densely wooded section that led to a small lake. He parked and then shifted in his seat to face her. She watched as he took a deep breath and exhaled slowly. "Ronnie, I can't forget…"

"What do you mean?" She knew exactly what he meant.

"You. I can't forget you." He rubbed his temple. "I didn't get much sleep last night. Or the night before." He let out a husky laugh. "In fact, you've kept me awake and thinking since you spun out before my eyes."

Ronnie felt her heart pulsing, trying to anticipate what he was going to say next. And how was she going to respond…

"I wasn't looking for anything like this to happen. I didn't think I was ready." He shrugged. "But it happened anyway."

Her heart was going to rocket right out of her chest. "Wh-what, exactly?"

He looked at her as if she were a student who just wasn't getting it. "I fell. Head. Over. Heels."

"For...?"

"For Ginger." At her stunned look, he added, "No, Ronnie. For *you*."

She blinked at the sudden tingling behind her eyelids, wanting to both laugh and cry.

"That has got to be the most original way to get yourself invited to a birthday party," she finally managed to say, trying to keep her voice steady.

It was Red's turn to look stunned. "That's all you can say?"

She wanted to climb over the truck's middle section and kiss him oh-so-thoroughly, but something in her resisted. "You could have just asked nicely for a piece of cake—"

He groaned and leaned toward her, cupping the back of her head while he kissed her. "I'll take this over a piece of cake any day," he murmured before his mouth closed over hers again.

Ronnie lost all sense of time and space. Red Brannigan II had ignited her appetite. And she wanted to have her fill.

She wrapped her arms around his neck. Brought her hands to touch both sides of his face. Ran her fingers through his hair. And kissed him with a hunger that matched his.

Red looked deeply into Ronnie's eyes. This was what he had been waiting for. Everything he had gone through to get to this point had been worth it. He gently traced his fingers over the contours of her face. She was real. His feelings were real.

"We have to get back, Red."

Red traced the outline of her mouth. He loved the sound of his name on her lips.

"Okay," he murmured. "I'll be back later in time for cake…"

After dropping Ronnie off, Red headed to one of the malls. He couldn't very well show up empty-handed for Andy's birthday. He wished he had asked Ronnie what Andy might like. Halfway there, Red changed his mind. He had the perfect gifts for Andy at his place. *In Toronto.* He had intended to give them to Marco last year, but the breakup happened and he had shoved the items into a spare bedroom closet.

Andy was a Leafs fan, just like Marco. Red couldn't remember if it was Casson or Ronnie who had mentioned it, but it didn't matter. All that mattered was that he knew Andy would like the gifts. What kid wouldn't like an official hockey jersey of his favorite team? And a hockey stick signed by all the players? Red had bid on the latter at a charity event in Toronto and had triumphantly brought it home, excited to give it to Marco.

Red felt a twinge of sadness, but he knew in his heart that he had accepted his loss. Now he had the chance to give these gifts to a little boy who had no idea yet that Red loved his mother and wanted to start a new chapter of his life with her. And *him.*

He checked his watch. If he wanted to be back in time for the party, he'd have to leave now for Toronto. It would take a couple of hours there and back, depending on the traffic, but it would be worth it, seeing Andy's face when he opened up the gifts. Red approached the merging lane and put his foot on the accelerator, zooming onto the 400 South.

CHAPTER TWENTY-THREE

RONNIE WAS FLOATING ON AIR. She couldn't think of a better cliché for how she felt. But she wasn't ready to tell Justine about her and Red. Not yet. Today was about Andy, not her.

Casson and Andy hadn't returned from their walk. Ronnie told Justine about inviting Red to the party to thank him for keeping Ginger and then drove back to her cottage to change. She went to her room and looked through her closet. She hadn't chosen an outfit yet, and now, knowing that Red would be there, she wanted to pick something extra special.

Ronnie finally decided on a tailored burgundy dress with three-quarter-length sleeves. She liked its classic rounded neckline and below-the-knee straight skirt. She had bought it two years ago, but hadn't had the opportunity to wear it since. Until now. Her son's seventh birthday and Red's declaration warranted a celebration. A double celebration. And this was the perfect dress to celebrate in. She would wear it with black pantyhose and a low-heeled pair of pumps. And the only piece of jewelry she'd put on would be her locket.

Ronnie laid the dress on her bed and ran her palm over one of the sleeves. A delicious shiver skittered through her at the thought of Red running his hand over the fabric…with her in it.

She couldn't wait to see Red again. She wanted to sing, she was so happy. Whatever feelings she had had previously about not wanting or needing a man had dissipated when Red had revealed his feelings to her. And kissed her.

She had been afraid to trust again, she realized. But looking straight into the crystal-clear depths of his eyes, Ronnie's fears had melted. Along with her heart.

She groaned. Another cliché. But true.

When she drove back, Ronnie was disappointed to see that Red's truck wasn't in the driveway. What was keeping him? She went to check on Ginger and let her out of the carrier for a few minutes. Her footsteps slowed as she heard Casson mentioning Red's name.

He must have called…

"He said he had made a mistake, and he should have never started up with her. He said he couldn't face her…" Casson's voice drifted off.

Ronnie had heard enough. She backtracked quietly up the stairs and into the guest bathroom. She sat on the edge of the tub and stared numbly at the opposite wall. *He wasn't coming.* She felt as if a slab of ice had rammed into her stomach. He had seemed so genuine earlier. She had believed his words, felt the passion of his kisses. How could he have suddenly changed his mind about her? About them? Yes, he'd been hurt. So had she. But she had been ready to let him into her life, and she had believed that he had felt the same about her. Tears of shock and frustration spilled onto her cheeks.

Maybe reality had hit him square in the jaw, the reality that by wanting Ronnie, he'd be getting a two-for-one deal. And maybe that had scared him enough to make him back off. She frowned, mentally playing the reel of what he had said to her in the truck. He couldn't forget her. He had fallen head over heels for her…

Ronnie's heart froze. He hadn't once mentioned Andy.

And she had been too caught up with the fantasy of Red loving her—

But no, he hadn't used the word "love" either.

Ronnie's stomach vaulted. How could she trust and have faith in someone who wasn't ready to accept her child? No matter how attracted she was to Red physically, there could be no going forward if he couldn't see himself including Andy in the picture.

This was a bad dream. She would wake up and see Red walking into the house, his eyes twinkling. Reflecting his love. And trust. And desire to get to know and love Andy.

Ronnie walked to the window and looked out. No truck. It wasn't a dream.

The chunk of ice that had struck her in the stomach now seemed like it was breaking off into icicles down her limbs. Casson's voice came back to her: *he said he couldn't face her…*

Her heart twisted. Red had ruined everything. Her day, her hopes and her dreams. He had destroyed her trust. *She* should have never started up with *him*.

Ronnie was done with trusting men.

And she never wanted to see Red's face again.

She dabbed at her eyes. She had Andy to think about now. Her beautiful, courageous little boy. And she was not about to ruin his birthday. She checked her watch. With a leaden heart, she opened the door and went downstairs.

Red looked at the endless lines of backed-up traffic ahead of him and behind. He had just passed Barrie and like a thousand other vehicles, he was stuck in a traffic jam on the 400 North. He rubbed his temples, then glanced at his watch. Damn. He had been so happy, getting to Toronto fairly quickly, grabbing the jersey and hockey stick in his new penthouse and wrapping them up before immediately heading back to Parry Sound. From his memory of a photo of Andy at Casson's house, and his photo in the locket Ronnie had shown him, Red kept picturing Andy's face lighting up at seeing Ginger and the hockey gifts.

When he finally pulled into Winter's Haven, he was relieved to see Ronnie's car still there.

The shocked look on Ronnie's face when she opened the door made him frown. Something had happened. "Is Andy okay?" he said, reaching to clasp her hand.

Ronnie pulled her hand away. "He's fine," she said woodenly. "I wasn't thinking of my son earlier," she said stiffly. "I made a mistake. Just like you."

"I don't understand, Ronnie." Red stared at the woman standing across from him, a look of aloofness and disdain on her face. He felt as if he had just stepped into a twilight zone.

"Just go," she snapped before turning away.

CHAPTER TWENTY-FOUR

RONNIE STARED AT JUSTINE. "What did you say?"

"Casson had been filling me in on what had happened with Red and his previous girlfriend. And her son, Marco."

Ronnie blinked, stunned. She had gone to find Justine and had burst into tears in the baby's room as she explained what had happened.

"I really messed up, didn't I?" Ronnie wiped her eyes. "I treated him like…like dirt down there."

At the sudden rumble outside, Ronnie rushed to the window. Red was putting on his seat belt.

She flew down the stairs, slipped on her boots, but didn't bother with her coat. She rushed out the door and down the steps, only to catch a glimpse of Red's back bumper before it disappeared.

Ronnie's heart plummeted. She turned and began to walk slowly toward the house.

A crunching noise in the driveway made her look back. Her heart began to clang. Red was driving back. She couldn't move. The truck came to a stop and Red jumped out. He took one look at Ronnie and gathered her in his arms. "Get in," he said huskily.

He helped her up, closed the door and got back in. He handed her some tissues, and after she had dabbed at her eyes, he took her hands in his. "Okay, Forrester, let it out. All of it."

She couldn't stop shivering. He took off his jacket and put it over her shoulders. "I'm listening," he murmured.

His gentle tone was enough to cause another round of sobbing. When her tears had subsided, she explained what had happened, how she had misinterpreted the conversation she had overheard. "I was so mean, turning into an ice queen and ordering you to leave."

"I'm pretty sure I can melt your icy heart," he murmured, before explaining why he had been late.

"You went all the way to Toronto to get those gifts for Andy?"

"I did."

Something flickered in his eyes, and Ronnie felt her heart tumbling in her chest. If she hadn't expressed it before, she had to tell him now. "I love you, Red Brannigan II." She cupped his face. "Do you hear me?"

"Loud and clear, Ronnie Forrester. And I love you more." He grinned before leaning forward to kiss her deeply.

"I can't exactly get down on my knee in this truck," he murmured in her ear, "but I plan to do so very soon in a more comfortable place. In the meantime, could I have the honor of attending Andy's birthday, and accompanying both of you to the grand opening of Franklin's Resort next week?"

"I'll say yes, but you'll have to run it by the little guy too."

He chuckled. "I think I can handle that. Now how about we go back inside so I can meet the birthday boy and watch him open his presents. And have some cake, of course." His eyes glittered. "Although I plan to drop by your place later...*much later*...for some real dessert."

Ronnie felt her heart skip a beat. Oh, yes. That was exactly the dessert she had in mind.

* * *

Red suggested that Ronnie go in the house first, while he grabbed the presents for Andy. He felt excited and a little nervous at the same time. What if Andy took a disliking to him? What if he didn't want to share his mom with anybody else? The poor kid had already dealt with his dad leaving him for a period of time; would he be wary of another man coming into his life?

Red knocked on the door, and when Ronnie opened it moments later, his pulse leaped. He searched her face, wondering if there was any sign of regret at having him come to Andy's birthday, but all he saw was a shy smile and luminous eyes with lashes that fluttered with restrained excitement.

"Hi," he said huskily. "Have you cleared my entry with the boss?" He waved over her head to Casson and Justine, who had entered the kitchen.

"Don't kid yourself," Casson replied with a laugh. "Ronnie's her own boss."

"I actually meant Andy," Red said with a smile.

"Oh, that boss. He's in the living room, playing with our dog, Luna." He checked his watch. "I think we can head there now and get this party started." He took the packages from Red.

Red followed them all into the living room, thinking about how just mentioning Andy's name had felt as if the child were already in his life… He watched Casson zigzagging around Andy and Luna before placing the two parcels in a corner with the other presents. When Andy noticed the packages, he came to a sudden stop and Luna careened into him, knocking him off balance.

Red swooped forward in a rush of adrenaline and caught the boy before he went crashing to the floor and ended up with a concussion. For several moments time stood still. Andy blinked at him with a mixture of surprise and curiosity in his dark eyes. Everyone else in the room faded from Red's view, even though they were just steps away, leaving the next few seconds to play out in slow motion…

The boy's hair was tousled, and his plaid shirt had flopped out of his pants. His cheeks were flushed, and his eyes—Ronnie's eyes—brought a lump to Red's throat, in addition to igniting an accelerating drum beat in his chest. The kid was so vulnerable. No wonder Ronnie was such a protective parent.

And he could be, too… He was ready…

Red knew in that instant that he would love this little imp as if he were his own…and maybe one day in the future, he and Ronnie could give him a special gift of a baby brother or sister…

He wished he could hug Andy right this minute, and tell him that he'd be there to catch him in the years ahead but that moment would have to wait.

As Red set him down, everyone came back into focus. Red's gaze flew to Ronnie, and he knew immediately that she had been touched by these past moments too…

"Thanks, mister." Andy's voice brought his attention back to the boy, who was stretching his neck to the max to talk to him.

He smiled and crouched down so he could be at eye level with Andy. "No problem. And you can call me Red."

"Red?" Andy's gaze flew to Red's hair.

Red chuckled. "Well, my mother couldn't exactly call me Purple with hair like this, could she?"

Andy giggled. "No." He suddenly turned and scampered off to the corner with the pile of presents. "Can I open my presents, Mummy?"

Ronnie walked across the room, squeezing Red's hand

slightly before joining Andy. "I guess we can switch the order of things," she said, ruffling Andy's hair. "Presents, then lunch, then cake. How does that sound?"

"Yay! That sounds great!" Andy clapped vigorously, and Luna bounded toward him, her tail wagging.

Andy had opened up Casson and Justine's gift—a high-powered telescope and an astronomy book for kids—hugged them both, and was now eyeing Red's gifts. Red handed the smaller gift to him with the Toronto Maple Leafs hockey jersey first, and smiled when Andy opened it and cheered. And although the shape of the next gift had made it pretty obvious, Andy jumped up and down when he saw all the signatures on the hockey stick.

"Okay, sweetie, put it down now before someone loses their head," Ronnie said firmly. "Your next gift is upstairs. Close your eyes and count to twenty while I go and get it."

Moments later, Ronnie returned with the carrier concealed under a box that had holes cut out strategically in it. "Okay, Andy, at the count of three, you can open your eyes and lift the box." She set the box down in front of him. "One, two, three. Okay, lift...and meet Ginger!"

Andy's eyes grew wide. "Mummy, Mummy, you got me a kitten!" He threw his arms around her neck. "Thanks, Mummy!"

Red was glad that Casson had been taking photos with his cell phone. These were memories that Ronnie would cherish forever. Seeing her gaze at Andy with such love made his heart ache with love for her.

At the sudden cry coming from the baby monitor, Justine went upstairs to check on A.J. Casson followed, with Luna bolting after him.

Ronnie let Ginger out of the carrier. Andy picked her

up right away and kissed her before walking over to Red, who stroked the kitten's back, smiling at the memories he already had of her. Ronnie sat next to Red on the couch and watched with an indulgent grin on her face.

Andy was a lucky kid to have Ronnie as a mother. And she was lucky to have *him*.

Here was a little guy who had gone through an ordeal no kid—or parent—should have to go through, and had finished his treatment with positive results. Results worth celebrating. No wonder Ronnie had wanted to get Andy something superspecial for his birthday.

"Her fur is the color of your hair, Red. It's so nice," Andy said, making the back of Red's eyes suddenly start to prickle.

His heart swelled. This was what he had always dreamed of, sharing special moments…with his family.

EPILOGUE

Along with the thrum of the helicopter's engines, Ronnie felt a warm thrum in her chest. Andy was sitting next to her, and Red was in the seat directly across from them. They were all wearing protective headsets, and Andy looked so small in his. Her eyes began to mist. This was a dream she had never envisioned, flying over Toronto at night, viewing the jeweled skyline and multicolored beams of light from the skyscrapers reflected in the shimmering waters of Lake Ontario.

And sitting across from the helicopter's owner, Redmond Brannigan II.

In the couple of weeks since Andy's birthday party, Ronnie had felt like she was on top of the clouds. Red had taken her and Andy for an extensive tour of his Victorian mansion, and Andy had been delighted with the secret nooks and crannies, and the hidden staircase up to the attic. Red had shown him and Ronnie the designed templates on his laptop for the pool and water slide, basketball court, treehouse, and mini movie theater, and Andy had looked at him with big brown eyes and said eagerly, "Can we come and visit you when they're done?"

Red had exchanged a smile with Ronnie, a smile that had filled her with such emotion that she had had to discreetly blot the tears that were starting to blur her vision. She and Red had agreed that they would let Andy get used to the idea of them being friends and sharing some good times together before letting him know that they would be sharing the rest of their lives together as a family…

Casson and Justine had invited them all to their place for skating on the frozen stretch of bay, and then later, dinner and a bonfire, roasting marshmallows and drinking hot chocolate. Red had taken turns with Ronnie skating alongside Andy, and at one point, Red had asked Andy if he was up to speed skating—which meant being carried as Red speed skated. Andy had said yes and Ronnie had watched with a thumping heart as Red zoomed around the ice, with Andy's little arms around his neck and his face registering both excitement and joy.

Ronnie's heart had done a pole vault a couple of days later when Andy had asked Ronnie if Red could come over to help them make peanut butter cookies. "He's funny," he had said matter-of-factly to Ronnie, "and he said he would help me build something awesome with my LEGO set."

Later that evening, watching them both on the living room floor, working together with the colored blocks, Ronnie had taken the tray of cookies that Andy and Red had made out of the oven. She had noticed that R+R+A had been etched into one of them and had looked up quickly to find Red's gaze fixed on her. And then he had winked.

Yes, she had been floating on top of the clouds…

And now she almost *was*, soaring in Red's helicopter over Toronto.

Red had reminded her of their conversation about returning to the city for a night view. Ronnie had thought to herself that returning alone would be bittersweet, like taking in a star-studded sky alone, without anyone to share the magic of it.

Well, she had returned with the man who had put stars in her eyes, and it felt so, so sweet. Last night, Red had told her to clear her schedule for midafternoon; he had a surprise for her and Andy. The only instructions he had given her were to go to Casson and Justine's place and to look out the big bay window at 4:00 p.m. She and Andy had done so, with Casson and Justine looking on, and at precisely 4:00 p.m., they heard an approaching rumble. Andy had let out a squeal when the blue-and-white helicopter had come into view and not long afterward, started to descend, whirling to a stop on the frozen bay, yards away from the skating surface.

Red had emerged wearing his headset, and carrying a bag. He glided across the ice and minutes later was in the house, inviting Ronnie and Andy to go for a ride in his helicopter, and handing them their headsets. Ronnie had caught the gleam in Casson's and Justine's eyes as she and Andy had gotten dressed. "You knew about this," she accused them, and they laughed and waved her off.

The pilot had greeted them and, after they were all safely secured in their seats, started the engines. Andy had been mesmerized the whole time as they flew past Parry Sound and the Thirty Thousand Islands along Georgian Bay, and over the Muskokas. The vast wooded areas looked like an enchanted wonderland with their snow-dusted boughs sparkling in the sun along countless lakes. Sitting next to her, Andy was practically glued to the windowpane, and when they reached Toronto and the CN Tower came into view, he cried out, "Look, Mummy! Look!"

Ronnie was in awe herself, and despite her initial worry that she would become light-headed or queasy as she had been on Red's penthouse terrace, she had experienced none of those symptoms so far.

Red had intermittently pointed out buildings that Brannigan Architects International had been commissioned to design, and when he indicated the Four-Leaf Clover, the residence tower with his penthouse, he told Ronnie that he had been the one to design it. When she looked up at him in awe, the gleam in his eyes as his gaze dropped to her lips made her pulse quicken.

He, too, was thinking of the kiss they had exchanged there…

When daylight turned to dusk, the pilot circled back toward the entertainment district. Looking out the window to the dazzling lights of the city against a backdrop of apricot and red-orange sky blotted with indigo clouds took Ronnie's breath away. The multicolored lights emanating from the skyscrapers were reflected in shimmering beams in the dark waters by the Harbourfront. The alternating lights of the CN Tower, both on 360 and along the length of the tower, made her catch her breath with their flashes of red and yellow, purple and electric blue.

"I love the pulsating energy of the city," he said, leaning forward, "but I also love the quiet and tranquility of Parry Sound." His eyes probed hers. "Do you think you can handle being a country *and* a city girl? I want to make some new memories with you and Andy in Toronto."

Ronnie swallowed a lump in her throat. She sensed that Red was referring to the time she and Andy had spent here in hospital. When they had passed over the downtown core, Ronnie had felt a momentary sadness, peering down at the cluster of hospitals that included SickKids. And then she was overwhelmed with a feeling of gratitude for everyone there who had helped her little boy… like guardian angels.

"I think I can handle it," she said breathlessly. Parry Sound was only a couple of hours away from Toronto.

"Good. No, *great*!" He squeezed her hands and brought them up to kiss them. "We'll enjoy the best of both worlds…" He glanced at Andy, who was still scrunched up against the window.

Suddenly Red looked at Ronnie's left hand and frowned.

"What's the matter?" Ronnie stared down at her hand.

Without letting go of her hand, Red unbuckled his seat belt, slid off his seat and knelt on one knee. He reached in the back pocket of his jeans and pulled out a small black velvet box. "Something's missing on your hand, that's the matter…" he said huskily.

Ronnie's heart stopped for a moment and then began pulsing at the sight of the large marquise-shaped diamond nestled inside. She blinked up at Red and back down at the platinum ring that he now held in his fingers.

"You are the jewel in my life, Ronnie."

Her head snapped back up and she realized that Andy had turned to look at them with interest.

"This ring doesn't compare in value to *you*, Ronnie," he said, his eyes bright. "I offer it to you with my promise to love you and your little squirt over there for the rest of my days. To cherish our family, and to always be there for you both. And for any little carrottop or rabbit that might join us in the future… Veronica Forrester, will you—"

"Yes! I will, Red Brannigan II!" She took a deep breath as he slid the ring on her finger, and thought her heart would burst when Andy started clapping.

"I'll take that as a sign of approval," Red laughed, before kissing her soundly. He gazed at her hand. "I hope you like it."

"It's beautiful," she told him. "I want to pick out a special ring for you, too, Red, but for now—" she shrugged and gave him a teasing smile "—all I can offer you is a plate of peanut butter cookies when we get back to the cottage."

"Mmm… Deal!" He stood up and turned to Andy, raising his hand, and Ronnie's heart swelled as the two loves of her life gave each other a high five.

* * * * *

MAKING ROOM FOR THE RANCHER

CHRISTY JEFFRIES

Prologue

Good evening, Wyoming, we are reporting live from the Twin Kings Ranch following the funeral of United States Vice President Roper King, who was born and raised right here in the small town of Teton Ridge, in the heart of Ridgecrest County.

As many of you know, Roper King was a well-respected war hero and successful cattle rancher who started out in local politics, then served two terms as the governor of Wyoming before becoming vice president. The guest list of attendees read like a star-studded who's who of celebrities, foreign dignitaries and politicians, including the president of the United States and her husband.

The service began as a somber and dignified celebration of life, then took an unexpected turn when political analyst Tessa King, one of Roper King's daughters, collapsed on the front steps of the church and was quickly spirited away by the Secret Service. While we don't have an update on Tessa's condition, there are reports that she was later seen at the private graveside service along with her five siblings.

Hold on, I'm getting word that one of the Kings is driving this way through the gates and it might be... No, it's just one of the other family members. Possibly one of Roper's less famous daughters.

We will update you with all new developments. Now, back to our news desk for more highlights from today's event...

Chapter One

"Will Grandpa Roper have any friends in Heaven?" five-year-old Amelia asked as they took a right onto Ridgecrest Highway, which wasn't so much a highway as it was a two-lane road that cut through the middle of downtown Teton Ridge, Wyoming.

"Mmm-hmm," Dahlia King Deacon murmured in response.

In fact, all of Dahlia's answers since her father's death were either nods, shoulder shrugs or noncommittal mumbles. Although, to be fair, her daughter hadn't ceased her rapid-fire questions since they'd said goodbye to the rest of the family and driven away from the Twin Kings Ranch ten minutes ago.

"Do you think Gan Gan is gonna move to Heaven, too?" Amelia asked next.

"Someday, but not anytime soon." Dahlia put her elbow on the windowsill of her truck, using one hand to prop up her pounding head while the other hand steered them down the familiar route. Normally, she would encourage her only child's inquisitive mind and happily engage in the back-and-forth. But today had been emotionally draining, and she was trying to hold it together as best she could.

Plus, Dahlia's twin sister, Finn, had already answered most of Amelia's questions when they'd been in the back seat of the limo, going from the church service to the family cemetery, and then back to the main house for the somber reception.

So far, Amelia's questions today included:

Did Grandpa Roper really know all these people?

Why are there so many movie cameras outside?

Do all those policemans work for Uncle Marcus?

Is it okay if I ask the President for one of her candies?

Can I be the president when I grow up?

When can we go home?

The last question had been exactly what Dahlia needed to hear to snap her back to reality.

Instead of saying goodbye to her mother, Dahlia had made a quick excuse to one of the Secret Service agents on protective detail before taking Amelia's hand in her own and sneaking out through the kitchen, past the catering staff who were hauling the leftover food to the matching bunkhouses behind the stables.

As soon as she'd gotten Amelia buckled into her booster seat, Dahlia had driven home on autopilot. She hadn't expected so many news vans to still be parked outside the front gates of her family's cattle ranch, and breathed a sigh of relief when none of them followed her.

Nobody ever expected the daughter of the third richest man in Wyoming to be driving a fifteen-year-old Ford F-150 crew cab with a cow-sized dent in the front grill and a Follow Me To Big Millie's sticker on the back bumper. They especially didn't expect it when that same man was Roper King, vice president of the United States.

Make that the former vice president of the United States.

To everyone else, Roper had been larger than life—war hero, politician, billionaire, national icon. But to Dahlia, he'd simply been Dad.

And now he was gone.

A ribbon of pain curled around Dahlia's throat, all the pent-up emotion of the day's orchestrated funeral threatening to suffocate her. She choked down a rising sob, telling herself it was only a twenty-minute drive to their little apartment in town. Twenty minutes before she could put on a Disney movie for her daughter, and then go have a good cry in the shower where nobody would be able to see her. Or ask her if all mommies got red-faced and snot-nosed when they cried.

The dark sunglasses she'd been hiding behind all day were no match for glare reflecting off the snow-covered Grand Tetons as the bright sun lowered along the opposite end of the sky. Dahlia was so busy adjusting her sun visor she almost didn't see the ball of white fur dart across the road in front of her.

Slamming on the brakes, she yanked the steering wheel to the right, keeping her grip on the worn leather as the truck skid off the road and shimmied to a stop. She threw the gearshift into Park and turned around before she could unbuckle her seat belt.

"Are you okay, Peanut?" she asked Amelia, hoping her daughter couldn't tell that Dahlia was still trying to catch her breath.

"Why did that doggy run into the road like that?" Amelia replied, whipping her neck around for a glimpse of the white ball of fur who'd nearly caused them to career into the ditch. "Where is his mommy? Is it a boy doggy or a girl doggy?"

"Amelia." Dahlia reached between the seats and put a hand on her daughter's bouncing leg. Other than a sagging black hair bow and matching snags across both knees of the white tights (which had come courtesy of the child's earlier visit to the stables with her twin cousins), Amelia appeared none the worse for wear. "Focus over here. Are you hurt at all?"

"I'm fine." Her high energy daughter barely glanced her way before unbuckling herself from her seat. "Can I go pet the doggy?"

"We don't pet strange do—" Dahlia started, but Amelia already had the back door open.

"Is that the doggy's daddy?"

Dahlia fumbled out of her own seat and dove into the back, trying to snatch the corner of Amelia's black velvet skirt before her daughter could climb out the door that should have been set to childproof lock. She had no idea who her daughter was talking about, nor would she unless she could get her hips unstuck between the driver's and passenger seats and follow after the girl.

Could this day get any worse?

Dahlia had to simultaneously wiggle at the waist while doing an elbow crawl over the discarded patent leather shoes on the floorboard before she could pull her legs the rest of the way through. By the time she was able to use the armrest of the wide-open door to pull herself upright, Amelia had already made her way to the front of the hood and was talking to someone.

A man.

"Is that your doggy? What happened to his leash?

What's his name? Is it a boy? Why aren't your shoes tied?" The steady stream of questions didn't provide the man with any opportunity to respond. But it did buy Dahlia a little bit of time to get her bearings, allowing her to push her sunglasses back in place and adjust the pencil skirt that had twisted up like a corkscrew during her ungraceful descent from the truck.

It also gave her a second to study this irresponsible dog owner, who was now holding his palm cupped against his forehead like a visor as he scanned the dense trees lining the road.

And really, a second was all she needed to make a snap judgment. Dahlia owned the only bar in town and could read a person the second they walked through the door. Five bucks said this guy was just another hipster tourist lost on his way to nearby Jackson Hole.

The man was over six feet tall, lean but muscular. He wasn't completely winded by the recent chase of his dog, so he must work out somewhat regularly. His faded Aerosmith T-shirt could've been well-worn, or it could've been one of those hundred-dollar designer shirts that people paid extra to achieve the same look. His stiff jeans still had the fold creases down the leg, and a pair of high-top basketball sneakers were in fact, as Amelia had just pointed out, untied.

"You want us to help you find your doggy?"

her daughter asked before Dahlia could stop her. "Mommy is the bestest at finding my shoes and my crayons and my grandpa's glasses. Gan Gan says that Mommy could find trouble in a haystack without even looking."

The stranger turned toward her, his eyes shaded behind his hand. Dahlia forgot about searching for the runaway dog, and instead concentrated on finding a deep enough hole that she could hide in.

It was a mistake to stay quiet for any length of time around Amelia, because that only encouraged the child to continue talking. As if to prove her point, her daughter added, "But Grandpa doesn't need to look for his glasses no more because he went to Heaven."

Amelia's voice had gone softer with the last sentence, the young child's sadness creeping into her normally exuberant tone. Dahlia's throat did that constricting thing again, and she didn't trust herself not to start bawling in front of a perfect stranger. Instead, she sucked in her cheeks, trying to take a few steadying breaths through her nose.

The man finally parted his lips, opening and then closing them before kneeling down so that he was eye level with Amelia. "I'm very sorry for your loss."

"That's what everyone keeps saying to us. But we didn't *lose* Grandpa. He went to sleep and didn't wake up. Right, Mommy?"

Two curious gazes turned up to Dahlia. One set was the same blue as her own, full of curiosity. The other set was an unfamiliar golden brown with flecks of green, full of uncertainty and maybe a hint of pity. Or maybe the guy just wanted them to think he was some stranded motorist in order to lure them into a false sense of security.

Crap. Getting abducted would be the green olive garnish to this four-martini day.

"That's one way to put it." Dahlia used her trembling fingers to push a fallen strand of hair behind her ear. She stepped closer to Amelia, putting her arm around her daughter's shoulder while simultaneously easing the five-year-old back a few paces so that she wasn't within snatching distance of a potential kidnapper.

Maybe Dahlia had been a little too quick to refuse the Secret Service's offer of an escort home. She'd always felt perfectly safe in her small hometown, well-known by the locals, yet pleasantly anonymous to most outsiders. Now, though, she'd broken all of her own rules about talking to strangers. Sure, there might not be a windowless panel van parked nearby or lollipops falling out of the man's pockets, but helping a random guy find his "lost dog" was supposedly one of the oldest tricks in the book.

The stranger in question rose to his full height, which was still several inches taller than her—even in her uncomfortable high heels. Stepping backward again, she glanced down at his large hands and the skin on the back of her neck prickled. He wasn't holding any sort of weapon, but he also wasn't holding a leash.

If she could get Amelia anywhere close to the rear door of the truck, Dahlia might have a better chance of making a run for it and locking them both in the cab. She spoke without taking her eyes of the man. "Peanut, go back to the truck and get your shoes on so we can help look for this man's lost dog."

Luckily, Amelia's need to ask a million questions was usually only superseded by her need to help an unfortunate animal, and she quickly obeyed.

"No." The man lifted up those same hands, palms out. "It's not *my* dog. He was on my property and I thought he might be lost. So I was tracking him, trying to get close enough to see if he had a collar. I almost had him, but then he heard your truck and took off running across the highway."

She noted the golden skin of his uncovered forearms. Nobody who lived in Wyoming this time of year had a sun-kissed tan like that.

"So you're saying you live in Teton Ridge?" she asked, knowing full well that if anyone new had moved to town, she would've heard about it. Amelia was now by the passenger side door, and Dahlia took another step in retreat.

"Lady, if you want to run back to your truck and lock the doors, I'm not going to stop you. I get it that you're out here on this road in the middle of nowhere and you think I'm some sort of madman chasing after a dog that clearly doesn't want to be caught. I'll just head on back to my ranch and everyone can go about their business."

"How?"

"How what?" He tilted his head, his dark copper hair cropped short, almost military-length.

"How are you going to get back to your ranch?" she asked, sounding like Amelia, who was now sitting on the loose gravel buckling her patent leather shoes onto the wrong feet.

He rocked back on the heels of his untied sneakers. "The same way I got here, I guess."

She didn't mean to let out a disbelieving snort, but the only ranches between the Twin Kings and the heart of town were the abandoned Rocking D Ranch, which was at least another eight miles south, and the Ochoa family's Establos del Rio. Most of the Ochoas had been at her dad's funeral, though, and they certainly hadn't been wearing Air Jordans and an Aerosmith T-shirt.

"I'm Connor Remington. The new owner of the Rocking D." He glanced at the sun sinking behind the trees, but didn't seem especially concerned by the fact that, in less than twenty minutes, it would probably be pitch-black outside and at least twenty degrees colder.

His story was at least plausible, considering the owner of the neighboring ranch had recently passed away. Besides, if the man was going to pretend to be a local rancher in order to flag down a passing motorist, he would've at least tried to dress and act the part. Which meant he wasn't pretending.

Lord, save her from dumb city boys who had absolutely zero sense of direction. Dahlia sighed in resignation. "Hop in the truck. I'll give you a ride."

Connor Remington hadn't been planning to meet any of his neighbors on his first day in town, but here he sat. In the front seat of an older truck, next to a quiet woman whose face was obscured by the largest sunglasses he'd ever seen, and fielding questions from a magpie of a little girl who was making her mother's white knuckles—no wedding ring on the left hand—grip the steering wheel tighter every time she asked a question.

"So I take it you live nearby?" he asked, trying to be polite.

The woman gave a tense nod. Her hair was a dark blond and twisted into a tight knot on top of her head. Her somber black outfit, coupled with the little girl's comments about her dead grandfather, suggested they'd just come from a funeral.

"We live in town" the little girl offered. "Gan Gan wants us to live at the big house on the ranch, but Mommy says she'd rather live in Siberia. Have you ever lived in Siberia?"

"Actually, I've stayed in a tent there once." Connor turned in his seat to smile at the child in the back seat. "It was summer, though, so it wasn't as cold as you'd think."

"You don't have to play along," the woman murmured out the side of her mouth. "It'll only make her ask more questions."

"I don't mind," Connor answered honestly. Besides, he was getting a free ride back to his ghost town of a ranch. The least he could do was be hospitable. Even if only one of the other occupants in this vehicle felt like engaging in conversation. "So since you're the first neighbors I've met, what else do I need to know about living in Teton Ridge?"

"Well, my Mommy's name is Dahlia but my aunts and uncles call her Dia. 'Cept Grandpa. He was the only one allowed to call her Dolly."

Connor caught a slight tightening of the muscles along the woman's already rigid jaw line and again felt the need to apologize for their loss. However, when his own father had passed away all those years ago, Connor hadn't been comfortable being on the receiving end of condolences for a man most people never really knew. It had felt forced and overly polite. So instead, he remained silent as she took a right onto the road that led to the Rocking D. Clearly, she'd been here before.

The adults' awkward silence, though, didn't stop the little girl in the back seat from continuing. "All of Mommy's brothers and sisters have nicknames. 'Cept Uncle Marcus. But he kinda has a nickname because everyone calls him Sheriff. Do you have a nickname?"

"Some of my friends at my old job call me by my last name," he replied, but the child squinted at him as though she were about to tell him that didn't count. "My dad used to call me Con."

Whoa. Now that wasn't something he'd thought about in a long time. Maybe it was being here in Wyoming, fulfilling a promise his dad broke, that had Connor thinking so much about the old man. Or maybe it was all this talk about dead fathers and their unique names for their kids.

"Well, I'm Amelia, but my friends call me Bindi."

Dahlia whipped her head around, a line creasing the smooth area right above her sunglasses. "No, Peanut, nobody calls you that."

"They will. When I go to school, I'm gonna ask Miss Walker to tell all the kids to call me Bindi Irwin from now on because I love kangaroos and doggies and owls and hamsters and someday I'm gonna be a zookeeper for all the animals and be on TV like my aunt—"

"Here's the Rocking D," Dahlia loudly cut off

her daughter. The truck hit a huge pothole in the rutted-out dirt driveway, but the woman didn't seem to notice as she murmured again to Connor, "They were having a *Crocodile Hunter* marathon on the Animal Planet channel last week."

"Where's your chicken coop?" Amelia asked, her head on a swivel as they pulled into the driveway between the farmhouse and the barn. "Where are all the cows and horses?"

"Well, I just moved here today so I don't have any animals yet. At least none that I know of." Hell, he'd only had one real conversation with his great-aunt before she'd passed away. At the time, he'd been so busy trying to absorb the shock of having a long lost relative that he hadn't thought to ask her about the livestock. "In fact, I haven't even gone inside the house yet. All my stuff is still in the car over there."

"That car's just like the one in the Princess Dream House commercial. It's even white like Princess Dream's."

"It's actually a rental," Connor explained when Dahlia parked behind it. He wasn't the flashy sports car type, but when his plane was diverted to Rock Springs late this morning, the white convertible had been the only option available. Having lived on military bases the past twelve years, Connor was in a hurry to finally settle into a place of his very own and gladly took the keys to the last vehicle in the lot.

Plus, in his one and only conversation with his

great-aunt, he'd promised her that he'd take care of her ranch and make her proud. He didn't have much experience with fulfilling dying wishes, but from what he'd learned from her probate attorney about the state of things out here, Connor was already way behind.

Amelia burst out of the truck before either of the adults, but luckily didn't go too far. Dahlia was quick to follow and caught up with the little girl by the overgrown bushes that were blocking the path leading to the house.

"So you bought the old Daniels ranch? Sight unseen?" Dahlia finally removed her sunglasses, and Connor was rendered almost speechless at the clear blue depths. They were slightly red-rimmed—from crying?—but that didn't take away from her beauty.

"Actually—" his own eyes followed hers and he saw what she saw "—I inherited it. My great-aunt was Constance Daniels."

"So you're the one she always talked about?" she asked, her words crashing into him like a wave of guilt. Before he could explain the unusual family connection, she added, "The one who was supposedly going to bring her ranch back to life?"

Something about the sarcasm in her tone immediately put him on the defensive. "That's the plan."

"Let me guess." She glanced down at the creased jeans he'd bought at the mercantile on his way into town. "You've just moved here from the big city, but you've always dreamed of being a cowboy."

"The way you say it makes me sound like a cliché who is destined to fail." He was repeating the same words his own mother had used when he'd told her about the Rocking D and his promise to his dying great-aunt. Connor narrowed his eyes slightly, practically daring this woman to doubt him, as well.

She returned his challenging stare, her expression completely unapologetic as she boldly sized him up. "*Destined* might not have been the word I would have used. But tougher men than you have tried their hand at making a name for themselves out here in the wilds of Teton Ridge and most of them gave up before their first full winter."

Fortunately, Connor had a history of proving people wrong. He crossed his arms in front of his chest, his biceps muscles flexing on their own accord. "How do you know how tough I am?"

Dahlia's lashes flickered ever so slightly as her pupils dilated, but she didn't break eye contact. Her full lips pursed ever so slightly, as though she were holding back the perfect retort, and his eyes dared her to say it out loud.

"So where is the white doggy now?" Amelia interrupted the adults' intense but unspoken staring competition. "Do you think it'll come back here? Do you have food for him? Where will he sleep if it snows?"

"Amelia," Dahlia sighed and finally looked down at her daughter. "Let Mr. Remington settle into the place before you start bombarding him with all your questions."

It was a little too late for that. The corner of Connor's lip tugged up in a smirk. Not that her mom's warning would do any good. The child hadn't stopped asking questions in the entire thirty minutes he'd known her.

He bent down because he could see that the girl was genuinely worried about the lost dog. Hell, Connor had been worried about the scruffy thing himself, otherwise he wouldn't have tracked it on foot for almost seven miles. He guessed he was like Amelia that way, too. Once he got on a trail, he didn't like to veer off course until he had all the answers. "I'll leave a little bowl of water and some blankets outside on the porch for him in case he comes back. Hopefully, he's at home now, all cozy in front of the fire and dreaming about his next adventure tomorrow."

The child nodded, but the concern didn't entirely leave her face. She tilted her head and started a new line of questioning. "Why is there still a sticker on your leg?"

"Because the boots and jeans I was wearing when I first got here were all muddy." He didn't mention the abandoned well he'd nearly fallen into when he'd been exploring earlier. That would've only given

Dahlia more ammo for her claim that he had no business owning a ranch. "But then I saw the little white dog and these new pants were the closest thing I could put on before the dog ran off."

"You mean you took your pants off outside?" she asked, her round eyes growing even rounder.

He dared a glance at Dahlia, whose cheeks had gone a charming shade of pink. "Well, nobody was out here to see me."

"One time, Mommy went into the river because my pet salmon was stuck on a rock. She had to take off all her clothes so she didn't catch the new-moan-yah. Aunt Finn said cowgirls gotta do what cowgirls gotta do. But Gan Gan says a lady never knows who could be watching."

Connor really needed to hear more about this pet salmon, he thought, smothering a laugh. Although, it wouldn't be appropriate for him to ask for any more details about a naked and soaking wet Dahlia while her daughter was standing between them.

Instead of offering an explanation, the supposed fish rescuer rubbed her temples, which didn't lessen the rosy color now staining her cheeks.

"Okay, Peanut, we really need to get back on the road. We can look for the dog on our way into town." The promise did the trick because Amelia waved goodbye and skipped toward the truck. Dahlia stuck out a hand. "Good luck with the Rocking D, Mr. Remington."

"Thanks again for the ride home." He took the smooth but firm palm in his own and an unexpected current of electricity shot through him. The jolt must've made its way to his brain because before he could stop himself, he added, "Maybe I'll see you in town some time and can repay the favor?"

She jerked her hand back quickly, but her face went perfectly neutral, as though she'd used the same thanks-but-no-thanks expression a thousand times before.

"I'm sure you'll be far too busy out here." She gave a pointed look to the broken wood slats in a fence that might've been a corral at one point. Then she glanced at his favorite basketball shoes, which felt about as out of place on this rundown ranch as her black high heels. "A city boy like you is going to have his work cut out for him."

As she and her daughter drove away, Connor recalled his aunt's probate attorney making a similar comment when she'd offered to sell the property for him. The lawyer had warned him that it was going to take a lot of determination and a hell of a lot more money to get the place operational again.

Yet, he was just as undeterred then as he was now.

Clearly, Dahlia wasn't going to be the only skeptical local who doubted his ability to make this ranch a success. The prettiest, maybe, but not the only one.

Good thing he hadn't come to Wyoming to make friends.

Chapter Two

Connor slept like crap in the musty-smelling, knickknack-filled three-bedroom house his great-aunt had bequeathed him. Thank goodness some thoughtful neighbor had cleaned out the fridge and shut off the gas and water pipes long ago. At least he hadn't arrived last night to a flooded living room and the smell of rotting food.

Growing up, his old man had told plenty of stories about spending his summers on a ranch in Wyoming, but never once mentioned the woman who'd owned the place. Even if he had spoken about his aunt Constance, Connor's mom wouldn't have believed a word Steve Remington said.

That was why nobody was more surprised than Linda Remington when Connor got a call from an assisted living facility in Wyoming. Because of Steve's transient lifestyle—bouncing in and out of different correctional facilities in between his occasional visits to his son and wife in Boston—followed by Connor's numerous military deployments, it had taken a dedicated social worker and a wily trusts-and-estates attorney nearly three years to help a determined Constance Daniels track down her next of kin.

Connor had only met his great-aunt a few weeks ago—via video chat and a spotty satellite connection onboard an aircraft carrier in the Pacific Ocean. She'd passed away before he'd returned from his final deployment. However, her probate attorney informed him over the phone that the ranch had been abandoned since Connie's first stroke, nearly three years ago.

So it wasn't as though Connor had been expecting anything fancy when he'd arrived at the Rocking D yesterday afternoon. Besides, he'd slept in worse conditions when he'd been on assignment with his scouting unit in the desolate regions of the Altai Mountains between Kazakhstan and Russia. He hadn't been lying to Amelia when he'd said he'd once been to Siberia.

He was no longer in the business of tracking people, though. Which was why Connor tried not to look for the little girl and her mother as he drove into downtown Teton Ridge the following morning. Actually, *downtown* was a generous name for the center of a city with a population of less than two thousand. So he was sure that if he wanted to find them, it wouldn't be too difficult.

There were a handful of restaurants and shops, a sheriff's station attached to a county courthouse that likely housed all the local government offices, a giant feed-and-grain store, and a small nondescript hardware store. If residents needed anything more than that, they'd either have to order it online or drive into Jackson Hole or Pinedale to get it.

Most of the buildings appeared to have been built in the heyday of the Wild West, a combination of wood and brick structures constructed so close together only a horse could pass between them.

His first order of business would be to go to the hardware store with the long list he'd made last night in Great-Aunt Connie's empty kitchen. Then he'd go to the market down the street for some groceries.

Scratch that. He needed a hot coffee and an even hotter breakfast before he did anything. He slowed his rental car and pulled into a parking space in front of a place called Biscuit Betty's. The smell of bacon hit him as soon as he climbed out of the convertible and his stomach growled. He was halfway to the front entrance of the restaurant when he caught sight of a blond girl skipping out of the bakery next door.

Amelia.

His skin itched in recognition, and then tightened when he saw Dahlia exit behind her, a stack of pink bakery boxes stacked so high in her arms he could only see the top of her bouncing ponytail.

Connor jogged over and took the top three boxes before she could object. "Let me help you carry these."

Dahlia's smile faded when she realized who'd relieved her of her load. Was she expecting someone else? A boyfriend, perhaps?

"I can get them," she insisted, her face now slightly pinched in annoyance.

"Oh, hi, Mr. Rem-ton." Amelia smiled brightly, the opposite reaction of her mother. "Mommy said we wouldn't see you again for a long time 'cause you'd be too busy working on your old junky ranch."

"I didn't say junky," Dahlia interjected a bit more quickly than she had yesterday when Amelia had made similar candid comments. She must've gotten a good night's sleep last night because she gave her daughter a discreet but pointed look rather than a resigned sigh. "I said run-down."

"It's both run-down *and* junky," Connor admitted, holding back a smile at their honesty. "And I plan to get busy on it as soon as I buy some supplies."

"Mommy told Ms. Burnworth at the bakery that the inside of your house was probably worse than the outside and that—"

"Here, Peanut." Dahlia shoved a pink box into Amelia's arms right before she could get to the good part. "Carry this for me and you can have one of the apple spice muffins when you get inside."

The little girl tipped the box sideways, the flimsy lid threatening to spill the contents, as she ran down the sidewalk.

Connor smothered his grin when Dahlia darted a glance his way. "Sorry about that. I should remember to watch what I say around her. I never know what she's going to blurt out."

"Like I told you yesterday, I really don't mind talking to her. She's a smart girl and…" Connor's voice trailed off as he saw Amelia rush inside a wide door below a wooden sign that read Saloon. He had a sudden flashback to his own childhood and his old man taking a way-too-young Connor to some of the less finer drinking establishments in Dorchester, Massachusetts. "Did she just go inside that bar?"

"Oh, yeah." Dahlia began walking that way, but not with any sense of urgency. As though it were totally natural for a five-year-old to hang out inside the local pub. "I should probably get in there."

"Isn't it a little early in the day for a drink?" He heard the judgment in his own voice and tried not to wince. He didn't know this woman. Who was he to project his own childhood insecurities on her daughter? "Sorry, I guess it's none of my business."

"You're right." Dahlia turned to him, her shoulders thrown back and her eyes almost a violet shade as they filled with anger. "It's *not* your business or my mom's business or anyone else's business where and how I choose to raise my daughter."

Wow. The woman had been quiet yesterday, letting her five-year-old do most of the talking. But clearly, she wasn't shy about choosing her battles and speaking up when she felt threatened.

"I didn't mean to imply that it was. I was just making an observation based on my own experience—"

"Can I make myself a drink, Mommy?" Amelia used her little body to prop open the thick wooden door. She had a half-eaten muffin in one hand and a smear of cinnamon crumbs across one cheek. "I promise not to put too many cherries in it this time."

"Sure, Peanut," she replied, but it wasn't in the same dismissive way as when she'd given in to her daughter yesterday. Dahlia put one hand on her hip and lifted her brow at Connor, all but challenging him to make another comment about her parenting decisions.

She'd been attractive before when her eyes had been red-rimmed and tired after the funeral yesterday. But her razor-sharp focus and the firm set of her sculpted jaw made her damn right sexy. Both intrigue and desire weaved through his gut, and Connor knew that if he didn't voice his concerns now, he would get blinded by her pretty face. Just like he'd gotten blinded by his dad's pretty words all those years ago.

"Anyway, I drove by a library on my way into town earlier and a smart girl like Amelia would probably love to, you know, go there instead of a saloon…" Connor stopped talking when Dahlia's eyes narrowed and her mouth hardened. Maybe he'd gone too far.

"Don't stop now, Mr. Big City Rancher." Dahlia put her other hand to her hip and leaned slightly forward. "I'm sure you have so many more words of wisdom to impart. I'd especially love to hear your advice about family matters, considering you never even met your great-aunt Connie—who was a wonderful woman, by the way, and didn't deserve to die all alone in an assisted living facility without so much as a visit from a single relative."

Ouch. Not that Connor didn't already feel guilty about that last part.

"Technically, I *did* meet her," he said. FaceTime counted, right? "And I would've visited her sooner if I'd known that she existed."

"Well, you were certainly eager to meet your inheritance," Dahlia shot back.

They were faced off on the sidewalk and he could practically see the steam rising from her. Maybe it was more recognizable, considering he was equally angry about the assumptions she'd automatically jumped to concerning *his* decisions. He'd never asked for an inheritance or anything else in his life. In fact, he seriously doubted—

"There's the doggy!" a voice called out and broke his concentration. He turned just in time to see Amelia race into the street, her muffin still clutched in her grip.

Connor had already dropped the pink bakery boxes and was running after her when he heard the horn of a big truck.

The scream of warning froze in Dahlia's throat just as Connor swept Amelia into his arms, yanking the child into the center median with him just before the orange big rig could smash into them both.

Dahlia, whose response was only a few seconds behind Connor's, almost got hit by a red compact car in the oncoming lane after she sprinted into the middle of the street to ensure her daughter was unharmed. Her voice returned just in time to yell some choice words at the taillights of Jay Grover's flatbed truck. The damn fool had been repeatedly warned to slow down whenever he drove through town, but warnings only made the contrary jerk want to drive faster.

"Is she all right?" Dahlia asked Connor between adrenaline-fueled breaths. The three of them were now standing in the center of Stampede Boulevard. Well, technically, only two of them were standing there. Her daughter was still in the man's arms.

"How come it's okay for you to say the *F* word, but not me?" Amelia asked, and Dahlia let out a shaky breath.

"I think she's fine," Connor replied, a smooth spot on his neck jumped visibly with his pulse, which was apparently pumping equally as fast as Dahlia's.

As much as she wanted to tear into him just a few moments ago, she couldn't stay mad at the guy for his earlier judgments. When it came to looking out for her daughter's safety, he'd actually put his money where his mouth was, and had been the first to run into the street to save her.

"Where's the doggy?" Amelia squirmed in his arms as her head twisted to search for the scruffy white mutt that had been the cause of yet another near accident.

"Oh, Peanut, let's get you inside right now. We can come back and look for the dog later." Preferably when Dahlia's nerves were more settled. And after she scolded her daughter for running into the street without looking for cars. Unfortunately, neither of those events would likely happen if Connor was hanging around.

"But what about school? I can't be late again."

Dahlia checked her watch and saw that it was

nearly 7:30 a.m. Amelia made it sound like she was chronically tardy, when in fact her daughter simply liked to be the first kid to arrive so she could be the one to feed the class hamsters.

"Well, I might need a few minutes." Dahlia shoved her still shaky hands into the pockets of her jeans, not relishing the thought of hopping behind the wheel of her truck until she was a little less rattled.

"But I promised Miss Walker we'd bring the muffins for the bake sale."

"I can drive you guys." He hefted the child higher, the muscles in his biceps flexing under a plaid work shirt. His jaw was set in a rigid line and his soft tone suggested he was well aware of the fact that Dahlia was still shaken by her daughter's near fatal encounter with a speeding madman.

"Fine," Dahlia said, almost a little relieved to have someone else there with her. Being a single mother meant she didn't always have someone sharing the physical burden. Micah, Amelia's father, was financially supportive and rarely missed his nightly calls with his daughter to talk about her day. But it wasn't the same. Even with most of her family living nearby, there were still times when Dahlia felt like she was going at it alone. Right now, she was still shaky enough to appreciate Connor's steady voice and quick reflexes. "I need to run inside and get something real quick, though. Can you salvage what's left of those muffins?"

She waited for a motorcycle to pass before leading them back to the sidewalk and toward the building she'd bought and lovingly restored. She saw Connor's eyes dart up to the second floor and stare at the freshly painted blue sign that was at least a century old, the gold block letters large and unmistakable: Big Millie's.

To his credit, though, he didn't ask any questions. Probably because the pink bakery boxes were upside down and Amelia was already talking his ear off about the little white dog. Dahlia slipped inside and grabbed the Safari Park lunch box and her daughter's pug-shaped backpack, then followed him to his rental car parked in front of Biscuit Betty's.

By the time they got to the drop-off line at Teton Ridge Elementary School, both Dahlia and Connor had made several assurances to Amelia that they'd keep their eyes open for the stray and try to help it if they could.

Several sets of curious eyes turned toward them as Dahlia climbed out of the convertible—which was thankfully closed this cold morning—to help her daughter unbuckle.

"Can I help you with the boxes?" Connor asked.

"Yes," Amelia said as Dahlia practically yelled, "No!" The last thing she needed were the other parents asking her what she was doing with some wannabe cowboy nobody in town knew. "The crossing guard will yell at you if you don't keep traffic moving. Just park over there and I'll run her inside the building."

"Don't forget to take care of our dog," Amelia shouted from the sidewalk before she waved goodbye to Connor.

"What dog?" Marcus King, dressed in his county sheriff's uniform, asked before the car door was even closed.

"Jeez, Marcus. You scared me half to death," Dahlia told her big brother, who was walking his twin sons, Jack and Jordan, to the flagpole.

"The dog me and my new friend, Connor, found and then lost again. Bye, Mommy," Amelia waved before running to catch up to her cousins.

Marcus wasn't the least bit subtle as he studied the license plate of Connor's rental car as it pulled into a parking spot. "Who's that?"

"Connie Daniel's nephew who just inherited the Rocking D. I'll fill you in later. But right now—" Dahlia pushed the pink bakery boxes into her brother's arms "—I need you to take these to the bake sale table before Melissa Parker comes over and invites you to the monthly mingle happy hour at the bar tonight."

The threat of having to actually socialize with other single parents was enough to get her nosy brother moving along without asking any more questions.

When Dahlia climbed back into Connor's convertible, she adjusted her dark sunglasses and slid low in the seat until he drove out of the parking lot.

"Careful, or I might think you're embarrassed to be seen with me," he said as he pulled out onto Stampede Boulevard.

"I just don't want to have to answer any questions."

"Like from the cop back there?" Connor asked. "He seemed pretty interested in committing my license plate number and physical description to memory."

Was that a note of jealousy she detected in his tone? History had taught her to be wary of insecure men. Not that she wasn't already wary of Connor Remington. Annoyance prickled her skin. "That's my brother. He's the sheriff and he's very protective."

"Cool," Connor said.

"Why is that cool?" She felt her eyes narrow behind her sunglasses.

"I guess because I always thought it would be neat to have a protective older brother or sister. Someone to look out for me when I was young."

Her heart softened, but only slightly. "Did you get picked on a lot as a kid?"

"Not any more than anyone else. But my dad

was gone a lot and my mom worked two jobs. So I was on my own for the most part. I'd always wanted siblings."

Dahlia thought about the other five King siblings and relaxed against the leather seat. "Trust me. It's not all it's cracked up to be. They're always up in my business or arguing with each other. If you think my daughter is a talker, just wait until you meet the rest of the—"

She caught herself before she revealed too much about her family.

"Anyway, thanks for getting to Amelia just in time this morning. And for the ride to the school."

"No problem." He turned his eyes away from the road long enough to smile at her, and something in her tummy went all topsy-turvy. Connor Remington might be completely out of place in a town like Teton Ridge, but he was still a damn good-looking man. And it had been a while since Dahlia had been alone in a car with a man she hadn't known since childhood, good-looking or otherwise.

"Where should I drop you off? Burnworth's? It's kind of an odd name for a bakery."

"Just pull in here." She pointed to the open parking spots near the old-fashioned hitching post in front of Big Millie's.

He surprised her by exiting the car when she did.

"You don't have to walk me inside," she told him

when he followed her to the wood-planked walkway that lined this side of the street.

"Actually, I was on my way to get some breakfast earlier." He stared at the overhanging cedar awning she'd replaced three years ago, keeping it as authentic to the historical building as possible. "So do you work at this place?"

His earlier words criticizing her for letting her daughter hang out in a bar hovered between them. Defiance made her square her shoulders. "I *own* this place."

"There you are, Dahlia." Ms. Burnworth, the older woman who was a co-owner of the bakery next door, made her way toward them so quickly, her apron with the words Taste The Burn stenciled across the front flapped in the breeze. "Another one of your daughter's critters is hanging out in the back alley again. Kenny is in a foul mood, complaining about the allergies he doesn't even have. But I wanted to get out here first and warn you that he's threatening to report you guys to the health department this time if you try and sneak it upstairs."

"Is it a scruffy white dog?" Connor asked.

Ms. Burnworth eyed him over her bright pink reading glasses. "Are you with Animal Control?"

"No, I'm—"

Just then, a yelp sounded from somewhere behind the building and Dahlia unlocked the heavy oak door and rushed through the bar and toward the back entrance, the quickest way to get to the alley. She'd no more than gotten the heavy screen security door open when a dirty ball of fur dashed straight through the kitchen and launched itself right up into Connor's arms.

Kenny Burnworth, Ms. Burnworth's brother and one of the biggest hypochondriacs in town, was giving chase with a rubber spatula as his only weapon of defense. Dahlia had to quickly put up her hand to stop the cranky old man from coming inside. "I'll take care of it from here, Mr. Burnworth."

The dog, now huddled safely in Connor's arms, let out a small whimper, and the baker let out an obnoxiously fake sneeze. "You better, Dahlia. This is the second one this month. Say, are you with Animal Control?"

She followed the older man's gaze toward Connor, who cradled the dog protectively. "No, sir, I'm not."

"Too bad." Mr. Burnworth fake sneezed again. "I would rather this place was still a brothel rather than a damn halfway house for every stray animal wandering around town."

When her neighbor left, Dahlia closed the screen door before finding a small stainless-steel bowl that she could use as a makeshift water dish. Connor followed her out of the kitchen and into the refurbished saloon.

He set the dog on the recently sanded hardwood

floor so it could drink, then stayed down on one knee near the scared animal. Dahlia's heart gave a little jump at his tender concern and she distracted herself by trying to find the dog something to eat. Right in the middle of the massive twenty-foot-long oak panel bar, she spied half a glass of orange juice and one of Amelia's leftover muffins and broke it into smaller pieces.

The animal took the offered piece and gulped it down in one swallow. When the pup gobbled up a second chunk without so much as a growl, Connor slowly stood up and began studying the open floor plan of the high-ceilinged room. He lifted one copper brow and asked, "Was this place really a brothel?"

Normally, Dahlia got a kick out of her not-so-well-known family legacy and being related to a self-reliant woman who'd made quite a name for herself at the turn of the last century. After Connor's earlier unsolicited advice, she hesitated for a second before remembering that she was raising her daughter to be just as strong as the rest of the women in their family.

Dahlia straightened her spine. "Yes, it was. Back in the 1890s, women didn't have a lot of options when it came to supporting themselves. They had even less when their husbands took off and left them with a small child to raise. So my great-great-grandmother did the best she could."

"Your great-great grandma is Big Millie? Is that her?" Connor zeroed in on the sepia-toned photograph framed above the antique cash register. "She doesn't look all that big."

"Well, her daughter was also named Amelia and the townspeople referred to them as Big Millie and Little Millie. Her portrait is…" Dahlia tried to think of the most polite way to describe the less attractive and downright intimidating woman who was rumored to have strong opinions and a supernatural sense about her neighbors. "It's a bit less inviting and currently on display somewhere else."

Actually, the life-sized portrait of the not-so-little woman hung above the mantel at the main house on Twin Kings Ranch where Dahlia's father insisted she was able to watch over the family. Her mother hated it, which was all the more reason for Dahlia to insist Grandma Millie the Second stay put.

"And did Little Millie, your great-grandmother, take over the family business?"

"Yes, right before prohibition. By then, they were making so much money as the only speakeasy between Casper and Idaho Falls, the bootleggers couldn't keep up with the high demand. They closed down the upstairs business and started manufacturing their own booze."

Connor's mouth formed a small O of surprise, and Dahlia bit back a smile. If he was so easily shocked by her deceased relatives, just wait until he met some of her living ones—like her sister Finn or her aunt Freckles. Now there were a couple of women who weren't afraid to make a grown man blush.

Not that she had any intention of introducing Connor to them anytime soon. Or at all. Her jaw tightened and she tried not to stare at him as he appraised the saloon, not bothering to hide his curiosity. Especially when she was equally as curious about him.

Before she could ask him something about himself, though, he nodded at the walls covered in shiplap and the huge antique gilt-edged mirror hanging behind the bar. "Is this what it looked like back then?"

"I tried to keep as much of it as original as I could." What had once started out as a fixer-upper project soon became Dahlia's refuge, a place to invest in herself after her divorce. "Except I converted the smaller…ah…*rooms* upstairs into one big apartment."

"And you're not allowed to have any pets in your own apartment?" Connor was now eyeing the very shaggy dog who was currently stretched out on its back in front of his cowboy boots, exposing its matted belly for a rub. In that revealing position, it was easy to see that the dog was in fact male.

Sure, they probably could keep the animal since she did own the building and the living quarters were separate from the commercial area. However, if Dahlia didn't draw a line somewhere, they'd have every dog and cat for miles around sheltered at Big Millie's.

Today, it was time to draw that line again. Her daughter had a way of bringing home strays, Dahlia thought as she studied the newcomer who had bent down again to rub the dog's belly. If she gave in now, she'd likely have two unwanted strays on her hands.

She sighed. "Even if my neighbor didn't make a big stink about it, we just don't have the room for another animal. A sweet pup like this needs room to wander and explore. He'd probably do great out on a ranch. A place with plenty of land and an owner who needs the company…"

She let her suggestion hang in the air, but Connor immediately shook his head. "Nice try, but I'm not in the market for a fluffy white ball of mischief."

"That's weird. I thought you wanted him." Dahlia tried a different tactic. If Amelia were here, she would've fluttered her eyelashes several times in confusion. Her daughter couldn't imagine anyone *not* wanting an animal—or ten. "You followed him from your ranch all the way to the street."

"Yeah, I was trying to see if he had a collar or needed help."

There it was. His admission that he'd gone after the animal first. Finders keepers and all that.

"That must be why he's already so attached to you." Okay, so maybe she was laying it on a little too thick. But the dog seemed to be in agreement with Dahlia's assessment because it chose that exact moment to stick out its small pink tongue and lick Connor's hand. She could tell by the softening of Connor's lower lip into a near smile that he was already a goner.

Feeling relieved, Dahlia knelt down to scratch the tangled and dirty fur between the mutt's ears. Unfortunately, her lowered position put her face only a few inches from his, and that rip current of awareness shot through her again. He must've felt it too because his hand froze just before it could graze hers.

His hazel eyes locked onto hers and Dahlia couldn't have looked away if she'd wanted to. His voice was deep and low as he lifted one side of his mouth. "Fine, I'll help. Just so we're clear, though, I'm only doing this because I promised Amelia I would. I have no intention of actually taking on a responsibility that belongs to someone else."

"Of course." Dahlia immediately stood back up, not entirely sure he was only referring to the dog. "Dr. Roman has a microchip scanner at her office over on Frontier Avenue. I'm sure she can help you find the owner."

"Dr. Roman, huh?" He easily scooped the dog into his arms as he rose to his full height. "Why do I get the feeling that you and Amelia are used to passing off stray animals to unsuspecting strangers?"

"Who else would we pass them off to?" She walked behind the bar, needing to put some distance between them. "Everyone else in town knows better than to get within a twenty-foot radius of my daughter when she's got an animal in her sights."

Plus, if Connor wanted to be a real rancher, he needed to get used to caring for all types of animals. Really, she was doing the good-looking city boy a favor. Maybe giving the man a little bit of responsibility of his own would teach him not to offer up his unwelcome opinions about Dahlia's responsibilities.

And if she could keep him from interfering in her personal business, then it would be a hell of a lot easier for her to stop thinking about his.

Chapter Three

"Let me guess." Dr. Roman chuckled to herself after Connor had explained to the vet how the scruffy white pooch ended up in his care. "Amelia Deacon was the little girl who talked you into adopting a stray?"

So Deacon was their last name. Connor tucked that tidbit of information into his mental file in case he needed it later on. "I'm guessing you know Amelia and her mom?"

"Yeah, my oldest son went to school with Dahlia and Finn." The veterinarian removed her reading glasses from the top of her black corkscrew curls, setting them on her nose before turning most of her attention to the new patient. "That family sends me more business than I can handle."

Finn. Another name, another breadcrumb. Connor collected clues the way Amelia Deacon apparently collected stray animals. Only he didn't know where this particular trail would lead or why he was on it in the first place. He had his hands full with getting the Rocking D running again. He shouldn't be out chasing after dogs *or* single moms. No matter how beautiful they were.

The single mom, not the dog.

The scared mutt was anything but beautiful, and smelled even worse than he looked. He watched the vet make soothing noises as she examined the little ball of white and mud-stained fur crouched low on the stainless-steel table. Connor was going to have to pay the car rental company an extra cleaning fee just to get rid of the stench from the short drive over here from Big Millie's. And if they ever found the owner, he was also going to have a serious talk with whoever had neglected the most basic of their pet responsibilities. This scrappy little guy deserved better than whoever had let him get this bad.

When Dr. Roman finished her exam, she pulled a small treat out of the pocket of her lab coat and fed it to the dog. "I'm not seeing anything out of the ordinary, but one of my vet techs is going to need to get him cleaned up a little before we can be sure.

His hair is so matted our microchip scanner might have missed something."

Connor had never been a big spender and rarely took paid leave, which meant he still had a few paychecks coming his way before his official discharge paperwork got finalized. Unfortunately, he needed most of that money to get the ranch operational again. He had no idea how much this vet bill was going to cost.

Growing up, his mom had never let him have a pet because she'd said they were too expensive and too much work. Was it more or less than what the military paid for the horses in their Calvary units? During his first day of training at the Marine Corps Mountain Warfare Training Center, one of the instructors told them how much the hay and grain alone cost, and Connor had almost fallen out of his saddle.

"Don't worry," Dr. Roman said, probably seeing the color drain from his face as he tried to add up how much money this would set him back. "Dahlia will want me to bill her for the exam and grooming and any necessary medications."

Having a single mom covering the cost didn't sit well with Connor. Especially because owning a saloon in a small Wyoming cattle town—no matter how authentically refurbished Big Millie's was—probably didn't generate a huge amount of extra cash. "No, I'll pay for whatever the dog needs."

* * *

Connor seriously regretted those words two hours later.

He'd gone to breakfast, the hardware store and the grocery store before returning to Dr. Roman's clinic to pay the final bill—which, thankfully, was a lot less than what it would have cost for a horse. The receptionist had him sign some papers and was swiping his credit card when the vet tech handed him a leash attached to a clean, freshly trimmed white dog that looked nothing like the dingy mutt he'd dropped off.

"What am I supposed to do with him?" Connor asked, staring at the colorfully striped bandanna jauntily tied around the dog's neck.

The man whose purple scrubs matched his dyed Mohawk gave him a sideways look. "Take him home, bro. Feed him. Play with him. Go on walks with him. You know? All the normal things people do with their pets?"

"But he's not *my* pet," Connor tried to explain as the receptionist handed him his credit card receipt. "Isn't there a shelter or a humane society or something that could take him?"

"Bro. You signed the form and paid the bill, so that kinda *does* mean he's your pet now. Or at least your responsibility. If you want to—" the tech lowered his voice and spelled out the next word,

"—R-E-L-I-N-Q-U-I-S-H him, the nearest shelter is in Pinedale. About an hour away."

Connor, though, had a trunk full of frozen dinners and rocky road ice cream he had no intention of wasting. And that was how, less than twenty-four hours after arriving in Teton Ridge, he ended up with a little white dog riding shotgun in his sporty convertible, both of them appearing about as citified and uncowboy-like as they could get. If he wanted any of the other ranchers in town to take him seriously, his next order of business would be to find the keys to the old Chevrolet truck he'd seen in the barn this morning.

How had one attractive woman and one little girl so thoroughly put a wrench in his carefully constructed plans? And how had he let them? His old man had always said that when Remingtons found "the one" they knew it. That was why his dad was always so determined to come back to his wife and son time and again and promise to change. But it didn't explain why his mom had kept taking Steve back.

In fact, Connor's disappointing experiences with his father had made him reluctant to form attachments, emotional or physical. As an adult, he'd been trained to get a job done and move on to the next. So settling down on the Rocking D, investing in the property and his future, was already putting the unfamiliar concept of permanency in his mind.

Then he'd met Amelia, who was open and honest and had such pure intentions, Connor already knew he'd be unable to tell the child no. His reaction to her mom, though, was a whole other thing. Not that he believed his dad's claims of his genetic ability to know when he'd met "the one." Hell, Connor learned early on not to believe most of his father's outlandish claims.

Still.

There was something intriguing about Dahlia, and if he had more downtime on his hands, he might have looked for answers.

He meant to take the dog to the shelter in Pinedale the following day, but then one thing after the next happened and he was too busy to do much of anything that first week on the ranch.

First, he had to find a nearby auto parts store to get a replacement battery and a new fuel pump before he could even get to work on the truck. Then Tomas Ochoa, who owned the ranch just north of him, paid him a call about the broken fence between their properties. Connor offered to pay half the costs and Tomas offered to have his son and a school buddy help with the labor so they could get the railing in place before calving season. The teens did such a great job, Connor hired them to come over the following weekend and help him rebuild the corral.

One of his great-aunt Connie's friends from the

community church showed up with a casserole and the name of a local woman who did some house-keeping. While Connor had learned how to make hospital corners on his bunk in boot camp, having someone do a deep clean on the house while he saw to everything else that needed fixing on the ranch might be worth the expense.

The delivery guy from the hardware store gave him the names of some local ranch hands who might be looking for some extra work, but Connor still didn't have horses, let alone the money to pay some-one else to care for them. One of the sheriff's depu-ties, not Dahlia's brother, saw him grabbing dinner to go at Biscuit Betty's one night and invited him to the rec center to join a game of pickup basketball if he ever found the time.

Everyone he met was warm and welcoming and they all asked about the white pup, who by now wouldn't leave Connor's side, following him around as if his pockets were full of Dr. Roman's dog treats. When he explained how he'd ended up with the stray, everyone would laugh and make a reference to Dahlia Deacon and her daughter. He'd yet to come across anyone who didn't know them. But any time Connor would ask about the woman—no matter how casually—the trail would go cold and the townspeople would essentially close ranks and not say another word about her.

Having moved from place to place all his life,

Connor was accustomed to feeling like the new kid on the block. However, this small town was different from any of the heavily populated neighborhoods he'd lived in growing up. The inhabitants of Teton Ridge were as nosy as he'd expected, but also extremely friendly (except for Mr. Burnworth at the bakery who never threw an extra muffin in the bag for the dog like his generous sister and co-owner did). Everyone was free with words of advice and recommendations, but they were also strangely protective. There was no way to blend in, nor was there a way to keep his head down and mind his own business. He stood out everywhere he went.

Which was why two weeks later, when he was at Fredrickson's Feed and Grain pricing galvanized steel troughs and controlled aeration storage bins for hay oats, he was approached by yet another new face.

An older gentleman with a bushy gray mustache and a set of wiry eyebrows shooting out below the brim of his straw cowboy hat moseyed up beside Connor. The man's shiny belt buckle might've been a rodeo prize at one point, but it was hard to tell since his barrel chest and rounded belly shadowed the waistband of his jeans.

"Are you that kid who inherited Connie Daniels's old place?"

Connor was thirty-two and a decorated military veteran. But even he knew that when a bristly old cowboy called you *kid*, you didn't correct him. Especially when Connor was shaking his work-roughened hand, which had a grip likely earned from decades of wrestling steers. "Yes, sir. I'm Connor Remington."

"Name's Rider. I remember your dad, Steve. Used to get himself in pretty deep with those Saturday night poker games over at Big Millie's. I was there the night he lost the Rocking D's prize longhorn while holding nothin' but a pair of nines. Ol' Connie finally put her boot down after that." Rider made a tsking sound, but before Connor could offer his standard apology for his father's lack of control around whiskey and card games—the older man went on. "I heard you were looking to breed some Morgan horses on your great-aunt's ranch."

Yep, there was no such thing as minding one's business in Teton Ridge. Not that Connor had anything to keep private. In fact, with his own memories of his old man already fading, it might be pretty informative to befriend the people around here who could give him a bit more insight into Steve Remington, and more importantly, his great-aunt Connie. "Yes, sir. That's my plan."

Rider crossed his arms over his massive chest and planted his boots a few feet apart, as though he was going to be standing there awhile. "What are you starting with?"

Connor told Rider about the three-year-old untried stallion he'd bought at an auction in Cody after he'd returned his rental car to Jackson last week. The stud would be delivered in a few days and Connor was in a hurry to make sure the small stables were ready. The conversation shot off from there and the two men stood in the aisle for a good twenty minutes or so discussing the safety of in-hand breeding versus pasture breeding as well as MHC proteins playing a role in genetic differences and horse compatibility.

When the old cowboy seemed convinced that Connor actually knew what he was talking about, Rider said, "I have a couple of mares that'll need to be covered at the end of the month. Why don't you bring your new stallion to my ranch? We can see how he does with the ladies, and if any of them take a liking to him, we can work out the stud fees."

Connor's chest suddenly didn't feel so heavy. It was the break he didn't know he'd been hoping for. He'd planned to invest in a few broodmares himself, but he also needed extra cash to pump into the infrastructure at the Rocking D while he waited for his investment to produce several—or hopefully more—foals.

"Sounds like a plan." Connor again shook the man's hand. "Where is your ranch?"

Rider's wiry eyebrows dipped low and he took off his cowboy hat to scratch the steel bristly hair underneath. "A few miles down the road from yours?"

Connor had the feeling that the older cowboy expected him to know every single ranch and cowpoke in Ridgecrest County. Sure, he'd heard of some of the bigger outfits nearby, like the Twin Kings and Fallow's Crossing, but it wasn't as though Connor'd had a ton of downtime to figure out who worked where yet. He'd rather remain quiet than ask an obvious question. Or worse, make a wrong assumption.

A few seconds of silence hovered between them before Rider finally replaced his hat. "By the way, I know the sins of the father don't always pass to the sins of the son. But just in case you're lookin' for a good poker game, you won't find that at Big Millie's anymore. My niece runs a respectable establishment nowadays."

Connor's ears shot to attention and his pulse spiked. "So Dahlia is your niece?"

"That's right." One side of Rider's gray mustache hitched upward. "I heard you'd been askin' about her around town."

Okay, so apparently Connor's horse breeding plan wasn't the only thing folks in Teton Ridge were talking about. He hoped his gulp wasn't noticeable. "I don't suppose you'd buy the excuse that I was just being neighborly?"

"Ha!" The old man's laugh was loud enough to

draw the attention of several customers and Freddie Fredrickson behind the register. "If I had an acre of property for every young buck who wanted to be *neighborly* with my nieces, I'd have the biggest spread in Wyoming."

A woman wearing denim overalls and a cap embroidered with the words Crazy Chicken Lady made a sniggering sound as she pushed her cart full of organic scratch grains past them.

"Sir, with all due respect, Dahlia Deacon seems like a perfectly nice lady and a great mom. And yes, I can see how many men would be interested in getting to know her better. But I assure you, all of my energy is focused on getting the Rocking D up and running. I don't have time to be pursuing anyone, let alone someone who so clearly doesn't want to be pursued."

"Did Dahlia tell you she didn't want to be pursued?" Rider asked.

"The subject never came up." And it likely never would.

Rider leaned in closer and lowered his voice. "Can I give you a word of advice, son?"

Nobody had called Connor *son* since his dad had died, and he didn't know how to feel about it. While he could use all the advice he could get, a warm sensation bloomed at the nape of his neck and all he could manage in response was a gruff "Hmm?"

"Dahlia will never raise that particular subject. She has good reason to keep her business to herself. But when the right guy comes along, Amelia will let her know." With that, Rider walked to the opposite end of the aisle, and then to the cash register up front.

Remingtons always know when they've found "the one."

Connor shook off the eerie sensation of his own father's words echoing back to him. All this talk of his old man was putting strange ideas in his head.

Not to mention the fact that Connor didn't believe a mom would actually take relationship advice from her five-year-old. Especially when Amelia hadn't proven herself to be the most discerning when it came to liking every person and animal that came along.

Sure, the little girl could outtalk anyone he'd ever met, and even *he* had already given in to the child's appeals once. But Connor had lived through too many of his own parents' battles to ever feel the need to win someone over. Besides, he hadn't been blowing smoke when he'd said his sole focus was on his ranch. It had to be. If Connor failed at this unexpected shot to fulfill his lifelong dream—as well as his promise to his great-aunt on her deathbed— then, like his old man, he wouldn't have anyone to blame but himself.

* * *

"C'mon, Mommy. We gotta check on him. It's been a whole month."

"It's barely been two weeks," Dahlia corrected Amelia way too early on a Saturday morning. "I'm sure Mr. Remington is taking wonderful care of the dog."

"But I don't even know if it has a name." Her daughter's eyes filled with that infamous King determination. Finn, Dahlia's twin sister, had once given her niece a book entitled *Girls Can Do Anything They Want*. Ever since she'd first read it, Amelia had taken the words to heart. It was a great motto for empowering young women, but only when it didn't undermine the mothers of those same women.

Nobody could always get what he or she wanted. In fact, just a few days ago, Amelia *wanted* to eat a bowl of chocolate chip ice cream for breakfast before school. But Dahlia *wanted* her to eat a bowl of oatmeal. Neither of them got what they wanted after *that* particular standoff.

Dahlia quickly weighed her options. She could say no and hold her ground—which was what every parenting advice guru would probably tell her to do. Or she could say no, and then later in the day when the negotiations continued—because they would always continue with a determined Amelia—Dahlia might be tempted to give in, thereby becoming a pushover.

Which left a third option. Instead of simply giving in, she could make Amelia think it was Dahlia's idea to go and visit Connor all along.

And that was why forty-five minutes and a quick shower later, Dahlia and her daughter were pulling into the driveway of the Rocking D with a box of doughnuts and a bag of squeaky toys.

Putting the truck in Park, she fought the urge to check her reflection in the review mirror. Why should she care how she looked when Connor saw her?

Maybe because she and her daughter were barging in on someone, unannounced, at eight thirty on a Saturday morning. Or maybe because the man walking out of the stables carrying a bundle of wood planks under one strong arm and a ladder in the other sent an unexpected thrill down her spine.

"There he is!" Amelia exclaimed as she unbuckled herself from her booster seat before Dahlia had even switched off the ignition. She really needed to remember to get that childproof lock fixed on the back-seat doors.

Hurrying after her daughter meant there was no time for Dahlia to give a second thought to her appearance. Luckily, instead of running straight to Connor, Amelia ran straight for the dog, who'd cleaned up even better than his new owner. Not that Connor needed to clean up. But at least he'd traded in those sneakers and that stiff denim for worn cowboy boots and a pair of faded jeans that settled low on his narrow waist.

Whoa.

Wait a minute. What was that all about? Why was she even paying attention to his jeans?

"Sorry for showing up unannounced." Dahlia slid her palms in her back pockets.

Connor's only reply was to set the bundle of wood down on the ground, his broad chest stretching against the fabric of his chambray work shirt. Her mouth went dry and, even though he hadn't asked what they were doing there, she swallowed before pouring out an explanation.

"I had the morning off and Amelia was really insistent about checking on the dog. She wanted to find out if you'd named him yet. I told her I was sure you had, but with her being in school during the week and me working in the evenings, the weekends are pretty valuable as far as quality time goes and I didn't feel like wasting a whole Saturday arguing with a five-year-old. I didn't have your number or I would've given you a heads-up. Or just sent you a text asking about the dog. Not that I'm fishing for your number or anything. Because I really don't need it and I'm sure that this is a onetime thing. I promise that my daughter and I don't make a habit of showing up at strangers' houses unannounced. Especially because you're probably super busy getting the ranch working again. The new roof on the stables looks great, by the way. Oh, we brought doughnuts."

What had gotten into her? She was talking even more than Amelia usually did. Dahlia squeezed her eyes shut, took a deep breath and counted to three before she embarrassed herself any further. When she dared a peek at the reaction on his face, she realized he was smirking at her.

"That sounds great," Connor said simply. Almost too simply.

"Which part?" Dahlia asked, pretending that her cheeks weren't the same color of pink as the strawberry smoothie she'd downed on the way over here.

"All of it." His smirk turned into a knowing smile. "But especially the doughnuts part. I worked through breakfast this morning."

He turned to Amelia, who was sitting in the dirt with the white pup licking the smeared glaze frosting and sprinkles off her face. "I have some chocolate milk in the kitchen."

That was it? Dahlia thought as she walked around to the passenger side of the truck to retrieve the pink bakery box and bag of dog toys. She'd just rambled on and on, talking more to Connor in the past thirty seconds than she had the entire first two times she'd met him. And all he could offer her in return was some chocolate milk and a *that sounds great*?

She bit her lip as she approached the man, who was kneeling next to her daughter and the dog, discussing the possible breeds in the little white stray's ancestry.

"Maybe he's part poodle," Amelia suggested.

Connor shrugged. "It's possible. The vet thought he might be part terrier. He definitely knows how to pick up a scent and track the badgers that keep trying to build their home under the old henhouse over there."

"Are there any roosters in there? Uncle Rider has a rooster that's meaner than lizard poop, 'cept Uncle Rider doesn't really say the word *poop*. He says the other one that I'm not allowed to use. His rooster is called Diablo and pecks at people when they hafta collect the eggs. 'Cept for me. Diablo likes me 'cause I have a sweet tem-pre-mint 'round animals. That's what my aunt Finn says." Instead of waiting for an answer, Amelia took off running toward the dilapidated chicken coop that looked like a razed tree fort and was apparently the last item on Connor's fix-up list.

"I actually met your uncle Rider the other day at the feed store," Connor said casually, and Dahlia felt the hairs on the back of her neck stand at attention. As soon as the man found out who her family was, she'd never get rid of him. Men and women alike loved hitching their lassos to the Kings. Or at least to their money and prestige.

She'd been dealing with it her whole life, and it was one of the reasons she'd never really dated much after her divorce. She could never tell who genuinely liked her, or who simply wanted to get closer to one of the wealthiest and most successful families in Wyoming. But Connor's next question convinced Dahlia that he still hadn't put all the pieces together yet.

"He took down my number and when my new stallion arrives, I'm going to bring it out to his ranch to see if any of his mares are compatible. He said his place is close to here, but I've met so many people in town, I don't really know who lives where."

Rider never felt the need to tell people his last name, let alone his address. He might not be as world famous as his twin brother, former Vice President Roper King, but as an old rodeo star and the co-owner of the second largest ranch in Wyoming, he was notorious in his own right.

"How'd you know Rider was my uncle?"

"He mentioned meeting my father once at Big Millie's. He wanted me to know that you run a respectable establishment and warned me that if I was anything like my old man, I should stay far away."

Dahlia tilted her head as she studied him. "And are you?"

"Staying far away?" Connor shrugged. "I've tried to, but you keep finding me."

"I meant are you anything like your father." Not that she had any idea who his father was or what that would prove. "Wait. Did you just say you've been trying to avoid me?"

"I meant that in a good way," he said quickly, but she was already rocking back on her boot heels.

That was certainly a first for Dahlia. Not that she thought the man—or any man—was dying to spend time with her, but she was usually the one to do the avoiding. The unexpected disappointment kind of stung. "So I should be flattered that you don't want to be around me?"

"I never said that I don't *want* to be around you, Dahlia. Obviously, I do. That's why it's been a struggle."

His insinuation, along with his use of her name, turned that disappointed sting into a warm tingle. She knew why she'd been keeping *her* distance from Connor, but now she was intensely curious about why he'd felt the need to do the same. Before she could ask him, though, Amelia and the rather adorable mutt were running back toward them.

"Hey, Mr. Rem'ton. Look at him following me everywhere I go with no leash. Aunt Finn says that if you got the goods, you can get 'em to follow you anywhere you want. That means I have the goods. Just like Mommy."

"Oh, jeez, Amelia." Dahlia would've covered her blushing face, but Connor was already covering his, his broad shoulders shaking. "Please don't repeat what Aunt Finn says."

"Is your uncle Rider married to your aunt Finn?" Connor asked Amelia when he finished laughing. He clearly was still trying to piece it all together and Dahlia wasn't going to make it any easier for him. Especially when she should be more focused on watching what her sister was saying in front of her daughter.

Amelia giggled. "No, silly. Uncle Rider is married to Aunt Freckles but they don't live together 'cause Aunt Freckles said she's too old for that nonsense. Aunt Finn is Mommy's age so they're only kinda old. They're twins. I wish I was a twin, but it's just me. Mommy said she's done having babies, but Aunt Freckles told Mommy not to count her chickens afore they hatch. When do your chickens get here?"

And just like that, Amelia spun the conversation right back to her favorite topic—animals. Thank goodness, because her daughter had just delivered a mouthful of information, potentially providing Connor with all types of details about their family if he could've gotten a word in edgewise to ask for clarification.

"I don't have any roosters or chickens yet. But I do have my very first stallion being delivered this afternoon."

"I can't wait to see your new horse. What color is he? What's his name? Where are you gonna put him? Do you have a saddle? Aunt Finn said all cow-

girls need their own saddles. Can I go see his stable?" Amelia shot off toward the large outbuilding
sporting a fresh coat of red paint.

For the next thirty minutes, Connor patiently
showed Amelia around the stalls, which were empty,
the tack room, which was only half-empty, and a
feed storage area, which was stocked completely
full. Dahlia and the white dog both trailed behind
them obediently—except Dahlia was the sucker still
holding the doughnut box.

Or maybe Connor was the sucker, since he was
the one stuck answering all of Amelia's constant
rapid-fire questions. She loved her daughter's curious nature, but sometimes Dahlia's own brain felt
as though she were trapped in a perpetual game of
fast-paced trivia and she had to know all the answers all the time.

Dahlia's mother, the former first lady of Wyoming and second lady of the United States, was
the opposite. Sherilee King would prefer to host a
head-of-state dinner for a thousand of her closest
friends rather than enjoy a quiet meal at home. She
often cautioned Dahlia about being overshadowed
by anyone—especially a five-year-old. However,
being the King who didn't fit the mold made Dahlia
want to encourage her daughter's natural personality all the more.

Of all her siblings, Dahlia was the least like her
parents. She was the reserved one, the one who pre-

ferred staying behind the scenes. Marcus was the Sheriff of Ridgecrest County. Duke had been a football hero before becoming a highly decorated pilot in the Navy. Tessa was a political analyst with her own show on a cable news channel. Finn ran their family's multi-million-dollar ranch and was responsible for several dozen employees and some of the best livestock in the state. MJ, the baby of the family, had gotten into some trouble recently, but Dahlia was sure the eighteen-year-old would get his act together and come out on top. Because that was what Kings did. They excelled.

Except for Dahlia. She'd been the one who dropped out of college one semester shy of earning her interior design degree. She'd been the one who'd ended up pregnant after a one-night stand during the height of her dad's hard-fought election campaign. She'd also been the one who'd insisted on marrying that same guy, knowing full well the improbability of a lasting marriage with a famous musician who was always gone on tour.

Not that she regretted her very brief relationship with Micah Deacon. After all, she'd gotten Amelia out of the whole deal. Plus, she and Micah got along pretty well, and Amelia loved her regular video chats with her daddy and spending time with him whenever he got a break in his schedule.

While Dahlia was happy and fulfilled with the life she'd made for herself here in Teton Ridge, there was always the unspoken expectation that she could have been so much more than a mother and a bar owner. She was a King, after all. Yet, nobody seemed to care that in reality, she'd never wanted anything more than what she already had.

She was perfectly content being herself and living life on her own terms. Just as she was content allowing Amelia to be *herself.* Even if that meant the little girl repeated things at the worst times or came up with the most inappropriate questions.

"But how does the baby get *inside* the girl horse's tummy?" her daughter asked Connor, who suddenly tugged at the collar of his shirt.

Instead of focusing on the smooth sun-kissed skin along his neck, Dahlia jumped into the conversation in the nick of time. "Peanut, why don't we let Mr. Remington get back to work?"

"Fine." Amelia gave a dramatic sigh. "Aunt Finn promised to let me watch a horse baby get borned next time they have one at the ranch. So I'll just ask her."

Heat spread across Dahlia's cheeks and she made a mental note to talk to her sister about how much exposure to the natural mechanics of animal procreation a five-year-old should have. Even one as precocious as Amelia.

"Thank Mr. Remington for giving us a tour of his ranch," Dahlia instructed her daughter, who immediately obeyed.

"You're very welcome." Connor's smile was directed at Amelia, but Dahlia's insides quivered at its charming effects all the same.

She shook her head quickly, reminding herself not to get drawn in. "And tell… Sorry, what's the dog's name again?"

Connor took off his ball cap and scratched his head. His close-cropped hair had grown at least half an inch since they'd first met. Not that Dahlia was paying attention to such things. He sucked in one of his lightly stubbled cheeks before admitting, "I haven't exactly given him a name yet."

Amelia gasped. "But he hasta have a name."

"What about Casper?" Connor asked. "Because he's white and follows me around everywhere like a friendly ghost."

"No. You can't name a dog after a ghost. All the other animals will be scared of him. Even though ghosts aren't scary to me anymore because I'm a big girl and met one once." Amelia tapped her chin, thoughtfully and Dahlia pretended like her daughter's fanciful imagination about ghosts was totally normal. "How about I think about it tonight and we can come back tomorrow with a perfect name."

"Peanut, we can't keep bugging Mr. Remington."

"Please, call me Connor." This time when Connor smiled, he looked directly into Dahlia's eyes. The earlier quivering was nothing compared to the ripple now coursing through her rib cage and settling in her tummy. "You both are welcome to come visit the Rocking D anytime."

"Woo-hoo!" Amelia did a little jump and then skipped to the truck.

"Be careful, Connor," Dahlia told him. "Amelia will hold you to that."

"I never offer something unless I mean it." He took a step closer to Dahlia and her breath caught in her throat. This wasn't good. "I was hoping that if I gave you some time and space, you'd eventually figure out that I'm a decent guy. So earlier when I said I was trying to stay away from you, I didn't mean to imply that you have to stay away from me."

"Nice to know." She shoved the doughnut box at him, quickly putting a stop to any flirtatious thoughts he might be harboring. "Now you won't be surprised if my daughter turns your ranch into a full-blown refuge for stray and injured animals."

"I have a feeling both you and your daughter are always going to keep me on my toes with your surprises." He took a maple bar out of the pink box and held it up like a salute. "Thanks for the warning, though. And thanks again for stopping by with breakfast, Amelia!"

Her daughter heard only the last sentence and waved enthusiastically out the back window. "See you next time!"

"Looking forward to it." Connor winked at Dahlia before taking a big bite of his doughnut.

When he licked the corner of his mouth, she knew she had to get out of there. Fast.

She mumbled a goodbye and turned to retreat to the truck before she started licking her own lips.

Driving away, Dahlia kept herself from looking in the rearview mirror. Obviously, she had no intention of showing up unannounced again and dumping any more of Amelia's lost causes on the unsuspecting rancher. But somebody needed to tell him not to get his hopes up, thinking there might be something to this spark between them.

Clearly, nobody else in town had bothered to warn Connor Remington that Dahlia King Deacon and her family would always be a whole lot more than he bargained for.

Chapter Four

"So what's up with you and this new guy who inherited the Rocking D?" Dauphine "Finn" King asked her twin sister as they sat on the top ledge of the smaller indoor corral, watching Amelia's riding lesson.

"Nothing is up with us." Dahlia hadn't gone back to Connor's ranch the following day like Amelia had wanted to. Nor did she have any intention of returning. Ever. Instead, she focused on her daughter sitting high and proud in the tiny custom-made saddle as her uncle led the five-year-old in slow circles. "Remember when Dad taught us how to ride? It's weird to think he's gone now and our kids won't get to know him like we did."

"One, I'm never going to have kids. And two, Dad didn't teach me. Uncle Rider did. Probably because I didn't need as many lessons as you." Finn, who was an accomplished horsewoman, gave Dahlia a light shove. "And don't change the subject. I heard this new guy was asking about you around town."

Out of all the siblings, Finn was probably taking the loss of Roper King the hardest. But she was the most stubborn and refused to talk about her feelings. So Dahlia didn't push. Her tough-as-nails sister would talk about it in her own time and under her own terms.

Instead, Dahlia sighed and answered, "He's probably only asking about me because he was there when Amelia spied a stray dog and talked him into keeping it."

"Amelia could sell a drowning man a glass of water." Finn laughed. "I heard about the stray. I also heard that the mutt follows him everywhere. He was sitting outside on the patio at Biscuit Betty's with the thing. And nobody sits on the patio at Biscuit Betty's before March."

"Foolish man. The guy is a total goat roper," Dahlia said, using the slang term for a wannabe cowboy. "He has no business trying to play rancher out here in the middle of Wyoming."

"Look at me, Aunt Finn." Amelia waved as she rode by. "I'm doing it all by myself."

"Stop waving and keep both hands on her reins,

Peanut," Finn coached. "Gray Goose will be more comfortable if you're in charge."

Dahlia shook her head. "I can't believe you have my daughter riding a pony named after vodka."

"I can't believe you would mind, considering y'all live at a brothel."

"It's a saloon," Dahlia replied. Finn was always teasing someone about something. So Dahlia indulged her by engaging in yet another argument about her choice of profession just so she could distract her sister from the real topic she wanted to avoid: Connor Remington.

"So what's his story?" Her twin must've sensed the one thing Dahlia didn't want to talk about. "Why's he here? Is there a Mrs. Goat Roper?"

Good question. The guy had to be single, right? He certainly acted as though he was, with that sexy smirk and those heat-filled stares. Besides, Dahlia could usually spy a married man a mile away. Still, she chose to ignore the second part of Finn's question. "Judging by his tan, I think he's from California, maybe? Or some big city. I'm pretty sure he was in the military at some point because he stands like he's constantly in the 'at ease' position. He never knew about his great-aunt Connie until just a bit before she passed away. From what I could tell, he was pretty shocked about inheriting the ranch, but he's intent on making it work. Which tells me he probably has all his savings riding on this and nothing else to fall back on. Oh, and I did find out that he was an only child. But I didn't pry into his personal business because it's personal."

"Yet, you felt comfortable foisting one of your daughter's strays off on him?" Finn asked, one eyebrow lifted.

"It was either *I* take the dog or *he* takes it. Have you met Mr. Burnworth?"

"Mr. Burnworth is a cranky pile of bones who told me I smelled like I'd been rolling around in manure last time I was in the bakery. How does such a skinny and bitter old man manage to make the best damn pies around? His baking skill is the only thing that's kept him in business all these years. It certainly isn't because of his customer service."

"Well, his baking and his sweet sister. She deserves a medal for putting up with him for so long."

"That's the same thing people say about you." Finn made her voice high-pitched as she mimicked most of their elementary school teachers. "Dahlia's so chill and gets along with everyone. What in the world happened to Finn?"

"Oh, please." Dahlia playfully shoved her sister. "Deep down, you're the softest one of all of us Kings. You just have the toughest exterior. And the hardest head."

"Take it back. I am not soft." Finn's boot swiped at Dahlia's, but she dodged the kick just in time. Her sister stuck out her tongue in response, then added,

"I'm certainly not soft enough to let you and your sweet-talking daughter pawn off any more animals on me. Unlike that so-called cowboy of yours."

An image quickly appeared in Dahlia's mind—of the wannabe rancher's broad chest and flat stomach in that snug T-shirt he'd been wearing the day they'd first met. There was certainly nothing soft about Connor Remington. Except maybe his lips…

"Whoa, that's a look I haven't seen in a while," Finn interrupted her thoughts. "You're interested in this new guy."

"No I'm not. I merely took pity on him because he has a decent-sized ranch without a single animal on it."

"So you've been spending time at his ranch?" Finn raised an eyebrow.

"Only twice. You make it sound like I'm stalking the man. I dropped him off the first time we met." She told her sister the story about how he was out on the road looking for the stray in a T-shirt—*don't think about the shirt*—crisp new jeans and sneakers. "And then a few days ago when Amelia wanted to check in on the dog."

"But he's getting more animals, right? I heard Uncle Rider wants him to bring his new stallion out here to see how he does in the breeding stalls. Rider actually got a kick out of the fact that the man had no idea who he was when he ran into him at the feed and grain."

"See. That's my point," Dahlia told her sister. "How can any legitimate rancher in a thousand-mile radius *not* know who Rider King is?"

"Fair enough. At least you can be assured that he isn't using you to get closer to the Kings." This time, Finn's voice was more solemn than playful. Both sisters unfortunately learned at a young age to be wary of men wanting to lasso themselves to their family's ranching connections. "Speaking of which, what's the latest on the donkey's behind, anyway?"

"I'm assuming you're referring to the father of my child?" For some reason, Dahlia's twin had never really taken to Micah Deacon, even though there was never any animosity between Dahlia and her ex. Besides, Micah was a good dad and would drop anything for Amelia if she needed it. "You know full well that Micah was never using me to get close to the Kings. That was the drummer in his college band. Remember, you had him in your Intro to Animal Science class our freshman year at UW?"

"Oh, yeah. That guy who tried to move in on you before the divorce papers were even signed, then tried to get his name on the deed for Big Millie's."

"It didn't go quite that far." Dahlia's lower spine stiffened at the reminder. "I had a lot going on at the time."

"Speaking of staying busy, I heard Micah was going to be doing another tour this summer. Does Amelia ever get to see her dad?"

Dahlia straightened her shoulders. "They Face-Time on the phone a few nights a week and he bought her that iPad to make the video calls easier and so she could text him whenever she wants. And, of course, so she can play her favorite games. He might be able to fly in from Nashville for spring break. Everyone's doing their best to make it work."

She often got tired of explaining her unique co-parenting situation to people, including her own family. Someone always wanted there to be a bad guy when a relationship ended, but the truth was that she and Micah were both the good guys, they just weren't good together.

"Lil' Amelia looks like a natural up there," Aunt Freckles called from a few feet away. Technically, Freckles was no longer their aunt since she'd been separated from Rider longer than she'd ever been married to him. But she loved the King children like her own and when Roper died, she'd dropped everything and came out to Wyoming to help.

"She's sure got it, all right." Finn hopped off the fence and walked over to Freckles.

"That reminds me." Dahlia jumped down and followed. "When you teach my daughter expressions like that, she usually repeats them at the most inopportune times."

"Expressions like what?" Freckles asked.

"The other day she told some random man that

her aunt says when *you got it*, the guys will follow you."

"Got what?" Freckles narrowed a teal-shadowed
eye and put her hand on one leopard-printed span-
dex covered hip. The older woman had to be pushing eighty, but she wore more makeup, hairspray
and Lycra than four twenty-year-old beauty queens.
Combined.

"Itttt," Dahlia repeated, pointedly sounding it
out. Although, Amelia had no idea what she was
even referencing at the time. And to be honest, now
Dahlia wasn't quite sure, either.

"Oh." Freckles nodded. "*Itttt*. Well, the girl ain't
wrong. Men are easily led around by their—"

"She was trying to explain why the guy's dog was
following her," Dahlia quickly cut off Freckles. "So
she was repeating a phrase she'd heard from Finn."

Finn shrugged. "Sounds like the phrase works
in both situations."

Freckles smiled, revealing a bright red streak of
lipstick on her front tooth. "Any chance this *random man* with the dog is that new rancher in town
who's been asking about you?"

"My guess is yes," Finn replied. "Otherwise,
Dahlia wouldn't be so embarrassed about it. She
has a thing for him."

"Who do you have a thing for, Mommy?" Amelia asked as she led the gray pony out of the corral.

"No one," Dahlia said a little too quickly and the

women beside her shared a knowing look. Finn and Freckles might not be related by blood or fashion sense, but they were definitely two birds of a feather.

Everyone was reading way too much into Dahlia's nonexistent dating life. There was nothing going on between her and Connor. But if she protested, they'd only become more suspicious.

So Dahlia shoved her sunglasses higher on her nose and quietly vowed to stay away from the man before the rumors really started to spread.

When Amelia and Dahlia didn't show up on the ranch the following day, Connor told the dog, "I should still call you Casper."

Of course, as soon as he settled on a name, he'd likely run into the adorable and persuasive child who'd insist on renaming the mutt, anyway. After all, it wasn't a matter of *if*, but *when* he'd see Amelia and her mom again. He'd learned a lot since he'd moved to Teton Ridge, but the one thing that still kept him on his toes was the small-town rumor mill. He might be able to physically avoid seeing the co-rescuers of his new pet, but he wouldn't be able to avoid hearing about them. Or vice versa.

So he spent the following week the same as the past two weeks, working on the ranch, meeting more townspeople and not referring to the dog by any name. Oh, and thinking about Dahlia when he wasn't busy with everything else.

It helped that his new stallion arrived on Monday and he didn't have as much time on his hands to think about anything but his ranch. By Friday, though, he needed to go back into town for a specialty feed Dr. Roman had recommended for Private Peppercorn.

The three-year-old stallion's grand sire was a proven Morgan stud who successfully covered more than fifty mares a season. Technically, he'd been registered as Colonel Peppercorn on his official papers, but Connor gave the untried stallion a demotion until he proved himself and earned his rank.

"Well, boy, if we go now, we can grab you a muffin before the feed store opens." He held open the truck door as the shorter dog defied gravity and easily launched himself into the cab of the truck.

When he parked outside Burnworth's—which had to be the worst name for a bakery ever—he cracked the window. The dog's ears perked up and he bounced across the bench seat, but Connor held up his hand, using the command signal he'd used in the Marine Corps when they'd had to silently post up outside a suspicious location.

"Stay," he told the dog before shutting the truck door. The animal's ears fell and its eyes blinked in confusion. "Come on. Don't look at me like that. Mr. Burnworth threatened to cut us both off if I brought you into the bakery again. Just wait for me here. I'll be right back."

But Connor was no more than halfway across the sidewalk when he heard an excited yip and turned around in time to see the scrappy white mutt wiggle out of the opening in the window. Instead of running toward Connor, though, the animal ran straight for Amelia who dropped to her knees just in time to be greeted by a wet nose and an even wetter puppy tongue.

"Hi, Goatee! I've missed you, too. How's my best boy?" As Amelia rambled on, the dog responded with more licking and tail wagging. "I've been wanting to come visit you at the ranch again, but Mommy said we should let you get settled and… Oh, hi, Mr. Rem'ton. Look, Mommy, Mr. Rem'ton and Goatee are here."

"I see that," Dahlia said as she balanced a travel mug of coffee in one hand and a red backpack in the other. She was bundled into a coat and scarf, her honey-blond hair hanging in loose curls under a Dorsey Tractor Supply ball cap. "Hi, Mr. Remington."

"Connor," he reminded her. "And apparently, this is my dog, Goatee? Is that what we're calling him?"

"Yeah. Don't you love it?" the little girl asked.

Connor squinted at the animal who, despite his recent grooming, still had a slight patch of longer hair that the clippers must've missed. "I'm guessing because that fur on his chin makes him look like he has a little beard?"

"No. Because Mommy and Aunt Finn were talking about you being a goat roper, even though you don't got no goats on your ranch."

"What's a goat roper?" he asked. But he could tell by the pink staining Dahlia's cheeks that the term wasn't complimentary.

"Amelia, how did you even hear that? You were supposed to be paying attention to your riding… Never mind." Dahlia turned toward him, but seemed to have trouble making eye contact. "It just means you're new to ranching."

"When I talked to Daddy on FaceTime last night, I had to ask him what it meant, too," Amelia reassured Connor. "He said that if I heard it from Aunt Finn, it couldn't be good. But I told him it was Mommy who called you that and then he just laughed and laughed and said Mommy has lots of experience with goat ropers."

Dahlia's face was now so red she almost matched the kid-sized backpack, which was sliding off her shoulder. "Peanut, why don't you go ask Ms. Burnworth for a muffin for both you and Mr. Remington. I mean for you and *Connor*," she amended with a bit too much emphasis. It was almost as though she wanted to remind everyone that he actually had a real name and not the unexplained nickname.

Feeling a mischievous grin tugging on the corners of his mouth, Connor reached into his pocket for a twenty-dollar bill and handed it to the girl. He wasn't about to let Dahlia off the hook with this one.

"And will you get something for *Goatee*, too?" Just in case Dahlia didn't hear him emphasizing the goat reference, he repeated it. "*Goatee* likes the banana muffins best."

"What about for you, Connor?" Amelia asked. His name had never sounded so innocent or so endearing. "What kind do you want?"

"Oh, surprise me." As the dog started to follow the girl, Connor swooped him into his arms. "Not you, Goatee. You're staying here with us. Even if your name is the result of someone's trash-talking session about your owner."

"It wasn't trash-talking so much as me voicing concern that perhaps the Rocking D is a bit more than you can handle." Dahlia lifted her own chin proudly before petting the dog under his. "Besides, he *does* look like he has a little goatee."

"How do you know what I can handle?"

With the dog still secured in his arms, Dahlia stood only inches away. The tip of her tongue darted out to touch her lips before she cleared her throat. "I don't. I really don't know you at all."

"Exactly. So maybe you should get to know me a little better." Even to his own ears, the words sounded like an invitation. A dare. "I mean, before you jump to any more conclusions."

"Just because you figured out how to dress the

part—" her eyes slowly traveled the length of his body to his boots and then back up again. The tilt of her mouth suggested she appreciated what she saw and his jeans suddenly felt tighter "—that doesn't make you a real cowboy."

Now he was the one whose skin was heated. Except, instead of blushing from embarrassment, his blood was pumping from arousal. He returned her earlier appraisal of him, allowing his eyes to scan just as slowly from her bulky jacket to her long legs encased in fitted denim. As he lifted his eyes back to her, he took a step closer. "I've never pretended otherwise."

"Have you ever worked at a ranch before, Connor?" Was it his imagination, or did she step closer, as well? Her face was tilted at an angle to look up at him while his head was lowered close enough that the brims of their hats threatened to collide.

He opened his mouth leisurely, taking his time with a single-word response. "No."

He was rewarded with the thrill of satisfaction when Dahlia's gaze dropped to his lips. And stayed there as she asked her next question. "Ever been in the saddle before?"

Oh, if she only knew.

Before he could tell her exactly how experienced he was, though, Amelia returned and Goatee reminded the two adults that he was the only thing wedged between them and full-body contact. The girl must not have noticed her mother jumping away as though she'd been startled.

Amelia pulled a muffin out for the dog before handing the white bag to Connor. "I got you blueberry. That's my daddy's favorite kind. He eats them all the time when he's on his tour bus and then his fingers turn all blue and so does his guitar strings."

Tour bus. Guitar. Deacon. Everything suddenly clicked together as he watched the girl feed the dog still balanced in the crook of Connor's arm. "Is your dad—"

Dahlia quickly interrupted. "We need to get to school, Amelia. You don't want anyone feeding the hamsters before you."

"Wait," he said to Dahlia, but her expression had gone blank, her mask already back in place. "Are you married to Micah Deacon?"

The last thing Connor wanted to be doing was standing on a public sidewalk in the middle of his newly adopted hometown publicly lusting over a famous musician's wife. Or anyone's wife, really.

"No, I'm not." Dahlia pulled her hat lower on her brow.

"Mommy and Daddy got dee-vorced when I was a baby." Amelia's casual response was the exact opposite of her mother's tense one. "We do co-parenting. Just like Peyton's family. Except Mommy and Daddy don't ever yell at each other like Peyton's parents do."

Dahlia stiffened and took a step back. "Okay, well, on that note, Amelia, we really do have to be off to school." She managed a polite wave at Connor, but it didn't take a psychic to know that the whole dynamic between them had shifted.

Amelia gave him a fluttery little wave, too. "Bye, Connor. Bye, Goatee."

As Connor watched the duo walk away, he wasn't sure whether to feel relief or confusion. If Amelia's assessment was correct, it was great that Dahlia and her ex got along so well. For their daughter's sake. But if they did, in fact, get along so well, then why hadn't they stayed married?

Not that any of it was his business. But if there was still some unsettled business between them, it did explain the woman's standoffishness. She probably didn't want people speculating about her and her famous ex-husband. Then again, maybe she was holding out hope of reuniting with the man and keeping her family intact. She certainly wouldn't be the first woman to do so.

Speaking of which, Connor probably should call his mother this afternoon and check in. His mom loved to remind him of how many times she'd given his father a chance to prove that he'd changed, that things could be different for the three of them once Steve sobered up. His mom also loved to remind him of how wrong she'd been to believe in such a pipe dream.

Connor had grown up determined to be a better man than his father, which meant he wasn't about to make a promise he couldn't keep. He'd also grown up determined not to be like his mother and fall for someone who couldn't love him back.

He wasn't sure exactly what was going on between him and Dahlia, but whatever it was, he'd better walk a fine line of not breaking either of his childhood resolutions.

Chapter Five

Dahlia usually worked the lunch shift at the bar, then flipped the closed sign at two o'clock so she could pick up Amelia from school. As business had steadily grown over the past year, she'd hired another bartender to cover more of the evening shifts. However, Dahlia usually liked to be downstairs when the weekend manager clocked in to go over any details that needed her attention.

Since Fridays were paydays for most ranch hands, Dahlia was currently adding more beer mugs to the custom-made glass chiller installed under the old-fashioned bar—right next to the very modern ice machine. Amelia sat on a bar stool across from her,

her iPad propped open against her Shirley Temple as she FaceTimed with her dad.

"And then Miss Violet pushed Uncle Marcus into the pool while he was still wearing his policeman's uniform and everything. Aunt Finn said he needed to cool off, anyway, and me and the twins laughed and laughed because he looked so silly, Daddy."

"Aw, man, I wish I could've been there to see it. Did you practice your backstroke while you were at the pool?" Micah asked his daughter. He'd taught her to swim over the summer and had been instrumental—both vocally and financially—in getting the city council to add an indoor pool when the town voted to renovate the old rec center.

"Yep," Amelia replied. "I practiced real good. Even after I got water up my nose. Aunt Finn got me some new goggles. Hold on, I'm gonna go upstairs and get them. Talk to Mommy while I'm gone."

Her daughter quickly angled the device toward Dahlia before rushing up the stairs to their apartment. "Hey, Micah," she said as she straightened the screen so that her ex-husband was vertical.

"Oh, wow, Dia, the new shelves turned out nice." Micah nodded toward the thick halves of reclaimed pine logs holding up the colorful bottles of premium liquor.

"Thanks. It was touch and go with the install, but you were right about using the iron brackets. Anyway, did you see that email from the school about how they printed the wrong Spring Break dates on the upcoming calendar?"

"Yeah, I forwarded the correct dates to our tour manager so she doesn't schedule anything for the band that week. Listen, I have to run into a doctor's appointment right now. Tell Amelia to text me a pic of her in those new goggles. I'll call her after her riding lesson tonight."

Dahlia gave Micah a thumbs-up before disconnecting the call.

"I can't believe how well you guys get along," Rena, her weekend manager, said as she breezed in from the swinging kitchen door. Rena was the same age as Dahlia, but she was petite and outgoing and had way more experience when it came to dating. She was also enrolled in the online program at UW working on her masters in hospitality, so Dahlia valued her professional opinions even more than her relationship advice.

"Really?" Dahlia shrugged. She couldn't imagine not getting along with Micah. Probably because there weren't any unresolved feelings lingering between them. Just mutual respect and a common goal—to make sure their daughter was happy.

"Does he know you have a new man?" Rena asked. "'Cause things might change when the old guy finds out about the new guy."

Dahlia's stomach dropped and she tried to sound

as casual as possible when she asked, "Who says I have a new man?"

Rena double knotted a short black apron around her tiny waist. "Everyone is talking about you and that dude from the Rocking D and how you guys can't take your eyes off each other when you see him in town."

"Pfshh." Dahlia picked up a discarded white dishrag and twisted it in her hands. "I barely know the guy. We've only met a handful of times."

"Uh-huh," Rena said, her tone full of doubt. "We'll see how long that lasts."

As if to prove Rena right, though, Dahlia ran into Connor four more times the following week and then five the week after that. Not that she was keeping count. Fortunately, Amelia was always with her, which prevented another close encounter like the morning in front of the bakery when she'd gotten so close to the man she could smell the minty toothpaste on his breath and the woodsy sage-scented soap on his skin. On the other hand, having her daughter there as a de facto chaperone meant Dahlia couldn't keep her personal business from spilling out of Amelia's mouth, either. And right there on the public sidewalk for anyone to hear.

Whether it was at the market or the hardware store or even once in front of the vet's office, Amelia and Goatee seemed to have a second sense about each other, zeroing in on each other before the adults could take cover and hide. Not that Dahlia would actually hide from anyone. But she'd been known to slip into the bank or the post office or even the sheriff's station if she saw someone coming her way and wasn't up for conversation.

Not that Connor seemed to be the type to hide, either. He always appeared happy to see Amelia and patiently listened to everything she said, no matter how embarrassing it might be. However, two nights ago, when they ran into him picking up one of the famous chicken pot pies at Biscuit Betty's, Amelia had invited him to join them for dinner and he'd been especially quick to make an excuse about having to run off and do whatever it was he normally did in the evenings.

What did he do with his free time when it got dark on the ranch? Did he call his girlfriend back home? Did he watch sports on TV or sappy Lifetime movies? Did he go for a jog or lift weights? Dahlia imagined him shirtless, tan, perspiration trickling along the ridges of his muscles as he did biceps curls—

"Can't we just stop by for a second?" Amelia interrupted Dahlia's inappropriate thoughts from the back seat as they passed the turnoff for the Rocking D the following Friday afternoon.

"Not today, Peanut. We're already late for your riding lesson as it is. Last time we were late, Uncle Rider made us muck the stall, remember?" And frankly, Dahlia was much too old to relive her least favorite childhood chore, even if it supposedly built character. In fact, she was seldom late for that very reason. While growing up, the only saving grace was that Finn often got the same punishment for talking back, which meant her twin sister shoveled a lot more manure than she had. Dahlia still grinned at the memory.

"But Connor said Goatee has been getting too close to Private Peppercorn lately and isn't allowed in the corral no more when they're working. He probably could use an extra cuddle so he doesn't feel left out."

Left out. It was exactly how Dahlia felt right that second. She didn't remember hearing Connor say any of that the last few times they'd seen him in town. In fact, she didn't even know that he'd hired anyone else to work with him on the ranch. "Who's Private Peppercorn?"

"His new horse. Mr. Connor said when he got him, the paperwork said Colonel Peppercorn but he hadta give the horse a dee-mo…a dee-mo…"

"A demotion?" Dahlia prompted.

"Yeah, a demotion 'cause Peppercorn is too young. Connor said that when he was a Marine, only the old people were colonels and they hadta work real hard for it."

When did he say any of that? Dahlia was sure she would've remembered it. Especially since the military reference confirmed her earlier suspicion that he'd served in the armed forces. "Was I there when he was telling you about Peppercorn?"

"I think so. But you were busy talking to Mr. Thompson about beer."

Woodrow Thompson, better known around town as Woody, had gone to high school with Duke, Dahlia's favorite brother. He used to say that Woody would've easily beat him out as the class valedictorian if he'd actually shown up for classes. Micah used to love it when Woody would randomly stop by and jam with the band who practiced in Micah's garage. He could play any instrument he picked up, but would never show when they were hired to play at an actual venue. In fact, Woody had kept the same part-time job at the Pepperoni Stampede for the past thirteen years and lived in an old Airstream behind his grandma's house off Moonlight Drive. He volunteered once a month at the vet's office, but otherwise didn't do much of anything. Nobody understood how someone so smart and so talented could be such an underachiever.

When Dahlia took Amelia to the library after school yesterday, she'd seen Woody checking out books about yeast and hops, and he mentioned that he'd been brewing his own beer in a kettle on his cookstove. For some reason, Dahlia had always felt an odd kinship with Woody. Maybe because people seemed to expect more of out of guys like him when they were perfectly content with their lives as they were. So she'd asked him to bring a few bottles by Big Millie's and he'd left. When she'd caught up with Amelia, she was giving Connor and Goatee a tour of the new audiobook listening center in the children's section.

It was also the same time that the no-nonsense librarian whispered a stern reminder to Connor that only service animals were allowed inside the building. Dahlia never even got the chance to ask him why he'd been in the library in the first place. Probably looking for a copy of *Horseback Riding for Dummies*.

Okay, that was mean. But seriously. What was the man always doing in town with his funny-looking dog, casually running into Dahlia and charming Amelia? He should be spending more time on that ranch of his. And she needed to find a hobby of her own to get her mind off him. Maybe Finn would let her redecorate one of the bunkhouses. Again.

Dahlia kept her foot on the accelerator as they continued past the spot on Ridgecrest Highway where they'd first met Connor. Her daughter was being unusually tight-lipped today, probably because she hadn't given in for once. But since this wasn't Dahlia's first rodeo with Amelia, she made a mental note to start thinking of excuses for why they couldn't stop at the Rocking D on their way home.

Because there was no way her daughter would simply give up on asking.

Up ahead, she spotted several black SUVs stationed along the road just inside the entry gates to the Twin Kings. But seeing Secret Service units parked on the grounds was just as common as seeing work trucks and delivery vehicles lately. In fact, a couple of weeks ago when she'd brought Amelia, there'd been a sleek black helicopter lifting into the air and Amelia hadn't even blinked twice.

That was what it was like growing up as a King, the daughter of one of the wealthiest families in Wyoming. The children had all been raised to expect the unexpected. Whether it meant entertaining a last-minute royal guest or foreign dignitary, or their father canceling all of his campaign events spontaneously to hop aboard the private jet and fly the entire family out to Albuquerque to visit one of his buddies from Vietnam.

So fifteen minutes later when she saw the reverse lights on a horse trailer backing into the stables, she didn't think anything of it. In fact, it took Amelia shouting, "He's here!" before Dahlia felt that shiver of awareness she got every time—

No. Her stomach sank when she recognized the distinctive red truck in front of the horse trailer. Not everything in her body sank, though. Her nerve endings betrayed her by zipping to life.

"What's he doing here?" Dahlia mumbled, but

Amelia had already abandoned the pony to go running toward Goatee, who'd let out an excited yip the moment the driver's-side door opened.

Connor's jaw was set and his expression was schooled, probably because Rider and Mr. Truong, the stable foreman, were already approaching his trailer, saying something about the stallion in the back. But she could tell by the slight widening of his eyes that he was definitely confused. When he saw Amelia, he blinked several times before his smile finally softened his face.

Was it because he was genuinely happy to see her daughter? Or had he just figured out exactly who her uncle was? A horse breeder trying to make a name for himself was certainly going to appreciate landing the Twin Kings as one of his clients. But Rider King, and more importantly Finn King, wouldn't do business with the man if he couldn't deliver.

Connor might've been trained as a tracker for one of the world's most elite fighting forces in the world, but as soon as he pulled up to the address on his GPS, he was sure he'd made a wrong turn.

This was the Twin Kings? Connor had only done some preliminary research about the local ranches, and while he'd known this one was the biggest on this side of the state, the owner was listed as King Enterprises, LLC. Was Rider the foreman here?

The overly official-looking guard at the front gate

asked him for his name and then checked his ID. He said something into the clear wire attached to his earpiece, a military-grade communications system, then instructed Connor to take the *main road*—because apparently there were non-main roads—to the *big stables*—because apparently there were multiple smaller stables—and then someone would show him where to back in his trailer.

"This place is a far cry from the Rocking D," he muttered to Goatee as he crested the hill where an enormous house sat at least a football field away from a matching stone-and-timber building that had to be the Big Stables. The dog only barked in agreement, then peeked out the window.

A man in a straw cowboy hat came outside and made the universal hand signal to roll down the window. When Connor complied, the man introduced himself.

"I'm Mike Truong, the stable foreman. Rider and Finn were hoping we could unload your stallion directly into the southwest chute. We have several mares separated in the adjacent stalls, but they're not twitched yet. We like to have all our gals comfortable in their familiar surroundings so we can keep things as natural as possible for them. Two of my best handlers are with them to watch for aggressiveness and compatibility. Usually, with untried studs like yours, we have them stay overnight and act as a teaser of sorts to confirm which mares would be receptive. But we can wait and see how the courtships go. Now, if you want to back in, my guys will guide you."

Connor might be good with horses, but he'd never had to tow them in a trailer until recently. The transportation unit had always done that for him. It took him several attempts to navigate the trailer into the wide-open doors of the stables and then line it up perfectly with the gate to the southwest chute where someone had hung a wood-carved sign that read Tunnel of Love.

"Feels like we're both under some serious pressure, Pep," Connor said to the horse who couldn't hear him, anyway. To say he was already overwhelmed by the time he caught sight of Rider in his rearview mirror, arms crossed over that distinctive barrel chest, was an understatement. He wanted to yell out the window that he was way better with a horse than he was with a trailer, but he'd show them soon enough.

Shoving the stiff truck gear into Park, Connor gulped in a deep breath before opening the door to exit. It took every ounce of control he possessed to stand there and pretend that he always drove up to multi-million-dollar cattle ranches and wasn't completely starstruck by the vastness of the successful operation. Hell, even the *stable* was more like an indoor arena, with several corrals and hundreds of paddocks. It was tough to act like any of this was normal. Especially when he couldn't even keep his own dog from leaping out excitedly.

Instead of one of the nearby stable hands catching Goatee, though, it was little Amelia Deacon who lifted the dog in her arms and rubbed her face against its scratchy white fur. Connor could feel his eyes widening in surprise at seeing the child here, but there was also something about her familiar face and excited greeting that made him feel as if he were on his own turf. As though he weren't a complete fish out of water. But then his eyes landed on Dahlia holding on to the lead of a gray pony and suddenly it all snapped into place.

The funeral Dahlia and Amelia had been coming home from the night they'd met on the side of the highway.

The ranch security detail, who dressed like Secret Service agents.

Twin *Kings* Ranch.

Holy crap.

Dahlia's father was Roper King, the former vice president of the United States.

Which meant her uncle was Rider King.

Connor hadn't followed the news much since his discharge, but how'd he miss something this big? He was a neighbor to one of the most powerful political and cattle families in the world.

His forehead broke out in a sweat and he quickly slammed the felt brim of his Stetson lower on his brow as Rider approached the window of the horse trailer first. The stallion's impatient snorts coming from inside grounded Connor, immediately returning his pulse to a steady rate. Being around horses always made things simpler. And this was just a job, same as any other.

"So you're Private Peppercorn, huh?" The older man lifted a weathered hand between the bars and stroked the horse's silky black forelock. "Lil' Amelia tells me you got a demotion, young fella."

"That's true," Connor admitted, watching Dahlia as carefully as she was watching his meeting with her uncle. A tingle traveled up the back of his neck. She was probably too far away to hear them, which likely explained the crease in her forehead. Clearly, she didn't trust him around anyone in her family. "His previous owner gave him a rank he hadn't earned yet."

"Smart decision. What branch were you in, son?" Rider asked, and it took Connor a moment to pull his eyes away from where Dahlia was directing Amelia to stop giving Goatee chunks of carrots she had in her pocket—no doubt for the pony.

"The Corps."

"I knew I liked you," Rider replied, his beefy hand slapping Connor on the back. "I was Third Recon Battalion. From '67 to '71."

Amelia approached with the gray pony. Goatee was now in Dahlia's arms, looking perfectly content to be carried around as if he were the emperor of the stables.

"Sorry to do this to you, son, but I accidentally double-booked this afternoon." Rider's bushy gray brows and mustache made it difficult to determine whether or not he was truly remorseful. Or if it was in fact an accident. The glint of satisfaction in the older man's blue eyes—the same shade as Dahlia's and Amelia's—seemed almost scheming. "I've got a riding lesson with this fine cowgirl right now. But Lil' Amelia's mom will keep you company while you introduce your stallion to the ladies over there."

"I'll what?" Dahlia blinked several times and Connor would've laughed at her trying to contain both her surprise and annoyance at the assignment her uncle had just dealt her.

Rider threw a heavy arm around Connor's shoulder. "Now Dahlia, we can't keep this young stud in the prime of his life pinned up when there are plenty of gals practically lined up to meet him."

"You better be talking about the stud in the back of the trailer." The look she shot her uncle would've broken lesser men. But apparently the older man wasn't the least bit fazed.

"Who else would I be talking about?" Rider's hearty laughter rang out as he squeezed Connor's shoulder with enough force to practically steer him toward Dahlia. "Look at those fillies over there just waiting to be neighborly. Love is in the air, all right."

"What does *be neighborly* mean?" Amelia asked, and Dahlia shot her uncle another withering look.

Rider cleared his throat before giving the child a leg up into her small pink saddle. "Never mind all that, Peanut. Now take the reins like I showed you…"

The older cowboy quickly led Amelia and her pony to a smaller corral inside the stables. Which left Connor and Dahlia alone near the horse trailer.

"Sorry you got ditched like that," she said to him. "I'm sure you were pretty excited to score the Twin Kings as a potential client, but, well, my uncle takes his family responsibilities pretty seriously."

"I would've been excited to have anyone as a potential client." Although, there definitely was the potential for some professional recognition if one of the most successful ranches in the state recommended him. "But I never got a chance to get excited because I was still processing it all when I finally put two and two together. I'm guessing there's a reason why you didn't want to give me the heads-up?"

"Yes. Millions of reasons." She didn't expound, but he guessed that she was referring to the financial ones. "Men tend to act differently around me when they know my last name."

He lifted a brow. "Only men?"

"No, but they're typically the ones who are bold enough to actually think that if they can get into my pants, then they can get into my family."

Whoa. Connor's fingers flexed impulsively at her candor. He didn't like the idea of anyone using Dahlia. Or getting into her pants. "If it makes you feel any better, I didn't know you were related to the Kings until right now. But it certainly explains why you were so standoffish before. And why everyone in town clammed up the second I asked about you."

"First, I'm not standoffish. Second, you were asking people in town about me?"

Should he deny it? Connor might not have time to invest in a full-fledged relationship, but he also didn't have time to play games.

"Of course I asked around. I'm not going to pretend that I wasn't interested in you. I still am, even though I'm way more cautious now that I know how it might be perceived." Hearing a whinny and the stomp of an impatient hoof reminded Connor that he wasn't here to flirt with the single mom. "But right now, I need to see to my horse."

Connor hadn't asked Dahlia to keep Goatee in her arms as he unhitched the trailer, but it gave her something to do instead of standing there awkwardly and thinking about his admission that he was in fact interested in her.

Her knees had gone a little wobbly and if more people hadn't been standing around the stables staring at them, she might've made a similar admission. Of course, it didn't help that some smart aleck, probably Finn, had hung up a sign over the entrance to the breeding chute that read Tunnel of Love.

It must be all the equestrian pheromones in the air that were throwing her off balance. Since she had no intention of following her uncle's request to walk him into the enclosure where the waiting mares had already caught Peppercorn's scent, she made her way to the cab of the truck and found a leash for the dog.

The stallion was young and, from the looks of things, eager to strut its stuff in front of his female audience. Connor had to circle the animal around several times to get it calm enough to lead the animal into the enclosure. Mr. Truong and several other experienced handlers watched Connor and the stallion intently, probably in case they needed to jump in and help control the reins.

Dahlia held her breath for a few seconds when Peppercorn reared back on his hind legs, but Connor proved to be more than capable of redirecting the horse. A warmth spread to her lower extremities as she watched him maintain control with a steady hand on the bridle and gentle words in the horse's ear. His command over the situation in the stables suddenly made her wonder if he'd just as easily take charge in other places. Like the bedroom.

Oh, Lord. Dahlia quickly clipped the leash to Goatee's collar and decided to go get some fresh air and cool down before someone confused her for one of the mares in heat.

When she returned an hour later from her walk, Finn had finally arrived and Rider was balancing Amelia on his shoulders as they watched Connor loading a very reluctant stallion into his trailer.

Her family wasn't only sizing up Private Peppercorn, they were sizing up Connor, as well. Seeing how he handled himself. And apparently, they must've approved of something because when Amelia caught sight of her and the dog returning to the stable, she yelled, "Hey, Mommy, Private Peppercorn picked Rita Margarita to be his new girlfriend. Connor's gonna bring him back tomorrow morning to visit again, but Aunt Finn says I don't get to be here for that."

"Aunt Finn is right," Dahlia replied loudly, before murmuring to Goatee. "For once."

"Aunt Finn says that Connor and Goatee can stay and have dinner with us, though."

"As long as Gan Gan doesn't mind," Dahlia replied as she kept her expression neutral. If she hinted at the slightest protest, her family would know something was up. But if she acted happy to have him stay, then he'd get the wrong impression.

"Actually, I should probably get Private Peppercorn home," Connor replied, saving both of them. "He's had a bigger day than I was expecting and needs his rest before he meets Rita Margarita's friends tomorrow."

"Speaking of military ranks, son," Rider said. "What was your MOS when you were in the Corps?"

"Here comes the inquisition," Dahlia murmured to Goatee, while a small part of her hoped the man passed her family's test with flying colors. "Let's see if your owner holds up to the spotlight."

"Initially, I was Infantry. After my three years were up, though, I had a buddy from boot camp who talked me into applying to MARSOC."

"What's MARSOC?" Finn asked.

Rider answered before Connor could. "It stands for Marine Forces Special Operations Command."

"Wait." Dahlia narrowed her eyes. "You didn't tell me you were Special Forces."

"You never asked." He smirked, before returning his attention to her uncle. "I was selected for the Marine Raider Regiment."

Rider let out a whistle. "So you were a Raider. Pretty impressive. Almost as impressive as Private Peppercorn's charm with those mares over there."

"Let me ask you this, Mr. Remington." Finn winked at Dahlia and she knew exactly what was about to come next.

"Please don't..." Dahlia said despite the already sinking sensation in her stomach. But her twin ignored her.

"My sister told me you were new to owning a ranch."

Connor was now staring directly at Dahlia, his knowing smirk making her go weak the knees. She suddenly felt the need to sit down. "I believe the exact term she used was *goat roper*?"

Finn laughed. "Her words. Not mine. But what I wanna know is how does a newbie cowboy who grew up in… Where did you grow up?"

"Primarily Dorchester. We moved around a lot."

"So how does a kid from one of the toughest neighborhoods in Boston know so much about quality horseflesh? Clearly, you picked a winner with your first stud over there."

"When I was an operator, my company commander made us attend a course at the Mountain Warfare Training Center. He wanted us to learn how to hump our supplies into some rough desert terrains we couldn't get to with a Humvee. Turned out I was pretty good with the pack animals and outdoor tracking. Several of us from my unit were integrated with various Army Operational Detachment Alpha teams. As one of the intelligence sergeants, I spent the last two years of my career tracking enemy combatants on horseback."

"Dang," Finn replied. "I knew Dahlia had you all wrong."

Crap. Dahlia usually prided herself on her ability to read people, yet she'd totally missed the mark on him. Although, in her defense, the man didn't really dress like a cowboy. And how was she supposed to know that the military still used horses?

As if the embarrassment and awkwardness coursing through her wasn't enough to make her want to hop in her own truck and take off, the well-dressed and overly protective Sherilee King appeared at the stable doors.

"Dinner was ready ten minutes ago," Dahlia's mother scolded the group still standing around the trailer before her eyes landed on Connor. "Are you who I think you are?"

"Jeez, Mom," Finn chastised the former socialite who was normally well-known for her diplomatic hostessing skills. "Is that any way to greet our new neighbor?"

"Is this Dahlia's new man?" Aunt Freckles appeared behind Sherilee.

"He's not my new—" Dahlia started at the same time Amelia replied. "Yes. This is our new friend Connor and his dog, Goatee. Mommy said they could stay for dinner if it was all right with you, Gan Gan."

"That's not exactly what I said," Dahlia pointed out, not daring so much as a glance in Connor's direction. Her family was overwhelming enough under normal circumstances.

"You might as well join us, Mr. Remington." Sherilee sighed, a rare sign that the perfectly composed King matriarch was at her wits' end. "I mean, why *wouldn't* you want to sit at our table and bear witness to my oldest son arguing legal defenses with his ex-girlfriend. Or enjoy the hospitality of my youngest son pouting while he spends the whole evening texting with his underage drinking buddies about how the Secret Service is trying to ruin his life? Unless, that is, you care at all about your arteries. My *former* sister-in-law made enough fried chicken and country gravy to clog even the healthiest of hearts."

"And *my* former sister-in-law," Freckles countered, "already ate enough biscuits and freshly whipped honey butter to choke a small horse."

"I had half a biscuit, maybe two." Sherliee began launching an intense argument about how stress eating actually burned calories.

Finn, who usually loved watching a good verbal sparring match, used an elbow to nudge Dahlia in the rib cage. "They really know how to sell the King family dining experience, huh?"

Dahlia shook her head, then dared a glance at Connor, whose face was pivoting back and forth as though he were watching a tennis match between the two older women who had never really gotten along.

Pushing through her own growing headache, Dahlia said, "Please don't feel like you have to accept my mother's not-so-tempting invitation. Our family dynamics are a little…off…since my dad passed away, and I'm sure you have more important things going on tonight."

It was a weekend, when most single men in town showed up at Big Millie's. Her manager Rena would've said something if Connor had so much as stepped foot inside the bar. So maybe he was finding his weekend entertainment elsewhere. Not that it was any of Dahlia's business.

"What's more important than getting to know your new neighbors?" Finn asked Connor, although she didn't do that obnoxious wink in Dahlia's direction this time. "You can pull the trailer up to the house and Private Peppercorn should be fine thinking about his fruitful endeavors."

"Plus…" Dahlia's uncle lifted Amelia off his shoulders and easily transferred her onto Connor's before he could object. "My wife makes a mean fried chicken and uses real cream in her mashed potatoes."

Freckles paused mid-argument with Sherilee to point a long acrylic fingernail at Rider. "I'm not your wife anymore, you addle-brained cowboy."

"That's not what you said last night when you snuck out to my cabin."

Dahlia groaned at the implication, Finn covered her ears and made a gagging sound, while Sherilee pinched the bridge of her surgically-enhanced nose.

"Everyone get up to the house before dinner gets

cold," her mother finally snapped. Then she smiled sweetly at Connor. "You, too, son. That's an order."

"Yes, ma'am." Connor did a mock salute, then winked at Dahlia. "How can I refuse an order?"

Chapter Six

How could Connor refuse the order, indeed?

The main house was unlike anything he'd ever seen. He'd entered through the massive kitchen, which was fancy enough to be in one of those magazines his mom used to subscribe to. The formal dining room had a table big enough for thirty and the living room looked like the lobby of a five-star hotel. That is, if five-star hotel lobbies had six-foot tall portraits of a fearsome King ancestor creepily staring down her hawkish nose at him from over the fireplace.

Dahlia's aunt, who insisted he call her Freckles, set up a little cushion beside a water bowl for Goa-

tee. And then she gave Amelia an apple to take outside to Private Peppercorn in the trailer.

Rider had been right. The fried chicken really
was amazing. And Mrs. King had also been right in
asking what was one more person added to the mix.
Besides Dahlia mouthing the word *sorry* to him
several times, he wondered if anyone else noticed
his presence. But that didn't stop him from enjoying the teasing and bickering and liveliness of it all.
Having eaten most of his meals the past few weeks
with just Goatee, Connor sat back and took it all in.

There was so much going on at the table and not
even all of the family was here. Nor did everyone
present make it through the entire meal. When Amelia and Marcus's twin sons went into the kitchen to
help Freckles with dessert, Mrs. King declared she
had a headache and excused herself. Not wanting
to wear out his welcome, Connor said, "I should be
getting my horse home."

"I'll walk you out." Dahlia rose from her seat so
quickly she nearly knocked over her upholstered
chair. Judging by the way her eyes had alternated
between rolling in annoyance at the upscale but
rustic-looking chandelier above and glancing at the
clock on the mantel all throughout dinner, she had
to be eager to see his taillights disappear.

For a second, he thought Goatee would prefer to
stay on as a house dog at the Twin Kings, lounging on his plush pillow and eating the table scraps

Amelia kept sneaking him. But the dog proved to be slightly loyal when he stretched before reluctantly following Connor toward the open entryway and the monstrosity of a front door.

They were on the front porch before Dahlia exhaled a ragged breath. "Sorry for all the drama tonight. My family can be pretty overwhelming. And that's if you know them. I can only imagine how we must look to outsiders."

"I actually enjoyed it," Connor said honestly. "One of my favorite things about living in the barracks was going to the mess hall to eat with everyone. For the most part, when I was growing up, it was just me and my mom. And on the nights she worked, I only had the TV to keep me company."

"What about your dad?" she asked. "Did he ever visit?"

Connor didn't like talking about his father's criminal record under normal circumstances. And standing on the front porch of a prosperous cattle ranch surrounded by Secret Service agents was anything but normal. "He was in and out of the picture. Out of it more often than not. Whenever he'd get released, he'd make all the usual promises about changing for the better, but it never lasted more than a few weeks."

Her full mouth opened, then closed again. He could tell that she wanted to ask him all the questions, and maybe he owed her that, considering many of her family secrets had pretty much been revealed now.

Since he wasn't quite ready to say goodbye, he asked her a question instead. "So Rider and Freckles are divorced, I take it?"

"Correct. Freckles owns a café over in Sugar Falls, Idaho, but she came out for my dad's funeral. We all adore her, but as you witnessed, she and my mom don't get along very well. They never have. I once asked my dad if it was a power struggle thing, with both of them being married to twins, and he told me that they each wished they could be more like the other. I know," she added when Connor tilted his head in confusion. "It's crazy since they're complete opposites. But my dad and Rider were complete opposites, too. Kind of like me and Finn."

"Finn definitely takes after your aunt more." He chuckled, thinking about both women's colorful personalities and irreverent humor.

Dahlia crossed her arms over her chest, which served to lift her breasts higher against her soft gray sweater. "Does that mean you think *I* take after my mom?"

She looked so adorable when her eyes narrowed at him like that, he couldn't help the chuckle escaping his lips. "Not exactly. Your mom seems very... How do I say this tactfully?"

"Controlling?" Dahlia prompted. "Overly concerned about appearances? Calculating? Almost mob boss–like in her ruthless attempts to keep everyone under her thumb?"

This time Connor did laugh. Loudly. "No, she just seems very intent on holding her family together no matter what."

"She is." Dahlia sighed before running her fingers along her scalp and shaking out the curls. "None of us will admit it, but she's usually pretty good at it, too. It's just that her methods can be incredibly frustrating at times. You saw how she was with Marcus and Violet tonight, right? How she finds ways to force them to interact?"

"Yeah, what's the story with them? Were they also married?" This family certainly kept in touch with their exes more than usual. Including Dahlia, who was currently co-parenting with Amelia's father.

"They never married, although I think they came close. Violet was in town for the funeral, which was the same night one of Marcus's deputies arrested MJ for underage drinking." This was the conversation that had dominated the family discussion tonight. "Marcus thinks our eighteen-year-old brother needs to learn a lesson, but my mom hired Violet to represent him in court. So that's why Marcus was in such a bad mood tonight. Although, to be honest, he's been in a bad mood for the past few years."

"And you have another sister? Tessa? Is she that famous news anchor?"

"She's a political analyst. She had a little moment with a Secret Service agent at our father's funeral. It's been all over the news, so she was hiding out here for a while. I'm guessing you haven't been on the internet lately?"

"Only if it involves horse testosterone levels, roof leaks or pasture enclosures." Connor scratched the stubble covering his chin. "Looking back, I should've at least done a simple Google search of your name. Or even Rider's. I mean, obviously I knew who Roper King was and that he was from Wyoming. But I guess I just assumed he'd be buried at Arlington National Cemetery. And that his children would be older. I guess it never registered that the funeral you'd attended the day we met was for the vice president. Although, I'm still kicking myself that I hadn't put two and two together sooner."

"To be honest, it was actually quite refreshing to have someone not know who I was. Or who I was related to." She smiled halfheartedly. "Oh, well. It was nice while it lasted."

"Don't worry. I won't hold all of this—" he gestured at the grand house and the even grander cattle ranch surrounding him "—against you."

"How accepting of you." She lifted one brow and he winked to let her know he was teasing.

Then he counted off on his fingers. "So that's four siblings?"

"Five. My brother Duke had to return to his ship

the week after the funeral. He's a pilot in the Navy and the perfect son. Ask any of my siblings whom they're closest to and they will all say Duke. Probably because he's the most like my dad."

Roper King had been a legend—a war hero and a well-loved leader. "I knew you'd lost your father recently, but I hadn't imagined *that* type of loss."

Now it was Dahlia's turn to tilt her head. "Didn't you tell me your dad had also passed away?"

Connor lifted his face to the clear night sky sprinkled with bright stars. "Yeah, but it wasn't nearly as big of a deal."

"I'm sure it was a big deal to you, Connor. I don't feel my father's loss any more than someone else just because of who he was."

Connor's throat grew heavy, but he swallowed the emotion. "Except I was used to my father leaving and never knowing if he'd return. So when he died, it was almost as though I'd been preparing for it my whole life."

"That's tough." Dahlia nodded knowingly and for a moment, he could almost believe that she hadn't grown up with a life of wealth and privilege. She had such a sympathetic expression as she listened intently. It probably made her a great bartender. "How old were you when your parents split up?"

"Which time?" Connor shoved his hands in his pocket. "The first time I remember him leaving was when I was about Amelia's age. The last time was when I was sixteen."

Right before Steve Remington had died.

"Divorce is so hard on kids." Dahlia exhaled deeply, bringing his attention to the condensation of her breath as it expelled in a long silky cloud from her lips. "I was blessed to have an amazing father. When I ended up pregnant a bit sooner than I—or anyone else—anticipated, it was my bond with my dad that made me vow that I'd never deny Amelia the same opportunity to have a relationship with hers."

The cool night air was thick and heavy between them and he felt like he should say something, but for some reason he held back. He'd already told her more than he'd ever shared with anyone else and she seemed to be lost in her own memories, looking off at the moon in the distance. Besides, his parents had never technically divorced—nor had they valued a healthy relationship with him over the dysfunctional one they shared with each other.

He cleared his throat. "I should probably get back to the Rocking D. Tell your aunt that her fried chicken was the best I've ever had."

"Yeah. I bet you didn't think you'd be getting both dinner and a show tonight. Everyone always expects the Kings to be this perfect version of the all-American family. But when they're behind closed doors, they're usually more than most people bargain for."

Connor grinned. "Once I realized none of the wisecracks or arguments were at my expense, I actually enjoyed your family."

"I'm glad someone did," she replied with a little wave before going back inside.

Connor hadn't been lying. Dinner with the Kings had started off overwhelming, but in the end he'd become mildly entertained and almost flattered that they were comfortable being themselves in front of him.

So much so that he'd felt totally comfortable opening up to Dahlia on the porch about his father. In fact, the only time he'd been uncomfortable all evening was the unexpected uneasiness he'd felt when she'd briefly mentioned her ex-husband. Probably because he didn't know the man and, therefore, couldn't separate the guy from his own experience with having a father so far away. Silently, though, he hoped Micah Deacon was worthy of Amelia's love and Dahlia's dedication to co-parenting.

From where he was standing, though, the man had to be a fool. Because if Connor would have been lucky enough to have Dahlia as his wife, or Amelia as his daughter, he couldn't imagine ever leaving them.

Dahlia had a love-hate relationship with the Spring Fling Festival that took place in the nearby

town of Fling Rock every year on the first weekend of March.

As a child, she'd loved the bright lights of the
Ferris wheel, the thrill of the carnival games and the
towers of fluffy cotton candy she and Finn would
mash into balls before shoving the quickly dissolv-
ing wads of sugar into their mouths.

As a parent, though, she hated the rickety nuts
and bolts of the quickly assembled rides, as well as
the money losing odds of the carnival games. But
she still loved the cotton candy. So much that she'd
invented a signature cocktail at Big Millie's called
the Sweet Circus, a sugar-rimmed martini glass with
a pink candy-flavored vodka. Finn was usually the
only one who ever ordered it.

In fact, it was Finn who'd insisted they bring
Amelia to the festival tonight and promised to go on
all the world-tilting, hair-whipping, nausea-inducing
rides with her. But then her sister had an issue with
an employee's workers comp claim and canceled at
the last minute. Amelia begged to go anyway, and
that was why Dahlia was currently walking down
the midway, trying to patiently explain why they
didn't need to go to the livestock auction scheduled
to start in thirty minutes.

That was also a new development in the love-hate
equation Dahlia now had with the Spring Fling. She
would love seeing the animals with her daughter,

but she would hate telling Amelia no when the child would inevitably insist they take one home.

"Peanut, where would we even put a sheep?" she asked her daughter when those blue eyes threatened to produce a few tears. It was tough to use rational logic with a five-year-old who thought about everything emotionally.

Amelia stopped in her tracks. "How about the parking lot behind Big Millie's? We can build a sheep pen there."

Dahlia was about to look up toward the sky for some sort of divine intervention, but her eyes landed on the cowboy who was waiting for them to move out of the middle of the midway.

"Excuse me, ladies, do you know where I could find a good sheep for my ranch?"

"Connor!" Amelia squealed with joy. Then she quickly scanned the area around his feet. "Where's Goatee?"

"I had to leave him at home. The organizers of the Spring Fling are pretty clear about no pets allowed at the fairgrounds. So I left him with a new squeaky toy and promised to bring him back something."

"Are you really looking for a sheep?" Amelia asked hopefully. "Because they're gonna have an auction and you can buy one right there inside that big red barn."

"I'm thinking about it. But I'm still doing my research." He winked at Dahlia and she was reminded of their conversation on the Twin Kings porch exactly a week ago. Had he finally done an internet search on her family? Her stomach felt like she was back on the Tilt-a-Whirl until he added, "I have several acres of pasture full of weeds that need to be chomped down before Private Peppercorn can get out there and graze on the grass. But then again, Dorsey Tractor Supply has a display of lawn mowers over in the home and garden sec—"

"You don't need a lawn mower." Her daughter jumped up and down before tugging his hand toward the arena. "I know where you can get a sheep instead."

Ha, Dahlia thought as she followed along. Connor might've proven himself when it came to horses, but there was no way he knew what he was about to get himself into. Within ten minutes, Amelia had fallen in love with three potbellied pigs, six dairy calves, two pygmy goats, an angry bighorn ram who Amelia insisted *just needed a hug*, and a forty-five pound turkey who most definitely did not need or want a hug.

"Don't look now." Connor moved behind Dahlia and spoke so low and so close she could feel his warm breath against her ear. A spiral of heat swirled its way from her jaw line to her toes. "But there's a Radical Reptiles snake exhibit just through those open doors. Do you want me to distract her when we go by so she doesn't add a boa constrictor to her list of animals to take home?"

Dahlia threw back her head to laugh, but Connor was so close behind her that her ponytail brushed against his shoulder. She took a step forward too quickly, and her boot heel caught on something in the straw, causing her to stumble.

Connor's firm arm snaked around her waist and hauled her against him. Drawing her in the opposite direction of where she was trying to go. Before she'd lost her footing, she'd been trying to avoid feeling the rounded muscles of his chest against her shoulder blades. But now that she was in this position, she was having a tough time pulling herself away.

He didn't seem to be in any hurry to yank his arm back, either.

Her daughter's eyes were glued to a pair of playful goats inside the pen in front of them, so maybe it wouldn't hurt for Dahlia to lean against Connor for just a few more seconds.

Ever since she saw him interacting with her family on the Twin Kings, she'd been allowing herself to consider Connor Remington in a different light. Not that his admission about being interested in her was some sort of big revelation. It was no secret that they were both attracted to each other. Although, it did make her pulse spike pleasantly when he'd said the words aloud.

No, the change came when he revealed that

he had prior experience with horses. As much as Dahlia hated being wrong about her earlier assessment of him, there was something comforting about the fact that he might actually have a shot at running the Rocking D. And if he was successful, then he might actually stick around. And if he stuck around, perhaps it wouldn't be such a bad thing for Dahlia to get to know him better. For them to explore exactly how deep this mutual attraction of theirs went. For them to get a little closer...

"Mommy," Amelia interrupted her thoughts. "Were you trying to climb into the turkey stall?"

"Huh?" Dahlia blinked several times to clear the confusion. "No, why?"

"Because Connor hadta pull me down, too, when I was getting a closer look at that big sheep with the horns." Her daughter's eyes flicked down to where Dahlia's hand now rested on top of Connor's, which was firmly planted above Dahlia's belt buckle.

When had their fingers gotten intertwined like that?

Connor's thumb lightly stroked another circle over the fabric of her shirt, making the sensitive skin underneath tingle with a delicious heat just before he slowly slid his hand away. "No, your mom was following the rules perfectly. She just tripped on that half-eaten corn dog someone dropped on the ground."

"Oh, no," Amelia gasped. Before Dahlia could

stop her, the girl swooped in to grab the discarded heap of deep-fried batter covered in mustard and bits of straw. "Littering is bad. An animal coulda tried to eat that and would've gotten the broken stick stuck in his throat."

"You're right." Connor deftly retrieved a dark disposable green bag from his back pocket. "I always keep these handy for Goatee. Let me take that and we can go find a trash can."

While Dahlia had been rooted to the ground, letting the panic at being caught in a semi-embrace wash over her, Connor once again sprang into action. Not only had he reacted calmly and quickly, he'd wisely led her daughter in the opposite direction of the Radical Reptile display.

By the time Dahlia caught up with them, she was relieved to see him already helping Amelia get a healthy dollop of hand sanitizer from the complimentary dispenser. As Dahlia watched them, a memory popped in her head of her own dad at the Spring Fling years ago. Dahlia and Finn had made a mess of their cotton candy and their hands were sticking to everything they touched. Roper had picked them up in both arms, walked them over to the open door of the men's room and called out, "Females on deck!"

Their dad had held them for what seemed like forever before several men trickled outside, then he took them into the empty restroom and helped both of the girls scrub all the stickiness from their hands and faces.

Dahlia had always assumed that her dad was so good with kids because he'd already had three of them by the time she and Finn came along. But the more she watched Connor's natural and easy interaction with Amelia, she had to wonder how a man with no kids, who'd only known her daughter for almost two months, could act so…well…fatherly toward her.

No. Amelia already had a father. Micah would've happily taken the messy half-eaten corn dog from their child and then helped her wash her hands. But Micah wasn't here, which made Amelia more susceptible to wanting to fill that void. It was one thing for Dahlia to get physically close to Connor. It was another to let her daughter develop an emotional attachment to him.

"Are you ready to go pick out Connor's sheep now, Mommy?"

Nope, Dahlia wanted to shake her head frantically. She wasn't ready to pick out a sheep and she certainly wasn't ready to encourage any sort of bond between him and her daughter, even a seemingly innocent bond over farm animals. But how did Dahlia explain her adult concerns to a small child?

She couldn't.

So Dahlia did what she always did, she distracted. "How about we get some kettle corn instead?"

And Amelia did what *she* always did. "How about we do both?"

"I think I saw a concession stand by the bidder registration table." Connor wiggled his eyebrows at Dahlia and her pulse skipped a beat when he lowered his mouth next to her ear again. "Not only did your daughter just call your bluff, she followed it up with some double or nothing."

The corners of Dahlia's lips couldn't resist smirking upward. "Oh, we'll see whose bluff gets called when she talks you into buying that ram with anger-management issues."

By the time the three of them made their way to the auction stage with a large bag of popcorn, three lemonades and two candy apples, the surrounding wooden bleachers were completely filled with potential buyers and spectators. In fact, it was so crowded that they had to make their way up the stands to the very back row, and even then Amelia had to sit on Connor's lap because there was only enough space for the two adults.

Luckily, she hadn't recognized anyone from Teton Ridge yet. Not that it should matter.

Dahlia's hip was wedged against Connor's and it took an act of supreme concentration to keep the rest of her thigh and her knee from touching his. Especially since there was barely any space on the narrow foot riser below after they set down their cups of icy lemonade. With the way her daughter was leaning forward excitedly, it would only be so long before the adults' entire bodies were pivoted together to keep Amelia's limbs from bumping into the people around them.

"Oooh, I like that one, Connor." Amelia tried to raise the bidding paddle, but Connor deftly switched it to his other hand, and hid it between his upper leg and Dahlia's. She shivered at the feel of his wrist grazing against her jeans.

If he was equally fazed by the contact, he didn't show it. Instead, he casually explained to her squirming daughter, "That's a pig. We're only interested in the sheep, remember?"

Five minutes later, Amelia tried again. "What about a baby pig? Like a really, really small one?"

"The small ones usually grow up to be big ones. Plus, horses and pigs don't always get along. Private Peppercorn already gets annoyed with Goatee's new obsession with his carrot treats. We don't want to have him fighting with a pig, too."

This prompted a discussion about whether or not the sheep would get along and where everyone would sleep in the barn. Her chatter would only stop each time a new animal came on stage, with Amelia avidly watching the bidding until the auctioneer yelled, "Sold!" Then she'd launch a different discussion.

Each time her daughter asked a new question—which had to be every thirty seconds—Amelia's tiny body would shift, which would cause Connor to bump into Dahlia, which would set off another alarm of sensations throughout her body. After a while, it seemed pointless to hold herself so rigid to avoid making contact with the man. Maybe if she relaxed and let the laws of physics run its course, her body would stop having such an intense reaction to his.

After the pigs paraded through, the goats came next and then the alpacas had their turn on the stage. By the time they got to the cows, Dahlia noticed that Amelia's questions were coming with less frequency and her posture was drooping. When the auctioneer finally announced the first lamb, her daughter was sound asleep, a fistful of buttery popcorn still clutched in her tiny hand and her sticky candy apple–smeared face pressed into the curve between Connor's shoulder and neck.

Dahlia's lungs felt like balloons inflating with way too much helium. It was too late to keep emotions out of it. The damage was done. She didn't think there could possibly be any sweeter sight in the world than her daughter happily exhausted and nestled comfortably in Connor Remington's strong arms.

He must've known the exact minute her carefully built walls began to crack because he caught Dahlia's gaze and whispered, "Should I wake her?"

She shook her head. "No, let her sleep. Unless she's too heavy for you."

Connor smiled. "Not at all. Although, it might help my balance to readjust just a little." His biceps, which up until now had been wedged against hers, eased behind her lower back. "There. That's better."

She gave a pointed look to where his hand casually rested on her opposite hip, then suppressed her own smile. "That was a pretty smooth maneuver."

Pressed against his side like this, she could feel his chest rumble as he chuckled lightly. "Thanks. I've been waiting to do that since they brought out the first goat."

"Only since then?" Dahlia asked, unused to hearing the flirtatious tone in her own voice.

"Okay, so maybe since that first time you and Amelia stopped at my ranch with doughnuts." That magical thumb of his traced a circle on her hip and it felt as though the denim fabric separating their skin would catch on fire. "I mean, I thought about it way before that., But I hadn't really hoped I might have a shot at it until that day."

She lifted her chin, bringing their faces closer together. "And is it everything you'd been hoping for?"

"Yes," he said, then swallowed. "And no. Hold that thought."

The couple who'd been sitting beside them had left and since the crowd had lessened as more and more animals were purchased, she watched him carefully ease Amelia's sleeping form along the bench, the kid-sized puffy blue jacket a pillow under her head and the backrest of the bleachers preventing her from rolling off.

When he turned back to Dahlia, she knew what was coming next. Anticipation rippled through her and she tilted her head up right as he lowered his.

"This is what I was really hoping for."

As soon as he kissed her, there was no denying that was the exact thing she'd been waiting for, as well. And oh, man, her expectations were definitely exceeded. Connor's mouth was firm and agile and tasted like sweet lemonade. When his tongue traced along her lower lip, she eagerly opened up to quench a thirst she hadn't known she had.

Her arms wrapped around his neck to keep her from completely falling into him as her body ached to get closer to his. His fingers splayed along her rib cage, holding her in place as his mouth thoroughly explored hers. When she tilted her head to allow him a deeper angle, he tightened his grip on her waist and yanked her against to him.

They were like two love-starved teenagers making out on the bleachers for all the world to see and Dahlia couldn't remember the last time she'd felt so reckless. So alive. So intoxicated. She couldn't be bothered to think that someone from their town might've been there to see them. All she could think about was how right all of this felt.

"Ladies and gentlemen," the auctioneer's voice rang out on the speakers above them. "This is the last animal of the night."

Connor pulled away and blinked several times before realizing the stands around them were empty. "Oh, no. I missed the sheep I'd wanted to bid on."

"Wait. You really were going to buy a sheep?"

"Yeah. Why wouldn't I?"

She resisted the urge to tap her swollen lips, which still felt as though they were on fire. "I thought you were just trying to make Amelia happy."

"Well, I was. But then I kinda talked myself into it along the way."

"So maybe you could go to one of the livestock auctions in Riverton," she suggested. "They have them once a month."

"That won't work. When Amelia wakes up, she'll ask why we didn't get one here. And do you want me to answer honestly and say it was because I couldn't keep my hands or my mouth off her hot mom?"

His tongue was skilled in more ways than one. Her heart was already skipping beats from his kisses. Now it threatened to shut down completely at his smooth words. Nobody had ever called her a *hot mom*, at least not to her face. And they certainly had never been equally as passionate about their commitments to her daughter.

Connor didn't release her hip as he leaned forward and squinted at the stage. "Now which one is left?"

Chapter Seven

"So how'd you end up with this feathered friend?" Dr. Roman asked when she made a house call on Monday to check on Peppercorn after his busy week at the Twin Kings. "I thought you were only setting up for horses out here."

Connor was still kicking himself over that acquisition. He hadn't been in the market for a sheep, let alone a damn turkey. In fact, the only reason he'd gone to the Spring Fling Festival was because Finn King said it would be a great opportunity to network with other ranchers from western Wyoming and eastern Idaho who'd traveled there every year for the event. She'd been right, although he now had a feeling that she'd also had ulterior motives.

Connor had met several other horse breeders at the rodeo exhibit and was about to drive back to the ranch when he caught sight of Amelia and Dahlia getting off the Tilt-a-Whirl. Sure, he'd run into them around the town of Teton Ridge before so running into them there wasn't shocking in and of itself. What had made his own heart tilt and whirl, though, was the realization that seeing them *away* from town had—for the first time in his life—made him feel as if he was finally home. As if he was finally ready to put down even more roots and invest himself into the ranch both physically and emotionally.

Buying a sheep seemed like a good way to further develop his holdings here at the Rocking D while simultaneously making Amelia happy. But unlike his adoption of Goatee, he couldn't totally blame the King-Deacon women for suckering him into this unexpected and very unnecessary acquisition.

He took off his hat and scratched his head before answering the vet. "I picked him up at the livestock auction at the Spring Fling Festival in Fling Rock."

"I love that festival. We take our grandkids every year." The vet jerked a thumb toward the chicken coop, which Connor had spent the rest of the weekend repairing. "And every year we see the same

Bourbon Red that never gets a single bid. I think he's getting bigger with age."

Great. Now Connor was the sucker who'd brought home a turkey nobody else wanted. Although it hadn't taken him long to figure out why the auctioneer had been so surprised to see his paddle in the air.

"Not only does the thing poop all over the place, he squawks and pecks at any human or animal that comes within a five-foot radius." Connor held up his bandaged left hand. "He did this when I was trying to let him out of his transportation cage."

Yet, the look on Amelia's face when she found out that Connor had *rescued* one of her favorite animals made the injury and the headache from the bird's nightly serenade of angry gobbles worth it.

And that amazing kiss he'd shared with Dahlia on the bleachers had been worth at least three more turkeys just like this one.

"How's his diet?" the vet asked.

"He eats anything he can get his beak on. Goatee was sniffing around a little too close to the chicken wire yesterday afternoon and now I can't find the little metal name tag that used to hang on his collar."

"Uh-oh. That might explain why he's so cranky."

"No, he was cranky well before he got here."

"Mind if I give him a sedative and try to do a quick examination?" the vet asked, but she was already pulling on a pair of latex gloves.

Connor couldn't help but wonder if there'd be an extra charge for that since this would be the second animal on his ranch she'd be seeing today. He'd already dropped a hundred bucks on the turkey and another three hundred on feed and fencing supplies to repair the coop when it became apparent that Peppercorn would kick out his stall door if he had to share the barn with the hot-tempered turkey on the opposite side of the stables.

Connor said a silent prayer of thanks that Peppercorn had several more live covers booked for this week and he was starting to see a return on his investment. Then he told Dr. Roman, "Knock yourself out. But I've got a load of hay arriving right now so I hope you brought some tranquilizer darts."

"I always come locked and loaded," she replied as she walked to the small mobile clinic trailer she towed behind her SUV.

The delivery truck from the feed store pulled up beside them and when the young driver climbed out, Dr. Roman asked, "No practice today, Keyshawn?"

"Nope. We didn't even make the playoffs this year. So my dad is having me do deliveries after school until baseball starts up next week."

Keyshawn Fredrickson was tall and muscular and, according to his dad Freddie, had recently gotten a full academic scholarship to Howard University. He'd also been one of the teenagers who'd come over with Luis Ochoa, Tomas's son, to help repair the fence. In addition to getting a sturdy enclosure for his pasture, Connor also got to hear about the drama surrounding the Teton Ridge High School basketball coach being fired during the back half of the season.

Connor might've only been in town six weeks, but he already knew all the local gossip. Unless it had to do with the Kings. Nobody had bothered to fill him in on any of that. He picked up a pair of hay hooks to help Keyshawn unload the bales of alfalfa.

"Whoa, is that the mean old turkey from Spring Fling?" The teenager paused with only one hook under the bale wire as he gaped in surprise at the vet entering the chicken coop.

Connor felt a resigned groan vibrate against the back of his throat before admitting, "That's the one. I'm guessing you're familiar with him, too."

"I won my girlfriend a goldfish at the Sink-A-Hoop game and as we're walking through the live-stock arena, that crazy dude poked his wrinkly bald head between the slats and ate my girlfriend's gold-fish. Tore right through the plastic bag and swal-lowed the thing whole. Then he almost ripped my thumb off when I tried to wrestle the bag away from him."

Connor again held up his bandaged hand. "Tell me about it."

The squawking started immediately and was fol-lowed by intense wing flapping. Connor was about to sprint over to the coop when he saw the flash of a syringe in the vet's hand and then the large bird flopped over in a heap of reddish brown feathers.

"He's a bit heavier than I was expecting," the vet called over to them. "If one of you can help me get him into the trailer, I have an ultrasound machine that might give me a better idea of what's going on."

"Man, Doc Roman is a badass," Keyshawn said after Connor helped her load the turkey onto the stainless-steel table in her tricked-out mobile clinic. "There's no way you could pay me to go into an enclosed space with that thing. Even if it's passed out cold."

"Who's passed out cold?" a little voice said and Goatee ran off the porch with an excited yip.

Connor had been so focused on getting the turkey into the mobile clinic without accidentally waking it that he hadn't heard Dahlia's truck pull into the drive.

"This crazy bird Mr. Remington found at the Spring Fling." Keyshawn answered.

"Oh, you mean Gobster?" Amelia smiled to reveal a new missing tooth. "Connor won him 'cause he was the highest bidder."

"Wait, you actually paid money for that thing?" Keyshawn's head whipped around to Connor, who would've felt suitably embarrassed if he wasn't feeling a rush of excitement at seeing Dahlia walking toward them. "And what kind of name is Gobster, anyway?"

"It's short for Gobble Monster," Amelia said. "I wanted to name him General Gobble 'cause Connor's horse has a soldier name, too. But Connor said he definitely didn't earn *that* rank. Look, we got him a silver ID tag to match Goatee's, but we haven't found a collar small enough for him."

Connor winced. He was *not* looking forward to the moment when Amelia noticed that Goatee's ID tag was now missing. As the girl continued talking to Keyshawn while he unloaded the hay, Connor used the opportunity to talk to Dahlia alone.

"Hey," he said. Because they weren't truly alone.

"Hi. Sorry for dropping in on you again like this, but I still don't have your number. Not that you need to give it to me. I mean, I know we, uh, you know, on Saturday night. But I don't want you thinking that *I'm* thinking that totally changes things between us or that I'm expecting you to give it to me. It's just that if I had it, I could've warned you that Amelia was insisting we stop by on our way to her riding lesson and check on the turkey."

"Dahlia," he replied when she took a short pause from her adorably sweet and nervous rambling. "We kissed on Saturday night."

Her eyes darted to where Keyshawn was telling Amelia about the biggest chicken he'd ever seen. But the blush that stole up her cheeks made her pretty pink lips seem that much more kissable. "Yes. That's what I said."

"No. You said we *uh, you know*. And I just wanted it to be super clear that we kissed and that I enjoyed it and that I would even like to do it again. Right this second, in fact. But I have a feeling you might not think now is the best time, what with the town veterinarian and the feed store owner's teenage son here to see us. So, please take my number and maybe we can find another time to make that happen. Soon."

"Well, I think I found the problem." Dr. Roman came out of the back of her trailer, and Keyshawn took a few steps closer to Connor. "It appears that the turkey has what looks to be a broken piece of wood lodged in its upper intestine. Almost looks like half of a Popsicle stick."

"The missing part of the corn dog!" Amelia shouted. Then her face went pale. "Is Gobster gonna die?"

"We should only be so lucky," Keyshawn mumbled, which Amelia thankfully did not hear. Connor nudged the teen with his elbow, and the young man scrunched his face. "What? You don't celebrate Thanksgiving?"

"I don't think he'll die," Dr. Roman said. "I can give him some medicine to help him pass the stick."

"You mean like poop it out?" Amelia asked rather

loudly. Keyshawn laughed and Dahlia pinched the bridge of her nose.

"Exactly," Dr. Roman told the child. "If he can't pass it by himself, then I can do a surgical procedure to retrieve it."

"Will it hurt him?" Amelia asked, her eyes full of alarm.

"Not as much as pooping it out would," Keyshawn answered.

"Then we should do it," Amelia declared.

Dahlia sighed. "Peanut, Gobster is Connor's turkey. He gets to make the decision about what's best for the animal."

Connor wasn't prepared to make this kind of decision. His eyes sought Dahlia's, but her only response was to lift one of her shoulders in doubt. Did he really want to shell out more money for the opportunity to keep a mean turkey around to continue wreaking havoc on his ranch?

"What's the success rate on an operation like this?" Connor asked.

Dr. Roman's lips pressed together in a crooked line, as though she were trying to keep a straight face. Finally, she said, "Well, I don't usually do surgery on a turkey. Why don't I give him some medicine for his digestive tract and see if that takes care of the problem naturally."

"As much as I'd like to hang around and see that,"

Keyshawn said, his face scrunched into a look of disgust. "I've got one more delivery to make."

The teen drove off, and Amelia followed the vet into the back of her mobile clinic, asking a million questions a minute.

By the time Gobster was returned to the coop— still sleeping, thankfully—and Dahlia was done putting away instruments and sterilizing everything Amelia had touched in the mobile clinic, Dr. Roman seemed more than eager to be on her way.

The dust was still settling on the driveway that led from the Rocking D to the highway when Amelia slipped her tiny palm into Connor's hand and said, "I hope Gobster is all better by Friday."

"Why Friday?" Connor asked, thinking there was no way it could take that long.

"That's the day of the father-daughter dance at my school and I want you to take me."

Dahlia's stomach felt as though someone had dropped a bale of hay on her midsection. And it didn't help that Connor's normally suntanned face had gone slightly pale.

"Amelia," Dahlia chided, her breath rushing out of her chest. "That's probably not something Connor would be comfortable doing."

"Oh. You don't know how to dance?" Amelia blinked at him. "I could teach you."

Connor knelt down to her daughter's eye level,

and Dahlia braced herself for Amelia's impending disappointment, no matter how polite the man was when he declined.

"I'm flattered that you invited me," he started before his eyes flicked up to Dahlia's, as though seeking her approval to break her child's heart. All Dahlia could do was nod. After all, she'd brought Amelia out here unannounced, putting them both in this uncomfortable situation. Connor continued, "Wouldn't you rather your dad take you to the dance?"

"Daddy is working and can't come. Besides, Miss Walker said it doesn't have to be a dad that comes with us. We can bring any grown-up we want and I wanna bring you."

This wasn't the first time Micah couldn't be here for an important event and Dahlia and Amelia were no strangers to making the best of it. "Peanut, why don't you ask Uncle Marcus or Uncle Rider to go with you?"

"'Cause Uncle Marcus has been grumpy since Grandpa's funeral. Jack and Jordan said it's 'cause he's secretly in love with Miss Violet. And last time Uncle Rider came to my school, Peyton said he looked like Santa Claus and then all the kids ran over to him and he didn't even get to hear the holiday song our class worked so hard on."

Connor lifted an eyebrow in Dahlia's direction and she nodded. "It's true. Rider showed up for the

Winter Wonderland performance last December wearing a red flannel shirt and the kindergarteners mobbed him. It was quite the scene."

"But Connor is the same years old as the other dads at my school." Amelia pointed to the Def Leppard T-shirt. "And he wears the same shirts like *my* daddy."

Dahlia would be lying if she hadn't also noted the similar tastes in classic rock fashion between the rancher and her ex-husband. But none of the other fathers at Teton Ridge Elementary—including Micah Deacon—were as good-looking as Connor.

"Come back, Goatee." Amelia took off running toward the dog who'd mustered up the courage to cautiously approach the chicken coop. "Gobster can't play right now. He's sleeping so he can go poop before Connor takes me to the father-daughter dance."

"Sounds like she isn't going to take no for an answer." Connor stood and ran his hand through his close-cut auburn hair.

"She usually doesn't. But don't worry. I'll talk to her tonight and find someone else to go with her."

"Like your little brother, MJ?" Connor asked.

Dahlia tipped back her head to stare at the clouds forming in the sky, as though an answer would fall down and land on her like a raindrop. "No, not him. You know how MJ got arrested and charged with drunk and disorderly? He happened to be with Kendra Broman at the time of his arrest, and her father, Deputy Broman, will most likely be at the dance with his younger girls. He still hasn't forgiven MJ for resisting arrest. I'd ask Mike Truong to take her, but he'll be going with his daughter." Now Dahlia was just thinking out loud. "Maybe one of the Secret Service agents still assigned at the ranch could take her."

"Or perhaps the friendly and personable Mr. Burnworth from the bakery," Connor suggested sarcastically—or at least she hoped he was being sarcastic—before shoving his hands in his pockets. "Anyone but me, huh?"

Great, now she'd insulted him again. "I'm trying to get you off the hook here, Connor. You've already done enough for Amelia with the stray dog and then the turkey. You don't need to take this on, as well."

"What if I want to go?"

Her heart caught in her throat, but then her brain shoved it back down as her senses went on high alert. *What's in it for you?* she almost asked. Instead, she narrowed her eyes. "Why would you offer?"

"Because I grew up knowing what it was like to be the only Cub Scout without an old man at the pinewood derby, or the third wheel with some other father-son team on the annual jamboree camping trip."

The red flag warnings inside her head immediately turned to white in surrender. A second ago, she'd been willing to send Amelia to the dance with a Secret Service agent, just so her daughter wouldn't feel left out. But that would only make them all stand out. Maybe going with Connor wasn't such a bad idea.

Amelia adored him and talked about him so much that people in town were already making assumptions about them. Hell, the guy had bought a stupid turkey at a livestock auction just to make her daughter happy. Then he'd paid to have the veterinarian come out to his ranch to examine the thing instead of ringing its neck, plucking it and turning it into his Sunday supper.

And Dr. Roman wasn't cheap. Dahlia had certainly paid more than her fair share of vet bills with all of Amelia's strays. So maybe Connor really was doing this out of the goodness of his heart.

Still. She had to give him one more opportunity to back out gracefully. "I should warn you that there will be lots of over-sweetened punch and pink cupcakes and Taylor Swift songs at this event."

"Doesn't sound much different from my usual Friday night." Connor smiled. "What time should I pick her up?"

Maybe there really was something about Remingtons knowing when they'd found "the one." Or the one*s* plural where the Deacon-King women were concerned. Because Connor was getting to a point where he couldn't explain this persisting connection he felt with both of them.

"How did you get yourself into this mess?" he asked his reflection in the dusty mirror above Aunt Connie's antique dresser as he knotted, undid, and then re-knotted the only non-military issued tie he owned. One minute, he'd been warning himself not to get too attached to Dahlia, and the next minute he'd practically jumped at the chance to take Amelia to the father-daughter dance.

A couple of hours later, Connor realized he wasn't the only man in town who was questioning how he'd landed himself in this situation.

"Got roped into playing rent-a-dad, I see," Deputy Broman said, raising his voice over the sound of a dance floor full of giggles and the latest Katy Perry song blasting out of the hired DJ's speakers.

Connor had met the man at Biscuit Betty's the first week he'd been in town. The deputy had been polite enough at the time, expressing his condolences about the loss of Aunt Connie and asking how Connor was settling in at the Rocking D. Then, after noticing Connor's Air Jordans, he'd made a not-so-subtle suggestion to stop by the new rec center in town to play a few games of pickup basketball.

But now the man's words were more insulting than challenging.

"Looks like your eye has healed up nicely," Connor replied, purposely referencing the shiner young MJ had landed when he'd resisted arrest.

"Humph. Kid's lucky his big brother is my boss. Or else he would've had more than a dislocated shoulder after getting my daughter drunk like that. The whole damn family is nuts if you ask me."

Connor hadn't asked him. But that didn't stop him from standing there silently and gathering intel. The dance had reached the point in the evening when most of the men were gathering on the sidelines, looking at their watches and asking their buddies the score of the UW game. Most of the girls were still swirling around the gym floor in big groups with their friends, their sugar highs peaking from all the buttercream frosting and fruit punch.

"Here, Connor, can you hold these for me?" Amelia shoved her glitter-encrusted silver shoes at him before running barefoot back to the center of the dance floor where a pile of pink and white balloons were being used as an impromptu trampoline. He added the shoes to the purple cardigan, white-sequined headband and rainbow unicorn purse already shoved under his left arm.

"She's a cute kid," the deputy continued. "Looks just like her dad, too. My cousin went to high school with Micah and played some jam sessions with him back in the day. I mean, I get that he has this big career and stuff, but it's just weird, you know."

Connor hated that his interest was piqued. But that didn't stop him from asking, "What's weird?"

"That he would've just taken off for Nashville and left his wife and kid here."

Wife? Connor swallowed the bitterness in the back of his throat. "I thought he and Dahlia were divorced?"

"Only because the rest of the Kings pushed so hard for it. If it had been me, I would've stayed here and fought for my kid. I mean, not to the level of Jay Grover over there." Broman jerked his chin at Amelia's friend Peyton's dad, who'd spent half the evening arguing on the phone with his divorce attorney and the other half complaining about his bitter custody case with any unsuspecting dad who walked by the punch bowl. "But I certainly wouldn't be riding around the country in a tour bus while some guy off the street waltzes in and takes over my parental role."

"I'm not taking over any role." Connor's shoulders jerked back instinctively, but he maintained his grip on his colorful collection of discarded accessories. "Amelia still has a father. He just isn't here right now."

"Don't get so defensive." Broman held up his palms. "You see a hot single mom and a kid who's so desperate for attention she talks to every stray animal who comes along. I don't blame you for wanting to step up and do the right thing. Plenty of guys would love to be in your shoes right now. Or at least they think they would until they find out what they're getting into."

Connor was seriously starting to get annoyed with people in this town making assumptions about him. His voice was tense when he asked, "Is this the part of the conversation where you tell me what I'm getting into?"

"Look, man," the deputy said right as the last song of the night ended. "I'm just trying to help."

"Help what?" Amelia asked from just a few feet away. The balloon in her hands was sagging almost as much as her eyelids, the sugar rush finally wearing off.

"Carry you to the truck," Connor said before using his free arm to scoop her up onto his hip. She immediately let her cheek fall on his shoulder.

"You don't need any help carrying me, Connor." Amelia yawned. "You're stronger than Gray Goose. And he's the biggest pony at the Twin Kings."

They were halfway across the parking lot when Deputy Broman and three of his daughters pulled up beside them in the Ridgecrest County patrol unit.

"Hey, kid," Broman called out his window, causing Amelia to sleepily lift her head. "Next time you talk to your *dad*, tell him I said hi."

Connor's fists clenched at the man's purposeful tone when he'd said the word *dad*. He had to practically shake out his knuckles before he started acting like angry Jay Grover back inside the gymnasium.

Instead of agreeing to pass along the message, Amelia just nuzzled against Connor's shoulder and mumbled, "I don't like that policeman. I wish Uncle MJ was allowed to punch him again."

Connor's chest shook from the laughter he tried to hold in. Apparently, Amelia wasn't that starved for attention, because she certainly recognized an antagonistic jerk when she saw one. As his smile faded, though, he wondered if she also recognized an envious jerk when she saw one, too. Not that Connor was actually jealous of Micah—a man he'd never even met.

But something about Broman's words had stirred to life an overwhelming sense of protectiveness toward the child. Connor had never experienced a paternal instinct like he had back inside that dance.

He wanted to be the one to protect Amelia, and he wanted everyone else in town to know it.

Chapter Eight

"Looks like the night was a success," Dahlia said as Connor carried a sleeping Amelia through her front door.

"I hope so," he whispered, following her down the hall to the bedrooms. "We all made it out in one piece, although the last time I saw my tie it was being used as the pole for the limbo contest."

Her heart melted at the tender way he carefully tucked her daughter into the twin-sized bed. When he returned from his second trip from his truck downstairs, everything inside her turned into a complete puddle of sappy mush.

"It's so loud downstairs at the saloon right now.

How do you guys get any sleep on weekends?" Connor asked as he crossed the threshold. Amelia's zebra-print booster seat was secured in one of his arms while the strap of the rainbow unicorn purse was falling off the opposite muscular shoulder. He dropped the sparkly shoes, hair bow and purple cardigan in a pile on the entry table and Dahlia thought her knees were going drop, as well.

"Like this." She closed the thick front door behind him. "I paid a fortune to soundproof the floor and walls. Can I offer you a drink? I have beer and wine or even fruit punch if you haven't gotten enough of that tonight."

"I would love a beer," he said, looking much more rumpled than when he'd arrived on their doorstep a few hours ago. His hair was barely mussed, but the sleeves on his now-wrinkled white dress shirt were rolled up and his gray slacks sported a pink frosting stain down the front. "In fact, I was surprised that the booster club at the school wasn't selling adult beverages at the dance. They could've raised so much money."

She retrieved two bottles of Snake River Pale Ale from her kitchen fridge before meeting him in the living room. "Plenty of other dads have suggested the same thing."

His eyes flashed with something—anger, frustration, annoyance...she wasn't sure—before he quickly blinked the emotion back and schooled his features. He took the beer from her hand and slumped onto her sofa. "Then I'll leave it to the *other dads* to bring it up to the booster club."

Dahlia could've sat in one of the custom uphol-stered chairs opposite him, but after making out with the guy on some bleachers and sending her daughter to a school dance with him, purposely dis-tancing herself from him would've seemed entirely too formal at this point. She chose the corner of the sofa beside him and asked, "Why did you say it like that?"

"Because I'm just a rent-a-dad, as someone pointed out tonight. So I don't really get a vote in the matter."

The muscles recoiled in Dahlia's shoulders. "Who would say something like that? Did Ame-lia hear them?"

"No. I would've probably given him another black eye if he'd said it in front of her." Connor tilted the beer to his mouth, and even though his frame was casually lounging against the decora-tive throw pillows, his knuckles were white from clenching the bottle so hard. "Maybe I still will if I ever play against him on the basketball court and he has his uniform off."

Realization crossed her expression, and Dahlia pulled her legs onto the sofa and tucked her bare feet under her. "Deputy Broman is such an ass."

"But he wasn't wrong." Connor's head fell to the

side as he turned his face to her. "I'm not a dad or even a relative. Which is fine. I'm not looking to replace anyone. But something about the way he said it just didn't sit well, you know? Like he was trying to put me in my place."

"Broman has had a chip on his shoulder ever since Marcus beat him in the election for sheriff. How does he know what your place is?"

"What *is* my place, Dahlia?" Connor shifted his torso, extending his arm to drape along the back cushions of the couch as he studied her.

She wasn't going to pretend like she didn't know exactly what he was asking. She'd spent the entire week since their kiss at the Spring Fling asking herself the same question. "I haven't figured that out yet. What do you want it to be?"

"I like spending time with you and Amelia. In fact, I'd like to spend even more time with you. But if things don't work out, it could be complicated."

"If things *do* work out, it could be just as complicated." Dahlia bit her lower lip, surprised she was open to the possibility in the first place. She'd only dated once since her divorce and that had been a disaster.

"How complicated?" he asked, dropping his hand so that the tips of his fingers were resting on her shoulder. A shiver radiated through her at his slight touch.

"I'm not just a single mom, Connor, all on my

own. Amelia and I might be a package deal, but my ex-husband is still a big part of our lives, and he always will be. Then there's my family. You might think that going to dinner at the ranch every once in a while is a fun spot of entertainment, but they actually can be a lot to handle."

He leaned forward to set his empty bottle of beer on the coffee table. "It's true that I don't need any extra complications right now."

Instead of getting up and leaving, though, he slid his body closer to hers. Dahlia's breath suspended while her pulse picked up speed.

"But you've seen my ranch. I don't know how to back down from a challenge. When I'm hot on the trail of something…" his voice was low and direct and sent a thrill all the way to her toes "…the twists and turns and roadblocks along the path aren't a deterrent for me. Only an enhancement on the way to my goal."

His lips lowered to hers, his mouth capturing Dahlia's breathy exhale.

Connor had only intended to kiss Dahlia briefly, just to confirm that after everything that had happened tonight with Deputy Broman, their attraction was still strong enough to steer them both down this trail together.

But this kiss was even hotter and more intense than the previous one. He'd barely begun exploring

Dahlia's mouth when she shifted her back against the arm of the sofa, sinking lower into a reclined position as her lips slanted over his, her tongue inviting him to delve deeper. Her hands slid across his shoulders until they were firmly planted on his upper back, encouraging him to follow her lead and lower himself until he was balanced on his elbows over her.

She brought one knee up alongside his waist, moaning deeply as his hips settled between her legs. His arousal pressed against the confines of his zipper as she arched against him and groaned.

Finding the hem of her shirt, Connor eased his hand underneath, the heat of her silky smooth skin skimming his palm as he maneuvered the snug fabric higher until he could cup her breast. Dahlia's moans turned into little pants as he used his thumb to trace circles around her tightened nipple.

When Connor had kissed Dahlia at the livestock auction, he'd been limited by the narrow bleachers and the public venue. Now, though, fully stretched out on her living room sofa, there was nothing stopping them from taking things to the next level. His body was already thrumming with anticipation.

Except, just like last time, Amelia was still asleep nearby. The realization made him lift his head and pull back slightly. Dahlia's lips were swollen and her lashes slowly fluttered open. "What's wrong?"

"Amelia could wake up at any moment and come in here and see us."

Dahlia's face lost some of its rosy glow. "If we go to my room, you could sneak out before she gets up in the morning."

"You have no idea how much I want to carry you to your bed right now." He groaned as he dragged himself away from her and plopped onto his side of the sofa. "But if we sleep together, I don't want there to be any sneaking around."

"That's fair," she replied, pulling her top down, which only emphasized the erect state of her nipples. His own chest swelled with pride that he'd been the cause of her arousal. Then it quickly grew hollow when he realized she wasn't going to insist that they didn't have to sneak around. Instead, she asked, "So we just go back to running into each other around town and pretending none of this happened?"

"Only until you realize that you want something more." His hand shot through his hair, trying to smooth it into place after the way she'd run her fingers over it.

"You seem pretty confident that I'm going to come to that realization." Her eyes traveled down the length of him, and Connor stood still, holding back a smile as she boldly assessed him. She would've had him questioning himself if her pink lips weren't so puffy and her pupils weren't still dilated.

"A man can hope, can't he?" He bent down to give her a quick parting kiss. He couldn't risk letting his mouth linger and still walk out of her apartment with full control of his libido.

If he was going to sleep with Dahlia, he needed her to be absolutely sure. Because once Amelia found out about them, there'd be no going back.

Dahlia stayed awake long after Connor left on Friday night, wondering if she should've convinced him to stay the night. In the end, though, he'd done the honorable thing by leaving. Plus, she'd never been very good at sneaking around. That had been Finn's specialty growing up. Dahlia had always been afraid of getting caught.

She'd barely fallen asleep before dawn when the theme song from *Top Gun* jarred her awake. She recognized the ringtone and reached for her smartphone.

Before she could say hello, her brother Duke asked, "Permission to buzz the flight tower?"

The phrase from their favorite movie was their inside joke and they used it instead of saying, "Brace yourself for this." Dahlia groaned and pulled the down comforter over her head. Last time Duke had asked to buzz the flight tower, it was to tell her that Uncle Rider had invited Aunt Freckles to the Twin Kings for their dad's funeral.

It had only been a couple of months since then, and the King family had been even more turned upside down since Tessa had been stranded at the ranch with that sexy Secret Service agent. Her sister had been so secretive about things before she'd left, Dahlia still had no idea if she'd decided to pursue anything with the guy. Then there was MJ's arrest and Marcus dealing with his ex-girlfriend staying in town to defend their baby brother. Dahlia didn't think she could handle any more King family drama. She pushed her hair out of her sleepy eyes before replying, "Negative, Ghostrider. The pattern is full."

Duke chuckled. "Well, I hope you have a huge cup of coffee because the controls are out of my hands on this one."

"Who messed up this time? Finn? Mom? Certainly not you."

"Of course not me," Duke snorted. "I'm the golden child, remember?"

"You never let us forget." Although, last time Duke had left town, something had been going on between him and his husband, Tom. Even Tessa, who'd been dealing with her own relationship issues, had commented on Tom leaving the Twin Kings a week before Duke had. But their brother was the family mediator and was always too busy working through everyone else's problems to bring any attention to his own. "So what's the latest gossip?"

"I got an email from Kenneth P. Burnworth about an hour ago."

"Mr. Burnworth?" Dahlia shot up in bed. "Since when does my annoying and grouchy neighbor from the bakery email you?"

"Since Tom and I hired him to do our wedding cake a few years back. Anyway, seeing as how I'm his favorite King at the moment, he thought I should know that Jay Grover was in the bakery this morning telling everyone that some hotshot new rancher out at the Rocking D took Amelia to the father-daughter dance last night."

"Well, he did." It wasn't like Dahlia expected it to be kept a secret. Nothing traveled faster than the news posted to the Teton Ridge Elementary Booster Club social media page. "And his name's Connor, by the way."

"Yeah, Uncle Rider told me about him last month. What's his deal?"

"Connor inherited the Rocking D from his great-aunt Connie. He's a horse breeder and Rider asked him to bring his stallion out to Twin Kings."

"I meant what's his deal as far as it relates to my niece? And to you, I guess. But especially to my niece."

"It's so nice to be loved, big brother." Dahlia

rolled her eyes. "Anyway, you know about the white stray dog and how we met, right?"

"Yeah, that all happened before I had to return to my ship. I remember being at Big Millie's that night with Tessa and her Secret Service agent when you told everyone you weren't interested in the guy."

Dahlia collapsed on the fluffy pillows. "Well, he's starting to grow on me."

"You know who he's not growing on?" Duke asked, but didn't wait for a response. "Mr. Burnworth. Your neighbor doesn't think it's natural for a grown man to be bringing a dog all around town with him. He thinks Connor is using the mutt to win favor with Amelia, which will in turn win favor with you, which will in turn get him one step closer to your trust fund and the deed to Big Millie's. Mr. Burnworth doesn't like having you as a neighbor, but…how did he phrase it… He'd rather trust the devil he knows than the one he doesn't."

That sounded like something her neighbor would've said. Despite their businesses running on completely different schedules, the older man's chief concern was that she'd expand the saloon into something bigger and drive away his customers. "So what did you reply to Mr. Burnworth?"

"I told him that I'd like to order five dozen of his famous chocolate chip muffins to be shipped to my squadron. I'm not going to argue with the best baker in Wyoming."

"You don't argue with anyone, Duke."

Her brother's pause was longer than she expected—even with him using the spotty reception onboard the aircraft carrier. Finally, he sighed before saying, "Depends on who you ask."

"Talk to me, Goose," Dahlia said, using another line from their favorite movie. "Is everything okay with you and Tom?"

Duke cleared his throat. "Yeah, we've just had some challenges with my latest deployment. It's what we signed up for, though, right? Look, I've got to meet my squadron in the ready room for a briefing. I just wanted to give you the heads-up that people are talking. Give Amelia a kiss from her favorite uncle."

The call disconnected, and Dahlia burrowed under her covers for a few more minutes before hearing the unmistakable clanging of pots and pans tumbling out of the kitchen cupboard.

"I'm okay," Amelia called down the hallway, but Dahlia was already out of bed.

"I hope you're not using the stove without permission," she said to her daughter as she trudged barefoot into the kitchen on the cold hardwood floors.

"No, Mommy. I'm just getting everything ready to make you and Connor pancakes."

Dahlia had to do a double take around the living room and entryway to make sure she hadn't missed something. Namely, an early-morning visit from an unexpected rancher. "Peanut, Connor's not here."

Amelia's lower lip curled downward. "But I thought he was gonna sleep over."

"Why would you think that?"

"Because Peyton's mom has a boyfriend and sometimes he spends the night at their house. Peyton's dad got real mad at her mom's boyfriend at the bake sale and dumped a tray of fudgy bars right over his head. But I don't think my daddy would dump fudgy bars on Connor's head."

"No, I don't think he would, either," Dahlia agreed, hoping she wasn't lying. But how was she supposed to know what would happen if Micah and Connor ever met? How they would react to each other. She'd like to think they'd get along, but she'd owned a bar long enough to see what happened to men when they got competitive or when their heated emotions got the best of them.

It was one of those unknown complications she'd mentioned to Connor last night. If they took their relationship to the next level and then things didn't work out, how would Amelia react?

It was why Dahlia hadn't seriously dated anyone since her divorce. Sure, there was Seth, the drummer from Tectonic Shift who'd tried to *comfort her* after she and Micah first split. But Amelia had still been a baby and Dahlia had soon realized what Seth's real intentions were. In hindsight, the experience had been a wake-up call for her. It had also cemented in the fact that Micah, despite their amicable divorce, would always put Dahlia and Amelia first. Even over his own band. Which made it that much easier for Dahlia to get along with her ex-husband and foster that bond between him and his child.

But this was different. Amelia was older and Connor's intentions—judging by his reoccurring thoughtfulness for her daughter, as well as his restraint last night—might actually be honorable. If things didn't work out with Connor, though, she wouldn't have the same compelling reason keep him in Amelia's life. Her daughter didn't necessarily need another father figure.

Dahlia bit her lower lip. Would it be worth the risk? Only time would tell.

Damn.

Sometimes being a grown-up sucked.

Chapter Nine

"With Tessa and Duke both gone now," Freckles told Dahlia that Saturday evening, "having the kids all spend the night here will help distract your mom from worrying about MJ's upcoming court case."

Normally, Dahlia loved the fact that Amelia got along so well with her cousins and that her family's ranch was close enough that someone was always willing to keep Amelia overnight when Dahlia needed a little time to herself. But after that makeout session with Connor last night, and then her talk with Duke this morning, she didn't quite trust herself to be alone long enough to think.

"What does Mom have planned for them?" Dahlia

asked, thinking about the last cousin sleepover when Sherilee King, who was constantly relapsing in her battle to be a vegan, tried to teach the kids how to make butterless carob chip kale cookies. After that failure, MJ ended up sneaking the kids into the bunkhouse's deep freezer where Gan Gan kept her secret stash of *emotional support* ice cream for an all-you-can-eat sundae party. Amelia had called home in the middle of the night with a bellyache.

"A tofu burger bar, but don't worry. I already have some ground sirloin patties pre-grilled and sitting in the oven warmer and that new cartoon movie cued up on Netflix. You know the one where the animals all sing 'Jolene' and '9 to 5'?" Aunt Freckles pointed to the extra-small T-shirt barely covering her extra-large bosom. It was lime green with the words I Beg Your Parton bedazzled above a picture of the famous country singer. "Can't ever go wrong with a little bit of Dolly."

"Maybe I should stick around?" Dahlia suggested, already envisioning the future conversation where she'd have to explain to her daughter why a chorus line of dancing giraffes would be singing the words *please don't take my man*.

"No way," Finn said as she entered the kitchen, the mud still on her boots from where she'd been working in the outer corrals. "No kids want their parents ruining the fun of a sleepover. Could you imagine if Mom would've shown up at Kelly Gladstone's house when she had her slumber party in tenth grade?"

"She *did* show up, Finn." Dahlia threw a piece of popcorn at her twin. "But you and Kelly had snuck out to watch Micah and Woody playing with their garage band at Big Millie's. I had to cover for you and say you were in the bathroom because you ate too much cheese on your pizza."

"Is that what got Mom started on her lactose-free kick?" Finn tilted her head. "I was wondering why she always watches me like a hawk whenever Mr. Truong gets the Pepperoni Stampede to cater lunch for the ranch hands. You've always been the worst at covering for people, Dia."

Dahlia immediately flashed to Connor's words last night about not being willing to sneak around. He was right. Even if it wasn't a small town and she wasn't from one of the higher profile families, she would no doubt get caught.

"You should bring back live bands now that you own Big Millie's," Finn suggested, snapping Dahlia back to the present moment. "In fact, I was going to meet Violet in town to have a drink tonight. Join us and we can figure out where to set up a stage."

"That wouldn't exactly be relaxing for me since the only place to have a drink in town is Big Millie's and it's supposed to be my night off." As a business owner who lived above her place of livelihood, it had been too tempting in those early months when

she was just getting started to not spend every waking moment at the bar being a helicopter boss. She'd
had to make a conscious decision that if she and her
daughter were going to live upstairs, Dahlia would
designate two days a week to completely distance
herself from her work. Originally, that had been on
Sundays and Mondays, when there was the least
amount of business. But when Amelia had started
school and Dahlia'd hired two trustworthy college
students as part-time bartenders, it worked out better for everyone's schedule for her to take the weekends off.

Freckles wiggled her penciled-in eyebrows.
"Maybe you should see if Connor Remington wants
to take you out on a date tonight."

"Yeah, I heard he went with Amelia to the father-
daughter dance," Finn replied, making Dahlia wish
she could be anywhere else but her family's kitchen
right now. See, there was no point in her and Connor trying to sneak around. Not when everyone was
already trying to push the narrative of them being
a couple. Oh, sure, right now, she could still pass
him off as a family friend. But it wouldn't be long
before someone said something in front of Amelia.

"Yes." Dahlia straightened her shoulders defensively. As soon as she exhibited any sign of doubt
or remorse, her family would take that as an open
invitation to pounce. Hell, they'd jump in with their
opinions no matter how she responded. But it was

always safest to hold her ground. "Amelia invited him and you know how insistent she can be."

"I also know how cautious her mother can be." Finn tapped her chin. "How did Micah feel about all of this?"

"Of course, he'd rather have been here himself, but he's used to his daughter having to attend things with her uncles."

"Yeah, but Connor Remington isn't exactly her uncle. Has he spent the night yet?"

Dahlia blushed, not from embarrassment but from guilt. Because the man almost *had* stayed over last night. She kept her voice resolved, though, when she answered, "Of course not."

"Why not?" Finn asked. "I saw the way you two were checking each other out when he was here with his stallion a couple of weeks ago and stayed for dinner. Couldn't tell the difference between you and the stall of pent-up broodmares panting after Private Peppercorn."

Dahlia's eyes threatened to pop out of her head and she had to snap her mouth closed before she could respond to her sister. "That's a real flattering comparison."

"It's also an accurate one. Come on, Dia. There's no shame in being attracted to a guy or even acting on that attraction. You're a single mom, not a nun."

"I can second that," Freckles said as she peeled the potatoes for her fresh-cut fries. "I may not be married to your uncle, but that doesn't stop me from slipping into his bed every few nights. It ain't a crime for a woman to enjoy a good roll—"

"Eww, Aunt Freckles!" Finn interrupted just in time. "We really need you to stop giving us those kinds of visuals."

"Finally, something I can agree with my youngest daughter on," Sherliee King said as she breezed into the kitchen in her expensive yoga clothes, not a drop of sweat threatening her professionally applied makeup. "Just because you're traumatizing our bodies with all that unhealthy cooking of yours, Freckles, doesn't mean you have to traumatize our minds, as well."

"Your mind could do with a little more dirtying if you ask me, Sherilee." Freckles pointed her potato peeler at their mother. "Don't forget, you and Roper stayed in the original cabin with us that first year before the big house was built. Your bedroom was right above mine and Rider's and when that headboard would get going, it sounded like a team of Clydesdales were storming through the roof."

Finn made a gagging sound, but Dahlia turned to her mom in shock.

Sherilee was the epitome of grace and class and everything one would expect from a famous politician's wife. Plus, Roper had always been surrounded by aides and friends wanting favors. Dahlia knew her parents had loved each other, but they never seemed to have much time together unless it was a formal event when there were walls of news cameras capturing their every move. "Really? You and Dad barely used to hold hands in front of us when we were kids."

"That's because they couldn't just stop with the hands," Freckles chuckled. "Why do you think your dad's campaign bus was nicknamed Ol' Faithful?"

"Because we lived near Yellowstone?" Dahlia asked and Finn covered her ears as though she already knew the answer was going to be something they wouldn't want to hear.

"Yes." Sherilee nodded earnestly at the same time Freckles shouted, "No! It was because the tiny bedroom in the back of the bus would spring to life at the same time every day. Just like clockwork."

Dahlia's jaw dropped in amazement. And slight aversion at the sullying of her childhood innocence.

"Your father was the love of my life." Sherilee held up her chin. "And what happened in our own private bedroom—"

"Or in the back of the campaign bus," Finn interjected.

"—was nobody's business but ours," their mother finished, narrowing one eye in her signature stern expression as she addressed all of them.

"See, Dia." Finn nudged her. "Even Mom agrees. What you and Connor Remington do out at his ranch is nobody's business but your own."

"Whoa." Sherilee held up a slim manicured hand displaying the fat diamond ring she never took off. "Who said anything about Dahlia and Connor Remington?"

"The whole town, Sherilee." Freckles rolled her eyes. "You've been so focused on MJ's arrest and Tessa getting tangled up with that agent, you haven't been paying attention to the latest romance brewing over at Big Millie's."

"I knew that saloon was gonna be the death of me." Sherilee opened the door of the hulking stainless-steel refrigerator. "Freckles, what have you got to eat in here?"

Uh-oh. Sherilee King was truly stressed if she was looking for her sister-in-law's calorie-filled cooking.

Dahlia braced her hand on the marble counter. "Actually, you guys, Connor has only been to the bar once—and we weren't even open at the time. So you can't blame my business. If anything, you can blame Amelia. She's the one who keeps me running into him."

"Amelia likes him that much?" Sherilee said around a mouthful of bacon Freckles had already precooked and hidden under a plate of foil for the burger bar. "Why didn't you say so? She's usually a pretty good judge of character, you know."

"She's five, Mom," Dahlia said, thinking this was another aftershock of the earlier confusion that had rattled her world. "She collects stray animals like other kids her age collect Pokémon cards."

"Yeah, but she has a second sense about these things. Your dad was the same way. He could read people."

"Can we go look at the ponies?" Amelia ran into the kitchen just then. Jack and Jordan, her two older cousins, followed behind her.

"Yes," Finn said to her niece. "But give your mom a kiss goodbye. She has to go see a man about a horse."

"Like a real horse?" Amelia asked with hopeful eyes.

"No, Finn is using one of her funny expressions again. Now, be good for Aunt Freckles and Gan Gan. I'll see you in the morning."

As Dahlia drove down the Twin Kings driveway leading to the highway, she couldn't stop thinking about Connor or the fact that *both* her mom and Finn seemed to be fine with the relationship. It wasn't that she needed her family's permission, or even their approval, to get involved with a man. In fact, the King women were very seldom in agreement on anything, and she couldn't help but think this was some elaborate plan of using reverse psychology to steer her in a different direction.

It wouldn't be the first time.

As she approached the turnoff for the Rocking D, a spike of rebelliousness caused her to jerk the steering wheel to the left. Like everyone else in her family, Dahlia had nothing to be ashamed of. She was tired of fighting this attraction between her and Connor. They needed to address it and deal with it once and for all.

She would simply stop by his ranch and explain that their relationship couldn't really go anywhere. Except, when she pulled into his driveway, she saw him sitting tall in his saddle as he rode Peppercorn along the fence line. He gave her a wave and then kicked his legs in the stirrups and set his horse on a furious pace, as though he was racing her back to the stables.

Dahlia was so impressed with his riding ability she pushed her foot down harder on the accelerator of her truck to match his pace so she could keep him in her sight. In fact, even after she parked, Dahlia was struck with a consuming need to continue watching Connor work with his horse that she told him, "Go ahead and finish up with him. I can hang out here with Goatee."

Connor removed Peppercorn's saddle and checked the horse's legs and hooves for injuries as the stallion drank from the water trough. As anxious as Dahlia was to talk with the man, she appreciated the fact that he took his time caring for his horse.

Dahlia sat beside Goatee on the porch steps, who was also breathing heavily as they both studied Connor. Of course, the dog had a good excuse for his panting. He'd just run like crazy to keep up with his owner.

Gobster, on the other hand, seemed to be the only living species on the ranch who wasn't staring adoringly at the man. In fact, the turkey ignored all of them as he roosted in his tree, poking his beak into a branch as he searched for bug snacks.

"I need to be more like that feathery one over there," she said absently to the dog as she scratched the wiry white hair between its ears. "He gets what he wants and then does his own thing. What do you think, Goatee? If I sleep with Connor once and for all, I should be able to get him out of my system, right?"

Instead of talking her out of the idea, the animal's response was to lower its furry chin onto its paws. But it didn't matter what Dahlia told the dog or told herself after Connor walked the horse into the stables and then emerged a few minutes later. His hat was gone and he was bare from the waist up, shooting a spiral of heat directly to her core. She would've gulped but her mouth had immediately gone dry.

His jeans hung low along his hips and his wet hair was dripping water onto the muscular ridges of his shoulders and chest. "Hope you don't mind, but I needed to wash some of the dust off me and I just got that old sink in the stables working."

Yep. Dahlia was totally going to sleep with him. She'd just have to deal with the what-ifs later.

Connor had braved colder water than what came out of the porcelain chipped utility sink inside the stables. But he'd needed some cooling down if he was going to have a civilized conversation with Dahlia, especially after the way she'd been studying him from the porch steps for the past ten minutes.

The woman had the ability to observe everything, without letting on that she was even paying attention. Like she was multitasking in her brain and filing everything away for later. She was usually very casual in her assessments, but she rarely missed anything. So when she directed the full scope of her attention on him, it was piercing.

His plan had been to wash up out here and then go inside the house to grab a clean shirt. Yet when she rose from the steps, her bottom lip clenched between her straight white teeth, Connor was pretty sure he felt the remaining droplets of water on his skin evaporate from the heat of her stare.

He opened his mouth to ask if she wanted to go inside, but before he could get the words out her lips were on his. Unlike their past two kisses, which were more leisurely and exploratory, this coupling of their mouths was frantic, intense. He backed her up the stairs and her arms clung to his neck as he felt around behind her for the front door.

Connor had won medals and commendations for his situational awareness, but he couldn't say how they'd gotten from the entryway to the bedroom. One minute he was unbuttoning her shirt and the next she was arching on the bed below him, her tight budded nipple in his mouth. He needed to slow down, to savor every second of having Dahlia in his arms, but all he could hear were her breathy moans encouraging him to go faster.

At least it *was* the only thing he could hear until the excited bark came from the furry bundle of energy who'd just jumped onto the bed with them.

"Sorry," Connor sighed.

Dahlia chuckled, the sound raspy. "He thinks its playtime."

"Not for you, though, boy," he told Goatee before scooping the dog off the quilt. "Let me take him to the other room. I'll be right back."

He hoped Dahlia didn't change her mind in the time it took him to find a long-lasting rawhide bone for the dog and then stop by his bathroom to get a pack of condoms out of the medicine cabinet. When he returned to the room, though, she'd pulled back the sheets and was propped up with her elbows behind her, wearing nothing but a pair of blue lacy panties and an inviting smile.

His heart stopped in its tracks, then resumed pounding at an uncontrollable pace.

Standing beside the bed, he began to unbutton his jeans, but her fingers stopped him. "Let me do that."

Despite the need vibrating through him, he held himself perfectly still as her fingers skimmed the sensitive skin below his fly. When his arousal sprang free, he closed his eyes and groaned. She took the condom from his palm and rolled it onto his hardened length, while he returned the favor, sliding the soft fabric of her panties downward and over her hips.

Yesterday, he'd told her that he wanted her to be sure about them before they took their relationship to this level. So far, her body's response to his indicated that she was more than sure. But he still needed to hear the words. As he settled himself between her thighs, he said, "There's no going back after this."

Her hands cupped his face as she pulled him closer. "Good," she replied before capturing his mouth with her own.

He entered her swiftly and she gasped. Holding the rest of himself completely still, he pulled back his head and asked, "Are you okay?"

"Yes. I just… It's been a long time and I don't remember it feeling this good. This right. Please, Connor…don't stop."

His heart thumped behind his rib cage as he resolved to make each sensation last for her. He retreated slightly before filling her again, yet with each thrust her hips arched to meet him. As her breathing hitched higher, he felt himself growing closer to his own climax. Next time he would make it last for both of them, but for now he needed to take care of her needs first. He reached between their interlocked bodies and used his thumb to brush against the sensitive bud centered just above her entrance.

It only took a few strokes before Dahlia threw back her head and called his name, her constricting muscles pulling him deeper inside her. She was still shuddering under him when Connor shouted with his own release.

The sun was barely rising when Dahlia heard the unmistakable gobble from outside the window. Stretching with a soreness and contentedness she hadn't expected, she rolled over in the bed to find Connor sitting up with just the sheet covering him from the waist down.

He was watching her intently, but she couldn't muster up so much as a single blush. Instead, she smiled deeply, feeling the happiness all the way to her toes, which had been properly curled a couple of times throughout the night. "I thought only roosters crowed at the crack of dawn."

"Gobster already thinks he's part peacock and part garbage disposal. So why not add alarm clock to his list of charming qualities?"

"I noticed Goatee won't go near him. Maybe Gobster needs a turkey friend to keep him company?"

"Tell that to the poor bird who'd be stuck in the cage with him. He'd probably peck it to death."

She smiled, then tucked her body against his side. His fingers brushed her hair away from her face and she thought she could certainly get used to waking up like this. Turkey noises and all.

She let her own fingers trail along the light dusting of copper-colored hair highlighting Connor's chest, following the curls as they narrowed across his abdomen and then lower. Lifting her face to his, she teased, "I hope you don't mind that I can't seem to get enough of you."

His arm flexed around her as he brought her closer. "Last night, when we were making love, you made a comment about it being a long time for you."

Now, Dahlia did blush. But only slightly. She remembered adding on the part about never feeling this way before, but thankfully Connor hadn't been arrogant enough to gloat over that bit. "It has."

"Am I the first guy you've dated since your ex-husband?"

Would this be considered dating? She and Connor had never really gone out together just the two of them. Also, was this a conversation she should sit up for? It felt better to talk about something like this while she wasn't making eye contact.

She laid her head on his shoulder and let out a deep breath. "Actually, there was a guy named Seth, one of Micah's band mates at the time. It was after we split up, and it only lasted for a few weeks."

"Why?"

"When the rest of the band moved to Nashville, Seth said that he was staying behind to help me with Big Millie's. Amelia was barely walking and I'd taken on this huge project partly because I loved the idea of owning and redecorating a historic saloon, and partly because I needed to prove to myself that I had my own life besides being Roper King's daughter or Finn King's twin sister or Micah Deacon's wife or Amelia's mom."

Connor didn't reply, but his hand continued a soothing circular pattern, tracing pleasantly along her lower spine.

"Seth would meet with the contractors if I was busy with Amelia, and it wasn't long before he started trying to make decisions that weren't his to make. And throwing around my family's name to build up his own list of people who would owe him favors. Turns out Micah had kicked him out of the band at the airport. He hadn't told me because he knew I had enough to worry about without adding his own career drama to the mix. When he found out Seth was still in Teton Ridge trying to cash in on his ex-wife's name, Micah wanted to kick his ass."

"Good," Connor said. "He should have."

"Except Micah had to get in line behind my mother, my siblings, and most importantly me. But not as much as I wanted to kick my own ass for letting the guy *help* me out in the first place. My dad told me not to beat myself up over it, but I'd never failed at anything in my life and I'd already dropped out of my interior design program and gotten a divorce in the same year. It sucked to have someone try to take advantage of me when I was already dealing with so much."

"I bet it did." Connor used his free hand to lift her chin so she was looking at his face. "Micah's leaving must've been rough on you."

"Not really," she said, then saw his eyes widen. "Okay, that sounds super shallow. I mean, the *idea* of divorce was a tough pill to swallow because it felt like I was admitting defeat. But it wasn't as if I really loved Micah in that way."

"Wait. You married someone you didn't love?" Connor shifted and his sheet dropped a bit lower, revealing the patch of bronze hair just above his... Dahlia had to shake her head to get back on subject.

"I should probably start at the beginning. When I was in my senior year at UW, Finn talked me into going to a bar nearby because Micah would be playing there. See, I knew Micah from school, but he was in the same grade as my brother Duke and normally played at some local places around Ridgecrest County. But Finn was the one who followed his music career and dragged me to this honky-tonk in Laramie. To be honest, I was more impressed with the old bar than I was with the band. In my defense, though, I was an interior design major and the saloon was a classic study in Wild West motif. It had stretched cowhides pinned up over the dark wood paneling and there were these antique red glass chandeliers hanging from the ceilings. And don't even get me started on all the polished brass and the exquisite ironwork…" She trailed off when she realized he was holding back a grin. "What's so funny?"

"Of course, you would be more impressed with the saloon decor than with a Grammy award–winning guitarist."

"Well, he hadn't won any Grammys at that time. But I'll stand by my original statement. The bar really was the perfect mixture of kitschy cowboy charm and old world elegance. Anyway, after their set, Finn and I were sitting with the guys in the band and Micah and I got to talking about Duke and Teton Ridge and our shared love of exposed log beams and brick facade architecture.

"We slept together and the following day it soon became apparent that the only thing we had in common was being from the same small town and our mutual love of interior design elements. When I found out I was pregnant, Finn—without my knowledge—paid him a visit and convinced him that the honorable thing to do would be to marry me. See, I was always the rule follower, while Finn was the rebellious twin. So to have her pushing for us to get married made it seem all the more reasonable. I remember thinking that if Finn, who could talk her way out of anything, thought this is the only way out of this mess, then that was my best option. Plus, my father was about to be announced as President Rosales's running mate and it just seemed like something we should do."

"How did the rest of your family react?" Connor asked.

"My mom said she would've expected something like this from Finn but not from me. So that stung. But my dad told me not to make any rash decisions. That I should do what feels best. It was actually his advice that made me think I should try to make a marriage with Micah work. I adored my dad and I wanted my child to have the kind of father I had growing up."

"But things didn't work out with you and Micah?"

Dahlia shrugged. "Up until the night I'd slept with him, I'd never really done anything impulsive or shocking. Looking back, it wasn't even all that reckless considering I'd known Micah all my life and he got along so well with everyone in my family. I figured it was a safe way to get a little rebellion out of my system, and then he and I could move on to being friends. But we just wanted different things out of life. He wanted to be famous and move to Nashville and I wanted to stay in Teton Ridge and carve out a quiet life for myself. So now we both live the lives we want and we make it work for Amelia."

"And you remain friends?" Connor prompted.

"I mean, we remain friendly with each other. We're co-parents, which means we have the same ultimate goal in mind and we have to work together to achieve it. But it's not like I'm confiding all my deep dark secrets to him."

"And what about me, Dahlia?" he asked, his finger now tracing along her arm, over her shoulder and down to her collarbone. "Am I a secret?"

"Not exactly," she said, giving an involuntary shiver at his caress. "Nobody can really keep a secret in this town. But…"

"But?" he prompted.

"I'd rather Amelia not know all the details."

"You don't think she's going to ask questions?"

"Of course, she'll ask questions." Dahlia rolled her eyes as she collapsed on her back. "Have you *met* my daughter?"

"So then what's your plan?" he asked before replacing his tracing fingers with his mouth, which now had full access to both her breasts.

She sighed from the scratchy texture of the stubble along his chin as it grazed her aching nipples and braced her hands on his shoulders. Then she pivoted her torso and pushed him until he was the one on his back. She deftly planted one of her legs on the other side of his hip in order to straddle him.

"Right now, my plan is to have my way with you one more time before I have to go pick her up and deal with those questions." Seeing his eyebrow raised at her avoidance of his question, she knew he wasn't going to drop the subject. So she smiled down at him and added, "Depending on how that goes, my next plan will be to casually run into you on occasion and act like I'm not imagining you walking out of your barn wearing just your jeans and cowboy boots."

He planted his hands firmly on each of her hips and pulled her against his hardened manhood. "Does that mean I have to act like I'm not imagining *you* in just those little blue panties laid out on my bed all ready for me?"

When that magical thumb of his moved from her hip to her inner thigh and then higher, Dahlia threw back her head to draw more air into her lungs. "Only until we get each other out of our systems and can move on to just being regular friends."

His thumb paused mid-flick and if she hadn't been so intent on finishing what they'd just started, she would've realized that Connor Remington had his own reservations about that plan.

Chapter Ten

Connor was finally getting a handle on being a rancher and, for the first time in his life, he felt as though the seeds of permanency he'd planted were coming to fruition. He'd bought himself a new flat-screen TV—Aunt Connie's old twenty-two incher still had the turn knobs for channels two to thirteen and wasn't compatible with an updated cable box—and even a new set of pots and pans that were from this century. In fact, he'd planned to pull them out of the box this morning and make Dahlia some pancakes. Another first for him, since he'd never cooked breakfast for a woman.

Then he'd been hit with the reality that they

weren't exactly on the same page about taking their casual relationship to the next level. Emotional attachments normally weren't his thing and just when he'd finally convinced himself that his growing connection with Dahlia would be worth the risk, she'd thrown out that offhand comment about moving on to being friends. He understood that she'd experienced that kind of one-and-done relationship with her ex-husband, but Connor didn't want to be lumped into the same boat as Micah Deacon.

He, unlike Micah, planned to stay in Teton Ridge—indefinitely. It was one thing to sleep with someone and then go about your business when you lived thousands of miles away. It was different when he was going to be running into her regularly at the bakery or the grocery store or even at her family's ranch.

In fact, tomorrow he was supposed to take Peppercorn to the Twin Kings for another group of mares whose cycles hadn't been ready the previous week. At this rate, his stallion's stud fees were bringing in enough money that he'd be able to buy a couple of broodmares himself so he could start his own program.

That reminded him that he needed to get the horse out later this afternoon for a good run so he'd be primed for tomorrow. Connor checked the time on his phone and saw that it was already noon. His mom always expected him to call on Sundays and she should be out of church by now. The phone rang three times before Linda Remington picked up.

"Connor? Is that you?" his mom asked, as though anyone else ever called her from this area code.

"Hey, Ma. How was your week?"

"Same as it always is. Except half the ladies in my bunco group came down with food poisoning after Carla DiAngelo brought something called bourbon-laced meatballs to the potluck on Thursday night. I didn't touch the things, obviously, because you know Carla has a heavy hand with the measuring cup and doesn't cook all the alcohol out." Connor's mom refused to go near an open liquor bottle, let alone partake in so much as a drop. Probably because her husband had such a problem avoiding the stuff. He wondered what his mother would think about Connor dating a bar owner. "And Dr. Ahmad is still trying to get me to see that dermatologist about the mole on my shoulder, but I told her it's always been that color since I can remember."

"Maybe you should have it checked out, Ma, just in case?" He made the suggestion, knowing it was futile.

"Bridget Shaw once saw someone about that little ol' sunspot she has on the tip of her nose and they talked her into getting something called a microdermabrasion peel. Her face looked like a scalded lobster for a whole month and her insurance didn't even cover it."

"That's because Mrs. Shaw went to her daughter's best friend's unlicensed beauty shop, not a dermatologist."

"Humph." His mother had some serious trust issues, not that Connor could blame her after dealing with his old man for so long. But her skepticism was getting worse lately. Thankfully, she changed the subject. "Father Brannigan asked about you at mass today. I told him to pray for you."

"Good. I'll take all the prayers I can get."

"So you're still planning to stay out there in Wyoming?"

And so it began. The same conversation they had every week. Where his mother forgot that she was talking to her son and began channeling some of the old conversations she used to have with her unreliable and untrustworthy husband.

"Yes, I'm still staying in Wyoming. The ranch is coming along nicely and I already have three animals now." He didn't admit that two of them weren't going to make him any money and one would end up being more of a headache than it was worth. "I plan to get another horse next week."

"Things always go well at first," she said, the cynicism heavy in her tone. "Then something'll happen to change your mind."

"If something goes wrong, then I'll stay here and deal with it. I made a promise to Aunt Connie, remember?"

"I'm sure your father used to make all kinds of promises to her. Then he named you after her and started making the same sorts of promises to you. We all saw how that turned out. I doubt she really expected you to keep your word."

"Well, *I* expect me to keep it. I'm not Steve Remington, remember?"

His mom exhaled loudly. "I know you're not. But as his son, it doesn't stop me from worrying that you'll fall into the same path eventually."

"I'm also *your* son. Give us both a little credit, Ma." Connor didn't like to brag about his accomplishments, but it would be nice if she could at least acknowledge that Connor was almost the same age his dad had been when he'd died. And Connor had yet to be arrested. Or fired from a job. Or in debt to any bookies. In fact, the medals on his dress blues (which had just arrived from storage last week) proved that Connor was more than capable of handling himself under pressure and not taking the easy way out of things.

"I just liked it better when you were in the military." His mom sighed. "I didn't worry about you so much."

"You know that most parents worry *more* about their kids when they're deployed to combat zones?"

"Yeah, but you were with other soldiers and officers and you guys had people watching over you." *Not always*, Connor wanted to correct her, but she was determined to see things her own way. "What kind of support system do you have in Wyoming? Have you even made any friends?"

"Yes, I have friends," Connor replied, trying not to think of Dahlia using that word to describe them. "And I have good neighbors and several of the business owners in town know me whenever I come in. It's a small town, Ma. Why don't you let me buy you a plane ticket so you can fly out and see for yourself?"

"I'll think about it," she offered, but Connor doubted that she would truly consider it. His father had had them moving around so much during their marriage, trying to escape his mistakes, his mother turned into a homebody in her older age. She rarely left her neighborhood now, let alone traveled out of state. At least she had a few dependable friends, even if they brought bourbon-laced meatballs to bunco night and got facials in the back room of someone's house.

By the time he hung up, Connor felt like he'd just finished a weekly chore. He loved his mom and appreciated the sacrifices she'd made working multiple jobs to keep a roof over his head and food on the table. But sometimes he felt as though he were more of a burden to her, a constant reminder of his old man. Sure, she loved him in her own way, but they'd never been especially close—probably because she'd built up so many of her own emotional walls. He couldn't imagine her patiently answering his questions the way Dahlia did with Amelia. Or her insisting on a family dinner every Friday night, the way Sherilee King did with her kids.

Maybe that was why he was hoping for something more with Dahlia. He wanted to feel that family connection. He looked at Goatee, who was taking the long way around the chicken coop to avoid Gobster. "It certainly would explain why I'm spoiling the both of you."

Connor saw Dahlia on Monday afternoon when he was getting ready to leave Twin Kings following a successful booking session with Peppercorn. She and Amelia were just arriving for the after-school riding lesson and he expected there to be some awkwardness because of Saturday night, but there was none. In fact, Dahlia even greeted him first and laughed along as Amelia told him all about how Peyton lost one of the class hamsters on the playground at recess and Mr. Tasaki, the PE teacher, found it scampering across the pull-up bars. Then, when nobody was watching, Dahlia walked him to his truck and gave him a kiss goodbye.

Clearly, she hadn't moved on from the physical attraction stage to the just friends stage yet. Which was perfectly fine with Connor.

On Tuesday morning, he ran into her at the grocery store and they ended up walking down the narrow aisles together, discussing the best flavors of cereal and Amelia's favorite lunch meat—ham, but not smoked or honey ham, just plain regular ham. Dahlia didn't seem to mind that Lupe Ochoa, Tomas's wife, kept giving them the side-eye when they were all standing in front of the dairy section at the same time. She kept right on talking about Greek yogurt versus Icelandic yogurt (Connor didn't know there was a difference), and he had the sudden realization that she could be nearly as chatty as her daughter. Dahlia didn't kiss him goodbye in the parking lot, though, because Lupe had followed them outside and wanted to say hi to Goatee, who was still having a hard time understanding why he'd had to stay tied up to the picnic table outside while his owner had gone into the market. But Dahlia had texted him later that night and told him that she'd wanted to kiss him goodbye. He'd almost driven into town to give her the opportunity to make good on her offer, but he knew she was working.

On Wednesday afternoon, the latch on the back of his horse trailer broke and he needed to run to the hardware store before they closed. He was coming out just as Dahlia and Amelia came walking past the door.

"Mommy and I are going to the Pepperoni Stampede for dinner because she doesn't feel like cooking." Amelia smiled as she pulled on his hand. "Come on. You can come with us."

He lifted his brow at Dahlia to ask if that was okay. Again, she surprised him with a wide smile and said, "It's all-you-can-eat salad bar night."

"There's my favorite air hockey player," Woody said to Amelia when it was their turn to order at the counter. "I built a couple of wooden step stools in my workshop since the last time you were in. The manager was worried about the liability, but all the kids love them because they can reach the pucks better."

Amelia let out a whoop and immediately ran to the arcade section of the pizza parlor to check out the games. Woody jerked his chin at Connor and said, "Are you that new rancher in town that everyone's been talking about?"

Woody, with his purple Mohawk, multiple piercings and sleeveless Pepperoni Stampede tee displaying an array of colorful tattoos, didn't fit the mold of what one might expect a typical small-town Wyomingian to look like. But he was just as much a part of Teton Ridge as Dahlia was and she watched Connor closely to see his reaction to Woody's unique appearance.

"Connor Remington." Connor smiled as he reached his hand across the counter to shake Woody's. "I think we met before, though, when I brought my dog into Dr. Roman's office?"

"That's right." Woody nodded in recognition.

"White terrier mixed with maltese. I remember animals better than I remember faces, bro. Did you end up taking it to that shelter in Pinedale?"

"Nope. He's most likely curled up at the foot of my bed right now or sitting in my kitchen tearing apart one of the million squeaky toys Amelia keeps giving him."

"Right on. Brenda, the receptionist at Doc D's office didn't think you'd keep him, but I knew you'd make the right call. You gotta be careful with those toys, though, bro. Some of the squeakers are super tiny and can get stuck in their throats when you're not watching."

"Yeah, I learned that the hard way." Connor leaned an arm on the counter between them. "So what I did is buy a box of tennis ball–sized squeakers online, right? Then I cut open the toys, replaced the small squeak with the bigger one and sewed them back up. It's loud as hell, but at least I don't have to do the Heimlich maneuver on my dog again."

"Now that's a genius idea." Woody pointed, his fingernail covered in chipped black polish. "If I wasn't already working ten hours a week here and volunteering at Doc D's one day a month *and* making my own brew on the side, I might want in on that business model. Do they hold up pretty well after you cut into them?"

"The trick is you've gotta do a zigzag backstitch,

then run it in the reverse direction to really lock it in there. Takes Goatee at least three hours to get the thing apart."

"Right on." Woody nodded, but Dahlia stared at Connor with a sense of awe.

"You sew?"

"Yeah. My mom couldn't really afford to replace my jeans every time I got a hole in the knee so our neighbor, who worked at a dry cleaners, taught me how to fix it myself. Aunt Connie had the same kind of machine in that back room at the Rocking D."

"That was her quilting room." Woody nodded wistfully. "Connie Daniels used to make the best quilts in town. She tried to teach me some of her techniques, but I didn't have the patience, bro."

A pointed cough came from someone in line behind them.

"Speaking of patience," Mr. Burnworth grumbled before raising his voice. "I'd like to order before Mayor Alastair over there makes his third trip to the salad bar. He always takes all the cherry tomatoes."

Dahlia asked Woody for their usual and Connor added a second pizza and a pitcher of beer, however, there was another delay as she and Connor argued briefly over who was going to pay. She ended up letting him because she didn't want to draw any more attention to the fact that they were having their first meal in public together.

When they finally got settled in a smaller booth

in the corner, Amelia reappeared and asked for quarters for the arcade. Before Dahlia could pull out her wallet, Connor was handing her a five-dollar bill. "Do they have a change machine?"

"Yes. Peyton is here with her dad, too, so can I share with her? She's real good at sharing because she and her dad only get one salad plate and one soda when they come here and they hafta take turns."

"Of course." Connor pulled out another five-dollar bill.

When Amelia ran off to rejoin her friend, Dahlia rolled her eyes. "You didn't have to do that."

Connor shrugged, looking a little uncomfortable. "I used to be the kid at the team pizza parties after baseball practice who didn't have any extra money for the games. My mom used to tell me that it would build character, but there was usually a generous parent who'd slip me a few quarters when nobody was looking."

Dahlia felt something tug low in her belly. His mom was probably right about it building character because Connor Remington had to be one of the most compassionate men she knew when it came to animals and children. Then she realized how shallow she must've sounded by casually dismissing his generosity to another child. "I only meant that Jay, Peyton's dad, is a notorious cheapskate when it comes to his daughter because he doesn't want his ex-wife coming after him for more child support. However, the guy is in Big Millie's at least once a week and easily runs up a hundred-dollar bar tab each time. Usually only on the weekend when I'm not working because he knows I'll call him out on it. Someone needs to build *his* character."

A server delivered a red plastic cup full of lemonade for Amelia and a pitcher of beer for her and Connor to split.

"Plates are already by the salad bar when you're ready." The young woman jerked her thumb toward Mayor Alastair and Mr. Burnworth who were fighting over the same pair of plastic tongs. "But you might want to wait until those two get through the line. Heather Walker got hit in the eye with a slice of cucumber last week when she tried to get between them."

Connor poured the beer into the frosted mug in front of Dahlia. "Yeah, I was at Biscuit Betty's last month when she officially called off Dollar Waffle Day half an hour after it started. Syrup is surprisingly tough to clean off leather cowboy boots."

The server shook her head and muttered, "I hate all-you-can-eat Wednesdays," before walking away.

"So, you seem to be learning the *Who's Who* of Teton Ridge pretty quickly." Dahlia took a sip of the icy cold pale ale.

"I'm trying. It helps being known as *the new guy with the little white dog who is dating Dahlia King*

Deacon." He used his fingers in air quotes for the last part.

Dahlia dipped her head nervously. "Someone already asked you if we were dating?"

"They didn't ask so much as assumed. I guess enough people have seen us together that they figure it's a safe assumption."

"Does that bother you?" she asked.

"Not if it doesn't bother you." He brought his beer glass to his lips, his eyes refusing to break contact with hers as he drank deeply.

She felt the blood rush to her brain. It was true, she wanted to keep whatever this was between them a secret, mostly for Amelia's sake. But Dahlia couldn't deny the way her body reacted every time she saw Connor around town. She should've been more guarded after they'd slept together, but she couldn't hide the fact that she was legitimately happy to see him. They talked about nothing, but everything, and there wasn't any sort of pressure to avoid him now that they'd already let the cow out of the barn so to speak.

"I think I am okay with it. I mean, as long as we take things—"

"Mommy, look what we won from the claw machine," Amelia interrupted, pointing to a stuffed panda bear in Peyton's arms. "If we can't win another one, then we're gonna co-parent this one together."

Peyton's dad chose that moment to suddenly stop scrolling on his smartphone and walk across the restaurant to check on his daughter. "Who won it, though? Whoever won it should get to take it home."

Amelia narrowed her eyes at the man. "Peyton won it, but with *my* quarters."

The other girl's lips curled down and she looked like she was about to cry. "Amelia, how 'bout you just keep it at your house?"

"No, it's both of ours and we're gonna share it," Amelia insisted and Dahlia's chest burst with pride.

"Come on, Peyton, don't be so quick to back down," Jay Grover told his daughter. "You gotta stand up for yourself."

Dahlia opened her mouth to tell Jay exactly what she thought about him and his inability to back down. But Connor beat her to it. "Buddy, why don't I buy you a drink and we let the children work this out for themselves."

Connor put his hand on the man's shoulder rather firmly—judging from the way Jay winced—then steered the man toward the front counter where Woody was still working. Dahlia had three brothers, grew up on a working cattle ranch with some of the best bronc busters in the business and she owned a bar. She knew how to break up a fight if she needed to. But right now, her priority was the two little girls in front of her.

"So what are you guys going to name the panda?" she asked them.

Neither child answered, though. In fact, Peyton was chewing on the end of her braid, her eyes huge as she watched Connor speak to her father. Dahlia wished she could hear what they were saying, but she understood why he was keeping his voice so low. The server brought out two pizzas and Dahlia, using the mouthwatering distraction to her advantage said, "Girls, I'll walk you to the bathroom so you guys can wash your hands. Then, Peyton, you can join us for dinner."

Amelia was having a difficult time peeling her curious eyes away from Connor—probably because she feared a repeat of the fudgy bar bake sale incident. Dahlia had to nudge her daughter toward the tiny ladies' room that barely had enough room for one person at the pedestal sink. She waited outside the door for the girls, watching as Jay nodded grudgingly at Connor, his mouth clamped shut in an angry line.

Woody went to the drink station himself to retrieve a red plastic cup, filled it with soda, then handed it to Jay. Dahlia let out the breath she hadn't realized she'd been holding as the man returned to his table, slumped lower in his seat and picked up his phone to continue his scrolling.

The girls came out and she led them back to their booth just as Connor returned. The muscles in his shoulders seemed more relaxed and he smiled, even though she could tell he was keeping Jay in his field of vision. "You ready to hit the salad bar?"

Dahlia nodded and followed him to the other side of the restaurant. When he handed her a chilled plate, she asked under her breath, "What'd you say to him?"

"I reminded him that his daughter was watching his behavior and that he didn't want to set the example that grown men fighting with women or arguing with young kids was ever acceptable." Connor settled a heaping pile of romaine lettuce on his plate. "I might have suggested that he doesn't want her marrying a guy who treats her that way or even dating someone who is too cheap to buy her a soda."

"That's all?" she asked as she followed him down the row of cut vegetables. The conversation would've been a lot quicker if that was the only thing Connor had said to Jay.

The cherry tomato bowl was completely depleted so he added a carrot stick to her plate. "I told him that if he didn't agree to let the girls share the panda, then we were going to be stepping outside to discuss the matter more thoroughly."

Dahlia shuddered. Her uncle Rider had talked enough about his elite Special Forces training and how the Marine Corps had taught him to *discuss the matter more thoroughly.*

Amelia and Peyton sat together on one side of the

booth with the stuffed animal between them. Which meant Dahlia got to enjoy the warmth of Connor's long leg pressed against hers all through the meal. The girls finished their pizza and were just about to take Andy Pandy, as they'd named him, to visit the arcade again when Jay shuffled over to their table to tell Peyton it was time to go.

Amelia's bubbly smile quickly turned into a frown when her friend gave a last longing glance at the panda before walking out the door. Her daughter sniffed and said, "But we didn't get to decide how we would share Andy Pandy."

"Why don't we take him to the Frozen Frontier next door?" Connor nodded at the toy bear. "Maybe we can distract him with an ice cream sundae while we come up with a visitation schedule for you and Peyton."

Dahlia could kiss the man for once again having the perfect suggestion where her daughter was concerned. In fact, she barely waited until they were outside on the sidewalk, then quickly planted her lips on his when Amelia skipped off ahead of them.

"You're so good with her," she whispered as she pulled away before they could be caught kissing.

Amelia was already to the corner and holding open the door to the ice cream parlor when they caught up to her. Connor swung the girl into his arms so she could see the all the flavors in the glass case before placing their order, and Dahlia didn't think her heart could handle the cuteness overload.

They had just squeezed into wrought-iron chairs crammed tightly around a minuscule table when Dahlia's cell phone shot to life with the opening bars of Foreigner's "Jukebox Hero."

"That's Daddy's ringtone," Amelia said excitedly, reaching for the phone and pushing the speakerphone button before Dahlia could stop her. She glanced at Connor to see how he would react to her taking a call from her ex-husband while they were in public. But he was biting into his homemade chocolate dipped waffle cone as though he didn't have a care in the world. "Hi, Daddy! We're at the Frozen Frontier with Andy Pandy."

"Hi, Andy and Pandy," Micah said. "Are those the class hamsters you get to take home for spring break?"

"No, Daddy. We can't bring hamsters inside the ice cream place. We came here with Mommy's new boyfriend, Connor."

Dahlia gasped and Connor nearly choked on his mouthful of Rocky Road. But Micah didn't comment on their daughter's awkward announcement before he started talking about something else. In fact, Dahlia couldn't even focus on what he was saying because she was mentally calculating how long Amelia had known about her and Connor. Clearly, they hadn't been as stealthy as she'd hoped.

"Did you hear me, Dia?" Micah asked from the speaker on her phone. He and her siblings were the only ones who called her by the nickname.

"Sorry, I missed that."

"I said that the orthopedic specialist thinks I'm going to need to do that wrist surgery after all. It's an outpatient procedure, but the rehab is pretty intense and I won't be able to play for a while. So I'm going to have to miss both the European and Asia legs of the world tour."

"Ms. Betty at the diner said her husband went to rehab, but it didn't work. Will your rehab work, Daddy?"

"It should, baby doll. It's not the same kind of rehab. Plus, I'm planning on doing it out there in Teton Ridge. There's a therapist in Jackson Hole who does home visits for…uh…clients who prefer to keep a low profile."

Dahlia knew she should reply—should say *something*. But for some reason, her ears weren't quite processing Micah's words. Maybe it was because of the way Connor was now sitting like a stiff wall of tense muscle beside her. Was he mad about having to listen to Amelia's conversation with her father?

"How long will you be here, Daddy?" Amelia asked. Okay, so Dahlia must've heard right. Micah *was* coming to visit.

"Two to three months depending on my physical therapy. I was hoping to plan it for summer break when you're out of school and we can spend more time together, baby doll. But the doctor says I already waited too long. He had a spot open up tomorrow, so as long as the procedure goes well, I should be on a plane to Wyoming by this weekend."

"Yay!" Amelia was now sitting on her knees, her hot fudge sundae threatening to topple over in her excitement. Connor's face was completely devoid of emotion, but his whole body was rigid. He was clearly way less thrilled than her daughter, who eagerly asked, "Are you gonna stay with us this time? You can sleep in my room."

Dahlia gulped, but resisted the urge to look at Connor to see how he was reacting to the suggestion that she and her ex-husband sleep under the same roof. She immediately set the record straight. "No, Peanut. You know Daddy never stays with us because our apartment is too small."

"But he can't sleep at Grandpa Tony's no more." Amelia pointed out. Micah's dad had sold his house a few months ago and moved to a retirement community in Tennessee to be closer to his son. The nearest hotel was in Fling Rock, and Micah wasn't really a nondescript motor inn kind of guy anymore.

"My publicist is working on lining up a place for me," Micah replied. "I told him there are usually vacation rentals available near Jackson Hole now that the ski season is winding down."

"But Jackson Hole is so far away," Amelia

moaned as she propped her elbows on the table in defeat. "Like almost a whole hour."

Then her daughter's eyes landed on Connor's stoic face and suddenly lit up. Dahlia knew exactly what the girl was thinking and shook her head in warning. But Amelia shared her ill-fated idea, anyway.

"Hey, maybe my daddy can stay on the Rocking D with you, Connor!"

Chapter Eleven

"No!" Connor said a bit too quickly, only to hear Micah Deacon on the other end of the line echoing the exact same word. And just as emphatically.

Amelia's face fell, Dahlia dropped the spoon she'd been clutching, and the teen employee of Frozen Frontier chose that exact moment to wipe down the other tables nearby that were already cleaned.

Connor cleared his throat, feeling as though he'd just thrown Andy Pandy out of a moving car window. He'd just finished giving Jay Grover a lecture about putting his daughter's needs first, so how did it look now for Connor to refuse to host Amelia's father out on his ranch?

But seriously, he and the man weren't friends. They didn't even know each other. Clearly, Micah knew how awkward it would be to stay with the guy who was sleeping with his ex-wife because he'd had the exact same response as Connor. Even Dahlia looked like she would rather be any place but here, having this exact conversation.

"But why not?" Amelia asked, looking at the only two adults who were physically present and had to actually witness the disappointment crossing her sweet face.

"Because, baby girl," Micah finally said via speakerphone. "That would be kinda awkward."

"But why?" Amelia insisted.

"Well, because I've never even met Connor in person. What if we don't like each other?"

Don't like each other? The ice cream cone in Connor's hand cracked under the pressure of his tense grip. Broman had made that comment about jealous dads at the dance, but Dahlia had brushed it off as the deputy being bitter. Obviously, though, Micah already had his own reservations and wasn't afraid to voice them.

"But why wouldn't you like each other?"

Good question, Connor thought. Unless Micah was hoping to get back together with Dahlia, what reason would he have to not like the man currently dating her?

Now Micah cleared his throat. "Who knows?

Maybe he'll think my cooking is terrible. Or maybe I'll think that he snores."

"I don't snore," Connor said, surprising himself with his defensive tone.

Amelia turned to Dahlia who'd managed to find a new spoon and was now shoveling ice cream into her mouth so quickly, it was a wonder she didn't have brain freeze. "Mommy, does Connor snore?"

He lifted a brow at her, daring to admit in front of her ex-husband and the eavesdropping teenaged ice cream scooper that she'd already spent the night with him.

"Okay, everyone," Dahlia said after she swallowed a final gulp of mint chip. "Here's what's going to happen. Connor is going to stay at his house on the Rocking D. Amelia is going to stay our apartment above Big Millie's. And Micah is going to stay...wherever he finds a place to stay that isn't the Rocking D or Big Millie's. And I am going to go home right now before I keep stress eating ice cream and barking orders like my mother usually does."

"Don't let Sherilee hear you saying that," Micah said, then chuckled. Because of course he was already privy to all the inside jokes about the King family. "Alright, I'll talk to you tomorrow, baby girl."

Amelia grudgingly told her father good-night and when Dahlia disconnected the phone, she shoved it into her jacket pocket. As though she was shoving from her mind all the drama the little device had just conveyed.

"So I guess this is what you meant by complicated?" Connor offered, trying to make light of the situation.

"What's complicated?" Amelia asked.

"Life, Peanut," Dahlia answered truthfully, then shook her head as if to clear it. "Anyway, tell Connor thanks for the pizza and the ice cream. Let's get Andy Pandy home so you can read him a book before bed."

Amelia picked up the stuffed bear and gave a dejected sigh. "Thanks for the pizza, Connor."

He walked them home, which was only a block away, and then spent the next twelve hours trying not to think about how one phone call had steered him so thoroughly off course.

The following morning, his phone vibrated in his back pocket and his senses went on full alert when he saw his mother's contact info on the screen.

They usually only talked on Sundays, so it was pretty out of character for her to be calling him in the middle of the week. "Hey, Ma. Is everything okay?"

"Well, I guess that depends. I went to see the dermatologist and he removed the mole to test it for cancer."

"Did you get the biopsy results already?"

"No. But that's not why I'm calling. When I was in the waiting room, I ran into someone."

Connor put the call on speaker and set the phone down on the workbench so he could talk while repairing the sliding mechanism on the trailer door latch. When his mom didn't continue talking, he asked, "You still there?"

"Do you remember when we lived in that apartment off Melville?"

"I remember living in a couple of places off Melville."

"The one by the park where you played Little League?"

"Oh…yeah, sure."

"Do you remember playing on that baseball team with the coach named Greg? He…uh…he and I went out a few times?"

"Of course. I loved Coach Greg. He had all those cool stories about being a Marine. He was probably the biggest influence on me enlisting."

What Connor didn't say was that the months his mom had dated Greg had been the best of his childhood. The guy had been easygoing and treated his mom right and would've made a great stepdad.

Of course, his parents weren't divorced at the time, which posed a problem. Whenever Connor's dad would be in jail, his mom would swear she was going to leave him for good. That year, he'd hoped that she would keep her promise because he really liked Coach Greg. But then Steve got released, and just like every other time when his old man was fresh out of jail, he'd sworn he was going to stay sober, and his mom had gone back to him.

"Well, that's who I saw at the doctor's office. I guess he had a few sunspots he was getting checked out. But we started talking and one thing led to another and, well, he asked me out to dinner this weekend."

"That's great, Ma. What's the problem?"

"I wasn't sure if you would approve or not. You were pretty mad at me when I broke up with him."

"I was twelve back then. I'm thirty-two now. You don't need my approval to date anyone."

"It probably won't work out, anyway. I can't believe he even recognized me with all my gray hair. Maybe I should just call the whole thing off."

"Ma," Connor said, pinching the bridge of his nose. "Stop being so cynical all the time. What do you have to lose by going out with Greg? You deserve to be with a nice guy."

There was a long pause on the other end of the phone before she finally sighed. "Okay. Then I'll meet him for dinner. He asked about you, you know? You should've seen him smile when I told him you'd joined the Marines. He said he'd always known you'd do big things."

Hearing his mom repeat Greg's words made Connor's rib cage ache with the gratification he'd never gotten to hear from his own father. How could a man who'd only been in his life for six short months have made such a big impact on him?

After he hung up with his mom, he sat on the stool and stared emptily at the workbench. Wow. How much different would his life have been if she'd stayed with Greg instead of going back to Steve?

How much different would Amelia's life be if Dahlia dated Connor instead of going back to Micah?

Not that she was going back to her ex. Just because the man was coming to town for a few months didn't mean that Dahlia would throw Connor over for him. Or that Micah didn't deserve a chance to win his family back.

Great. Now he was sounding like his mom, focusing on everything that could go wrong. Still. He knew all the signs of what was coming and he didn't want to influence what was ultimately Dahlia's decision. She alone needed to figure out what would be best for Amelia. In the meantime, maybe he should distance himself a little while they sorted out what Micah's return might mean to all of them.

Dahlia was foolish to think she could simply get Connor out of her system after just one night together. If seeing him with her daughter these past couple of months wasn't enough to make her fall for him, seeing him sharing common interests with

Woody and then putting Jay Grover in his place would've cemented things for her. In fact, she'd wanted to invite him back to her apartment instead of going to the Frozen Frontier with him. Amelia already referred to him as her boyfriend, so would it be a stretch to explain that Connor wanted to have breakfast with them when her daughter saw him at the kitchen table the following morning?

She'd been hoping to ease everyone into the idea of Connor becoming a part of their lives, but then Micah announced he was returning to Teton Ridge, which immediately threw them all into a tense discussion she hadn't been ready for. Then Micah made that stupid crack about the possibility of them not getting along and Connor had snapped back, and Dahlia wasn't entirely sure she wanted to take on the role of mediator.

When she saw Connor at the bank on Thursday, Dahlia asked if he wanted to grab some lunch at Biscuit Betty's or even take a sandwich over to the park. She'd hoped that spending a few minutes alone together would help her get a feel for how he was handling the recent development. Although he was friendly, his eyes didn't quite meet hers when he said he had Goatee in the truck and needed to get him home. Everyone knew that he took his dog to "socialization" classes at the dog park at least once a week.

She couldn't read his mind, but it didn't take a

fortune-teller to see the writing on the wall. While she had no intention of getting back together with her ex-husband, they were also navigating what had become a multi-pronged relationship. Micah was the father of her child, and if that wasn't enough, he was also good friends with several members of her family—Duke and Marcus, not Finn—and they'd grown up in the same town. Hell, they were friends with many of the same people. Of course, Connor would have doubts about where that left him.

Maybe he was pulling back to protect himself. And maybe she should let him.

As Dahlia was finishing the inventory in the stock room on Friday morning, a task she always did before taking off for the weekend, the motion sensor at the front door of Big Millie's chimed. When she went to see if it was a delivery, she was shocked to see Sherliee King standing right inside the door, her knit suit and Italian leather pumps looking completely out of place in the Wild West–styled bar.

Aunt Freckles slammed into the back of her sister-in-law. "Something wrong with your legs, Sherilee? You're holding up traffic here."

Now, *there* was a woman who looked completely at home in a honky-tonk. Freckles's jeans were painted on legs that weren't quite as slim as they had been thirty years ago, and her black leather jacket boasted a motorcycle club patch that was probably as authentic as she was.

"Well, I'd move, Freckles," her mom snapped, "but your tacky rhinestone belt buckle is now stuck to the back of my knit jacket. You should be more careful. I mean, this is St. John, for God's sake."

Dahlia sprang into action and came around the bar to help her mother disentangle the tiny crystals snagged between the delicate knitted fibers of the silk. "What are you doing here, Mom?"

"I figured it was finally time I come check out this place for myself." Her mother had never been shy letting Dahlia know exactly what she thought about the family heritage behind Big Millie's. Sherilee nodded at the ornate staircase that led to a remodeled balcony with only five feet of the original railing remaining. "I see you got rid of all those doors upstairs where the former residents used to entertain their customers."

"Not totally rid of them. I just walled off everything past the balcony and turned them into our private apartment."

Her mom's cosmetically sculpted nose barely quivered as she sucked in a deep breath of indignation. "Really, Dahlia. You're as bad as Finn sometimes."

Freckles winked at her as she bit back her smile. It was a King family pastime to shock the normally unflappable and tightly reserved Sherilee King. Dahlia was glad to know she hadn't lost her touch since moving off the ranch.

"Since you're here, can I get you a glass of wine or a vodka soda or something?"

"I'll take a margarita if it's no trouble," Freckles replied.

"It's ten o'clock in the morning," her mom said. "What kind of self-respecting establishment sells liquor at this time of day?"

"Luckily, I know the owner," Dahlia replied as she walked behind the bar. "And if you're real nice, I'll give you the family discount."

Her mother rubbed at a nonexistent crease on her Botox-enhanced forehead. "Fine. I'll take a vodka martini. Extra dirty."

"Ooh, change my margarita to one of those." Freckles snapped her fingers, the long nails painted the same shade of coral as her lipstick. "We might need the big guns to get through this."

Dahlia grabbed the stainless-steel shaker from the shelf under the bar. "What happened?"

"I found out I'm receiving the Presidential Medal of Freedom this weekend," Sherilee said the same way one might say that they found out the Easter Bunny wasn't real. "Several of the representatives from the charities I've worked with will be there."

"Wow!" Dahlia blinked. "That's an incredible honor, Mom. Why are you so worried about it?"

"Because we've got a lot riding on this plan."

Dahlia was afraid to ask, but couldn't help herself. "What plan?"

Freckles then went into detail about an elaborate scheme she and Sherilee had plotted to get Tessa to the White House, where they'd have Grayson Wyatt, the Secret Service agent her sister had fallen in love with, waiting there to propose.

"Yeah, I can see why you'd think that something like that could totally backfire on you." Dahlia was tempted to pour herself a martini, as well. "So you came here to have me talk you out of it, right?"

Her mother and aunt exchanged a look before her mom shook her head. "No, the plan is in place. But we need all you kids there so Tessa doesn't get suspicious."

"*This* Sunday? As in less than forty-eight hours?"

"Actually, we would need to take the Gulfstream over to DC tomorrow so we can get everything in place."

Dahlia shook her head. "No can do. Micah is supposed to arrive first thing tomorrow morning. Amelia is spending the day with him."

"Perfect." Her mom clapped her hands together. "That means you're free to go with us."

"You want me to leave my child behind?"

"No, I want you to leave her with her father. Micah Deacon is perfectly capable of taking care of his daughter for one night. Possibly two if things go sideways and we have to chase after Tessa."

"But she's never stayed anywhere without me, other than at the Twin Kings with you guys. Even when I take her to visit Micah in Nashville, we usually stay together in the guesthouse on his property." Oh, jeez. Hearing the words coming out of her own mouth, Dahlia realized she sounded exactly as controlling as Sherilee. Was she really that much of a helicopter mom?

"You could have Micah stay with her here. I mean upstairs." Sherilee shuddered as she said the word. "Where she'll have her own bed and toys and everything is familiar to her."

"No, Mom. I don't want my ex-husband sleeping in my bedroom."

"You only have the two bedrooms upstairs now?" Freckles looked up at the ceiling. "I could've sworn there used to be at least eight of them up there back in the day."

Her mother threw back the rest of her martini. "Then have Micah stay with her out at the ranch. Only the staff and a small security detail will be there since we'll all be in DC. Amelia'll be comfortable and it has a ton of extra bedrooms that were never used for illicit purposes."

"Not as far as you know," Freckles murmured into the rim of her glass. She swallowed, then added, "Honestly, darlin', I don't think lil' Amelia is gonna want to go to DC. Could you imagine having to sit through that boring presentation and all the ridiculous speeches?"

"Hey!" Her mom shot her aunt a pointed look. "I'm *making* one of those ridiculous speeches."

"My point exactly." Freckles made a saluting motion with her martini glass. "Let her stay in Teton Ridge with her daddy and enjoy some one-on-one time with him."

Dahlia slowly felt her resolve slipping. Then Sherilee played her final hand. "Even Duke will be flying into DC for the occasion. Hopefully, Tom won't have any surgeries scheduled and can drive over from Walter Reed to meet us."

Not only did Dahlia miss her big brother, she needed to find out what was going on between him and his husband. "Fine. I'll ask Micah if he's okay with it when I talk to him tonight. But you better not let Finn know he's staying at the Twin Kings."

"You don't have to tell me twice." Her mom held up her empty glass. "This was one of the best I've ever had. And for what it's worth, I really do like what you've done with the place. It's got both charm and that bit of Western rustic chic that probably makes it a big draw for all those people on social media trying to post whimsical old-timey pictures. In fact, you know what would look great right there on the wall by that picture of Big Millie? That portrait of your dad's grandma. I'm thinking of redecorating and, needless to say, it really doesn't go with my vision."

"You mean the portrait of Little Millie?" Dahlia

scrunched her face. Her great-grandmother might've been an excellent businesswoman and gambler, but the painting of her hanging over the fireplace at the Twin Kings was equal parts gawdy and intimidating. She always seemed to be watching everyone. "No, thanks. Aunt Freckles, maybe you and Uncle Rider would want it for the cabin?"

"Are you kidding?" Freckles shook her head so hard the loose skin around her neck jiggled like Gobster's. "That woman scared the hell out of me when she was alive. I don't want her mean, judgy face looking over me and Rider when we're getting naked on the bear skin rug in front of his fireplace."

"For the love of God, Freckles!" Sherilee slapped both of her palms over her eyes like a blindfold. "I'll never be able to unsee that image."

"I'm serious, though," Freckles said. "Ol' Grandma Millie gives me the creeps. Did you know that Rider once told me she still talks to him? Gives him advice and such?"

"That's ridiculous," Sherilee scoffed, right before she shoved three blue cheese–stuffed olives in her mouth in quick succession. "She's been dead for fifty years now. If the talking portrait of a dead woman was giving advice in my home, don't you think I'd know it?"

Freckles tsked. "She probably doesn't talk to you because she knows you wouldn't listen, anyway."

Dahlia was still chuckling when her mother and

aunt walked out of the bar a few minutes later, bickering as much as they had been when they'd first arrived. She finished her inventory, then spoke to Micah after his procedure. Even though he was still a bit loopy from the anesthesia, he was looking forward to having Amelia with him for the whole night. He'd also suggested that Finn not know he would be staying at the Twin Kings, but that could've just been the aftereffects of the pain meds talking.

That night, even though things were still awkward between her and Connor, she didn't feel right leaving town without talking to him. She dialed his number, and he answered on the second ring.

"Hey, is everything okay?"

"Yes, why?" she asked, pulling her small suitcase out of the closet and hefting it onto her bed.

"Because you've never called me before."

That was true. They'd texted a few times, but usually, they talked in person...like when they ran into each other in town. "I just wanted to let you know that I'm going to be out of town this weekend."

"Oh." He paused, and she wondered if she was making a bigger deal out of this than it was. For all she knew, he couldn't care less that she'd be gone. He probably wouldn't have even noticed. Then he asked, "Are you taking Amelia to stay with her dad after his surgery?"

"I wish," she quickly replied then heard his sharp

intake of breath. "I mean, that would be way easier than what my mom and aunt talked me into."

Connor actually chuckled at that, which made Dalia smile in relief. But he didn't ask for any details, which made her determined to continue talking and keep the conversation going.

"Anyway, Amelia is going to be staying out at the ranch with Micah. I've never really left her overnight so I'm kind of worried, even though I know her dad will take good care of her. But it's weird knowing that I'm going to be so far gone and not actually in control of the situation." Dahlia hadn't noticed that she was piling way more clothes into her suitcase than she'd ever need for an overnight trip. But it kept her hands busy as she continued to talk and talk and talk. "You probably think I'm acting like a helicopter mom, which is totally a fair assessment given how neurotic I must sound. God, I'm turning into my own mother who is right this second interfering in her grown-up daughter's love life. Tessa's love life, not mine. Our love life is going fine, I hope. Don't you think it's going fine between us? Oh, jeez, now I sound like my mother again putting you on the spot. Except, I'm not nearly as crazy as her, I promise. Speaking of crazy, did I tell you how she's talked all of us into going to DC, even though, it's a horrible plan that's never going to work—"

A bark thankfully cut her off before she could keep rambling on. "Is that Goatee?"

"Yeah, he's mad at me because I stopped throwing the squeaky toy for him so I could answer the phone."

"Oh, I didn't mean to interrupt you guys," she said, finally drawing in a long breath.

"You can always interrupt me, Dahlia." When he said her name like that, his voice equal parts silky and husky, her legs threatened to give out. "Besides, I like listening to you when you do your nervous talking thing. I always wonder how long you'll go before you finally run out of something to say."

"Well, I'm glad one of us enjoys it." She collapsed onto the bed, thankful he couldn't see her do a nosedive into the pillows to drown out her embarrassment. When she came up for air, she heard her phone beep and said, "Listen, my aunt is calling through on the other line and I have to answer it or she'll tell my mom and *she* will send my brother over here to check on me. Maybe we can talk more when I get back?"

"I'll be here," Connor said.

It wasn't until Dahlia was trying to fall asleep later that she realized he hadn't assured her that their love life was, in fact, fine.

Saturday morning, she and Amelia pulled into the nearby airfield, her daughter as excited as Dahlia was nervous. Micah's chartered plane arrived just before the Twin Kings jet was scheduled to depart for DC. Amelia ran to her father, who easily lifted her up into his arms, despite the fact that he had a cast on one hand and a guitar strapped to his back.

All of her family was already waiting onboard the private jet for her and she saw her sister glaring out the oval window at her ex-husband and then tapping impatiently at her watch to indicate that they were already late.

"Okay, so Amelia's suitcase is packed and in my truck. Can you drive with your hand and wrist like that?" Dahlia asked before handing over her keys to Micah.

"Of course," Micah said. "There's still only that one stoplight in town, right?"

"No, there's two now. We're quite the metropolis. Anyway, Amelia has a duffel bag packed with her favorite stuffed animals. And she still uses that green blanket at night and won't fall asleep without it. Aunt Freckles said the kitchen at the ranch is already stocked with premade meals that can be microwaved." She bit her lip. "I feel like I'm forgetting something."

"Don't worry, Dia. We'll be fine." Micah bounced Amelia higher on his hip and she giggled. "Tell your mom congratulations on her medal and try to talk Duke into coming back here afterward for a jam session. Maybe we can get Woody to join us."

"You could ask Connor to play with you guys,

too." Amelia said, and Dahlia rolled her eyes behind her sunglasses.

"Oh, yeah?" Micah wiggled his eyebrows at Dahlia before returning his attention to his daughter. "What does Connor play?"

Dahlia frowned because she hadn't seen an instrument at his house when she'd stayed the night last weekend. Of course, she hadn't seen the sewing machine, either. Was there something else she'd missed about him?

"I don't know," Amelia said. "But Miss Walker says everyone gets an instrument when we do Music Mondays. She has extra triangles and maracas and even a tambourine he could probably use."

"Let's worry about that when Mommy gets home tomorrow," Dahlia said, then gave her daughter one last hug and kiss goodbye.

She gave a final wave at the top of the steps before stepping onto the plane and taking her seat. And just because it seemed like the right thing to do, she sent Connor a text letting him know that her flight was leaving. That way, she couldn't be held responsible for anything that happened while she was gone.

Such as her persuasive daughter talking her dad into stopping by the Rocking D unannounced with a pair of maracas.

Chapter Twelve

Connor saw Dahlia's truck spitting up dust in the distance as she pulled onto the driveway leading to his ranch. No, that couldn't be Dahlia. She'd sent him a text less than an hour ago saying her flight was leaving, but nothing else to indicate she would be missing him while she was gone. So then who was driving her Ford to the Rocking D and why?

A twinge of jealousy spun itself into a rock-sized lump when he saw who was behind the wheel. Micah Deacon hadn't shut off the engine before Amelia unbuckled herself and jumped out the door.

Goatee came tearing across the yard with a chorus of excited barks to greet her.

"Hi, boy." She dropped to her knees, giggling at the slobbery kisses. "I brought my daddy over to meet you and Connor and Peppercorn and Gobster."

"Man, she's fast," the man said as he came around the front of the truck. "I'm Micah. I'd shake your hand but…" He held up his right hand covered in a white cast-like bandage. Only his fingers were exposed. "Sorry for barging in on you like this."

"No problem," Connor said, a tenseness in his stomach as he sized up Dahlia's ex-husband while pretending any of this was normal. "I'm starting to get used to it."

Both men fell in step behind Amelia and Goatee as she led the tour to the chicken coop first to meet Gobster, who was flapping his wings and making threatening caw sounds. As soon as the turkey's caws turned into screeches, Goatee made a detour straight to the safety of the porch.

"Whoa. That's one angry looking bird." Micah kept his good hand on Amelia's shoulder to prevent her from getting too close to the wire fencing. Seeing the man's quick instinct to protect his daughter eased some of the heaviness in Connor's stomach.

"Tell me about it. I went into the coop this morning to feed him and he took a bite out of my favorite shirt." Connor held out the cotton tee with what used to be an image of the Beatle's *Abbey Road* album. "Tore a hole right through Ringo Starr."

"At least he didn't go after Paul or John," Micah

replied. "That would've been a one-way ticket on the stuffing express."

"What's the stuffing express, Daddy?" Amelia asked.

Micah winced like a preacher's kid who'd just gotten busted saying a curse word. "Oh, just one of those weird farm terms I heard your aunt Finn use once. Now where's this horse I've been hearing all about?"

"He's in the stables!" Amelia grabbed Micah's unbandaged hand in one of hers and then reached back for Connor's. "Let's go."

If Micah Deacon thought it was odd having his five-year-old daughter literally forming a link between him and his ex-wife's boyfriend, the man didn't say. And if he wasn't going to complain, then Connor certainly wasn't going to bring it up.

But he had to think it was weird, right? Even the most easygoing guy on the planet would know that the situation could go sideways pretty quickly. Just as it had on the phone call earlier this week.

They made their way to the stables. Just a trio of two men and a little girl who had no idea how awkward this was. As they stood in front of the stall, Micah stared at the hand-carved sign hanging from the fence that read Sergeant Peppercorn.

"I thought you said his name was Private Peppercorn?" Micah asked his daughter.

"It was. But then Aunt Finn said that he earned

a promotion and made him that sign. Did you know that he has eighteen girlfriends right now? Aunt Finn said it's fine for stallions to have that many but if a *man* does it, we can kick him in the—"

"How about we show your dad where I'm going to put the new mare when she gets here?" Connor interrupted just in time. Then he forced himself not to make eye contact with Micah, who was clearly having a tough time keeping a straight face.

"It's over here, Daddy," Amelia said, happily skipping ahead of them. Goatee returned now that they were out of Gobster's field of vision and he jumped up onto one of the straw bales, yipping until Amelia followed him.

As the little girl and the dog played hide-and-seek in the barn, Micah turned to him. *Here it comes*, Connor thought. The real reason for this visit.

"Just in case you're wondering—" Micah rocked back on his heels "—this whole thing is awkward for me, too."

Connor's only response was a single nod of acknowledgment. Although, he did resist the urge to fold his arms defensively over his chest. Instead, he assumed the military at ease position, clasping his hands behind his back.

"You probably think I'm a deadbeat dad who ditched my kid to run off and become famous."

"Actually, I never really thought that," Connor admitted. "Dahlia is pretty clear about your co-parenting situation and I know that you're active in Amelia's life, even when you're out of town."

Micah shrugged. "Well, I think that about myself sometimes. Back when she was a baby, it was easy to tell myself that Dahlia could handle things. That Amelia was too young to even notice that I wasn't around. But now she's getting older and more aware of everything. Man, she's so damn smart, you know? It's a trip talking to her on FaceTime and hearing about her day and it's starting to eat at me that I can't be with her all the time. Sometimes I regret not staying here and making things work."

Connor felt his last statement like a swift kick to the chest and dragged a deep breath in through his nose. Micah must've seen his reaction because he held up his unbandaged palm.

"No, man, not like that. It never would've worked between me and Dahlia. She figured I was safe because we'd known each other forever and a lot of the guys she'd met in college didn't make it a secret that they were mostly interested in her family name. Anyway, we both knew it was hopeless before we even walked down the aisle. What I meant was that I regret not making things work by staying here in Teton Ridge, staying closer to my daughter. Don't get me wrong, Dahlia's done an amazing job. She's such a great mom, and I appreciate the way all of the Kings have stepped in and helped while I've been away on tour. And I can't even begin to thank *you* for being involved and taking her to that dance and just, you know, being good to her mom and… crap…this is starting to sound really weird." Micah scratched his head. "Anyway, what I'm trying to say is that I'm glad Dahlia has you and I don't want you to feel threatened in any way now that I'm moving back to town. Unless I find out you're not the man they think you are."

Connor blinked twice, but chose not to focus on Micah's last sentence. "*Moving* back to town? Or just staying here for a couple of months for physical therapy?"

"Here's the thing. I haven't told anybody this, not even the guys in my band. But the surgeon says my wrist is pretty messed up." He sighed, finally appearing as though he might actually be stressed. "It's going to be a long time before I can pick up a guitar again and even then, it probably won't be at the same level I was playing before. So it kind of seemed like the universe was telling me that it was okay to take a break. To return to Teton Ridge and be a normal dad again."

Connor didn't want to think about what this new development would mean as far as his relationship with Dahlia. Or the bond he'd established with Amelia. But then he saw a little blond ponytail poke out from behind a hay bale and knew how he *should* feel. He cleared his throat. "Yeah, well, that'll be great for Amelia."

"I hope so." Micah was also watching Amelia, a determined look in his eyes. "I guess we'll all just have to figure out how to make things work."

Connor hoped it would be just that simple. But there were a lot of lives and personalities at play here. Things had been complicated enough before her ex-husband returned full-time.

If his past training had taught him anything, he knew that once he made the decision to go down this trail, he'd have to stay the course and keep his senses on high alert. Because his emotions weren't the only ones at risk of getting lost.

"Hey, man." Micah's voice was rushed when Connor answered his phone later that evening. "I hope you don't mind, but I got your number from Mike Truong, the stable foreman."

Connor gripped the rope he'd been coiling tighter. "Is something wrong with one of the mares?"

"No. I wish it were that simple." That was when he heard Amelia's hiccupping sobs in the background.

"Is she okay?"

"Physically, yes. But I can't get her to stop crying. Something about a panda and Peyton, and I can't really understand the rest through all the tears. I was gonna call Dahlia and ask her to interpret for me, but I don't want her thinking I can't handle my own daughter for the night. So I called you."

Connor didn't know whether to be flattered or confused. But then he heard Amelia do that hiccupping sob again and it no longer mattered how Connor felt. "Can you put the phone on speaker so I can ask her?"

"There," Micah said. "Amelia, can you tell Connor what's wrong?"

"Tonight is s'pose to be my night to co-parent Andy Pandy." Hiccup. "But when I used my tablet to talk to Peyton, she said she forgot him at her dad's house." Hiccup. "And her dad won't bring him to her mom's 'cause they're fighting." Hiccup. "And now Andy Pandy won't know that I love him." Two hiccups.

"Did you catch all that?" Micah asked.

"I think so. Do you know Jay Grover?"

"Unfortunately. Let me take you off speakerphone so you can fill me in."

Connor explained about the claw machine at the Pepperoni Stampede and the co-parenting agreement between the girls and his subsequent conversation with Jay.

Micah snorted. "Did you really tell him you were gonna kick his butt if he couldn't get on board with the co-parenting plan?"

"I might've used more colorful language at the time. But he shouldn't be such a crappy dad just to get back at his ex-wife. And I didn't like the way he spoke to Amelia, either. Tell her I'll drive over to Jay's to pick up Andy Pandy and bring him out to the ranch for her."

"I'll come with you," Micah said, but before Connor could protest, he added, "Not that you couldn't take him. From what I remember, he lost every single wrestling match his sophomore year before Coach Plains cut him from the team. But the guy is a yeller and knows how to cause a scene. You don't want to risk having Deputy Broman responding to a disturbing-the-peace call. With Marcus out of town, Broman is probably looking for an excuse to lock up someone else important to the Kings."

Connor shoved down the thought that he was actually significant enough to be considered as someone important to the Kings and instead asked, "But I thought you and Broman were good friends? At least that's what he said at the father-daughter dance."

"A lot of people think they're my friends," Micah replied. "They're usually full of it. I'll be by to pick you up in fifteen minutes."

The line disconnected and Connor thought about taking off on his own and going to Jay's without Micah. However, by the time he fed Peppercorn and Gobster—he didn't want to risk delaying their dinnertimes and have the turkey try to eat a hole through the chicken wire again—Micah was bouncing up the drive in Dahlia's truck.

Connor whistled for Goatee before he opened the back door. The dog sprang onto the back seat beside

Amelia. Micah squinted at the small white dog, who was in need of another haircut. There was no mistaking the sarcasm in his voice when he asked, "Do you really think we need to bring the attack dog?"

Connor climbed into the front seat. "I figured he'd be a good distraction to keep Amelia occupied in the car so she doesn't hear us talking to Jay."

Micah nodded as though any of this made sense. "So just to be clear. We're two grown men, taking a five-year-old and a white fluffy dog with us to possibly go kick another guy's ass over a doll?"

"Andy's a panda bear," Amelia corrected from the back seat. "And Mommy said A-S-S is a bad word."

"Mommy's right," Connor told the girl before lowering his voice to talk to Micah. "Let's hope things don't escalate that far. But if they do, you take care of Amelia. I'll deal with Jay."

"I know I'm not Special Forces," Micah said, surprising Connor with his intel. Not that he blamed the man for doing his research. "But I got my start playing in some of the roughest honky-tonks and dive bars on the rodeo circuit. I can throw a mean right hook."

"Not with your wrist like that, you can't." Connor pointed to the street ahead. "Turn here."

"Crap. I guess I'll have to use my left hand."

"Look, if one of us goes to jail for hitting him,

it should probably be me since you have Amelia tonight."

"I can probably afford a better attorney, though," Micah replied, then shot him a sheepish smile. "No offense."

"Maybe we should focus on a plan that doesn't involve either of us getting into a fight or getting arrested?"

"Peyton says Andy Pandy sleeps on her bed," Amelia said, clearly listening to every word from the back seat. "Maybe we can just sneak in the window and get him."

"No," both Connor and Micah said at the same time.

"Baby doll, you can't just sneak into someone's house," Micah said as he turned onto Jay's street. "Your mom would be so mad at us if we let you do that."

"But I know which window is hers."

Connor turned around in his seat. "Amelia, I need you to stay here and keep Goatee from barking or getting out of the truck, okay? He doesn't know this neighborhood and we wouldn't want him running away again and getting lost."

"Maybe you're right." The little girl nodded solemnly as she stroked the dog's back.

"Besides, I'm sure if we just knock on the door and talk to Peyton's dad, he'll be happy to give us

Andy Pandy," Micah said, and Connor almost believed him.

Of course, Jay's flatbed truck wasn't in the driveway and his house was dark when they parked at the curb. When nobody answered the door, Amelia rolled down her window and yelled, "Oh, no! Andy Pandy is all alone in there. We can't just leave him here. It's *my* night."

"Hey, baby doll, which room is Peyton's?" Micah called back to Amelia.

"You can't be serious," Connor said, looking up and down the darkened street. "That's breaking and entering."

"Are you going to go back to the truck and tell her that we can't get her doll? Because I'm not gonna break her heart like that."

"It's a bear," Connor corrected absently. But one look at Amelia's tear-stained face was all it took to agree to something so ridiculous. "Okay, you go into the room. I'll stay out here as the lookout."

After all, Connor had done way more dangerous missions than this in enemy combat zones. In fact, he was the third wheel in this situation. His role was secondary to Amelia's actual father's. How bad could it be?

"Can you say that again, Peanut?" Dahlia asked her daughter, thinking the cell phone might've cut out. "Where's Daddy?"

"The deputy put him in the back of the police car."

Dahlia's stomach dropped. "What deputy?"

"The deputy that Uncle MJ punched."

Oh, hell. Dahlia needed to go get Marcus. She walked out the door of her hotel room and, trying to keep her daughter talking, asked, "What are you doing right now?"

"Eating an ice cream with Keyshawn. Did you know he lives next door to Peyton's dad's house?"

Dahlia had to breathe through her nose. "Why are you at the Fredricksons' house?"

"I'm not. I'm in the truck. No, Goatee, dogs can't have chocolate ice cream."

Dahlia stopped in the middle of the long hallway between her and Marcus's room. "Goatee is with you?"

"Yeah, he got in the car when we picked Connor up."

They picked Connor up? What in the world was going on? "Can you put Connor on the phone?"

"I don't think he can talk right now."

"Why not?"

"'Cause he's in the front seat of the police car."

"Oh, my gosh," Dahlia said, then caught herself. *Stay calm.* "Amelia, I need you to tell me what happened."

"Nothing really. We just came to get—" The call cut out for a second. When her daughter's voice returned to the line she heard "...that's all."

It sounded like a lot more was going on. "Is Keyshawn still there with you? Can I talk to him at least?"

"Hold on a second," Amelia told her, then forgot to move the phone away from her mouth before yelling, "Hey, Keyshawn! My mommy wants to know if you can come talk to her." There was a pause and then Amelia said, "He said he'll be right over when he finishes giving his witness statement."

Dahlia slid down the wall of the hotel hallway until she was sitting on the plush carpeting. Thankfully, Marcus came out of his room at that exact second and saw her. "Dia! I was just coming to find you."

"Keep eating your ice cream, Peanut. I'm going to stay here on the phone with you and wait," she told her daughter in the calmest voice she could muster. Then she covered the mouthpiece on her phone and asked her oldest brother, "What in the hell is going on back in Teton Ridge?"

"Apparently, Micah was breaking into Jay Grover's house with the intent to remove an item from the premises. Connor was in the front yard, acting as the lookout."

"Wait, back up. They took Amelia with them? My daughter was an accomplice to a burglary and my truck was the escape vehicle? I knew I shouldn't have left. Please tell me Jay wasn't there. The last thing I need is for that guy to try to sue me."

"They're still getting witness statements, but it sounds like Amelia wanted to let Goatee out of the car to pee. Then Amelia had to pee, so Connor walked her over to the Fredricksons' and asked if she could use their restroom." Marcus put his hand over his mouth and his shoulders shook several times before he could continue.

Dahlia wanted to shake her brother by the front of his shirt. "I'm glad you think this is funny."

"No, no. It gets better." His mouth twitched several times and he had to look away briefly. "So Amelia had just gone inside the Fredricksons' to use the bathroom when Connor heard Jay's truck coming down the street. He tried to run back to the house to give Micah the signal, but Micah had gone in the wrong room and was wandering around the house in search of a—" Marcus paused to wipe the back of his hand across his eyes, but the tears of laughter were already escaping "—a panda bear. Apparently, they'd broken into Jay's house to steal a stuffed animal."

Dahlia gasped. "Not Andy Pandy?"

"That'd be the one. When Jay pulled up, Connor tried to waylay him in the yard so Micah could make his escape. Except Micah, not knowing Jay had returned, throws the panda out the window and it lands in the boxwood shrubs below. According to witnesses—"

"Oh, great. There's witnesses?"

"Whole damn block. At this point, Jay starts yelling, 'Thieves, thieves,' at the top of his lungs and races to the bushes. Connor is faster, though, and beats him there, getting the bear first. Jay attempts to sucker punch Connor, but his fist glances off his cheek. So Connor returns the hit and lays Jay flat. Now Jay is out for the count and Micah is trying to shimmy himself down the trellis, but he only has one good hand so he slips right before he lands in the bushes by Jay. His elbow lands in Jay's solar plexus, which wakes the man up and he starts yelling again and raising holy hell. Broman and a junior deputy are now on scene and an ambulance is there on standby."

"So did Amelia see any of it?" Dahlia asked and didn't realize she'd dropped her hand from the mouthpiece of the phone until she heard her daughter's response.

"No, me and Goatee missed the whole thing 'cause the Fredricksons have a cat and Goatee wanted to chase it. Mr. Freddie said that maybe Goatee should sit in the truck and give his cat a break, so he gave me an ice cream and asked Keyshawn to watch me until the policemen decide what to do with Daddy and Connor. Oh, here they come now. And they have Andy Pandy with them!"

"Here, you better talk to them." Dahlia passed the phone to Marcus. "I don't trust myself not to completely lose my cool, and my daughter doesn't need to hear that."

She rubbed her temples as her brother spoke to her ex-husband, wincing every time he'd have to pause to recover from his sudden bouts of laughter. When he hung up, he told Dahlia, "Everyone is fine. Micah's taking Connor home and then he and Amelia will head straight to Twin Kings."

"Thank God." Dahlia sagged against the wall. "I can't believe Broman didn't arrest them."

"Oh, he still plans on it. But I told him to hold off on filing the official charges until we get back. Mom will kill you if you leave early and ruin her surprise for Tessa tomorrow."

Chapter Thirteen

Dahlia stood outside the county courthouse steps on Monday morning when Connor and Micah came out of the adjacent sheriff's building.

Connor's lips were pressed in a firm line, looking suitably embarrassed by the whole affair. As he should. However, Micah had the audacity to smile and wave at her. "Thanks for posting bail for us, Dia."

"I didn't do it for you. I did it so my daughter doesn't have to come visit you guys behind bars. Can you even imagine how awful a jailhouse visit is for a kid?" As soon as she saw Connor flinch, she knew she'd said the wrong thing. "Oh, my gosh, Connor.

I'm so sorry. Of course you know exactly what that would be like."

"You're only speaking the truth." Connor rubbed the back of his neck. "Funny thing is I spent my whole life trying not to be like my dad and the one time I actually do something I think is fatherly, this happens. I promise, Dahlia, I'm not the kind of guy who normally gets into brawls and gets arrested."

"Technically, you weren't arrested. You just had to appear for an arraignment and then post bond," Violet Cortez-Hill said as she broke away from where she'd been huddled in discussion with the district attorney. "And you didn't get charged with the battery since all the witness statements reflected that you acted in self-defense."

"Thank God for that," Dahlia said, not only relieved but also touched by his admission that he felt "fatherly" toward her daughter. "I appreciate you always wanting to do what's best for Amelia, but what were you guys thinking? Now you have a burglary charge on your record."

Micah raised his bandaged hand. "I'm the one with the burglary charge. Connor just got accessory to burglary. For a former military scout, you're a real crappy lookout, man."

"I was taking your daughter to the bathroom. Besides, I told you which window to go in and you picked the wrong—"

"Hey," Violet quickly cut off Connor. "The DA is

going to be walking by any second. Let's not admit to the crime in front of him, shall we?"

Marcus came out the door marked Sheriff, took one look at Violet, then almost turned around and went back inside. Then he saw Dahlia and asked, "Seriously, Dia? You hired my ex-girlfriend as their defense attorney, too? Is my entire family suddenly getting a group rate?"

"Good morning, Sheriff." Violet's smile was so bright and taunting that Dahlia nearly laughed. "I was on my way to your office next to ask you about the alleged victim in my clients' case. Jay Grover?"

"What about him?"

"A little birdie told me that Mr. Grover was doing a little breaking and entering of his own right before he confronted my clients and accosted one of them."

"Is it considered an accost if he couldn't even land the punch?" Micah asked Connor, who lifted one shoulder.

Marcus didn't bother looking in their direction he was so focused on his ex-girlfriend. "Does this little birdie happen to work in my office?"

"You know I won't reveal my sources. But I've already gotten the DA to agree to reduce the charges from burglary to trespassing. As soon as he watches the video footage I obtained of his star witness, I have a feeling Mr. Grover is going to be so embarrassed, he'll want to drop the charges altogether."

"She's good," Micah said to Marcus, who only

clenched his jaw tighter. "Violet, any chance you do contract negotiations?"

"As mind-numbingly boring as that sounds," Violet replied to Micah despite the fact that her eyes were locked onto Marcus's stern face. "I've got a big case coming up this week and need to get through that before I can focus on my next career path."

"That's right. MJ's trial starts in a few days. Are you going to be at the family dinner tomorrow, then?" Micah asked, and Connor's eyes immediately shot to Dahlia's.

"Probably not," Marcus said at the same time Violet nodded and said, "Yes, I'm bringing a pie from Burnworth's."

After a couple more seconds of intense glaring, her brother stomped back to his office and Violet headed down the steps.

"Okay, then I'll catch everyone there," Micah said more to himself before addressing Dahlia and Connor. "I've got to run to my physical therapy appointment, but I should be done in time to grab Amelia after school. I'll call you."

And just like that, Dahlia and Connor were left standing alone on the courthouse steps. If he was going to tell her that he needed a break from her and all the trouble she and her family had caused him, now would be an opportune time. She swayed slightly before bracing herself for the inevitable.

"So you've got a big family dinner going on?" he asked, catching her off guard.

"Oh. Um. Yeah. My mom has this annoying PR person who wants us all to meet before MJ's hearing so we can best plan our strategy for a public show of support. Duke flew back with us from DC and invited Micah to stay on at the ranch. They were friends all through school and the best men at each other's weddings."

"You mean the wedding to you?"

Maybe Dahlia shouldn't have reminded him of that fact. But the past was there. It happened. She couldn't erase it. "Yes, Micah's wedding to me. The one we had before we got a divorce. Is that a problem for you?"

"I want to say it is. I even want to be jealous of the guy or find something to dislike about him. But I can't. It just might take me some time to get used to it, I guess."

An unexpected and very tiny drop of hope blossomed inside her. "I don't know if any of us will get used to it. I know you've been pulling away lately and I'm not sure if it's because of your own stuff you have going on. Or if it's because the attraction isn't there anymore..." She paused, letting her words hang in the air in the hopes that he'd fill in the rest for her.

Connor's head shook firmly. "It's definitely not because of you."

That blossom of hope got a little bigger before she realized that he hadn't denied the fact that he'd been pulling away. Dahlia was too invested at this point, though, to keep fishing for answers. Seeing Tessa and Grayson find their own happiness this weekend was all the encouragement Dahlia needed to be like her strong female ancestors and take matters into her own hands.

"Then it must be because of the situation," she said with more confidence than she felt. "If it's weird for you to be around my ex, I get it. I probably wouldn't enjoy being around your ex, either. But if you truly do want to give things a shot between us, then it's something you're going to have to get used to. And there's nothing like a King family dinner to get your feet wet."

For the first time in several days, she finally got a genuine smile out of the man. "Is that an invite?"

She leaned up on her toes and dropped a light kiss on his lips. "No, it's a warning. If you still want to run after that, then I won't stop you."

Connor sat in the living room at the main house on the Twin Kings Ranch, trying not to feel like the wannabe cowboy that Amelia had adopted like one of her strays. But everyone in this room had known each other for decades and he was clearly the newcomer. He would've been way more comfortable eating in the bunkhouse with the rest of the ranch hands, or even in the kitchen with Freckles as she finished cooking the dinner that Sherilee King was already complaining about.

The condensation on his glass of iced tea dripped down his hand before splattering on his jeans. He would've set it down on the end table beside his silk upholstered chair, but the wood finish probably cost more than his last pay stub.

Dahlia threw him the occasional smile, but she was sitting with Violet, Finn and Tessa, all looking overwhelmed at the stack of glossy bridal magazines Mrs. King had just dropped in front of them. Marcus and Grayson, the Secret Service agent who was now engaged to Tessa, were discussing law-enforcement training tactics. That conversation might've been more appealing to join if Connor wasn't awaiting a possible trial for trespassing and hoping not to draw any more attention to his potential criminal record. Duke and Micah were discussing their glory days playing high school football, and though Connor had played kick returner on his own varsity team, he didn't know most of the names they were referencing.

Normally, Amelia was the one who put him at ease in big situations like this, keeping him talking by asking him a million questions a minute. But she'd gone out for a ride on her pony with Rider and Marcus's twin boys. Connor had been tempted to join them, but then it might seem as though he were

steering clear of Micah or running away from interacting with Dahlia's overwhelming family.

And Dahlia was right. If he wanted to be in a relationship with her, he'd have to eventually learn to
deal with all of this. For years, this was the exact
type of emotional attachment he'd been trying to
avoid. Yet, now, he found himself wanting the one
thing he'd always wanted as a child. A family.

He was also on the edge of losing it, though.

"I'm gonna go check and see if Rider and the kids
are back yet," Micah told Duke before leaving Connor sitting alone by everyone's favorite King sibling.

"It's a lot to take in, huh?" Duke's voice was calm
and knowing. "Even for someone who used to be
Special Forces and probably saw a lot of action on
his deployments."

"Am I that obvious?" Connor asked.

"If it makes you feel any better, Grayson over
there was once a sniper on the Counter Assault
Team. After nearly a month of being assigned to
Twin Kings full-time and getting the full vetting
and approval of my eagle-eyed mother, he still can't
stop peeling the wrapper off that beer in his hand."

The words were probably supposed to be comforting, but only put Connor slightly more ill at ease.
"So, you're saying it won't get any easier?"

"Nah, it'll definitely get easier. Tom does just fine
with all the chaos and drama. Of course, he has ten
brothers and sisters of his own, so he's used to it."

"Ten? Wow. I was an only child."

"I know. I saw the briefing file in the Secret Service bunkhouse."

Connor gulped. "They have a file on me? Already?"

"Don't worry. It's pretty basic. They screen everyone who comes in and out of the Twin Kings. Once MJ's hearing wraps up, though, they'll be shutting down their operation and returning to DC."

That's right. Dahlia had explained to Connor that after the vice president's funeral, a few agents had stayed on at the ranch due to Tessa's recent media storm and MJ's arrest. Now that the new vice president was sworn in, though, the protective detail would be reassigned.

"I'm sorry to hear about your father, by the way," Connor offered. "He once visited the troops when I was still a grunt stationed at Camp Dwyer and he was larger than life. I didn't even know he was from this part of Wyoming before I moved here."

Duke's pleasant smile slipped and his brief nod was his only acknowledgment of the condolences. Damn. Maybe Connor shouldn't have brought that up. And here he thought he was doing so well and finally relaxing a bit.

Before he could change the subject, Micah burst into the room. "Hey, Rider and the kids aren't back yet. Mike Truong expected them over thirty minutes ago."

Dahlia sprang to her feet and, instead of running to her ex-husband, she turned her wide pleading eyes to Connor. He walked to her and kissed her temple. "I'll go looking for them."

"We'll all come," Finn said, but Connor was already heading out the door.

Mike had two trail horses saddled and was buckling a bridle onto a third.

"Do you know what direction they went in?" Connor asked the foreman.

"They took off toward the west, but the trail forks several ways from there. Two of the agents went out in an ATV, but there's a number of paths out there that are way too narrow for anything but horses."

"Can I take this one?" Connor pointed at the pale palomino whose saddlebags were already packed.

"She's all yours. Grab one of the red first-aid backpacks and a walkie-talkie from the tack room. They should all be charged."

Connor already had his foot in the stirrup when Finn grabbed his horse's bridle. He expected Dahlia's twin to question him about his abilities. Instead, she said, "Stick to the area south of the main trail. I'll take the north side. Hopefully, Rider kept everyone together."

Connor hadn't been past the stables on his prior visits to the Twin Kings, but he set the palomino on a dead run along the dirt road heading west. A two-seater ATV raced past him and he saw Marcus and

Micah inside. Maybe they should've formed a better plan or at least assigned designated search areas so they weren't all covering the same areas. But it was an eighty-year-old man and three kids on ponies. How far could they have gone?

The Twin Kings was a working cattle ranch and it hadn't rained in at least two weeks, so there were hoofprints everywhere he looked. But as he passed a smaller trail, he noticed a different set of prints. Rabbit. Several sets, including two tiny ones that likely belonged to a couple of babies. And they were relatively fresh. If Amelia had seen the bunnies, there was no doubt she'd followed.

Connor slowed the horse and scanned the shrubs and overgrown grass surrounding the trail for more clues. Then he saw it. One random leaf on a sagebrush had a damp dark spot on it. Keeping the reins in his hands, he slipped off the horse to get a closer look. His nose knew what it was before his eyes did. Chewing tobacco. Rider once offered him a dip when they were in the stables. He said he never chewed in front of Freckles or Sherilee and could only sneak it when he was out of the house.

Getting back into the saddle, Connor followed the trail as it narrowed. The sun had already gone down behind the Teton Mountain Range in the distance and there would only be about fifteen more minutes of natural light before he'd start wishing for his old pair of military-issued night-vision goggles.

After a quarter of a mile, he saw the thin trail again split into two smaller paths. There was a scrap of pink fabric sticking out of a rotted stump just past the fork, but Connor knew Amelia never wore pink. In fact, today she'd been wearing a beige long-sleeved sweatshirt with the bright green Australia Zoo logo on the front. Using his heels to nudge the horse's sides, he continued down the opposite path. He paused briefly at a creek, but didn't cross. He remembered Amelia telling him that Gray Goose, the pony Amelia had likely been riding, hated water and refused to set foot in it. Instead, Connor followed the river rocks along the creek bed north before finding a rabbit den.

Bingo. There were three sets of smaller pony-sized tracks in the dirt near the burrowed entrance. A few feet back were a set of larger horse prints; the hoof marks were sunk deeper into the ground and likely the result of Rider's heavier weight. So, the group had probably followed the bunnies here, but then where'd they go?

His radio crackled to life and he held his breath, hoping someone had found them. But it was Duke advising them that the rescue helicopter from the nearby airfield had just landed at the King's helipad and he and Dahlia would be flying overhead with a search light.

Just thinking about the terror on Dahlia's face back in the living room made Connor pick up speed.

After at least five more minutes, the walkie-talkie again sounded and he heard Finn say, "I have the boys. They were southwest of the Peabody Trail. They're tired and thirsty, but still in their saddles."

Relief washed over Connor before quickly fizzling out. Two people were still missing.

"Where's Amelia?" Micah demanded, the engine of his ATV revving in the background of the radio transmission.

"The boys say Rider got hurt and couldn't ride," Finn advised. "Amelia stayed to watch over him while the boys rode back to the stables to get help. But they got lost."

"Do they know where they left Amelia and Rider?" Dahlia asked over the radio and Connor could hear the strain in her voice. Determination kept him moving forward.

"Negative," Finn said. "I'll get these two back to Violet at the main house. You guys keep looking."

Connor wanted to relay his position and update them with what he'd found so far. But he didn't want to give anyone false hope. Of course, he only had a couple more minutes before he was going to need that search light. He held the walkie-talkie up to his mouth and just as he depressed the button, he heard something behind a wall of fir trees.

Was that…? A shot of adrenaline spiked through his already tense muscles and he tried to listen over the pounding of his heart.

He took a few more steps, then heard Amelia's voice clear as day. "Miss Walker said her Paw Paw once had a heart attack and it felt like a herd of buffalo were stomping around on his chest."

Connor charged through a narrow opening in the branches covered in pine needles just in time to hear Rider groan. "Right now, it feels like a herd of buffalo are stomping around my ears, Peanut. Do you think you could ask a few less—"

"Connor!" Amelia cried and ran straight for him. He was off the horse just in time to catch her jumping into his arms. Relief pulsed through him, causing him to crush her against his chest as he fought back the tears of joy. Amelia giggled, then squirmed until he loosened his hold. "I knew you'd find us, Connor. I told Uncle Rider you're the best tracker there is. Didn't I tell you, Uncle Rider?"

Connor's eyes fell to the older man who was sprawled out on the cold ground, his head propped up under a saddle blanket. "You sure did, Peanut. About a million times."

He carried the girl over to Rider and knelt down. "What happened?"

"Horse got spooked by a damn lizard of all things and reared back. When he came down, I lost my balance and landed on that boulder over there. I think I busted one of my ribs," the older man said, and even in the growing darkness, Connor could see that his face was nearly white under that bushy gray mustache. His breathing was definitely strained. "I used to break a different one every month back in my bull-riding days and then get back in the saddle. I should be fine as soon as I catch my breath."

Rider tried to sit up and cursed.

"Take it easy. There's already a rescue helicopter en route. You should probably keep still until a medic can check you out." Connor reached for the radio clipped to the back of his belt. "I've got Amelia and Rider," he relayed and could only imagine the cries of relief on the end. "Amelia is doing great and Rider is alert and feisty as hell. But he's going to need a medic and possible transport."

Connor transmitted their GPS coordinates, then went to his saddle to get the first-aid bag. He wrapped Amelia in his jacket before tearing open the emergency blanket to throw over Rider in case he went into shock.

Someone had already secured the reins of Gray Goose and Rider's stallion to a nearby branch, but judging by the loose knots, it had been one of the kids. Connor tightened them just as the helicopter made its first pass over the area.

"We're down here!" Amelia jumped up and down, waving as if she were on a parade float, having the time of her life. "We're down here!"

The headlights of the ATV with Marcus and Micah came crashing through a line in the fir trees on the opposite trail just as the helicopter began its descent. Micah was using his good hand to yank the harness-like straps off him as he climbed out of the off-road vehicle.

"Daddy!" Amelia cried with the same level of excitement she'd had when Connor first found them. Then she leaped up into her father's arms to hug him. And the weird thing was, Connor wasn't the least bit envious. In fact, seeing the raw emotion and relief on Micah's face almost made him tear up. Micah might share DNA with the girl, but there had been nothing less intense about Connor's own response just a few minutes ago. It was almost as though he were watching himself, reliving that same adrenaline rush and feeling of euphoria.

Then Micah made the moment even more emotional by turning toward Connor and pulling him into the embrace, as well.

"Thank you for finding her, man," Micah said, his voice scratchy and almost trembling. "I was so damn scared."

"Me, too," Connor admitted, patting Micah on his back. "But we've got her now."

"Okay, you two," Rider huffed as Marcus checked his pulse. "Don't make it all about yourselves. Leave some drama for everyone else."

"Mommy!" Amelia said, wiggling out of their arms before running toward Dahlia who'd had to make her way to them from the open clearing where the helicopter landed. "Connor found us."

"I know, Peanut." Dahlia dropped to her knees as she squeezed Amelia to her. There were tears in her eyes and when she lifted her face to Connor's, it was probably the most beautiful sight he'd ever seen in his life. "I'm so proud of him."

"Maybe we should buy him a muffin tomorrow to thank him," Amelia suggested.

Dahlia threw back her head, her laugh throaty and raw. When she made eye contact with Connor again, there was a fierce determination that sent heat ricocheting through him. "Oh, I think I owe Connor a lot more than a muffin."

"Come on. Now it's *really* getting dramatic," Rider said before passing out.

Dahlia sat on a sofa in the hospital waiting room with Amelia asleep on her lap, the rest of her family surrounding her as they argued among themselves. Freckles and Sherilee exchanged insults. Micah and Finn exchanged dirty looks. MJ and Tessa exchanged conflicting viewpoints about politics (although, it was honestly refreshing to see her baby brother get fired up about anything since he'd been so sullen and despondent lately). And Duke's frown and jabbing thumbs on his phone keypad suggested he was exchanging angry texts with someone. In fact, the only family members who weren't currently arguing in her presence were Marcus and Violet, but that was because they were together in the emergency room, likely arguing about what color of cast Jordan should get on his arm.

But tonight none of that bothered Dahlia in the least because she had her baby girl safe and sound in her arms.

The bickering stopped long enough for Grayson and Connor to carry in a tray full of coffees in to-go cups.

"Which one is the sugar-free hazelnut soy latte?" her mom asked. Dahlia almost giggled at the way Connor and Grayson stared helplessly at each other, neither one wanting to be the one to tell the formidable Sherilee King that they'd failed in their mission.

"You think there's a fancy espresso bar nearby open this time of night?" Freckles's plastic bangle bracelets jingled as she reached for the nearest cup. "They're from a vending machine downstairs, Sherilee. Stop being such a snob and thank your future son-in-laws for their efforts."

"Well, the cease fire was nice while it lasted," Dahlia sighed, then shifted Amelia's feet off the cushion so Connor could return to his seat beside them.

Connor leaned closer and asked, "Did your aunt just say son-in-*laws*? Plural?"

"Yep," Dahlia said. "And you didn't correct her. So now everyone is going to have expectations about the future of our relationship. If that doesn't scare you, ask Grayson what it's like having Sherilee King and Aunt Freckles plan and orchestrate your engage-ment and wedding."

"I don't know. Grayson seems pretty happy with Tessa if you ask me." Connor rested his arm along the back of the sofa. "Besides, I don't care about anyone else's expectations or plans for me. I only care about yours."

Two doctors in blue surgical scrubs kept Dahlia from having to answer.

"Mr. King is out of surgery and stabilized," the doctor spoke to the entire room. "One of the broken ribs punctured his lung, so we have him in ICU to keep a close eye on him. Only one of you can go back at a time to visit."

Freckles rose from her chair and nobody else even bothered standing up or objected to her going first.

"That." Dahlia lifted her chin at Freckles as the older woman quietly followed the surgeons down the stark white hallway alone. Then she faced Con-nor. "That's what I expect. I want you to be my Freckles. She's not related to any of us by blood— or even marriage, legally—and she and my mother can barely stand each other. But when it comes to Rider, there's no question that she's the one who is going to go to him first. I want you to be the person I call when my whole world gets thrown for a loop. I want you to be the one I turn to when my daugh-ter doesn't come back on her pony or when I have to find a way to explain to her that we can't take on another stray. I purposely built my life here in Teton Ridge because I wanted to keep things simple. I wanted to keep my daughter's life simple, away from the spotlight that I grew up in. But there is nothing simple about Amelia. There's certainly nothing simple about being a King. My family is messy and my life is complicated, no matter how straightforward I try to make it."

"Your family is just a tiny bit messy," he said before kissing her forehead. "And your life doesn't seem all that complicated to me."

"Connor. I'm a single mom who owns a bar in a former brothel."

"Well, I'm potentially a convicted felon and an alleged goat roper who owns a ranch that is barely turning a profit."

"Trespassing isn't a felony," Micah said out of nowhere, and Finn sent him a sharp elbow to his rib cage.

Dahlia rolled her eyes. "I also have an ex-husband who married the wrong twin and a daughter that will tell everybody anything that pops into her mind and only stops talking when she's sound asleep."

"I have a dog with codependency issues and a psychotic turkey I bought to impress the woman I love and her daughter."

"Goatee isn't codependent, he just… Wait." Dahlia's knees went wobbly and Amelia almost slid from her lap. "Did you just say you love me?"

"Of course, I love you. I know you have a lot going on and you were hoping to get me out of your system so we could go back to being friends. But I want to be your Rider, Dahlia King Deacon. I want to be the one you turn to first. Whether it's finding your lost daughter or finding a missing panda bear, I want to live in that complicated, messy world with you and enjoy every second of it together."

Then he kissed her, right there under the harsh fluorescent lights of the hospital waiting room with all of her family members looking on. His hands cupped the sides of her face as his lips sealed his commitment. When he pulled away, Dahlia's insides spiraled with a dizzying happiness that threatened to lift her out of her seat.

Pressing her forehead against his to keep her soaring emotions in place, Dahlia smiled. "I love you, too, Connor Remington."

The waiting room at the Ridgecrest County Hospital clearly wasn't the way Connor had envisioned hearing Dahlia utter those words to him. In fact, twenty-four hours ago, he'd doubted that he'd ever hear them at all. But when she declared her love for him, he knew that he couldn't go another day of his life without hearing them again.

Amelia lifted her head drowsily, her eyes still half-shut. "What's going on? Are we having a party?"

"Not yet," Sherilee King told her granddaughter. "But we're going to when your mom and Connor get married."

"Mom!" all five King siblings in the room yelled at once.

"They barely told each other *I love you*," Finn chastised her mother. "Why don't you give them a little time to get used to the feeling before you have them walking down the aisle. Especially before you say something in front of you-know-who."

Dahlia's twin gave a not-so-subtle pointed look at Amelia, who just shrugged. "I already know they're gonna get married."

Connor brushed the child's hair out of her face. "How'd you know that?"

"Grandma Millie told me."

"You mean the scary old lady in the painting above our fireplace?" MJ asked, the look of disbelief on his face matching everyone else's in the room. "She told you this?"

"Yeah. She talks to me all the time. I'm named after her, you know."

Dahlia's eyebrows slammed together. "Peanut, Grandma Millie passed away a long time ago. Before I was even born."

"I know. Uncle Rider says she talks to him, too. He heard her tell me to find a good one for my Mommy. So I did."

Connor had never believed in the supernatural,

but his very first conversation with Rider King came floating back to his mind and sent a shiver down his back.

"Did she say anything else?" MJ asked. "Like if the judge was going to find me guilty?"

Amelia scrunched her nose and forehead. "I don't think so. But she did say Uncle Marcus was too sad all the time and that Uncle Duke needed to be more trusting."

Duke's head jerked up. "What does *that* mean?"

"I don't know." Amelia shrugged. "Ask Uncle Rider. Oh, I almost forgot. She also said Aunt Finn was being way too mean to Daddy."

"Ha!" Micah shouted triumphantly.

"I am *not* mean to your father," Finn argued just as loudly.

"She didn't even mention me?" Sherilee King asked. "I'm the one who's had to live with her up on my fireplace for over thirty years, staring down her judgy nose at me."

Then Tessa asked Duke who he didn't trust, and as several arguments broke out around them, Dahlia put her head on Connor's shoulder. "Remember when you said my family wasn't messy?"

"I think I admitted they were a little bit messy."

"Was that before or after you found out my daughter talks to my dead ancestors and tells fortunes?"

"You know, the first time I ever met your uncle Rider, he said that Amelia would tell you when you found the right one. I thought he was crazy at the time, and I'm still not convinced he isn't. But maybe Amelia's onto something."

"Did I find you or did you find me?" she asked, a smile playing at the corners of her lips.

Connor kissed her tenderly, then said, "I'm pretty sure we found each other."

Amelia snuggled in between them and nodded to the duffel bag under Micah's feet, which the man kept shushing every time a scruffy white head popped out. "And me and Goatee found two daddies."

* * * * *

MILLS & BOON

Coming next month

FROM BRIDAL DESIGNER TO BRIDE
Kandy Shepherd

"I'm thinking of the questions people might ask us at the wedding."

"Where did we meet?"

"Perhaps we met in LA. At a party."

"To which, sadly, I was not invited," he said with a mock mournful expression.

"Shame. There was a party at a waterfront venue in Santa Monica. I went outside for a breath of fresh air. You were outside—"

"Taking a break from a particularly boring business dinner." He paused. "And I saw this dark haired girl leaning against a palm tree. I was struck by her beauty."

Eloise giggled. "I like that. So what happened?

"I opened a conversation with a witty remark."

"I responded with something equally witty."

"We struck up a conversation. You hung onto my every word."

"Huh! How about I made you laugh?"

"You do that in real life, so that could work. Then you said you had to get back to the party."

"No! I'm sure I would have wanted to stay with you."

"Would you?" he said.

"Yes." Her gaze connected again with his in that surprisingly intimate way.

"I got your number. And I called you straight away to check I got it right."

"So when did you call me?"

"I asked you to call me when the party was finished. You did. Then I took you back to your hotel room."

"And...?"

"We talked all night until the sun came up," he said a smile dancing around the corners of his sexy mouth. "I was a gentleman."

"And I was wishing you weren't." She slapped her hand over her mouth. "Scratch that!"

He laughed. "So I wasn't such a gentleman the next night."

"Really," she said trying to sound prim instead of turned on.

It took a real effort not to focus on imagining the exciting details of his fictional ungentlemanly behaviour and her fictional response. Since that first kiss she had spent too much time fantasying over the prospect of making love with Josh. Now he sat so near to her in the privacy of her home, it was impossible not to acknowledge that intense physical pull. "And we spent as much time as we could together before you had to go back to Boston."

"We did. In fact, we hardly left your hotel bedroom." His tone was so exaggerated in its lasciviousness it made her laugh.

"If you say so," she said.

"I wished so," he said with a grin.

She was glad she had decided not to sit next to him on the sofa. It would be only too easy to let this game get out of hand and practice for real.

Continue reading
FROM BRIDAL DESIGNER TO BRIDE
Kandy Shepherd

Available next month
www.millsandboon.co.uk

COMING SOON!

We really hope you enjoyed reading this book.
If you're looking for more romance, be sure to
head to the shops when new books are
available on

Thursday 18th March

LET'S TALK
Romance

For exclusive extracts, competitions
and special offers, find us online:

f facebook.com/millsandboon

🐦 @MillsandBoon

📷 @MillsandBoonUK

Get in touch on 01413 063232

For all the latest titles coming soon, visit
millsandboon.co.uk/nextmonth

MILLS & BOON

THE HEART OF ROMANCE

A ROMANCE FOR EVERY KIND OF READER

MODERN

Prepare to be swept off your feet by sophisticated, sexy and seductive heroes, in some of the world's most glamorous and romantic locations, where power and passion collide.
8 stories per month.

HISTORICAL

Escape with historical heroes from time gone by. Whether your passion is for wicked Regency Rakes, muscled Vikings or rugged Highlanders, awaken the romance of the past.
6 stories per month.

MEDICAL

Set your pulse racing with dedicated, delectable doctors in the high-pressure world of medicine, where emotions run high and passion, comfort and love are the best medicine.
6 stories per month.

True Love

Celebrate true love with tender stories of heartfelt romance, from the rush of falling in love to the joy a new baby can bring, and a focus on the emotional heart of a relationship.
8 stories per month.

Desire

Indulge in secrets and scandal, intense drama and plenty of sizzling hot action with powerful and passionate heroes who have it all: wealth, status, good looks…everything but the right woman.
6 stories per month.

HEROES

Experience all the excitement of a gripping thriller, with an intense romance at its heart. Resourceful, true-to-life women and strong, fearless men face danger and desire - a killer combination!
8 stories per month.

DARE

Sensual love stories featuring smart, sassy heroines you'd want as a best friend, and compelling intense heroes who are worthy of them.
4 stories per month.

To see which titles are coming soon, please visit

millsandboon.co.uk/nextmonth

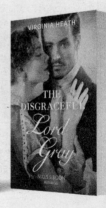

MILLS & BOON

HEROES

At Your Service

Experience all the excitement of a gripping thriller, with an intense romance at its heart. Resourceful, true-to-life women and strong, fearless men face danger and desire - a killer combination!